I0618452

Bait

Courtney Farrell

Fiction Foundry Press

Bait

Fiction Foundry Press
www.courtneyfarrell.com

Editor: Diane Reed
Cover Art: Liliana Sanches
Layout/Typesetting: C.L. Foster
Formatting: RikHall.com

ISBN: 978-0-9904449-0-9
E-ISBN: 978-0-9904449-1-6

Dedication

This book is dedicated to all the members of Fiction Foundry.
Because of you, it's a much better story.

Chapter 1

I was doing all right 'til the rats got the pox. That's when everything got personal. That was the day I stole a car, and started a war, and let the whole world find out I'm a girl. That last part really screwed up everything.

Gray clouds hung over the crumbling city, and the wind carried a bite of snow. Anybody with a shred of sense had already crawled into whatever hole they called home. I headed for the river, 'cause I'm stupid like that. I had boys to feed, seven or eight of 'em, depending on which strays showed up and how many of my regulars came back alive. I meant to bring home dinner whether I got soaked doing it or not.

The whole long riverbed stank, a rotten-egg smell of swamp gas and trash that sank under the good air and wouldn't blow away. I didn't care. The riverside warehouses creeped me out worse, with their peeling paint and dirty, broken windows. Anything could be inside, a pox-infected boy, or worse, a bunch of healthy men scouring the city for a rare surviving female like me. I pulled my baggy gray sweatshirt down over my little round butt and snugged a ball cap low over my eyes, hoping I looked like a scrawny boy. No girl in her right mind would go outside, not alone, and especially not here. I did it all the time, but I had to. My boys were hungry. Me and old Joe, we kept those kids alive, and I'd keep on doing it 'til the pox took me.

Scrambling down the rocky slope, I came to a shadowy place where bare-branched cottonwoods creaked in the wind and leafless brown willows tangled over frozen mud. The river ran shallow, black and sluggish, weaving almost silently between snow-covered rocks. I picked my way over old tires and broken chunks of concrete. A rustle came from the bushes. My head snapped around. Trash fluttered from its trap on a fallen barbed wire fence. I let out a breath and kept picking my way upstream. It was dangerous going, with evening coming on, but down low I kept out of sight of any scavengers who might be working the flats.

A flat, ice-slick stone tipped underfoot and I almost skidded into knee deep water. I bit back a girly squeal. Ahead, a pair of mallards squatted near the shore, the male's green head bright against the gray concrete that littered the riverbank. My stomach growled. I bent and picked up a big slimy rock, even though I didn't have a chance in hell of landing a duck. I had better luck with rats, and when I missed they didn't explode into the air to alert anybody who might be watching.

The wind picked up, making my wet fingers ache. I stopped for a second, just long enough to switch the rock to my left hand and jam my freezing right in a pocket. The ducks picked that moment to take off. They soared over my head in a spray of water, wings pumping fast. I took a left-handed shot at the little brown female, missed her clean, and then made eye contact with the male. That's when I knew he had the pox.

I knew it for sure, 'cause ducks don't make eye contact. Neither do rats or pigeons. Sure, they might see you, but they never really meet your eyes. Not unless they have the pox. It looked at me, the pox did, right through that duck's eyes, and I about choked on my tongue. The green-headed drake swooped and landed on the other side of the river. He waddled along the bank, fat and fearless. I practically drooled. Clenching my hands together in the big front pocket of my hoodie helped, but they still itched for a rock or a stick. I didn't grab one. The pox never gave up on tempting me, and I never quit resisting.

It jumped species, infecting one kind of animal and then another. Sick ones wandered around in the open like they wanted to get eaten. I think they did, 'cause that's how the pox spread. One-legged Joe called me crazy, but I knew I was right. That's why I survived, when just about every other female on the planet died. I looked the pox in the eye and I recognized it in a thousand different bodies. It slipped from one to the next, so I looked close, real close, before I made a kill. If I saw that gleam in the eye I walked away, no matter how hungry I was. Okay, that was kind of a lie. I didn't really walk away.

I got spooked and ran.

In the dying light, the ground looked flatter than it was. I stumbled, but didn't stop. *Forget the duck,* I told myself as I splashed through the shallows. Icy water stabbed my toes. *Get a few rats. Rats never get the pox. Won't be long, they come out after dark.*

The sound of men's laughter jolted my nerves. I plastered myself against the right bank, low and still as I could get. Heavy thuds of booted feet passed across the lip of the embankment, not ten feet from my head. Cold ground sucked the heat from my body, but they'd see me if I moved. They'd grab me and lock me up, like they did to all the girls. The pox hit us girls the worst, so we're valuable now. Only a few survived, and all of us young. Pox took the others, the mothers and aunts and grandmothers, leaving me alone. I hated it for that.

Up by the warehouse, a man grunted, like he was hauling something heavy. He set it down with a thud. Something squeaked, and it took me a second to recognize it as the springs of a car, groaning under a load. It'd been a few years since I'd ridden in one.

Old-man noises came from above. They reminded me of my grandpa getting out of a chair. A deep voice spoke. "Sophie, my back's shot. Let's finish up tomorrow. Besides, Rico wants us back before dark."

A woman's laugh cut the gloom like silver bells. "Rico can wait. You boys, bring over those last four crates for your Uncle Benny."

"He ain't my bleedin' uncle," one of them grumbled in a fake British accent. The other guys laughed. Even I smiled a little.

"Be a love and lift this one in for me," the woman said. "I think we can fit two more in the back."

I knew that voice. Sophia Arabola, the most beautiful woman in the city. The last free one, besides me, and I didn't count. To my crew I was just another brother, even if I am technically a girl.

Sophia Arabola. Even her name was beautiful. I'd peeked at her before, when I was sure the Zunos couldn't catch me. Her face came back to me, a perfect oval, nose straight and fine, lips full. A body so lush that men's heads turned whenever she walked by. Her eyes were too black for the pupils to show. Maybe that was the secret of her magic. Sophia had some secret way of controlling men, some way I didn't understand. They didn't lock her up and rape her. Instead, they fell all over themselves trying to please her. I kind of got that. Part of me wanted to run to her, too, but of course I didn't. She'd sell me out in a heartbeat.

Sophia's crew had the territory next to ours, and they didn't like us much. That gang gave me nightmares. The Zunos were grown men, with guns and gear and cars. They would've rolled over us already if we had anything worth stealing. Lucky they didn't know about me. I was worth stealing, big time. Besides Sophia, I hadn't seen another girl in years.

I had one thing in my favor—Flint's Army. Not that Flint was my guardian angel, or anybody's. Him and his douchebag band of wanna-be soldiers would rape me quick as the next guy, then sell me into some basement harem. But lately, Flint was pushing the Zunos hard, crossing their borders at night and picking off the occasional sentry. He probably suspected they had a woman. With an army breathing down his neck, Rico didn't bother with kids like us.

Shadows deepened as the sun went down, invisible behind steel gray clouds. The wind picked up. I curled on my side, hood up to hide my pale face. A rock gouged my hip, but that was okay. The pain kept me centered.

Men spoke from the warehouse parking lot, up the bank, out of sight. "We can't get the last of 'em. The roof could come down any second."

"To hell with it, then."

A mound of soil under my right foot gave way, and I slid a few inches downhill. Under my boots, a handful of rocks rolled into the water. *Did they hear that?* I gripped the red Colorado clay with my fingernails and listened hard.

Tiny scratching noises came from the riverbank, all around me, as rats came out of their burrows. A little early for rats, and too many all at once. Goosebumps spread along my arms and tingled up my spine to the base of my skull. Pushing myself up on my arms, I turned in slow motion and looked over my shoulder. A hundred pairs of beady eyes looked back at me. One rat, a big male, clawed his way up the riverbank and lunged for my boot. I kicked him into the water, whirled and yanked my hand back before another one sank his teeth into it. A little scream escaped me as I struggled to my feet. I spun in place, stomping and shaking my hands, imagining them clinging to me, their sharp little claws deep in my cotton sweatshirt.

Rats have the pox now, damn it! The last clean meat around. It sent them to bite me, since I won't eat anything infected. Clever.

An engine coughed to life above. Its headlights reflected dimly off the far bank, showing more rats coming my way from both sides of the river. A few brave ones plunged into the current and tried to swim. They got swept downstream. I scrambled up the rocky slope, sucking in air with rapid gasps. For a second I saw the big white SUV waiting there, and it gave me a blaze of hope. Then I put my hand on a rat's wriggling, furry back and squealed like a loser. I jerked back, slipped on the ice, and fell in the river. When that water hit my stomach I thought my heart would stop. The cold shocked a gasp out of me as the current dragged me along. Sharp stones and underwater garbage tore at my jeans. I rolled to all fours, heaved to my feet, and staggered for the nearest shore. Icy water streamed off my clothes.

Shaking with cold, I climbed up into the shadow of the warehouse. One of its walls had collapsed, and the roof sagged sideways. That explained the rich pickings there. None of the other scavengers could get to those crates, but the Zunos had a lot of manpower. Their old white Jeep idled in the parking lot, its headlights splitting the darkness. A man trudged past, a flashlight hanging heavily in one hand.

A busted Coke machine leaned drunkenly against the warehouse wall. I faded into the corner next to it, out of sight and out of the worst of the wind, too. If I had to, I could wait there 'til the Zunos were gone.

A rat nose touched my ankle. I couldn't help it—I jumped, sucking in a loud hissing breath. When the flashlight beam fell on me, the rat ran away.

"What's this? He ain't one of ours," a chunky man said. His fat jowls shook when he talked. He walked up to me, shining the flashlight in my eyes. "You okay, kid? Why ya all wet?"

"Rats chased me," I whispered in my huskiest voice. A couple of pairs of their bulging black eyes peered at us from the shadows.

"Rats? Chase 'em right back. Them 're good eatin', boy."

I shook my head, knowing opening my mouth was the last thing I ought to do. But compared to the pox, anybody was a friend. "Not these ones. Don't. They got pox." I walked away, wet clothes heavy on my skinny shoulders.

He spoke behind my head. "Everybody knows rats don't get pox."

I tried not to turn.

"Wait a minute," he said. Before I could run, strong hands grabbed the sodden hoodie on either side of my waist and yanked it up. The cold night air hit my wet skin and I let out a squeal. The man dragged me backward, running his free hand over my ass. "You ain't no boy."

"Get off!" I twisted hard in the fat man's hands, but he was a lot stronger than me.

"Mine!" A big dark-haired man bellowed. He barreled up to the chubby one and started wrenching the guy's arm. "Rico said, next one's mine!"

"Alright, alright."

Working together, the men pinned my wrists and lifted me clear off my feet. They slammed me face down over the hood of their car. A big hand on the back of my neck held me there. I struggled, tasting oily dust and my own blood. My hat fell off, and wet brown hair stuck to my cheeks. I cursed myself for not cutting it sooner, even though my small nose and delicate chin wouldn't let me pass for a boy, hair or no hair.

"Stop this, now!" Sophia Arabola's voice rang with power.

"If we let 'er go, she'll run," Chubby whined.

"That's no way to treat a *female*," Sophia snapped. From her tone, she might as well have said *Goddess*. "Release her."

They let me go. I would have run, but I couldn't. Knees shaking, I slid off the hood. Three men stared hungrily. My eyes cut from them to the rats and back again. The men edged in. Pox-infected rats crept closer. I pressed my back against the warm hood of the Jeep and didn't move.

"Sweetie, you're gonna catch your death of cold," Sophia told me. "Come with me and I'll get you something dry to wear."

I didn't answer. My eyes tracked rats through the shadows.

Sophia didn't seem to notice them. She bent to peer into my face. "How old are you, honey? Fifteen? Sixteen? You're small for your age, aren't you, but real pretty. I like your spiky hair. That retro punk look suits you."

I said nothing, and it wasn't just 'cause I had no idea what *retro punk* meant. Something in her eyes jogged my memory, like I knew her. I shook off the feeling. Of course I did. I'd seen her before, just not up close.

"This poor child's in shock," Sophia told the men, like they cared. She beckoned to me. "You just need a hot meal. Don't worry. I won't let them touch you."

I eyed the rats. Sophia's offer seemed like a good deal, especially at the moment. I took a couple of hesitant steps toward her.

"I know you're cold. We'll be on our way in a minute, and I'll get the heat on for you." Sophia gave me an encouraging nod and then moved to the back of the jeep. "Toss in the last crates, would you, Benny? Give him a hand, boys, those are big ones."

A couple of huge crates sat on the asphalt behind the open hatchback. Pairs of men bent and picked them up. I ghosted around the dented white Jeep until I stood even with the open driver's side door. With matching grunts, Benny and the chubby one heaved the last crate into the vehicle.

Sophia squatted behind the car to read the label on a box. "I can't wait to get these home and open them."

She looked up just in time to see me leap into the driver's seat.

Men pounded toward me, shouting. I slammed the car door and hit the lock button. The windows were open, I didn't know how to close them, and there wasn't time. I shoved the stick to 'D' for drive. The Jeep lurched forward, but I couldn't reach the pedals.

Quick as a cat, Sophia sprang forward and grabbed my neck with one hand. She pinned my head back, and I felt a rat wiggle behind my neck. It thrashed in my hood, tearing the thick cloth with its teeth. A naked, wormy tail whipped across my lip. I seized the horrid, infected thing, and I threw that rat right in Sophia Arabola's face. It clung, she screamed, and I slid my butt right off the seat and stomped on the gas.

Too bad I didn't know how to drive.

Chapter 2

Tearing out of the warehouse parking lot, I dropped a wheel in a pothole. The Jeep bounced, I flew off the seat, and when everything came down again the hatchback door slammed itself closed. Perfect! I let loose a howl. What a haul! All I had to do was get back to Joe's without crashing.

I'd seen my mom drive, like five years ago, so I had the main idea. Go with the gas pedal, stop with the brake, steer with the wheel. Even so, driving was harder than I thought, especially now that the roads were clogged with wrecked cars, potholes, and traps set by folks like me. I reached over to turn up the heat and nearly went in the ditch doing it.

Once my heart slowed back down, I felt around under the seat and found the lever that scooted it forward. Like most things, it was broken, and it only moved a notch or two. That helped some. The windows didn't want to close, though. They could have been broken, or maybe I didn't hit the right button. I finally gave up and clung to the wheel with icy hands.

I didn't drive fast, but it still wasn't easy, hanging on the edge of the seat and pressing the gas pedal with my big toe. I looped around a curvy road that took me east on what used to be a freeway. That's when the big man caught me. I heard a whoop and then his weight hit the roof of the Jeep. I screamed and mashed the accelerator. The rear-view mirror only showed me a rectangle of black sky, which didn't help, and then a couple of wrecks loomed out of the dark. I swerved hard and barely missed them. Well, I missed them, not counting the scrape on the side of the Jeep. Big Angry Man didn't. I unloaded him there and sped away, giggling.

My tension spiked when I made it back to home territory. Our crew had a decent spread—a couple blocks of slum, with a few abandoned buildings and the Bar and Grill. That was my home, cracked vinyl booths and all. The trick would be to get there alive, and there was a pretty good chance I wouldn't. I dreamed up the security system when I was eleven, but I never thought it could kill me.

I took a slow right turn off the main road onto a cramped side street lined with trailer homes, most of 'em empty. At that point, I should have turned off the headlights. I chickened out. Little boys and small dogs ran loose in the road, and I couldn't bear to squish one. Old Rob Perkins pointed at my lights and wagged a finger at me, but he didn't call his swarm of kids out of the street. Apparently I liked them better than he did. I scanned the roofs of the buildings on both sides, looking for telltale sparks. Nerves made my underarms damp, and I couldn't stop shivering.

Another right took me down into an alley barely wide enough for one car. I had to switch off the lights then, or the boys would put a bullet in my head. *Won't they be sorry when they find me, loaded with loot and dead as their mother,* I thought, trying to stay strong. My back ached from sitting on the edge of the seat, and it wasn't doing my butt any good either.

I missed my left turn in the dark. Swearing, I hit the brakes and struggled with the stick, trying to back that monster up. *I can pass with one miss. Two, and they'll open fire, just like I taught them to. Ditto if I hit anything, or even turn over a trash can.*

Leaning out the open window into the smoky night air, I saw the first rooftop spark. My miss had been noted. I swore again, more colorfully this time. My hands clenched the wheel. Nothing was scarier than a bunch of preteen boys with rifles. I knew, because I trained them. They moved over the rooftops like monkeys, with no fear of death at all.

The way I saw it, anybody who crossed our territory with headlights didn't know the place. People who lived there could come and go in the dark. Lights were nothing but a rolling advertisement saying *I'm trespassing, might as well shoot me.* My idea. Brilliant, huh?

Clouds hid the moon, throwing the alley into darkness. I sat stiffly, staring forward, as the big Jeep inched between two trash cans and a wrecked car. Would it fit? I resisted the temptation to get out and check. Anybody dumb enough to scout ahead would get shot.

I made the next left perfectly, clearing the brick buildings on each side by inches. Ahead, on top of a flat-roofed building, a boy struck a piece of steel against stone, and sparks flew. *Not fair! I made the turn,* I wanted to shout, but I couldn't. As close as I was to losing control of my crew, I couldn't show up crying for mercy. My boys would be off following Dakota before I was done bawling, and I needed them. That pack of young killers was all that stood between me and gangs like the Zunos. They had one woman already. Two would start 'em on a harem, like one of the big crews.

I gasped as my right fender bumped a rusted steel barrel. It rocked dangerously. I took a chance and edged the side of the Jeep in the way. With a metallic clang, the barrel bounced off, rocked, and stayed upright. I flinched at the sound. My jaw ached with tension. More sparks flew from the roof of Joe's diner. Boys crouched up there, rifles shouldered. They'd be watching me through their scopes. Without my hat I looked different. I hardly ever took it off.

This could be it.

I held my breath. Another hundred feet took me right to Joe's back door. Welcoming howls erupted from the rooftop and I nearly cried. Skinny, stunted boys surrounded the Jeep, pounding on the hood with the flats of their hands. "Jack, Jack, Jack," they chanted. It drove me crazy.

I turned the key in the ignition, trying to shut it off. It made a horrible high-pitched chatter instead. Joe reached in through the open window and turned the key the other direction. I could have figured that out.

He got the car door open, grabbed me by the arm, and marched me into the kitchen as fast as his wooden leg would carry him. "What the hell happened?"

"I jacked that car off the Zunos, and it's loaded, just *loaded*, but . . . but..."

"What?"

Tears threatened, and I choked them back. Boys packed into the run-down restaurant kitchen, all staring at me. I swallowed the bitter taste in my mouth and told them the truth. "The rats have pox now, and I think one of 'em might have bitten me."

"Shit! Where'd it get ya?" Joe grabbed my wet sweatshirt and pulled it off over my head.

"On the neck, maybe, if it did at all. I'm not sure."

"Dakota! Get the sulfuric acid off the shelf there." Joe lifted my short hair off my neck. In the glaring light of the single bare light bulb, he looked old and frightened.

Dakota carefully took the bottle off the highest shelf and set it on the counter. Freckles stood out against his pale face. I hadn't seen that look in his eye since I pulled him off his dead mother, five years ago, when he was ten and I was eleven. It made my heart ache.

"You boys, out, out, out! Dakota, keep 'em out," Joe bellowed. He put on a pair of dish gloves, using his left hand to tug the rubbery material over the terrible burn scars on his right. "It'll be okay, Jacqueline."

I hated it when he called me that. It reminded the crew that I was different. I opened my mouth to snap at him, but he spoke first.

"You're gonna need to strip down. Any little mark could be a bite or a scratch. You know what I gotta do." He picked up the bottle of acid. Tears welled up in his kind old eyes.

I couldn't look at him. Teeth chattering with cold, I pulled off my muddy socks and boots, and then my wet jeans. As the only girl there, I'd always been hyper-modest, hiding in my closet to wash or change clothes. I knew it was dumb of me to worry about stuff like that when my life was at stake, but I couldn't help it. A blush spread up my face in a hot wave, all the way to my hairline.

Joe wasn't a dirty old man, thank God. He scanned my body in a professional way, like a doctor, braced for what had to happen if I got the pox. He'd pull the trigger if I asked him to. He owed me that much. I'd saved his life, even if I couldn't save his leg.

"Everything has to come off, Jack. We can't risk missing a bite."

I stood still, absolutely mortified. Only my dread of the pox kept me there. Joe lit the expensive single burner of his stove. Propane was hard to find, so he never let us use it to warm the place. That night he fired it up just for me.

He picked up the bottle of acid. "I won't lie to ya. This is gonna hurt a lot. But it gives you a chance."

Shivering, I pulled off my wet tank top and underwear. My nipples tightened in the drafty room. "Burn it out, Joe," I said, throat tight. I rolled my stiff neck and stared at a yellowed water stain on the wall. "Wherever they bit me. Get it on there good. If I get sick anyway . . . I can't do that to my boys. Before it gets bad, can you . . . can you ask Dakota to shut me down?"

A quick intake of breath by the door made me look up. Dakota stood there, blue eyes wide. He'd put himself on guard at the threshold, keeping the boys out like Joe said to, but he faced into the room, not out. Dakota looked right at me, standing stark naked in Joe's kitchen, and I'd as good as admitted that he mattered more to me than anyone in the world. Too late for bullshit, as my dad used to say, before he died.

"Yeah," I told Dakota. "I want you to pull the trigger. Please. And take care of the boys—"

Joe dabbed acid on my scratched-up arm. I cried out in pain. "I think those cuts were from rocks, when I fell in the river."

"Those aren't claw marks? Hard t' tell," Joe said. "We gotta be sure." He dabbed on a little more. Acid hissed on the open wounds. I panted and tried not to scream. The kids were freaked out enough as it was.

I talked through the pain the best I could. "Dakota, make sure the boys bathe now and then, whether they want to or not. And remember, next summer, there'll be apples out on the west side. You know the place."

Dakota nodded, lips pressed together like he was trying not to cry or scream. I stood frozen, acutely aware of every square inch of skin Joe checked.

"Jack," Joe said. "Jackie!"

I flinched. "What?"

Joe grinned. "I'm pretty sure none o' these marks are bites. Rats got the pox, but chances are, you don't."

My head snapped around and Dakota and I locked eyes. Small boys peered around his legs, watching to see what their chief would do.

I burst into tears, just like a girl.

Chapter 3

Joe broke out his last stash of real shampoo that night, and a tiny bar of hotel soap too, not the homemade stuff that stung my skin. He lit this weird little propane burner he kept in the back, and I had my first hot shower in three years. Afterward, I came into the kitchen wrapped in an old wool army blanket, since I only owned the one pair of jeans. I had three or four shirts, though, or at least I did until the boys started borrowing them. That was so annoying. I looked for my jeans on the kitchen floor and found 'em boiling on the stove with the rest of my dirty clothes. Even my boots sat in a bucket of bleach. Joe wasn't taking any chances with the pox.

I stood there, barefoot on the torn linoleum, and no one noticed me. The guys had hauled the stolen crates inside. Dakota and Joe bent over them, slashing the tape with knives. Small boys practically hung on their arms, little faces lit with excitement. They all babbled at once. "What's in the box? Is it food? Ammo?"

"Toys," three-year-old Tito said. "I hope it's toys."

The scene brought back bittersweet memories of Christmas morning. Most of my boys didn't remember Christmas. Dakota did, though, and so did Keenan and Ash, since they'd been nine or ten at the change. I would have loved to start up the tradition again, but couldn't bear it if I had nothing to give them. I was lucky to keep people fed, and I dreaded their disappointment when I couldn't. Joe couldn't help much, with one missing leg, and those ugly burn scars that pulled his right hand into a claw. He'd been fat once, and he said it saved his life. Five years later, his skin hung in loose folds, too big for his shrunken body.

Usually I was the practical type, 'cause I had to be, but getting toys for Tito suddenly seemed like the most important thing I could do. *Must be stress,* I thought. *Hell of a day.*

A cheer went up when the crate came open, followed by a collective groan. I had to ask. "What is it?"

Fourteen-year-old Keenan rolled his eyes. "Ladies' things."

Joe muscled the crate onto the table. "Go through it, Jackie, see if there's anything that fits." He palmed one of the labels. "Size four, petite? Here's a two. What size are you?"

"I have no idea. Kind of small, I guess."

I wrapped the blanket tighter and squeezed up to the table next to Dakota. He grinned at me, and I couldn't help noticing he had to look down to do it. *Damn. I'm losing ground here.*

Little Tito turned away, his brown eyes sad.

"Hey, Tito," I said brightly. "The boxes are toys. I'll help you make a fort out of them, once we get 'em unloaded."

"Yay!" Tito's tiny feet danced. "Dump 'em out."

"Not so fast," Joe said. "Let 'er find something to wear first."

Keenan shoved his arm in the crate and pulled out a fistful of satin and lace. Sexy lingerie cascaded over his hand, shining in a rainbow of colors, and all the boys stared. Somebody made a loud wolf-whistle.

With an insolent smirk, Keenan held up a scrap of lavender that had to be underwear, even if the bottom was only a triangle held on with strings. "Maybe this would fit you, Jack."

I tried to backfist him in the face without letting go of my blanket. Keenan danced out of reach, laughing at the way I grabbed for the gaping folds of wool.

"Hey, hey, that's enough, there," Joe yelled. "Show yer chief some respect."

"Yeah," Dakota echoed, fixing Keenan in a glare. "Unless you wanna sleep outside tonight. The Zunos are pissed, y' know, and they can take it out on you."

"It was just a joke," Keenan growled. He left the kitchen through the big open archway, throwing punches at the air as he went.

I watched him go. *That one's becoming a problem, and he's too big to slap down. What am I gonna do, quit feeding him? There'd be war.*

"Here's something nice," Joe said, pulling out a long white dress. "This was worth a fortune once."

I shook my head. "No way. There's two things wrong with that. One, it's white. Two, it's a dress. Aren't there any jeans in there? Jackets?"

"Knives?" Dakota added. "Guns?" We shared a smile. At least somebody understood me.

Joe dug through the pile, unearthing more embarrassing thongs. "Not that I can find. Wear this 'til yer jeans are dry, you don't hafta go out in it." He tossed the dress over my shoulder.

I caught it with two fingers and couldn't stop the "oooh," sound that came out my mouth. The dress was pure cashmere, soft and warm. Dragging the hem of the blanket behind me, I went into my closet to change. My closet wasn't really mine, since mostly canned goods lived there, but one corner held a rack for my stuff. A single, bare bulb glared overhead. I locked the door tight, dropped my blanket and slipped on the long-sleeved dress. The fabric hugged my slim body past the hips and then fell to the floor. Silver buttons started at the low v-neck and went the length of the gown to the hem. I tugged the neckline up, but it slid right back down. The outlines of my small breasts showed through, and I wished I'd grabbed a bra out of that crate. No way was I going back for one, not after what Keenan did. I gazed at my reflection in the dusty strip of mirror glued to the inside of the door.

This is gonna make waves.

I left the blanket on the closet floor and walked into the diner, the long skirt swishing around my legs. A semicircle of booths ringed the perimeter, up against the windows. A long wooden bar separated the old restaurant from the kitchen in back. A delicious smell in the air made my stomach growl. It brought back Saturdays at home with my family, watching cartoons until lunch was ready.

I choked up for a second, remembering. "Is that…Spaghetti-O's?"

"Yeah! And there's more, lots more," Tito yelled from one of the booths. His face and hands were covered in red sauce.

When he crawled off his seat and tried to run to me, Dakota scooped him up under one arm. "Don't get sauce on Jackie's new dress, okay?"

"Jack," Tito stared at me, eyes round. "Pwetty."

"Rrrr," Dakota made the sound for him. "Prrretty."

"Pwetty."

"Try again."

Tito got it right that time. Dakota cheered and set him down. "Good job. Run back to the kitchen now and ask Joe to clean you up."

Tito made a beeline for my white skirt, and Dakota headed him off. "Don't touch! Go to the kitchen, now." Tito went.

"Thanks." I sank into my favorite booth. Every crack in the red vinyl seat felt familiar, even through cashmere.

Dakota slid in after me and looked down at my dress. "Wow. Nice." He ran his fingers lightly down the inside of my arm. That tingled, and I felt my cheeks get hot.

"Chef's special," Joe interrupted, setting down a couple of bowls of canned pasta in front of us. He still loved to play at running a restaurant, even though the place hadn't been open in years. "Here ya go, darlin'." With a flourish, he shook out a white cloth napkin and tied it around my neck.

I liked the napkin because it covered the low-cut part of my dress. From Dakota's grunt, he didn't. We filled up on pasta while Joe opened more cans to feed the boys. Soon the booths were full of slurping kids. I winced. I'd kind of dropped the ball on the whole table manners thing.

Two bowls later, Joe untied my napkin and disappeared into the back with a herd of young ones who needed a wash. I caught Dakota looking at me. He got that funny quirk at the corner of his mouth, like he did when he was trying not to laugh, but he didn't look away. He reached out, real slow, and touched my hair. A sweet shiver went down my back. Dakota noticed and shot me a grin.

That's when I knew I was in trouble.

The outside door opened and then slammed shut. Keenan and Ash ran in, laughing their asses off. "Did you see the look on his face?"

The boys piled into our booth, even though like five other ones were open, and both of them started talking at once. "We took all those empty cans."

"Down to the corner, where that flat-topped building looks down on Zunos territory," Ash filled in.

Keenan mimed dumping a load of garbage, and they both cracked up. "Oh, man! Direct hit!"

"Right on top of Rico's convertible. I thought that guy was gonna have a heart attack."

I sat up straight. "They saw you? Which one?"

"The older dude, with the big arms and the shaved head," Keenan gurgled, wiping tears of hilarity off his cheeks.

"Benny." I slumped back in my seat. "Shit. You had to rub it in." Keenan and Ash looked a little deflated until I added, "Benny probably loves Spaghetti-O's."

We all laughed then. I knew I shouldn't, since what they did really was dangerous, but it wasn't my fault if I had a teenaged-boy sense of humor. I hadn't hung out with a girlfriend in years.

I slowly shook my head. "They're gonna come after us now for sure."

"That didn't make no difference," Joe said from behind me. "They woulda come for us in any case. You took their frigin' car, Jackie."

"Great," Dakota muttered. He stood up on his seat. "Hey! Listen up! I want double guards tonight, all night. Locked and loaded! Be ready, 'cause they *are* coming. Hit the bell if you even think you see the Zunos."

"What's in it for me? Besides not dying, I mean," fourteen-year-old Ash said, and the younger boys giggled. "I want extra Spaghetti-O's."

"Fine. Anybody who does a double shift gets a whole can to himself," Dakota said.

I put my head in my hands. *This is my fault. I pissed off the Zunos. Stupid, impulsive thing to do.*

Dakota bounced over the partition into the next booth, hopped off that table, and stopped dead. "Oh, sorry, Chief. Did I, um . . . overstep there?"

"No, no, that was good, Dakota. Thanks," I said.

I'd always wanted my lieutenants to think for themselves. It hadn't occurred to me that once they did, they wouldn't need me anymore.

"Hey Jack," Joe said. "The little guy's asking for you. I got him all cleaned up."

I opened my arms to the toddler. "Come on up here, sweetie." Tito crawled up on my lap. I hugged him, cooing like a mother over his cuteness. It would have been nice to have a little girl too, but of course they weren't any.

Dakota gave me a soft smile as he hurried by. Then he snapped into lieutenant mode. "All right, you guys! Let's get that scrap metal up on the roof. Remember, the only car they've got left is a soft top."

That set off a round of howls. My crew streamed out the door, leaving me behind. I felt hollow inside, even with a sweet little kid to hug. *Is this what I have to look forward to?*

I leaned back with the sleepy child in my arms, overwhelmed with love. I was so glad I hadn't let Tito die. I almost did. I almost chose to leave him for the hunters.

Hunters. I shuddered. Those pox-infected people seemed to exist for only one thing—a chance to pass on the disease. They hid in places we had to go, near food and water, along roads, or inside camping stores. I saw a hunter catch a boy once, hold him down, and press his pox-slimed lips against the boy's screaming mouth. I never really got over it.

But that didn't happen to Tito. Me and Dakota, we saved him.

At the peak of the epidemic, people had swarmed the stores, trying to lay in supplies. Lots of them got infected and wandered off. Cars clogged the lanes outside the supermarket, blocking each other in. I closed my eyes, re-living the hot, hungry summer when I was fourteen.

My empty stomach aches. Dakota insists on risking the grocery store. I reluctantly agree. Nerves on edge, we slip between abandoned cars. Sun scorches my bare shoulders. Something rustles. I duck down in the shadow of an old pickup and freeze. A wadded McDonald's bag tumbles by, riding the dry Colorado wind. Dakota beckons me forward. I creep up to join him, keeping low to use cars for cover. Thirst burns my throat.

We peer into the dirty windows of every vehicle we pass, alert for hunters. I only see a few dead dogs on the seats. Those give me a pang. I watch Dakota's back while he uses his pry-bar on the dead automatic door of the Safeway store. Straining, he makes a crack wide enough for his skinny body to squeeze through. I gulp a last breath of fresh air and follow. Inside, the whole place stinks. Black mold coats the floor and drifts dustily along the tiles. We crouch behind a cash register and peek out. A sneeze threatens, so I press a finger hard under my nose to quash it. Good thing, too.

A pox-infected housewife trudges by, her fuzzy slippers crunching on broken glass. She's pushing an empty shopping cart. Gray, sticklike legs stick out from under her filthy dress. We hold our breath until she goes by.

"She's shopping?" Dakota mouths.

"Going through the motions," I whisper back. "It's kind of . . . mechanical."

If that woman spots us, she'll chase us for sure. But she's sickly, and we're faster. I like my chances. The poxy housewife rounds a corner and disappears, wheels squeaking. I pull a dusty plastic shopping basket off a stack and dart down an aisle. Working together, me and Dakota pile random cans in the basket and run for the door, holding the wire handles between us. We fit through the crack in the door better than our basket does, but we make it, loot and all.

Outside, we jerk to a halt. A minivan sits on the sidewalk, just outside the door. It hadn't been there before. A baby wails from his car seat. I cringe at the noise.

Dakota rubs dirt off the back window and peers in. "A live baby! Haven't seen one of those in years. We gotta get out of here. That sound's gonna bring down hunters for sure."

Inside the store, a woman screams.

"Too late. They just got his mom," I rasp.

Dakota's already moving. "Jackie, come on!" he says over his shoulder.

A rattling sound comes from the door. I should run, but I stand there, riveted. A young, black-haired Latina struggles in the grip of the poxy housewife. Silver drool drips from the infected woman's lips.

"Tito, Tito," the young mother sobs. She wrenches at the crack in the door. It's too narrow for her.

I take a step toward the door, and then stop. Long, red fingernail scratches mark the mother's arms. We can't help her. She's already infected.

The sobbing woman wrenches one hand free. She reaches into her jeans pocket, pulls out a set of car keys, and tosses them to me. I step back, shaking my head, and let the keys clatter to the sidewalk.

"Get Tito!" she shrieks. "Please! Take him, feed him, please, please."

With a final scream, the woman gets pulled back into the store. I hesitate, then dive for the car keys.

"Jackie, what're you doing?" Dakota bellows. "Seriously, you're taking the baby?"

***

I shifted on the red vinyl cushion, forcing the memory out of my mind. Around me, the diner was dim and quiet. I felt safe. Tito was safe.

I dozed off and barely cracked an eye when Joe gently scooped up the sleeping kid and limped off to tuck him into his usual booth. I sat up and stretched my arms over my head. “Everything okay?”

Joe reached past my head to tug the blue cotton curtain tight across the window. “Some kinda action outside.”

A tingle of adrenaline trickled through me. I scooted out of the booth and padded barefoot to the door.

Joe put a hand on it and held it closed. “Jack, I never did tell ya what to do, not even when you were a little girl. But I’m telling ya now. Stay inside.”

“Why? The Zunos know I’m a girl now! Our crew always sort of knew, but they didn’t care until you made me wear this stupid dress.”

“Too bad,” Joe said. “Yer not goin’ out lookin’ like that.”

I glared. “Like what?”

“Bait.”

Chapter 4

I couldn't sleep. Boys ran in and out of the diner all night, letting in cold air every time they opened the door. We couldn't afford to heat the place on a good day. That night, I could see my breath by the light of the beer signs in the window. I tucked my bare toes up under the cashmere skirt, wishing our last space heater hadn't crapped out. We used to be able to find those in abandoned stores, but not anymore. Stuff got picked over in the years since the epidemic began. I wrapped a blanket around my shoulders and worried.

Around two in the morning Joe caught me sneaking into the kitchen to check on my jeans, which hadn't dried much in the cold. "Go lie down, Jackie. You need t' rest up, after what you been through. You were exposed to the pox, whether you got bit or not. Bad time t' stress yourself."

The nasty sensation of the rat's tail whipping across my lip came back to me. But the boys all thought I was fine, and I wasn't about to scare them with that story.

I folded my arms and looked up at him. "Why are you suddenly treating me like this, Joe? I'm not fragile."

Joe huffed a tired sigh. "Yer the only girl we got. We need you. The whole damn world needs you."

"Sure," I spat. "To have babies. What, am I locked in now?"

I said it right as the back door opened. Dakota, Ash, and Keenan came in off their shift, all flushed with excitement. When they heard what I said, their chatter died.

"What's this?" Keenan stalked up to Joe. "Is she? Is she locked in now?"

"I never said that," Joe said.

"Don't even think it," Keenan snapped. He brushed past, crackling with aggressive energy. Droplets of drying blood stained the front of his shirt. My shirt, actually, one he'd borrowed without asking.

"You hurt, Keenan?" I asked softly.

He shook his tawny head. "It's not my blood." A feral light danced in his eyes.

Keenan looked me up and down with those gold cat eyes of his, making me wish I had something to wear besides that dress. Then he cruised off toward the darkened bar. I watched him go.

"Hey Dakota, you guys want some food before you go out on shift?" I asked, just to change the subject.

"That was it. I'm done," he told me. "I've got guys on the border with everything in the arsenal. It's quiet out there right now."

I knew what he was leaving out. Keenan had tangled with somebody, but we were all too tired to talk about it.

"Good," I said. "Let's get some sleep."

We headed for our usual booth. Dakota always slept on one side of the table, and I slept on the other. Years ago, when we were all smaller, we'd pile in four or five to a booth, leaving most of the benches in the diner empty. It was less scary that way, especially when homeless guys started kicking over garbage cans in the alley.

That night, when I crawled onto my bed, Ash and Keenan had already taken over Dakota's side of the booth. They sat shoulder to shoulder, stiffly, like they had something to say. I glanced at Dakota to see how he was handling that. He didn't seem to care. He just collapsed in the booth behind me instead. Since I couldn't flop down like I wanted to, I sat there, stared at Keenan and Ash, and waited.

That pair had been joined at the hip since they came to me as lost fourth graders. If the world hadn't gone to shit, Ash would have been the most popular boy in school. He could be deadly when pushed, but his mom must have raised him with all kinds of compassion. He used to rescue moths from windowsills and pick earthworms out of puddles after it rained. That night, I figured Ash meant to rescue me. Why he brought Keenan along, I had no idea.

Ash leaned forward, a sympathetic smile on his handsome face. Dim red and blue neon light shone off his perfect chocolate skin and wooly hair. "How you feelin', Jack?"

"Fine." I kept it short, hoping they'd go away so I could sleep.

"I got something for you. Or we do. It's from Keenan, too. I couldn't have got it without him." Ash dug into his pocket and pulled out a small leather bag. He pushed it across the table to me.

I poured out the contents and gasped. A handful of gold and diamond rings spilled out, along with a fat roll of hundred dollar bills. Paper money didn't mean much anymore, at least in my neighborhood, but those rings made the best trade goods ever. I flicked the bills aside and played with the rings, admiring their glitter in the neon light of the bar signs in the window. "Wow. This is really something."

"Spoils of war," Keenan said. "By the way, I didn't get the chance to tell you earlier, but you look gorgeous in that dress."

I felt my eyes widen in their sockets. "Uh, thanks," I choked out.

The back of my seat rocked a little as Dakota rolled to his knees and leaned on the partition between the booths. "Go to bed, you guys."

"Okay," Keenan said obediently. As if they'd rehearsed it, Ash and Keenan laid down in Dakota's spot, feet together and heads in opposite directions. It looked crowded and uncomfortable, but they settled in like they meant to stay.

Dakota shot them a murderous look. One on one, he could whip either of them, but together, those boys could kill him. I felt sick thinking about it. The winner—or winners—would lead my crew, alongside me. And from the way Keenan looked at me, that wasn't all they had in mind. I could have sworn fourteen was too young. Guess I was wrong.

Joe cut the dim light over the bar and left for his pallet in the back. I laid down on my right side, head by the window, facing the dark forms of Ash and Keenan. They didn't try to move any closer. If they had, I would have spent the night in my closet with the canned goods. The diner got quiet, but I didn't sleep. I laid awake thinking about Dakota. I couldn't believe they pushed him aside that easily. *How am I going to hold off both Ash and Keenan at once? What will they do when I refuse them?*

The back of the seat rocked again, and Dakota dropped down behind me, the length of his lean, hard body pressed against mine. I sucked in a startled breath. Dakota wrapped an arm around me and lay still. I trembled a little, ready to run, but he didn't move his hand off my stomach.

I lifted my head to look over my shoulder at him. He gave me the tiniest smile, just the corners of his lips, and his eyes were soft. I let my head down just as Dakota slid his arm under it. Pillowed on his shoulder, I felt warm and safe. I reached back with one hand and flipped half my blanket over him.

Ash and Keenan sat up for a second to look at us and then sank back down, stubbornly refusing to leave. That bothered me.

As the only girl around, I'd been pressured for sex since childhood. Some men wouldn't take no for an answer, so I got pretty good at taking cheap shots and bolting. That kind of thing got worse as I got older. Dakota watched out for me, sticking closer as I got into my teens and even normal, non-pervy men started taking an interest. That was when I cut my hair off and tried to look like a boy. We never talked about it—I was way too shy—but Dakota had to know I was still a virgin. Now he obviously wanted to be more than friends, and I couldn't get comfortable with it. I didn't want anyone else. Never had. Dakota was the only guy I ever dreamed about, ever pictured myself having babies with. The only one I didn't want to reject. But old fears die hard.

Tension began to leave my shoulders. As I relaxed, Dakota molded his body to mine. My heart raced, and I covered his hand with my own, pressing it close. I wiggled my hips, just a little, enjoying the feel of him through my cashmere skirt. Dakota's breath came faster, stirring my hair. He traced his lips across the nape of my neck. All at once I wanted him to kiss me, and I was afraid he'd try.

He must have sensed my fear, because he stroked my hair with one hand, whispering, "It's okay, Jackie, it's okay. Go to sleep."

I didn't want to. I didn't want to miss a second of that.

***

I woke up the next morning, still tangled in Dakota's arms. At some point I'd rolled over in my sleep and thrown a leg over his hip. Embarrassed, I edged it back.

Dakota caught the back of my thigh and stopped me. "Don't," he whispered.

I dropped my gaze, but left my leg where it was, despite my shyness. I had to admit, I suddenly wanted to kiss him. I wanted it bad. But the diner was full of boys who were probably giggling at us behind their hands. I peeked under the table. Keenan and Ash were gone, thank God. Sounds of ripping cardboard told me people were helping themselves to boxes of canned goods, which I strictly rationed.

Dakota's blue eyes smiled into mine. He slid his fingers up an inch or two and squeezed the back of my thigh. "Mmm. Feels good."

The pressure sent heat to my core. I felt my breath quicken. "Yeah," I whispered. "But it sounds like the kids are up. They're into the food."

"Can we let 'em, just this once?" Dakota murmured. "Maybe we all oughta grab the chance to be happy, before . . ."

"Before war breaks out?"

"Don't think about it right now, Jackie." Dakota put a hand on my ass and pressed himself against me.

I'd never felt anything like that in my life. I made a little sound, half moan and half sigh, and his eyes damn near lit on fire. I forgot all about war, with the Zunos or anybody else.

Dakota took a shuddering breath and his free hand came up to cradle the back of my head. We gazed into each other's eyes. His lips were parted a little, and his blue eyes looked gray in the hazy light. I stroked his cheek, the side with the scar from his first knife fight, and tangled my fingers in his dark hair. I loved every line of that face. He kissed me, lightly at first, then more insistently, our breath mingling, coming faster, until Keenan kicked the underside of the table with his boot.

That made a huge boom, right by my ear. I squealed. The old Formica table rattled against the bolts that held it to the floor. Diamond rings bounced off and rolled all over the floor. Kids giggled from all around the diner.

"What the fuck, Keenan?" Dakota roared, heaving himself up.

I shot out of the booth and tripped on the hem of that stupid dress. I would have fallen on my face if Ash hadn't caught me. I shook him off like it was all his fault and ran into my closet. The closed door muffled the sounds of the boys shouting. I flicked the light on and froze. The place had been transformed. The cans all sat on one side, and the flimsy curtain rod bowed under the weight of my new clothes. Joe must have done it for me.

My fingers automatically flipped through the hangers. They remembered the motion from long ago trips to the mall with my mom. *Mom.* I sank to the floor in a pile of cashmere and let the tears go. My thoughts jumped from her to Sophia, who probably would have shared all those clothes with me if I hadn't ripped her off. I would've loved to hang out with another girl. Too bad that friendship came as a package deal with three horny old men.

In a minute I stood and wiped my face. That skirmish last night was just the Zunos testing us. They'd come in force. If not tonight, then soon. We had work to do. I shucked the dress, grabbed an emerald-green sweater off the rack and slipped on my old jeans, even if they did stink of bleach. New socks, fresh from the package, made me feel crazy rich. I laced up my damp boots, pushed open the closet door, and stepped into our single, short hallway.

One end of it led into the diner, and the other dead-ended in the storage room that doubled as Joe's bedroom. About halfway down, an archway opened into the cramped industrial kitchen. Opposite that was our one tiny bathroom, which only worked when we poured water in the toilet tank. That was it. Not a lot of space for nine people. No wonder the place always smelled like dirty socks.

Joe muttered from inside his room. His gruff voice carried too well. "Better watch yer back, Griffin."

"No shit," Dakota answered.

"We don't need them two runnin' this outfit. 'Specially not that Keenan. He ain't been right in the head since dogs ate his sister, and her not even dead yet. Take this."

"Sweet," Dakota said, in that vaguely awestruck tone I'd only ever heard him use about weapons.

"The blade clips on yer boot, like this. Don't let nobody see it."

"'K. Thanks, Joe."

I hesitated in the hall, but decided not to interrupt, even to tell Joe that he ought to shut the door if he wanted to give away his boot knife in secret. For all I knew, he wanted to be overheard. Maybe it was his way of supporting Dakota. The old man's opinion sure carried a lot of weight with the boys.

I did a U-turn and wandered off toward the diner. Joe's motives had always been a mystery to me. Our crew had lived with him for almost five years, and I still didn't understand him. Crippled or not, the old man could be chief if he wanted. But he wouldn't take the job. He never said why, but I guessed his brush with death did it. The reaper took Joe's leg already, and most of the use of his right hand. When it came for the rest of him, he wanted us to be ready.

Back in the diner, first shift was already out on watch. The other boys were either sleeping or sitting around on top of the tables, eating cold food out of cans. Marc, the new kid, sat alone in a booth, knobby knees to his chest. That skinny white kid reminded me of a stray puppy, long legs and no meat on him at all. He watched the other boys with big, frightened eyes, and he didn't try and talk to anyone. Ash had found him in the alley a couple nights earlier, starved, frozen, and all bruised up from someone's fists. Marc swore he was eleven, but he looked more like nine. Whoever he lived with before didn't feed him much.

Marc saw me coming, jumped off his bench, and intercepted me before I got halfway across the room. "Jack, aren't I supposed to work? I'll pull my weight around here." He pushed a lock of tangled brown hair out of his eyes and snuck a glance at another boy's breakfast.

I felt sorry for him. The poor kid was hungry, too scared to help himself, and nobody had noticed. "Okay, if you're well enough to work, you can go out with me and Paco today," I said, pulling a can of refried beans from a box. I handed it to him, along with a can opener and a mostly-clean spoon. "Eat this now. You'll get one more at dinner time." I clapped Marc on the shoulder, grabbed my sweatshirt and went out the front door, leaving him to struggle with the can opener alone.

Outside, painfully bright sun glared off new snow. Ice glazed the cracked windshields of the wrecks in the diner's parking lot. I didn't dare wander too far that way, not without a gun. Instead I went left, around the outside of the diner, and then veered right, down the alley. That path led through the garbage maze and out to Zunos territory. Rico might be down there, or some of Flint's men. I'd rather see those guys from one of my rooftop hiding places, where they probably wouldn't see me.

Our homemade metal ladder clung to the wall of the four-story building next door. Half-hidden in shadow, it was hard to see. I started the four-story climb to the roof, ignoring the cold that bit into my bare hands. My arms ached by the time I got to the top. I pulled myself onto the gravel-strewn rooftop with a grunt and wiped my damp, freezing hands on my jeans. From up there, I could see the top of the Zunos' house, two buildings away. Their place had once been a fancy townhome. Now the lower windows were all boarded over, except for a few portholes to shoot through. A sloppy homemade barricade surrounded their winter-brown vegetable garden.

To my left, Ash sat cross-legged on the roof, over by the corner that looked down on the garbage maze. His rifle lay across his knees. "You're early for your shift, Jackie. The bell hasn't even gone off yet."

"I know." My eyes automatically scanned the rooftops for snipers, but the territory seemed deserted. I squatted down anyway, in case my outline showed against the sky. "I don't see any of Flint's men out there. Don't see anybody."

"There's at least two of Rico's guys behind the curtains on their top floor. If you watch long enough, you'll see light glint off their binoculars," Ash said. "Flint's not here yet. He doesn't usually hassle 'em 'til after dark."

I knew that much, but I didn't say so. Ash might've heard the fear in my voice.

When Flint says the word, his army will crush the Zunos. He'll take Sophia and move on us next. Then where am I gonna run?

Ash shoved a hand in his jeans pocket and pulled out that same little leather bag. "I know I gave this to you before, but here it is again."

"Oh, the rings! You picked them all off the floor for me. That was so sweet," I said, and I meant it. The roll of bills was in there too. Looking over the gray, run-down city, I got an idea. "You know, paper money isn't worth much around here. But I hear they still have shops at the Tech Center. There's supposed to be a whole complex behind that fence, with a university and everything."

"How you gonna get in there, Jack? With the fence they got around that place, it might as well be a prison."

"Maybe they'll let me in, if I look nice," I said. "I can dress up now, remember? I might pass as a student."

Ash shook his head. "Don't be stupid. You go in that gate, you're never coming out. The guards'll be like, free girl, thanks. That was easy."

I huffed a frustrated sigh. "The kids are in rags, Ash. There's holes in the bottoms of Zach's tennis shoes, and he wears 'em out in the snow. It's all he's got! I'm down to my last pair of jeans, and these aren't gonna last much longer." I ran a finger over the patch of chilly skin that showed through the hole on my knee.

"You have plenty of sexy underwear though," Ash smirked.

I punched his shoulder. "Seriously! People need stuff. I wish we could scrounge at the malls, but they're a nightmare." We both shuddered. Abandoned malls were usually crawling with hunters, and the other scavengers we might run into weren't much better.

Ash cradled his rifle, looking thoughtful. "You know that outlet mall up north? That's a possibility, now that we got a car."

I shrugged. "I haven't been there since before the epidemic. Could be bad now."

Ash's brown eyes lit with excitement. "Maybe it's not. That place is out on the highway, too far to walk. Could be loaded! Damn, I wish I knew how to drive."

"I'll teach you. I figured it out yesterday, more or less. Let's check it out this afternoon. But this might not work out. I don't want to get the kids' hopes up and then let 'em down. So can we keep this to ourselves?"

Ash grinned. "Sure, *Jacqueline*."

"Don't call me that." Laughing, I threw the leather bag at him, but I snatched it right back. I still dreamed of using those hundred dollar bills in the fancy shops at the Center.

From outside the diner, someone hit our scrap metal bell. Ash handed me his rifle and left, leaving me alone with my worries. I pulled up my hood, hunkered down, and stared out over the decaying city. Fear crawled out of my belly and made itself at home in my head. *Flint's coming. I don't have anywhere to run. Should I take off through the streets, alone, or with the crew? How can I ask them to give up their home? How long would Tito last outside, at night, in the bitter cold?*

I had no answers, so it was easier to focus on the things I could change. I could get shoes for the kids, and maybe some warm clothes. I could scrounge food to fill the storeroom. But our biggest problem was defense. *There might be something I can do about that . . . before it's too late.*

Three hours later, the bell rang, signaling the end of my shift, so I handed off my rifle to Dakota. He took it without a word. I hesitated before turning away. *What did last night mean? Are we different now? Are we together? Or was he just playing around, showing up Keenan?*

Dakota shifted his rifle into one hand and caught me around the waist with the other. He pulled me close. "You don't get off that easy," he teased.

My worries melted when our lips pressed together. By then, I didn't want to go inside, but I couldn't hang around distracting a sentry, either.

"See you later, after my shift," Dakota murmured.

"Okay. Be careful out here. Keep your head down." I gave him a last, quick kiss and reluctantly let him go.

By the time I got back inside, my mind was back in business mode. Food, security, survival. That's what mattered. Before my night with Dakota, it was all I ever thought about.

I walked into the diner and clapped my hands loud. "Hey, hey, babeees! I got plans for a wicked new trap. Who wants to help me set it up?"

A couple of bleary eyed twelve-year-olds crawled out of a booth and shuffled toward me. "She asks, like it's optional," Zachary said to Caleb.

"No, you guys did a late shift last night," I told them. "Go back to bed. You're not on again 'til three."

"Oh, good." The kids did identical face-plants onto red vinyl cushions, and they didn't move again.

I tried not to laugh. Both of them had dried-on goop on their faces. They'd obviously been up early, stealing extra food while I rolled around in Dakota's arms.

Dakota . . . That thought made me flush in places I didn't know could flush. Maybe the two of us would end up together, permanently. Dakota sure had the makings of a good father. He was already sharing that job with Joe. I forced my mind back onto business. I was Chief. We had work to do if we wanted to survive.

"Paco, Marc! Let's go," I called. The three of us cut through the kitchen on our way out.

Keenan leaned on the back door, smiling a little, his weird amber eyes on me. He stepped aside when he saw us coming. "Need some help, Jack?"

I felt like saying no, since he'd done two shifts already, but I really did need the help. Besides, if Keenan was gonna be an asshole, I figured I ought to squeeze some extra work out of him. "Yeah," I told him. "I need some muscle for what I've got in mind."

He puffed up a little, and I knew I said the right thing. Ash appeared then, Keenan's ever-present shadow, so I led my troops out into the cold gray day. We climbed the rusted ladder and trotted across the rooftop, faster as we warmed up. At the corner, an eight-foot gap yawned between one rooftop and the next. The jump itself wasn't that hard, but it was six stories down to concrete. A miss would be fatal for sure. That scared the crap out of me, but I hid it pretty well. My heart pounded. I sprinted for the gap and landed in a spray of gravel. Why they put gravel on rooftops, I never knew.

I got ready to spot the next kid in line, who turned out to be Ash. Ash didn't need anybody's help. He bounded the gap with the grace of a panther, landed way past me, and came back to crouch near the edge, about ten feet away. The two children watched us anxiously.

"You're next, Paco," I called. "You can do this. Take a big run at it."

Paco scrubbed his mouth with the back of one hand. He wiped his palms on his jeans and eyed the gap, dark eyes bright with fear.

"Right here, buddy." Ash patted a spot to his left. "That's your target."

Paco took a couple of big steps back, crossed himself, and started his run. His tennis shoes flapped on the rooftop. They were way too big for him.

My stomach clenched. "Jump hard," I screamed.

Paco's little legs churned. Everything looked good to the last second, when he came up short by half a stride and chipped in an extra one. He wasn't going to make it. His hands grabbed for the edge, stubby fingers clinging, and his legs kicked in midair. Ash hauled him up by one arm and the back of his jacket.

"Oh my God," I gasped. Paco crawled for my lap and I hugged him, stroking his coarse black hair. "It's okay, baby, it's okay now, you made it." Over the top of Paco's head, Ash and I shared a horrified look.

The last kid stood forgotten on the other side. After a minute or two, I looked up and signaled him to wait.

I patted Paco's back. "Sit down over there and wait for me." He obeyed without a word.

I turned my attention to the new kid, who looked like he'd lost all confidence in the leadership around here. I didn't blame him.

I stood up. "Marc! You're up. Go, go, go!"

He made it with inches to spare, but me and Ash both grabbed the back of his shirt, just in case. The worn cloth ripped. Marc gave me an irritated look.

"Sorry," I said. "I'll get you another shirt when I can." That seemed to satisfy him.

I stood up and stretched my back. I hadn't even gotten to work yet and I was already exhausted. A howl came from the other rooftop, where we'd just been. Keenan stood on top of this big boxy structure, where I guess the vents went in. That put him about fifteen feet up, and twice as far from the edge as he needed to be. Once he saw us watching, he ran a few strides and then hurled himself into space.

Keenan fell through the air in a gigantic arc, arms out to the sides and knees pulled high. He landed with a whooping war cry, which I didn't appreciate, seeing as how we were there on the sly to set a trap. Come to think of it, I'd been making way too much noise myself.

"Nice jump," I said, as he swaggered over. I opened my mouth to add a few things, like shut the fuck up and don't ever do that again.

I never got the chance.

"Thanks, babe," Keenan said.

"Don't call me that," I said. All the boys laughed, even Ash, and I couldn't help smiling. I led them across the roof. "Come on, I'll show you my evil plan."

Chapter 5

I had a talent for setting traps. Deadfalls, pits, trip wires—I loved them all. That day, I had a big idea. Big enough to make every trap I'd ever made look lame in comparison.

I pointed across the rooftop. "There it is. That will be my masterpiece."

A white plastic water cistern sat high on a platform. Even without the scaffold, the tank must have been twelve feet tall. Big bolts attached it to the roof of the old hotel, and a vertical pipe fed into the base. I didn't mind destroying it, since nobody needed it anymore. That red brick building had been abandoned as long as I could remember. We scrounged in there on and off for years, until the place flooded one rainy spring and everything inside molded.

What really made me drool was the building's location, overlooking the Zunos' parking lot. "So, if we drop this into the alley while Rico's driving out—" I started.

Keenan cut me off. "No way. I'm not moving that. It's too big."

I wanted to punch him, but I'd lose that fight. *How the hell does Sophia get all those men to obey her?*

"Keenan, be a love and bring me a crescent wrench, one that'll fit those big bolts on the bottom," I said, in my best Sophia Arabola imitation.

He used same fake voice back. "All right. Just for you, doll." Keenan bounced over the gap between buildings again, taking the easy way this time, and loped away over the rooftop.

"Doll?" Ash choked back a laugh.

I shrugged. "A small price to pay." Then we both busted up.

Pretty quick, Keenan showed up with the crescent wrench. He handed it to me with a flourish.

"Thanks, love," I said, with only a little snark. I squatted down and tried the wrench on the rusty old scaffold. Those bolts were stuck tight. I struggled for a while, gave up and sat back on my heels, panting. "Crap."

"Here's where the muscle comes in," Keenan said. He took the wrench out of my hand without even asking.

I pressed my lips together to keep from snapping. I really wanted those bolts out. That cistern would fill the alley perfectly. Targeted right, it could crush Rico's car. The thought made me cringe, but we didn't have to use it unless we really needed it.

Instead of using the tool like a normal human being, Keenan beat at the frame like an angry gorilla. First one corroded bolt popped loose, then another, until the scaffold came free from the roof. The cistern swayed, and water sloshed inside.

Ash climbed up and took off the bolts that held the tank to the platform. "Stay back, you guys," he told the younger kids. "It's just balanced up there now."

"When we tip it, I bet that pipe at the bottom will snap," I said. "If we can get the tank lose without draining it all the way, it'll land like a bomb."

The boys cheered. We all started pushing the scaffold. The tank rocked, farther each time, until the pipe at the base gave way with a scream. The whole thing crashed down. Our shoes got soaked, but plenty of water stayed inside, under the level of the central pipe.

"Oooh, this is going to be perfect," I chortled. While Ash and Keenan tore off the rest of the metal frame, I knelt down by the younger boys, who wouldn't have been out there in the first place if I had any brains. I opened my arms to them. "Thanks, guys. We couldn't have done this without you."

Paco and his new buddy came over for their hug and then shared the biggest grin I'd ever seen. Marc probably wouldn't wander off any time soon. We might starve, but we sure weren't boring.

"Don't we get hugs?" Keenan leered. "You couldn't have done it without us, either."

Dakota loped toward us across the rooftop. From his scowl, I could tell he heard that. He stared at Ash and Keenan, his dark brows drawn together. "No, but you can each have an extra can of food, though."

Keenan glared. "We ate plenty while you two were busy—"

Ash elbowed Keenan in the ribs. They both glanced at me, real quick, and shut up.

Dakota ignored them. "What are you guys doing, Jackie? Is this a new trap? It's huge."

I led him closer, eager to show it off. "Look, it'll fill the alley, so they won't be able to dodge, at least not side to side."

Dakota moved to the edge of the roof to look down. "It really will fit exactly. Great idea. Good job, everybody."

Keenan gave the tank a shove. The heavy cistern rolled toward Dakota's back.

"Look out," I shrieked. I pounced on the tank, clinging to the raised plastic edge. The massive cylinder slid under my hands and kept moving. Marc and Paco leaped in to help.

Ash stood frozen. Keenan folded his arms and sneered.

Dakota leaped the five-foot cistern almost from a standstill. I gaped in amazement. In his place, I would have gotten steamrolled right off the building. Those boys were inhuman on a lot of different levels.

The tank stopped just short of the edge. I wanted to run to Dakota, reassure myself that he was all right, but he went into full-on lieutenant mode. "Roll it back, people. Nobody get between the tank and the drop again."

Working together, me, Dakota, and the younger boys wrestled the cistern away from the precipice. Keenan leaped the gap between the buildings and headed home alone.

"Ash, haul some bricks up here and block it in," Dakota ordered. "Keep it lined up with the alley so it's ready to go."

I was kind of surprised when Ash obeyed.

We all got back to the diner without any more near-death experiences. On the back porch we ran into Caleb and Zachary, coming out for sentry duty.

"Yuck, Paco, you got blood all over the doorknob," Zachary said.

I hadn't even noticed the kid was hurt.

Zachary grabbed Paco's hand and took a look at the cut. "What happened, dude?"

Paco's stocky little body practically quivered with the morning's excitement. His breath blew clouds of steam into the winter air. "We set up an awesome trap over Rico's alley with an old water cistern. You gotta see it—it's a car crusher! The broken pipe at the bottom had sharp edges, I guess. No big deal. And then Keenan—" He cut himself off and glanced up at me.

I derailed that topic on purpose. "Paco, go find Joe. He'll help you get that cut cleaned up and bandaged."

Paco headed into the kitchen. I followed him inside and found the kid on his hands and knees, digging comic books out of a low cabinet.

"Keep your hand off the dirty floor, Paco. It's gonna get infected."

He rolled his eyes and huffed. "It's just a little cut. Not fatal, Jack."

I turned away. "Whatever." I had trouble on my mind—Keenan trouble. I'd just seen him out of the corner of my eye, slipping past the doorway of the kitchen on his way to the back room. That was Joe's private space. Keenan would only be going there for one reason—to hide.

Paco glanced after Keenan. "He better run."

I nodded. "Yep. Dakota's gonna kill him. I ain't stoppin' him, either." *Not that I could if I wanted to.*

In a few seconds, Dakota's footfalls pounded down the hall. "Keenan! Where the hell are you?" He stuck his angry, red face through the open archway to the kitchen. A big wooden club swung from his fist.

I pointed right. Dakota stormed that way. Me and Paco ran into the hall to watch him go. Dakota kicked open Joe's door, splintering the flimsy frame, and the shouting began.

Paco took a nervous step back, the stack of dog-eared comic books hugged to his narrow chest. "Glad he's not mad at me," he whispered.

I nodded. Not that I would've said so out loud, but I felt the same way. "This is gonna get ugly. Keenan's prob'ly got his knife on him."

The shouting got louder. "Fight, fight," boys shouted, crowding into Joe's doorway to watch.

"Some fool's gonna get in the way and get himself cut," I muttered. "Stay here, Paco." I squared my shoulders and strode down the hall. "Clear out, you guys. Clear out, I said! Let 'em work this out on their own."

Inside Joe's room, something crashed. Keenan yelped. Nobody listened to me.

I pulled my car antenna whip out of the back pocket of my jeans and tugged on one end, so it telescoped out long. I'd never hit anyone with it yet, but the crew didn't necessarily know that. The whip made an intimidating whine as it arced through the air, and the metal knob on the end hit the wall with a crack. Powdery, white drywall flew.

"Move it! Right now." Boys flinched. I whirled the whip one more time.

The crowd retreated halfway down the hall, which was far enough for me. I stepped into the small, windowless room. The stagnant air reeked of dirty socks, angry boy sweat, and fear. Keenan lay in a fetal position on a narrow strip of floor between Joe's low foam pallet and the wall. A long smear of blood told me he'd hit the ground hard enough to slide. Both arms wrapped around his head, and his knife lay out of reach against the far wall. Dakota stood over him, club raised. His hands trembled with fury.

"He had it coming," I said softly. "But that's enough. Don't kill him, Dakota. Not today, anyway. We're doing this by the rules."

Dakota looked right at me, chin tipped up like a gangster. Then he took a step forward and kicked Keenan hard in the stomach. Keenan grunted and curled into a ball. I shouldered past Dakota and got between them.

"Enough! We'll deal with this in front of the whole crew." I put an open hand on Dakota's chest and shoved.

He refused to step back, and I wasn't strong enough to make him. Heat poured off his body, and his muscles twitched with pent-up tension. Dakota stared me down for a long minute. I held my ground with an effort, looking up to hold his gaze. He abruptly turned away and strode from the room, the bloodstained club over one shoulder.

The car antennae whip slipped from my fingers. I sagged against the wall, pressing a palm against my damp forehead. For a minute there, it looked like my second-in-command was gonna launch a mutiny. If he did, I wasn't sure I could win.

Keenan moaned from the floor. "Help me."

"Like hell. You brought this on yourself," I told him. "And just so you know, it's not over. The whole crew's gonna hear how you tried to murder Dakota."

Keenan groaned. I left him alone to think things over.

***

Feeling shaky, I took my blanket out back and sat on our wooden porch. Our sagging privacy fence hid me from the burned-out neighborhood on the west, and the empty four-story office building across the alley blocked most of the wind. I leaned against the diner, letting the winter sun warm my face. Maybe ten minutes later, Dakota came out. He sat hip to hip with me, taking half my blanket without asking. I kind of liked that.

"Well, that assassination attempt failed," I muttered. "Bet they try again. What are we gonna do? Put 'em against a wall and shoot 'em?"

Dakota shook his head. "Only if we want this crew to fall apart. These kids never trusted anybody 'til they came here. I shoot a couple, and people are gonna wonder who's next. They'll start leaving. Some of 'em might go next door. Besides, we need Keenan to fight the Zunos."

"Keenan can join the Zunos for all I care."

"That's what you say now," Dakota snorted. "But if he goes, Ash'll go too. What does that leave me with? A girl, some little kids, and an old cripple."

Thanks a lot, I thought, but I didn't say it. Dakota was right. I plotted and schemed like a champ, but in an outright fight, Paco could kick my ass. The only reason I got to be Chief at all was because I'd been the oldest kid when all the parents died. That made a difference when I was eleven and Dakota was only ten. But now all three of the older boys were bigger than me, and my power was slipping away.

I stared down the dim, narrow alley into the garbage maze on the perimeter of Zunos territory. Nothing moved except a few drug addicts who camped in the abandoned office building across the lane. Rico and his men were hunkered down, too scared of Flint to even come steal their car back.

"Keenan's not in shape to fight anyway, after what you did to him," I pointed out.

Dakota shook his head. "Nah, he's fine. I didn't break any bones. Just busted his face up some. But now he's pissed. If the Zunos attack us, will he even fight?"

"He will as long as I'm here." I said it with utter certainty. *Keenan would kill for me. Once I'm gone, who knows?*

"I'd quit worrying about the Zunos if I were you. Flint's our real problem," I added, hating the insecurity in my voice.

Dakota turned to face me, and cold air flooded under our blanket. "The Zunos weren't even our enemies until you provoked them."

"Like hell they weren't." I shivered, clasping my chilly hands together. "They practically raped me, Dakota. You know that big ugly one? Rico promised him he could have the next girl they caught."

"That's 'cause Rico's got no use for girls."

"Oh. I didn't know." I added that tidbit into my reckoning about Sophia and her uncanny ability to stay free when all the other surviving women lived in in hiding, if they weren't already prisoners in some gang's harem. It still didn't add up, not with Benny and Chubby and Big Angry Man around. As far as I could tell, they weren't gay.

Dakota ran his fingers through his unruly brown hair. "We didn't need this shit with Keenan, especially not now. Flint's gobbling up all the little crews, one at a time. Some gangs are going belly up the second he shows up. Handing over their women just to stay alive. That's not gonna happen here, Jackie."

My stomach fluttered with fear, relief and gratitude. "What are we gonna do, then? Run?"

Dakota shook his head. "I don't know," he sighed. "Running would just take us into somebody else's territory."

I didn't know either, so I just leaned my head against Dakota's warm shoulder. He still smelled faintly of gunpowder and aggression, but that was good. It made me feel safe. I snuck a glance at his face, and he caught me looking. His fingers ran through my hair, sending shivers down my spine. Then he bent his head and kissed me. One of his warm, strong hands wrapped my slender waist, and the other cupped my cheek. My lips parted so the tips of our tongues barely touched. Afterward, I melted against his chest. We sat in silence, close together under our blanket. I didn't know what to do about Flint. But at least I was with Dakota. For the moment, it was enough.

After a while, I leaned in to whisper. "I'm so glad you came back to our booth last night. Please don't leave me alone with Keenan. At least not at night."

"I don't plan to," he said. For a second, his eyes lit with an inner fire. It scared me and I loved it, all at the same time.

"And Dakota? There's something else I need to talk to you about.

Remember that roll of hundred dollar bills? I want to try getting in the Tech Center to buy the boys some clothes and shoes."

Apprehension tightened Dakota's handsome features. "Don't. The Center's out of the question. That place is a fortress. Just throw those bills away. They're useless. Nobody takes paper money anymore."

"What are we gonna do, then? The kids need things," I said. "I guess we could risk the mall."

"No way, Jackie! It's too dangerous. Remember what happened last time, with those hunters? We have to be careful. Let's wait a few months, try again in the summer. Maybe some of the infected will die off by then."

"Easy for you to say," I huffed. "You got all Steven's stuff after he…"

Died. Neither of us said it out loud. But Dakota was thinking it too. I knew by the way he looked down at the old brown bloodstain on the sleeve of Steve's jacket. *One death this winter. One new kid to take his place. Most years are worse.*

Dakota sighed. "Jackie, even if you could get into the Tech Center, you shouldn't be spending Keenan's money. Even on the kids. That's…oh, forget it."

I blew out an aggravated breath. "What?"

"It's a guy thing. A point for Keenan's team. They're being providers, see? Lettin' you see how they'll take care of your babies." Dakota leaned back on the wall and closed his eyes against the sun. "Yep. They're movin' in, all right."

I got that, but then I started thinking about Paco's too-big shoes and Marc's ripped shirt, and the fact that I could dress up like a rich girl and walk right into those fancy shops at the Tech Center. I had the cash, and the Center had to have better stuff than our musty abandoned stores did.

Besides, I'm Chief. Have been since those boys were a bunch of scared children. Dakota doesn't get to tell me what to do. Nobody does.

I stood, leaving Dakota the blanket. "I'm going inside."

He tossed the blanket over a shoulder and followed me. "Yeah. Feels like lunch time."

Me and Dakota grabbed some Spaghetti-O's in the kitchen and wandered down the hall, eating cold pasta straight from the cans.

"See, I'm so much more sophisticated than you," I joked. "At least I use a spoon."

"Yeah, right." Dakota grinned. "You're such a lady, with your homemade sword and that car-antennae whip in your pocket." He raised the can like a cup and slurped up another mouthful, getting red sauce on his face. He wiped it off on a sleeve.

Sounds of laughter and running feet filled the diner. Tito and some buddies crouched behind some overturned crates—the fort I'd promised them and never made. A guilty pang got me in the heart.

"More ammo," Tito yelled. "Need mo' ammo!"

"Yessir," Keenan let out a mock scream and dive-rolled across the floor.

Dakota muttered, "See, I told you so." He was right. Keenan's black eye wasn't slowing him down at all.

"Here ya go, Cap'n." Keenan dumped a pile of foil balls in Tito's lap.

"Good job, men," Tito said in his best captain voice, and unloaded on Ash, whose long legs stuck out behind the enemy fort.

Marc popped up from Ash's side and hurled more garbage. The floor was already covered with trash. I stood back and watched, a fond smile on my face.

"Reinforcements! We need help over here," Ash bellowed. "Paco, save me!"

Paco dashed over, attacking both sides at once, and utter chaos broke out. I retreated behind the bar, giggling, until I noticed that Dakota wasn't laughing.

Dakota strode down the short hall back toward the kitchen, but stopped halfway there. He leaned on the wall, arms folded, an icy edge to his blue eyes. "See?" he hissed. "They're recruiting reinforcements."

I hovered at his elbow for a minute or two while he ignored me. "It's only a game, Dakota. Tito isn't gonna change the balance of power around here, no matter whose side he's on."

I slid my hand under Dakota's bicep and leaned on him for comfort. His muscles felt rigid under my fingers, and he pinched my hand a little too hard against his body.

He spoke over my head without looking at me. "Gimme some space, Jack. Don't be so damn clingy all the time."

I shrank away. "Hate Keenan if you want, but don't take it out on me. It's not my fault you let him sleep in our booth."

I slid into my booth and sat there alone. Just when I thought I had someone to lean on, Dakota had to go and be a dick. Should I take the hint and leave him alone? If he didn't want me, there were plenty of other guys who did. The trouble was, I didn't want anyone else. Me and Dakota had been partners from the beginning. And now everything was screwed up. He was mad, and I didn't even know what I'd done wrong.

Chapter 6

"Hey, Jackie." Ash reached over the table and jingled car keys in my face.

I snatched the keys out of his hand. My spoon and the empty spaghetti can clattered to the floor. "Where'd you get those?"

Ash didn't even pretend to be embarrassed. "Nail on the kitchen wall, where Joe left 'em."

I wasn't thrilled that people felt free to help themselves to my car. After all, I stole it all by myself. But this wasn't a good time to start a fight, not with our crew on the brink of civil war.

Ash stood by my table with a hopeful grin on his face. "Teach me to drive now, please?"

My heart melted. Keenan was the troublemaker, not Ash. Plus I needed a break from Dakota, if he was gonna be a jerk. "I did promise, didn't I? Okay. We could go scout out some stores. Wait for me? I gotta get my pry bar."

He quirked a lip at me. "I'm not goin' anywhere. You got the keys, Jack."

"Oh. I do. Right. Back in a sec." I hurried through the diner, dodging flying balls of foil, and ducked into my closet. My street pack hung on the hook behind the door, loaded with scavenging gear like lock picks and rope. I threw in the pry bar and my old scrap-metal sword, grunting under the added weight. The weapon slowed me down some, but if it kept me from getting captured, it was worth it.

I made it across the junior war zone and out the front door without seeing Dakota. Winter sun bathed the south side of the diner, where the restaurant parking lot used to be. Now the place looked more like a used car lot. I didn't like it because there was too much cover for hunters, but the boys loved to hang out in the derelict, forest green VW van by the front door. In winter, sun beat through the windows, and it got nice and warm inside. Me and Dakota sat in there sometimes, even though we didn't have a clue how to get the thing running.

That day, Ash leaned on the van's tall hood, waiting for me. He stepped forward when he saw me coming. "Finally. Let's go."

We followed the sidewalk around the building toward the alley in back. That's where I left the Jeep, as close to the diner as I could get. Didn't want to make it too easy for Rico to steal it back.

As I entered the alley and crossed the line from sun into shadow, a shiver came over me. I wasn't even cold. I scanned rooftops and checked the dirty, broken windows of the four and five-story brick buildings that lined our alley. Nobody watched us. Nothing seemed out of the ordinary. In a second, the feeling passed.

I let Ash's infectious grin get me in a good mood again. We climbed in the stolen car. I grabbed the lever under the driver's seat and rocked it, but the chair didn't move. "It's stuck. You'll have an easier time once it's your turn, since you're taller than me."

Ash reached down under the seat, right between my legs, and yanked on the bar. With one strong arm he shoved my chair forward. That time it moved.

I recoiled. My outraged noise came out more like a bleat. "Ash! Get your hands out of there!"

Ash pulled his hands back, palms out. "Whoa. Relax the rabid defense of your virginity, Chief. I'm no rapist. See? Now you can reach the pedals."

That virginity comment pissed me off because it was true. "If you'd been chased by rape gangs as often as I have, you'd be defensive too."

Ash winced and looked away. He had no answer to that.

I reached for the gas pedal, and my foot touched it that time. The seat really was a lot better. Ash still wouldn't look at me. "Sorry I was a bitch," I grunted.

"You can afford to be," he smirked. "You are the last woman on earth, after all."

I shot him a sideways look. "I'm *not* the last woman on earth."

"You might as well be, as far as I'm concerned."

"Do you want me to teach you to drive or not?" I snapped, all bitchy again.

Ash nodded earnestly.

"Then pay attention. Because I've never done this part."

We both laughed. I turned the key in the ignition. It sputtered and died. I tried again.

"I think you need to press on the gas a little when you turn the key," Ash said.

"How do you know?" I answered, concentrating on the Jeep.

"Because I was the oldest. I got to ride in the front seat when my dad drove."

"Oh." I turned my head in time to see a flash of pain in his eyes. I'd just trampled on our unwritten rule—never, ever ask anyone about their life before, or their family, or even their school. If people wanted to share, that was fine. But never ask.

I grimaced. "Sorry, again."

Ash gave me a good-natured smile. "Just drive, Jack."

"I'll try. You do understand I kind of figured this out on my own, right? So don't expect too much." I turned the key and touched the gas, like he told me to. It fired right up, and we cheered.

I inched the jeep forward and back about a hundred times before I got it turned around in the narrow alley. "Yay! Now we're going. I think the windows really are busted, unless you can fix those too. I can't get 'em to go up."

Ash tried the button on his side, which didn't work. "Can I reach over you, or are you gonna blow your rape whistle again?"

"I'd love to, but it would probably attract the Zunos," I said, navigating through our garbage maze. I'd designed it myself, in case of invasion. It really was a pain in the ass to get through, with too many dead ends to remember. At least we didn't have to worry about getting shot by our own guys anymore. I inched the Jeep through the narrow space between a pile of old tires and an old Mini Cooper. "Oh, go ahead. I can't drive like this and push buttons all at once."

Ash tried the buttons on my side, which were also dead. "Nope. They're dead all around."

"No worries." I cranked up the heat. Most of it blew out the windows. "Let's go to the Center first. We ought to look over the place. I haven't decided yet whether I'm gonna try and get in or not."

"You're not," Ash said. "You'll agree once you see their fence. It's a lot bigger than it used to be. Sneaking in is impossible, and they have armed guards at the gate. Like I said, they'll let you in. They just won't let you out."

That made me even more curious to see the Center—from a safe distance. It wouldn't do the crew any good if I got trapped in there, especially not with Flint's Army on the border.

Before Flint showed up, my problems at least made sense. All I had to do was feed the kids. Keep 'em alive until they could take care of themselves. Eighteen. In my mind, that was the magic number. If I could help each boy make it to eighteen, I'd done my duty. Whatever happened after that wasn't on my shift. But things weren't that simple any more. Problems tangled in my mind until I didn't know which to work on first. Starvation. The pox. Flint and Rico. Infighting. Each one made it that much harder to handle the rest. I resolved to keep on like I had been. Feed the crew. Get 'em some decent clothes. Don't get caught.

Ash was only fourteen. Four more years 'til he'd be eighteen. It felt like forever. Teaching him to drive might give him an edge, help him hang on. Then he could help me teach the rest of the crew. So I stopped next to the burned car that marked the edge of our territory. We traded places, and I settled into the passenger seat.

The sound of running feet shot me straight up. "Ash, go!" I yelled. A shadow fell over the open window. I whirled, grabbing for the hilt of my scrap-metal sword.

Keenan squinted at me through his one good eye. The black-and-blue one Dakota gave him had already swollen shut. He leaned into the back seat and laid a couple of shotguns on the seat. Then he grabbed the window with both hands, pulled his knees up, and bounced into the car, feet first.

"Keenan, you scared the shit out of me," I said, one hand over my pounding heart.

"You should be scared, Jack. Goin' out with no hat on, and only one guy for protection? In a shiny green v-neck sweater. Yep, you look like a girl to me." Keenan leaned forward to check out my nearly absent cleavage.

I put a hand on his forehead and shoved him back. "My hoodie's in my pack, and I don't even have a hat anymore. I lost my only ball cap when the Zunos grabbed me."

"When you stole this car, you mean," Keenan said. He slouched down on the back seat and got comfortable.

That was a problem. I didn't want to go anywhere with Keenan, but I couldn't see how to get him out of the car, either. Ordering him out would just switch him into asshole mode, and he wouldn't leave.

So I tried to be diplomatic. "Okay, you've got a point. A second guy isn't a bad idea, especially one with weapons."

"Obviously," Keenan said. His voice dripped with sarcasm, making me sorry I was nice to him. "So, where we goin'? Scrounge patrol?"

"Yep." In a fit of paranoia, I dug my shapeless hoodie out of the bag, yanked it over my head, and pulled on the hood. At least it kept Keenan from looking down my shirt. "There. Happy?"

"Better. You still look like a chick though." He leaned out the open window. "Zach! Caleb! Load up, we're scavenging."

Technically, Keenan was out of line, giving that order, but I didn't want to start shit with him. My place as chief was vulnerable as hell. I needed to inspire loyalty, and it sure wasn't gonna be with my fists. A big haul of badly-needed clothes would help.

Zachary and Caleb piled cheerfully into the back seat of the Jeep. I wasn't sure how much security a couple of twelve-year-olds added, especially since their sentry shifts just ended, so they'd handed off their rifles to the next guys in line. But if the kids wanted to come along, it was fine with me. The sun was shining, I had my own car, and we were gonna hit the jackpot!

"Alright then, I'm ridin' shotgun," I said with a grin, and put out a hand. Keenan handed me one of our two guns and our entire stockpile of ammunition, which came to nine or ten shells. I rode with the muzzle sticking out of the window, feeling like a badass. "Whohoo, we're goin' shopping! Let's check out the Center first, just for fun."

"Long as we don't try and stop there," Ash said. "I'm not kiddin' about that place."

"Deal."

We took off with a jolt, then Ash stepped on the brake too hard. The boys laughed, but he didn't get mad. Going out through the garbage maze, Ash only scraped the Jeep a few times, which wasn't bad. There couldn't be a worse place to learn to drive.

Zachary cheered him on. "It's okay, dude, you're doin' fine. Nobody liked that barrel anyway."

Ash took the long way out to the main road, a right turn through a two-lane industrial loop lined with warehouses and machine shops. The direct route wouldn't have been smart, since it went right past the Zunos' house. Passing them in their own car might get us shot, and I could hardly blame them. The warehouse territory technically belonged to them too, but I snuck through there sometimes on my way to the river. Lately it had gotten easier. Ever since Flint showed up, the Zunos stuck a lot closer to home. I still breathed a sigh of relief when Ash took us onto the highway and headed east.

Thirty minutes later, we came to a t-intersection and went north along the road that bordered the Tech Center. Double chain link fences, twenty feet tall, surrounded the place. Each one was topped with a roll of nasty looking razor wire. Watchtowers stood sentinel in the dry moat between the two barriers.

"It really does look like a prison," I breathed. "Except for all the fancy houses back there, under the trees."

Zachary made a low, impressed whistle. "That place is awesome. Imagine if we had security like that. No more worries."

"Bet they have craploads of food in there too," Caleb said, hanging out the open window to stare.

We came to the gate, where a short military caravan waited to get in. Four Humvees escorted a big semi tractor-trailer carrying a wide, tarp-covered cargo. A sign on the gleaming guard house read *National Space Center, Research and Development.* Overhead, an American flag snapped in the cold breeze. One at a time, drivers showed their IDs and rumbled through.

"Look at that guard," Zachary exclaimed. "He's wearing a helmet like a deep-sea diver."

"Yeah. Or an astronaut," Caleb added. "But why?"

I looked the guard over. With that reflective dome over his head, he looked like a robot. I couldn't see his face at all. He gave me the creeps. The man moved heavily, with a long, silver tank strapped to his back. I suddenly put it together. "Pox. They're all suited up in case of pox. He's even breathing compressed air."

"Chicken shit," Keenan crowed.

While we stared, Ash had been inching the Jeep forward behind the line of trucks. The wide load ahead of us blocked the road. Then the semi went on in, and it was our turn—only we didn't want a turn. I yanked in the muzzle of my shotgun and held the gun low. Too late.

A soldier's head turned. A deep, male voice crackled from a speaker on his helmet. "Hey, that's a girl!"

"Ash, step on it," I barked.

He floored the gas and whipped around the line of cars. We roared away. Zach and Caleb howled with excitement. Keenan rode facing backwards, his gun out the window, ready to shoot anyone who followed us. Ash took the frontage road and headed north, weaving too fast around derelict cars. His crazy driving scared me worse than the soldiers did, but I didn't tell him to slow down. I watched the rear-view mirror, gripping my shotgun with sweaty palms. Nobody chased us, but my heart still took a while to stop racing.

"If we're done bein' stupid, we could hit the outlet mall on the highway now," Ash said.

"Whose territory is it in?" I asked.

The boys shrugged. Nobody knew. They all looked at me, waiting for me to make the call.

"Let's drive by and take a look," I decided. "If it feels safe, we'll get some shoes."

The parking lot at the outlet mall was nearly empty. That was a good sign. When the epidemic hit, people hoarded food and ammo—not urban fashions.

"Ash, circle the parking lot. Stay on the perimeter in case we need to make a quick getaway," I said.

"Okay, Chief."

"Eyes up for hunters, everybody. Look in all the cars. Check store windows. Let me know if anything moves. There's our target, straight across," I murmured. "Famous Footwear."

"New shoes!" Zachary exclaimed. "You're the best, Jack."

"You can thank me after we get out alive."

We circled the deserted parking lot again. I fidgeted in my seat, nerves tingling with pent-up tension. Ash took us right past the stores. The dead eyes of the mannequins in the windows seemed to follow us as we went by. Faded red and white signs hung in the window of the shoe store. *Sale! 20% off!*

My lip twisted in a grim smile. *Not anymore. Everything's free now, if you don't pay in blood.*

A long, red awning protected the store fronts from the elements. Tumbleweeds and trash blew along the sidewalk beneath it. No doors gaped open to the winter wind. Not a single window was broken. The riots had completely missed this place.

Something else felt wrong, too. "There's no graffiti anywhere," I whispered.

Keenan answered in a low voice. "Yeah. Some crew shoulda taken a territory this rich."

"I don't like it."

"You always say that, Jackie," Zachary grumbled as we passed the darkened Starbucks.

"That's 'cause it's always true," I said. "Stores are traps. Usually there's only one way out. Half the people I've seen taken were caught in stores."

"We gonna pass on this one, then?" Ash asked.

"Oh, come on," Zachary begged. "I'll run in by myself if I have to. Just wait for me outside."

I shook my head without looking at him. Ash circled past Famous Footwear again. Had something moved inside the dimly lit shoe store, or was it just a reflection of our moving car?

"Please, Jackie," Zachary whined.

I twisted in my seat and gave him a level stare. "Zach, I know your feet have been cold all winter. I see you putting plastic bags over your socks when you have sentry duty in the snow. I care, okay? I care. But it isn't worth dying over. Or getting taken by the pox. It loves places like this."

"I don't know how a disease can love anyth—"

I cut him off. "Shhh! Eyes up. Mouth closed. We're gonna take a closer look."

Ash parked near the shoe store, but not so close that it gave away our position. I handed him the shotgun, pulled out my pry bar, and strapped on my pack. Nerves made my stomach all quivery, but I wasn't about to admit it in front of the boys. We got out of the car in silence. The thud of the doors closing made me jump. Clustered together, we walked toward the building. The pry bar hung heavily from my right hand. The Jeep waited behind us, its broken windows an open invitation for hunters.

"We better check the back seat before we leave," I muttered.

At the door, Ash and Keenan readied their shotguns. I gave the go-ahead. Caleb tugged on the door of the store, and it squeaked open. "Unlocked?" he mouthed. "That's weird."

I thought so too.

Caleb held the door open and we peered inside. The place smelled musty, with a hint of some rancid animal scent. Thick dust coated the orange benches and display shoes on top of the shelves, turning everything gray. Spider webs hung from every corner. The only sign that the last customer left in a hurry was a lady's purse lying in the grimy doorway. Bird droppings had splattered into the dust around it and dried there.

"No footprints. Nobody's been here in a long time," I whispered.

I waved Keenan through the door first. He crept in, shotgun levelled. Me and Ash followed, and the kids came last. We fanned out sideways to look down the aisles without getting too far from the door. Caleb cautiously dogged Ash's steps, staying behind the bigger boy's gun, but Zachary headed straight for the shoes. Without a word, I grabbed the kid and yanked him back into line.

The store looked deserted, and oddly untouched by looters. I faded left and peeked behind the checkout desk. Nothing was there but an open cash register, loaded with cash, and some neat piles of shopping bags. I left the useless money but helped myself to a fistful of dusty plastic sacks.

A faint sound came from somewhere inside the store, like a thousand tiny claws on paper. Goosebumps tingled along my arms as all the little hairs stood up. I froze, listening.

Nothing moved. The only sounds were Keenan's soft footfalls as he moved down the center aisle to check the back room. In a moment, he reappeared, an open hand raised in our "all clear" signal.

I handed a big plastic bag to each of the twelve-year-olds. "Go get yourselves shoes," I whispered. "Grab some for Keenan and Ash too. Be quick. Don't try 'em on, just take 'em."

"Size nine," Ash muttered from his post by the front door. "Keenan's an eight, I think."

The younger boys started going through boxes. I hated going over to the girl's side of the store alone, but I couldn't beg for help. Not and get any respect. I tiptoed past glittery little-girl party shoes that no child would ever wear. In the women's section, I dropped to my knees and slid out a box labelled *Ladies Tennis, Size 6.* Something rustled from the dark hole where it had been. My hands reflexively jerked back. The shoe box hit the floor with a hollow thump. I hissed a curse, imagining hunters hearing that, coming our way.

Dank, ammonia-laden air wafted out of the dark gap on the shelf, making my eyes water. I scrambled to my feet, wrinkling my nose against the moldy cat piss smell. The new shoes got stuffed in my bag without a second glance. They'd probably fit. We weren't sticking around long enough to try them on. Leaving the trash on the floor, I eagerly headed for brighter light.

Paper crackled behind me.

I jumped. That startled Ash, who swung his gun around. We both stared intently at the source of the sound. Nothing moved.

Probably just mice. I retreated into the men's section and met Caleb coming out of the running shoe aisle with a loaded bag. "I got Nikes for Marc and Paco too," he said softly.

"Good. Where's Zachary?"

Caleb pointed left. "He wanted boots."

Joe and Dakota needed new boots too, so I turned down that aisle. *Joe's a size twelve, and Dakota? Maybe a ten now?* Head bent, I peered at the labels on the boxes. The back of my neck prickled. I whirled, but saw nothing.

I quickly chose some boots for the big guys and stood up, the plastic handle of the loaded shopping bag cutting into my hand. I dropped it by the door, relieved to be done. Then one last thing occurred to me—warm boots for Tito. I moved through deepening twilight to the rear wall of the store, where the little kids' stuff was. Zach sat on the floor back there, all alone, peering into a shoe box.

I passed him, grabbed some bright yellow snow boots and teeny red sneakers for the three-year-old, and strode toward the door, relieved to get the hell out of there. Zachary hadn't moved.

"All done, Zach?"

The kid stood up and followed me. He cracked the lid of his shoebox and gazed into it while he walked. Ropy strands of dark hair fell over his eyes.

It was so sweet I almost laughed out loud. *He loves his shoes.* That made the whole ordeal worth it.

"Let's go, people," I called softly.

Boys headed for the front door, lugging armloads of loot. Keenan and Ash exchanged triumphant grins next to a poster of neon-colored running shoes.

"Just a sec," Caleb said. "I'm gonna grab some of those packs of socks. The ones from the Zunos' crate are all girlie."

"Okay, go ahead. Just hurry up," I said. Something small and dark moved along the top of a shelf. My head snapped around. "What's that? A mouse?"

The tiny, dark brown head peered down at me, with big perky ears over a pair of shiny rodent-like eyes. As the creature pulled itself forward on overlong forelegs, I realized it wasn't a mouse at all, but a cute little bat, no more than four inches long. Tiny claws on the front edge of each folded wing gripped cardboard, making scrabbling noises.

"Heads up," I said, pointing at it with the pry bar. "Might be poxy. I can't tell in this light."

Caleb turned to look at the bat and accidentally dropped his bag. Shoes and socks spilled all over the floor. "Shit," he hissed.

The bat's fuzzy body came upright. She looked right at me, spread her leathery wings, and made a single, high-pitched squeak. Faint scratching sounds came from everywhere at once. More bats poured from crevices between shoe boxes, cracks in the ceiling tiles, even from under the checkout desk.

Before the first one took to the air, I was already screaming. "Run!"

People stampeded for the door. Keenan grabbed my arm and hauled me through. Outside, I wrenched free, frantically counted my boys as they ran out, and came up one short. "Who's missing? Zach?"

"No, I'm here," Zachary yelled. He was already halfway to the Jeep. "Aw, hell! Hunters! Hunters at the car!"

Four or five ragged men clawed at the white painted doors. Another one was partway through an open window, legs dangling. When they saw the boys, the hunters sprang after them. Ash's shotgun boomed, blowing one of the infected men nearly in half. Guts spilled over pavement. The others charged. Keenan bellowed a war cry and joined the fight.

A child's high-pitched scream came from inside the store. A cloud of bats passed the big front window, so many that I couldn't see beyond them. Gunfire thundered from the parking lot, making me flinch. I shrugged off my pack, dumped it on the sidewalk and tore through the contents. Lock picks and coils of rope got pushed aside. One bright yellow lighter lay at the bottom of the bag. I seized it, ripped open the door of the shoe store, and ran inside.

The heavy glass door swung closed behind me. The mob of bats had stopped circling. Their restless wings whispered from the shadows.

Caleb yelled from somewhere in the back of the store. "Help! I'm trapped in the storeroom!"

"Stay put, I'm coming!" I dove for one of the empty shoe boxes that littered the floor. Five seconds with the lighter, and one end of it burned brightly. Gripping the bottom of the box, I held it high.

The lone bat still sat on the top shelf. Flames reflected off her black button eyes. Maybe she was sick. Maybe the pox was eating her up inside, and she didn't have the strength to fly. Somehow I doubted it.

She bared her teeth at me, revealing rows of miniscule, white needle teeth. One naked, semi-transparent wing arced forward, so I could see the outlines of the bones inside. Thousands of bats fluttered to the front of the store, clinging to the doorframe, the sale posters, to anything they could. Blocking my escape. Their massed bodies dimmed the room to a gray twilight.

The cardboard burned too close to my fingers, and I had to drop it. It glowed feebly from the tile floor as the fire died. I bent to snatch up another carton. The bat on the shelf leaned forward eagerly, eyeing the back of my neck. I spun to face her. Coughing from the smoke, I touched flame to new tinder.

The bat shifted anxiously, watching the flames, but she didn't fly away. Both wings swept forward, so the pointy tips met. Her colony instantly left the window and swirled around me in a moving cloud. Though I stood near the front of the store, the living tornado completely blocked my path to the door.

I let out a panicked gasp and spun in place, waving fire. *That one controls the rest! Normal bats don't do that. They're infected for sure. Oh my God, oh my God! What am I gonna do?* When I threatened from one direction, more bats darted at me from the other side. Outside, gunfire raged. *This can't last. They're going to take me!*

A grim smile touched my lips. "Fine. We'll all die together." I let the flame lick the side of another shoebox. That one had shoes in it. I didn't care. Black smoke rose around the boss bat's head.

She snapped her wings open. The cloud of bats split, clearing my path.

"Not that easy. I'm taking my kid with me." Holding the burning cartons over my head, I walked down the aisle toward the back. The room got darker as I moved farther from the big front window. "Caleb!" I yelled. "Where are you?"

His scared voice came from behind a door. "In here."

I yanked open the door of the dark room. Caleb's dirty-blonde head caught the faint light from my fire. He ran to me, a sob catching in his throat, and threw his arms around my waist.

"It's okay, honey. Careful, take this." I handed him a burning box. "Stay close. We're walking out of here."

"They're poxy, aren't they?" Caleb babbled. "The bats."

I gave him a short nod. We strode to the front of the store. Bats covered the door.

"Clear the door *now*, or I'm gonna burn this place down," I bellowed.

The press of dark bodies instantly split. Bats flapped in opposite directions and scattered.

Caleb was awestruck. "They understand English."

"Only 'cause they're infected," I said, head swiveling, looking all around. "Caleb. Get that shopping bag. Take every last sock. We are damn well gettin' what we came for."

He held up his burning box, eyebrows raised in a silent question.

"Toss it," I said.

Caleb hurled the smoldering carton onto a shelf and snatched up the shopping bag. We pounded toward the door as bats took flight. I pushed the kid through first. Then I threw my own burning box, ran out, and slammed the big glass door behind me. Inside the store, flames were already spreading.

The Jeep roared across the parking lot toward us, swerving around the grisly remains of the hunters. Ash slammed on the brakes, laying rubber. Keenan opened the passenger side door, dived out before the car stopped moving, and rolled to his feet in one fluid motion, shotgun ready. Staring open-mouthed at that epic move, I completely missed the hunter coming out of the food court.

A whisper of shoe on pavement alerted me. I leaped sideways, pulling Caleb with me. The hunter was a lot taller than us, with a tangled mat of dark, curly hair clinging to his skull. He was young, in his twenties, and he hadn't been infected long. Those were the most dangerous kind, with speed and agility intact. I know it sounds crazy, but the pox inside him saw me, and I saw her, too. I recognized her, even disguised as she was in a male body. I'd seen that predatory expression before, behind different eyes. Behind my mother's eyes.

"You," I mouthed. No sound came out. *"I know you."*

"Jacqueline," the hunter moaned through lips wet with silver drool.

I'd never heard a hunter speak. I didn't know they could. *He knows my name. He knows my name! How?*

I jumped between Caleb and the infected man. "Run! Run for the car!"

Caleb bolted without hesitation. The hunter let him go and came for me instead. I'd stupidly gotten myself trapped between the infected man and the burning shoe store. Plastic-laden smoke filled the air, making me sick. I was in trouble.

I shuffled backward, inching past the front window of the shoe store. Sometimes a slow retreat didn't trigger their chase reflex. It wasn't working. He still followed me. Inside the burning building, frantic bats beat their fragile wings against glass, trying to get free, get at me. I backed toward my scrap-metal sword, lying on the sidewalk inside my pack. Not that it was bright to stab a hunter, but I was scared enough to do something stupid. The infected man leaned forward, sniffed the air, and leaped.

I screamed and skittered sideways, barely avoiding his silver-tipped nails. The tips of my fingers snagged a strap of my pack. I snatched it up and fumbled for the sword inside.

Keenan stepped up beside me and pulled the trigger on his shotgun. It only clicked. "Shit! Out of ammo." He grabbed my shoulder, yanked me behind him, and brandished his gun like a club.

The hunter lunged and we both scrambled back, closer to the wall of heat from the burning building. My back was scorching, and my lungs burned from the oily smoke. The infected man kept coming, immune to pain, immune to fear. My hand touched cold metal inside my bag, and I pulled out the long, sharpened shard of metal.

Infected blood, infected blood, I thought madly. *Don't get it on you.*

With a squeal of tires, Ash sent the Jeep careening backwards with the passenger door flapping on its hinges. The rear bumper hit the hunter with a crunch, and one tire bounced over the body. I couldn't look. Someone kicked open the back door of the Jeep.

I jumped in the back seat, Keenan took the front, and we were out of there!

"Whoohoo," I howled. Boys shouted and cheered as we sped away.

Me and Caleb ended up next to each other. He hugged me, saying, "You came back for me. You came back. And we damn well got what we came for. Every last sock."

I squeezed the kid's bony shoulder and looked into his teary eyes. "Of course I came back for you, Caleb. You're my kid. You're *crew*."

"Yep. Right up to the second you get the pox. Then you're on your own, bitches," Keenan chortled.

I slapped the back of his head for that. The boys all laughed.

"Wish these windows closed," Zachary said, hitting the broken button again and again. "What if the bats follow our car? What if they fly inside?"

"Don't make me think about that, dude," Caleb told him. "Besides, we burned 'em up. Jack's a helluva chief, I'm tellin' you. Helluva chief."

The boys celebrated all the way home, except for Zachary, who quit worrying about the window and flopped back with his eyes closed. I could relate—I was exhausted myself, and my stomach felt hollow. Keenan passed me a bottle of water. Lifting it to my lips felt like an effort.

The boys laughed and talked, throwing a few good-natured elbows at each other as they bent to lace up their new shoes. Caleb hung his feet over the seat to show off his Nikes, and Keenan propped his black canvas Skechers on the dash.

I sat there with a silly grin on my face. *I saved Caleb. We won that one. We won!*

Going out of the outlet mall parking lot, Keenan twisted in his seat and gave me the thumbs-up. "You rock, Jack."

"So do you. And I really mean that." I turned to the other boys. "Did you guys see him? That was legendary."

Keenan gave me a wide grin, so his puffy black eye scrunched closed. Nervous energy poured off him, too much for the small space we all shared. "That's right, babe, I am a fucking legend. Move fast, or die young. Whoohoo!" That set off another round of howls from the crew.

"And Ash, you totally saved us both. That was some badass driving," I said when the shouts subsided. Leaning forward, I squeezed both their shoulders at once. "Thank you."

Ash kept driving, but Keenan turned and put his hand over mine. That kind of gesture wasn't like him. For a second I was captured, and I couldn't look away.

"You don't hafta thank us, Jack. We're crew."

Chapter 7

By the time Ash got us back home to the diner, the winter sun was sinking below the horizon. We trooped into the kitchen like heroes, holding our treasures high. Everybody not on duty packed excitedly into the small room. Joe fired up the single-burner propane stove to cook us a hot dinner. That didn't happen too often, since propane got harder to find every year. I took advantage of my position as chief to stand at his elbow and warm my hands.

Caleb picked up the shopping bag. Every kid leaned forward eagerly. "There's something for every single one of you, so don't worry," he told them. "I just gotta sort 'em out. Paco, I think these ones are for you. Trade with somebody if they don't fit."

Paco beamed like it was Christmas morning, and so did I. Caleb continued his rounds with the shopping bag, handing out new shoes, while Keenan told the kids all about the hunters who'd been waiting for us at the Jeep. He acted it out, doing claw-hands and making shotgun noises with his mouth.

Just after he finished his tale, the shift change bell rang from outside. Keenan headed for the door. "You tell 'em the part about the bats, Jack. I gotta go relieve Dakota on watch."

"Okay." I sat down at the table, blew on a bite of stew, and got my thoughts in order. Stories were our main form of entertainment, so I had to make mine a good one. Kids waited impatiently for me to begin. "You know, these new shoes weren't easy to get," I finally said. "There were thousands of bats in the shoe store, and they chased us!"

The boys made excited "oooh" sounds at that. I smiled and went on. "One bat was their boss. She seemed almost human. She gave orders by pointing with her wings, like this." I raised both arms like wings and aimed them dramatically at Paco, who shivered with delight.

"That's crazy talk," Joe muttered from over by the stove.

I ignored him. "The boss bat understood English, too. Bats covered the door, so they had us trapped. I told her if she didn't let us go, I was gonna burn the place down."

"They moved, all right. Like that!" Caleb split the air with his hands. "And then we torched the store anyway," he added with a grin.

I felt bad about that. Being mean was never my thing. I loved animals, even bats. I squirmed inside, thinking about what I'd done. *They were poxy, so that makes it okay...doesn't it?*

I didn't notice Dakota standing in the doorway until he laughed. "Bullshit. One bat is the chief? And she's a girl, of course."

I smirked right back, pushing Dakota's shoebox across the table to him. "Of course she is. Just like the girl chief who brought you these awesome, brand-new boots, and the hot dinner Joe's dishing up for you right now."

That changed his channel. Dakota tore open the shoe box, as thrilled as any kid. "Cool. And wool socks, too. Thanks!"

"Hey Jack, you're the only one not wearing your new shoes," Paco said.

I shrugged and took another bite of scorching-hot stew. "Zach's not wearing his yet either," I said, sucking air around a mouthful.

Zachary leaned back in the chair beside mine, his mop of curls dark against the white wall. He looked pale, and his brown eyes were too bright. They flicked around constantly, drawn to the slightest movement. That bothered me.

I bent to peer into his face. "Hey, Zach, you feelin' all right?"

"I'm fine, thank you," he said politely. "In fact, I brought you a gift."

Kids giggled at his overly formal tone. I shook my head in wonder. *Boys. Most days they're dropping the f-bomb. Then they trot out manners you didn't know they had.*

Zachary bent and pulled a shoebox out from under his chair. "This is for you, Jacqueline."

I shot him a raised eyebrow for calling me that, but he didn't seem to notice. Under the circumstances, I didn't slap him down, even though he knew better. The box felt super light in my hands. *Not shoes. What could it be?* "That's so sweet, Zach. A surprise, for me?"

I balanced my soup bowl on my lap and pulled the lid off. With a high-pitched squeak, the bat inside launched itself at me.

I shrieked and threw myself backward. Steaming stew seared my chest. The bat flapped at my face, tiny teeth bared. I hit the floor and thrashed, crying out, flailing like mad. Shouts and pounding footfalls filled the air as boys panicked and fled. Dakota whacked at the bat with one of Joe's aprons as Caleb ripped open the back door. I ran outside, screaming, ducking and waving my arms.

Zachary and the bat were on me like predators. I dive-rolled across the deck to avoid a sudden swoop, came up on my feet and slapped aside the boy's grasping hands. He lunged for me again, slipped, and crashed to one knee. Boots skidding on the icy deck, I dashed back inside. Dakota slammed the door and turned the deadbolt with a snap, locking Zachary out. The pox-bat disappeared into the night. The stunted boy stood on tiptoe to peer in the small window at the top of the door. His small hands gripped the frame. A tiny, clotted wound marked one forefinger.

And the pox stared out of his eyes.

I saw it and sobbed. "Zach's been taken. He's bit, see it? Look, right there on his finger, he's bit."

"He must have been taken hours ago," Dakota said grimly. "He brought that bat home with him."

"On purpose, to infect me?" I babbled. "Me, why me?"

"Did he scratch you? Did he?" Ash asked frantically, grabbing my hands and turning them over. "Are you bit?"

I held up my arms. "No. Not at all."

Zachary's silver fingernails dug into the weathered window frame. He began to pull. Out front, someone rang our alarm bell. Every clang sent a jolt up my spine.

Ash put an arm around me. "Come away, Jackie. Come away. Don't let him see you."

"Just a minute." I pulled away and walked toward the window. The child's gaze followed me with rabid intensity. "Zach? Zach, if you're in there, if you can still hear me, I forgive you. I know it wasn't your fault. And I'm really sorry I didn't take better care of you. I tried. I tried so hard." I put a hand over my mouth to stifle my sobs.

Zachary's eerily calm voice came through the closed door. "It's all right, Jacqueline. We've been looking for you. Time to come home."

That unnerved me. *Home? I am home.* I took a step back. "I'm not going anywhere with you."

My eyes met Caleb's. He shook his dirty-blond head. "That's not Zach. That's not even his voice! He sounds like some creeper now. And he never calls you Jacqueline. Jack, maybe Jackie, but never Jacqueline. You know that."

I nodded. Swallowed. Tried not to puke.

"Aw, hell," Joe said. He pulled a shotgun off the rack on the wall.

Caleb's fragile jaw clenched and released, over and over. He put a hand on the old man's thick, tattooed arm. "My job, Joe. It's my job. Zach was…" He choked up and then forced out the words. "My…best friend."

"Caleb, you don't have to—" I began.

Joe stopped me. "We got this, Jackie." He pressed the shotgun into the twelve-year-old's thin hands.

Ash and Dakota flanked me, took my arms, and tugged me toward the diner. "Come on. You don't need to watch this."

Behind us, Joe was doing my job, talking Caleb through the

nightmare. "All right. You tell me when you're ready. I'll open the door."

Caleb's voice sounded high and weak, like a much younger child. "Okay. Just gimme a second, Joe."

"That ain't yer friend no more, so don't you hesitate," Joe said. "Not for a second, or he'll get loose in here. More kids'll die."

Maybe I shouldn't have let them lead me away. Maybe it was my responsibility to stand by and witness that. But I caved and let Ash and Dakota win. They walked me into the diner, aiming for a corner booth, as far from the back door as they could get. We never made it.

Caleb's shotgun boomed. A shriek escaped my lips, and I flinched. Both hands flew to my cheeks. Dakota pulled me close. I wrapped my arms around him and tucked my face against his chest. Around me, children sobbed. Tears and spilled soup dampened Dakota's shirt. Normally, I'd never cry in front of the crew. That day, it didn't matter. We all cried together.

Five minutes later, Caleb drifted into the diner, moving in slow motion. He wasn't crying, but he had that wide-eyed, glassy look I'd seen on so many traumatized children. The kid crawled into the booth he'd shared with Zachary, pulled Zach's green wool blanket off the bench, and pressed it to his mouth. Without a word, I took a seat beside him. I wrapped him in the blanket and rocked him like a baby while he cried. Eventually Caleb fell asleep on my shoulder. I couldn't move without waking him, so I stayed there for hours, ignoring my aching back.

Deep in the night, Joe's deep voice came from the kitchen, startling me out of an upright doze. He was arguing with Dakota. "Leave 'im. Ya can't handle an infected body 'til the sun hits it. We'll deal with it tomorrow."

"After all the kids see him layin' there?" Dakota let out a deep, exasperated huff of air. "Why?"

"I dunno why," Joe said gruffly. "I jus' know what I've seen. You touch a pox victim in the dark, you're as good as dead yerself."

Their voices faded. I sat in the dark diner, listening to the soft sighs of sleeping children. Zachary's last words haunted me. *"It's all right, Jacqueline. We've been looking for you. Time to come home."*

That hadn't been our boy. Somebody was talking through his mouth. Somebody who knew my name. It didn't make sense, but I had a hunch it was the same somebody who controlled those bats.

Who's looking for me? The pox? Why me?

I knew one thing for sure. If whoever it was ever found me, they'd have a fight on their hands. Because I was already home.

Chapter 8

Boys came and went with their sentry shifts, but Keenan stayed on duty all night. Dakota wasn't around either. I wondered if he was out moving Zachary's pox-infected body in the dark, despite Joe's warning. We couldn't bury it, not in frozen ground. Maybe Keenan and Dakota were carrying the corpse to the river. Maybe it was still lying on our back deck, so children would have to step over it in the morning. My heart ached. *Zach trusted me to take care of him. And I tried. I tried!*

Around three in the morning, I managed to slide out of Caleb's booth without waking him and move to my own. I stretched out on my red vinyl cushion, a dish towel under my face to keep it from sticking. After a while Dakota came in, the soles of his new boots squeaking against the floor. I couldn't read his expression in the dark. He stood near my feet for a minute, and I thought he was about to take his old spot on the far side. Instead he slid behind the table and sat close to me. I rolled over on my side to make room. His hip felt warm against my stomach.

Dakota reached down and stroked my hair. I ran my fingertips along his arm. He traced my collarbone under the neckline of my emerald green sweater. "This top is so hot on you."

I almost thanked him, but then he added, "And you wore it out with Ash and Keenan."

I sat up and pushed his hand off. "I didn't wear it for *them*, Dakota. God, give me a break! Zach *died* tonight, and all you can think about is yourself."

He snorted through his nose. "I'm thinking about *you*, Jackie. It could've been you who got infected, instead of Zachary. What were you thinking, going off without saying a word to anyone? Wearing that? With Flint's men all over the place."

"Well, you weren't going to take me shopping, were you?" I snapped. "And besides, I only left with Ash. Keenan caught us at the corner and jumped in the car, shotguns and all."

"At least he had the sense to bring weapons," Dakota grunted.

"Yeah. Truth is, I was pissed when he showed up, but we would have been in trouble without him."

"Yep, they're heroes, all right. Good thing you took 'em along. Right after you begged me not to leave you alone with them." He mimicked my voice, making it extra whiny. "At least not at night."

I resisted the impulse to slap him for that. Instead, I did what I remembered my mom doing when my dad got in a bad mood. She used to get quiet and just sit with him, not moving much, not talking. After a while, he'd usually squeeze her hand or something, and the fight would be over. Was it the same with a boyfriend? Who knew? There was no one to ask.

All I remembered about boyfriends and girlfriends was how mushy they seemed when I was in grade school. Apparently, girls were supposed to giggle, flip their hair, and grab for their lip gloss whenever boys came around. Dakota would laugh his ass off if I acted like that. So I just sat there with him, saying nothing.

After a while I turned sideways on the bench, letting my thigh lie partway over his, and kept my voice soft. "You know, I really do appreciate that you're so concerned about me."

His expression started to soften, but then I added the kicker. "But I'm Chief. I go where I want, with who I want. So deal with it. Besides, I kept my hoodie on, and we never even saw Flint's guys all day."

Dakota swore under his breath. "There you go. Playin' the Chief card again."

I nodded. "Damn right. And one more thing. You might as well let go of the jealousy, because Ash is two full years younger than me, and Keenan's like a year younger. I'm never gonna hook up with either of them."

"I'm younger than you, too. By seven months," Dakota whispered, his face close to mine.

I put my arms around his neck and tilted my head. "I don't care."

Dakota kissed me then in a way he never had before, mouth open, with his tongue. I gasped and my lips parted, inviting him in. His hands moved over me, all sweet fire and barely restrained force. My heart raced, and I instinctively knew he was staking his claim. He wouldn't give me up to Keenan or anyone else—not unless I sent him away. And I had no intention of doing that. Not ever.

I trembled a little in his arms, but I didn't pull away. Dakota backed off a little and cupped my face in his hands. His eyes were lit with some emotion I didn't understand. "It's all right, Jackie," he whispered. "Don't be afraid. Do you trust me?"

I nodded. He kissed the palm of my hand. When he took my little finger in his mouth and let it slide back out, I moaned out loud. I leaned in for a kiss and felt him tugging up my sweater. He pulled it off over my head, and I let him. Dakota's hands slid over my silky camisole, making my pulse pound in all kinds of wild places. I buried my face in his neck, craving the sweet musky scent of his skin. I wanted it all over me.

With a sudden motion, Dakota wrapped his hands around my hips and lifted me so I straddled his lap. I cried out.

"Shhh," Dakota whispered, laughing low in his throat, but the way he gripped my hipbones and squeezed made it awfully hard to be quiet.

He slid his warm hands under my camisole and stroked them down my back. When they came to the waistband of my low-slung jeans, I tensed.

"We don't have to do anything you don't want to do," Dakota murmured. He lifted his feet off the floor, pivoted, and stretched out on his back, pulling me down on top of him. "There, see?"

I knew that meant he'd put me in control, at least for the moment, so I'd feel safe. I loved him for it. With my hands on either side of his shoulders, I leaned down and kissed him, then rocked my hips against his.

He groaned. "Jackie, you don't know what you're doing to me."

I leaned forward and kissed him again, but my arms didn't want to hold me up for long.

"You okay?"

"Just tired," I whispered. "I sat up with Caleb most of the night."

"It's all right. Come here, relax." Dakota pulled my head down to his chest and started massaging me, kneading the knots out of my arms, then my back and neck. It went on for a long time. I melted against him, absolutely in heaven, and fell asleep.

***

I woke up the next day to the sound of running feet. Kids raced through the diner in their new tennis shoes.

"I really am faster in these," Paco bellowed. "I really am!"

"Me too," Tito squealed. "Weally, weally!"

I marveled at how fast life went on for them, only one day after Zachary died. They'd seen a lot of death in their short lives, and I couldn't blame them for being happy when they could.

Dakota slept through it all. I rolled over on my stomach, warm under our blanket, and gazed at his sleeping face. A tousled lock of dark hair fell across his forehead. I sometimes felt a tug in my heart when I looked at Dakota, like I got when I hugged my kids. A huge rush of that feeling came over me then. I closed my eyes and pressed my cheek against his fleece sweatshirt. No way could I let Keenan try and kill him again. Something had to be done.

I reluctantly slipped out from under Dakota's arm, pulled on my soup-stained sweater, and went out into the kitchen. Someone had pulled back the blue cotton curtains, so sun streamed in the windows, warming the room. I consciously kept my gaze off the back deck, where Zachary had died. Instead, I set wash water to heat over the stove, and while I waited, I checked on my sentries. Everybody who had duty was on the job. Good.

After a quick sponge bath in my closet, I changed into another stolen top from Sophia's crate. Then I strode into the kitchen and banged on the pot that served as our bell.

Boys hurried out of the diner. Sentries loped in off the rooftops. Every single one of them used the front door. "Everything okay?" Caleb asked. His eyes were puffy from crying, but he hadn't missed his shift.

"Yeah. All quiet outside?"

He nodded.

"Good. Come on in, all of you."

"Seriously, you're pulling all the sentries off their posts at once?" Caleb asked. "Now, while the Zunos are watching our every move."

"Yes, I'm pulling sentries," I snapped. "This is important. We're having a meeting."

We all jammed into the small kitchen. Tito wove between our legs, all excited. I gathered the little one close and squatted down to get on his level. "I have a job for you, Tito. I picked you for this, 'cause I know you can do it."

Tito stuck out his tiny chest. "Yeah!"

"Okay. We're having a meeting in here. We just need to talk, but somebody has to watch our backs. Keep us safe. Can you do that for me?"

His little mouth hung open. "I'm a sentwy?"

"Yeah, you're a sentry," I nodded. "But only from inside. Don't leave the building. Sit by the windows and holler if you see anybody in our territory."

The toddler let out a high-pitched version of our sentry howl and ran for the diner.

"What's this all about?" Joe asked me. "Ash and Keenan?"

"Yeah. Only I don't want the little guy to hear it." I looked at Paco and Marc. "So don't tell him. And Joe, is Zachary's body still . . ."

"On the deck?" Joe nodded. "Yep. I want to make sure the sun gets on 'im good before anyone touches him."

Around the room, boys muttered and glanced at the back door.

"We'll take care of Zachary later," I told them, stretching the curtain tight over the kitchen window. "He's not forgotten. Joe says infected bodies have to lie in the sun first, or it's a risk for the rest of us."

They all looked a little nauseous at that, but Caleb's expression was the worst. I couldn't help them get over it. I couldn't get over it myself. But we had work to do.

"Everybody get in here," I yelled. "Meeting!"

From around the corner in the hall, Keenan said, "Watch out. She's doin' her queen bitch thing again."

"You bet I am, Keenan. " I said it real loud, so he'd hear me, and a few boys flinched. "Get in here. Sit down and shut up."

Keenan shuffled in, followed by Ash.

I pointed Ash to one of our four chairs. "Have a seat, Ash. Sit. Everybody sit."

Joe took a chair, and the kids sat on the counter or cross-legged on the floor. Dakota remained standing. I didn't tell him what to do. I was pretty sure at least a couple of people noticed that.

I stood in the middle of the room with everyone staring at me. "The reason we're having this meeting is because yesterday, Keenan tried to kill Dakota."

Boys gasped. Keenan turned red in the face. "I did not! It was an accident!"

Pointing at him, I snapped, "Shut up."

Keenan did.

Then I turned back to the group. "Right after it happened, I wanted to put Keenan against a wall and shoot him. Know why he's still alive?"

I waited. Scared-looking boys shook their heads. Keenan fidgeted, eyeing the door, but he stayed put. Joe watched us all grimly.

"Because Dakota told me not to," I finished. When I said that, eyes got wide all around the room. "Dakota said if we started shooting people, you guys would wonder who was next. He's right. We're not that kind of crew. So if we shoot Keenan, we're gonna do it by a vote."

"But I didn't do anything," Keenan yelled.

I shook my head. "We're not gonna argue about *if* you did it, Keenan. I saw you."

"I saw him, too," Paco said. His lower lip trembled. I wanted to kneel down and hug him, but I didn't.

"Me too," Marc said. "If it matters. I know, I'm new and all, and I don't get a vote. But I swear I saw Keenan try and ram Dakota off the roof with a big barrel."

"Actually, I think you should get a vote, Marc. You put yourself in danger yesterday, trying to protect our crew. Show of hands! Who says Marc gets a vote?" I put my hand up. Everybody else did too, except for Ash and Keenan. "Okay then."

A couple of guys patted Marc on the back. Not much of an initiation, but it was all I had in me at the time.

"So, do we vote now?" Caleb asked. He looked at Keenan with narrowed eyes.

"Not yet," I said. "Just to be fair, I have something to say in Keenan's defense." I couldn't look at Dakota when I said that. I fixed my eyes on Keenan instead. He gazed back at me pleadingly.

"Last night, we were attacked by hunters. Caleb was trapped in the store. Keenan and Ash came back to save us. They had the keys to the Jeep. They could've just driven away, but they didn't. I'm grateful for that. And here's the most important thing. There's a war coming. Ash and Keenan are both good fighters."

"If they don't stab you in the back," Dakota added.

Ash shot me his classic offended-innocent look. Keenan stared down at the floor.

"If you're in this crew, you can't pick and choose who you protect and who you attack," I said. "We're all on the same side. Right?"

"Right," the boys chorused.

"What about Ash?" Paco asked. "He didn't do nothin' to Dakota, but he didn't help him neither."

"Good question," I said. "I've thought a lot about that. We got a couple of options. He can live or die with Keenan, 'cause they're partners. We could kick him out. Or we could let him stay on probation." I turned to the younger kids. "Probation means he can live here, but if he makes another mistake, even one, that's it."

"Let 'im live or die with Keenan," Caleb yelled. "If we kick 'em out they'll join the Zunos."

I nodded. That was probably true. "Show of hands?" I asked. It was unanimous, except for me. Nobody seemed to notice I didn't vote.

"Fine. Paco, can we borrow your marbles for the vote?"

Paco ran out and came back with a cloth bag. I dumped the marbles into a bowl and pulled an empty glass bottle off the shelf. I set the bowl and the bottle in the bottom of a black plastic trash bag and left it on the table.

"Okay. Line up. Vote by dropping a marble in the bottle. A black one means death. Any other color is probation. Do it inside the bag. Votes are secret for the rest of your lives."

Joe got up, and the boys shuffled into line behind him. One at a time, people peered into the bag, stuck in a hand, and dropped a marble in the bottle. Each little clink made me want to scream. Some of the kids had tears running down their faces, but they all voted. I went last. Then I pulled out the clear glass bottle and held it up. Everybody watched the marbles roll around and around the bottom of the bottle.

Marc jumped up to take a closer look. "Four to two. They live!"

Keenan slumped on the floor against the wall, head back and eyes closed. Sweat dampened his hair. Ash looked too calm, almost dazed.

"Sentries, back outside," I called. "The rest of you can go."

Dakota's voice cracked across the room. "Wait." My crew skidded to a stop without even looking at me.

That irritated me, but I was too emotionally drained to fight over it.

Dakota stood over Keenan. "Conditions of your probation. You guys both report to me. You stand watch separately. Eat separately. Sleep separately. Somewhere other than me and Jackie's booth."

A few boys sniggered, and I realized our drama wasn't a secret. Everybody knew about it, but nobody dared say a word. At least not to me.

"You'll follow my orders in battles, too, or else." Dakota made a gun with his hand and pulled the imaginary trigger. Keenan winced. "You are both gonna work longer and harder than the other guys. We need to scrounge anyplace sketchy, I'm sendin' you in first. If I give you a stick and tell you to take the Zunos' entire goddamned territory, you will fucking take it or die trying."

A few people glanced at me to see if I'd slap Dakota down for overstepping his authority. I pointedly didn't.

Dakota whirled to face the rest of the boys, who clustered by the door, ready to run. "If Ash and Keenan can do all that for one full year, then they are back in the crew, no hard feelings. After that year is up, anybody who hassles 'em will deal with me. Now go!"

Boys stampeded out of the room. By Joe's old clock, me and Dakota were due on watch in ten minutes. I released my kindergarten lookout from his post by the window and made a big deal over him for doing it. Then I bundled up and headed out. Ash and Keenan hadn't moved from their chairs.

I stopped by the back door. "Can you guys please help Joe deal with Zachary's body?"

Keenan scrambled to his feet. "Sure. Sure, Jack. Right away."

"Do whatever Joe tells you to, exactly, so you don't get infected," I added, and then walked out into the cold.

Halfway to the cracked wooden stairs, I had to stop because tears blurred my eyes. Keenan and Ash had survived. Four people saved their lives, and I wasn't among them. Even after all they'd done for me, I voted against them. Keenan risked his life, jumping between me and that hunter. And I still voted against him. *I did it for Dakota, because I had to,* I told myself, but it didn't help.

I scrubbed my hand against my jeans. I could still feel that cold black marble between my fingers.

Chapter 9

The territory felt too quiet. The usual crowd of slackers that hung around the Zunos' parking lot had disappeared. Even Rico's spaghetti-splattered Camaro was gone. There had to be a reason. So I pulled up my hood and skulked across the alley to the ladder, heading for my favorite rooftop lookout. Up on top of the four story building, I jogged to a sheltered corner, crouched down, and peeked out. The two red brick buildings on my side of the alley were dead quiet. Only a few shadows moved behind the windows of the abandoned office building across the way. Maybe they were squatters. I hoped they weren't Flint's men, watching me through binoculars. The thought made me hunch even lower. Over my head, a little flock of pigeons cooed soothingly. I settled in, letting the sweet sound relax me.

About ten minutes later, Dakota came out to join me, carrying a blanket. "I figured I'd find you hiding up here." He settled himself against a low wall a few feet away.

I shrugged. "I guess it doesn't matter if I hide or not, since the Zunos found out I'm a girl."

"It's still better if they don't see you. They already want to raid us bad enough as it is," Dakota said, gazing out across our territory.

"The Zunos aren't gonna raid us. Not as long as Flint's around." I leaned against a wall, arms wrapped around my knees, and scanned for intruders anyway.

"So that's what's wrong. You worried?" Dakota asked. "Or just in a bad mood?"

"I don't know," I huffed. "Everything's different now. I feel like the crew just noticed I'm a girl. I know that isn't true—people always kind of knew, but it didn't matter. I was just another brother. And then, all of a sudden, everything changed."

Dakota leaned forward and looked at me, a hint of a smile on his face. In the morning sun, his eyes were the exact same shade of blue as the sky. "Got news for ya, Jack. It wasn't that sudden."

Dakota fell silent. The wind flipped a lock of dark hair over his forehead, and I had a sudden urge to touch it. I didn't. That whole conversation made me uncomfortable. I gazed away at the territory, doing my job.

Then he added, "I've loved you for years."

My head snapped around. "Years?" I whispered.

"Yeah, but what was I gonna do? I was shorter than you until last summer. And you were Chief."

I made a face at him. "I'm still Chief."

"See how hard this is for me? And then Keenan had the balls to make his move first. They were brilliant, teaming up on me like that. It could've worked."

Dakota offered a corner of his blanket to me. I reluctantly scooted over and sat beside him. He tucked me against his side. "What's wrong, Jackie?"

"I'm not being . . . too clingy?" I asked.

"Aw, I'm sorry I said that. I was just in a rotten mood." Dakota squeezed my hand. "You know, when you went off with Ash and Keenan, I thought that was why."

I smiled. "Oh, please. You think I'm that immature?"

"I told you not to try the stores, and you went anyway. Without saying a word," Dakota growled. "That pissed me off."

I tossed my head. "I listened to your advice. Thought about it. Made my own decision. That's what a chief does."

"It was stupid, Jackie."

"Of course it was stupid, since I got Zach killed," I said bitterly. "You think you can do better? Then go up against me for chief. Do it. I dare you. We'll take a vote. I'll be like, hey, how are those new shoes, guys? How 'bout that Jeep? Okay, let's vote, right now."

A half smile touched Dakota's lips. "That's not fair. You know I'd never do that to you." He bent his head and kissed my neck, feather light touches that moved down to my collar, sending tingles lower. My bad mood faded. Guilt welled up instead. How could I be enjoying myself, even falling in love, when my poor judgment had gotten a kid killed?

"Don't hang on to your failures, Jackie," Dakota murmured. "You do your best. We all do. Nobody wins 'em all."

That startled me, because it felt like he'd read my mind. "Yeah, well . . . I ought to," I said defensively. "I try so hard, every single day. I can't even remember the last time I got to have any fun."

"Stick around. I'll show you some fun," Dakota smirked, putting his hand on my thigh.

That made me laugh. I playfully pushed his hand off. He grinned and put it back, higher than before. "This isn't fair," I said. "We're supposed to be on duty, and you're distracting me."

Just to tease him, I gazed out across the rooftops, completely ignoring him. Nothing had changed, except that a bunch more pigeons sat on the wire now. They were all staring at us.

That bugged me.

I stood up without taking my eyes off the birds. "I'm gonna go check on something." I moved to the other side of the rooftop.

All the pretty purple and green necks swiveled to watch me. Goosebumps rose on my arms. The flock took flight, circled our roof, and landed on a different wire, closer to me. One of them caught my eye. I couldn't tell boy pigeons from girl ones, but for some reason I thought this one was a female. Something about her seemed familiar, but I couldn't be sure if I'd seen her before.

I fidgeted, wondering what to do. The female's little head swayed whenever I moved, and the flock imitated her a split second later, like we were all linked. Without picking up my feet, I leaned to the right. The whole line of birds leaned left, mirroring me. I took them back to the middle again, then the other direction.

Freaky.

I loved birds. But these pigeons were no more birds than my mother was the woman who raised me. Not after the pox took them.

"What are you doing, Jackie?" Dakota called from the other side of the roof.

"Watching the pigeons. They have pox."

"Then don't eat one," Dakota said. "Forget the birds. Come on back."

The flock took flight again. "Good, they're gone," Dakota said. "Now will you—"

Gray forms shot out of the air, right at his head. "Look out!" I screamed.

At the last second, they swerved and came for me. I wasn't ready. I threw up an arm, and one of the lightweight bodies smacked off it. Feathers blew across the rooftop. Dakota ran toward me, whipping his blanket at the flock.

I started hurling garbage, chunks of metal that we'd hauled up there to harass intruders. A window broke in the next building over. The squatters inside shouted. The flock scattered and came back, over and over.

"Her, get her! That one!" I pointed, but Dakota didn't see which bird I was talking about, or why.

I dashed away from Dakota, and the birds followed me. I knew they would. Without slowing down, I bent and snatched up a long piece of rebar, then spun around to face the flock. They shot into the sky and came back down in a tight v-formation, with the pox-boss three places behind the leader.

"I know who you are," I screamed, pointing at her with the rebar.

"You are gonna die!"

I saw the surprise and shock in her eyes, and I saw her fear. Then the pox left those birds. Seriously. It winked out of them, leaving their little red eyes normal and nice again. I'd never seen that happen. I didn't know it was possible.

Birds landed all around my feet. Cooing softly, they began their strutting walk, pecking for whatever pigeons eat. I didn't try to hurt them. They weren't my enemy. *She* was.

***

I slid down the ladder and raced around the perimeter of our territory, checking with all the sentries. Nobody had any problems with pigeons or anything else. After my shift, I ran to find Joe. I felt like throwing myself onto his lap and sobbing, but I couldn't do that, not anymore. Instead I slid into his corner booth and told him everything.

The first thing Joe said was, "Pigeons don't fly in a V-formation, Jackie."

"I know that. She probably learned how when she jumped into a goose," I blurted. "Remember how we used to have Canada geese on the golf course?"

Joe gave me a concerned look. "She? Who?"

"The pox, Joe. It's alive, aware. Or she is. I'm pretty sure she's female."

Joe shook his head. "That's crazy. The pox is alive, alright, but it's some kind o' germ. It can't think."

"It can, too, and it's after me," I insisted. "Poxy animals have chased me a bunch of times lately."

"Aw, come on," Joe groaned. "Infected animals can't hardly walk. They ain't gonna chase nobody."

"I'm telling you, they chased me, just like the bats!" My shrill voice cut across the diner. Boys' heads turned. "The exact same person was in the bat, I swear. She's out to get me. It's personal."

Dakota showed up just in time to hear that. "Who's out to get you?" He and Joe shared a glance. I could tell they both thought I was nuts.

"Tell him, Dakota," I said. "Tell him how the pigeons dove at me in a v-formation."

"They did," Dakota said. "It was wild. They dove at her head and tried to peck her. I tried to chase 'em off, and they kept comin' back."

Joe didn't say anything for a minute. Then his big, square head swung back toward me. "This female you were talkin' about. Was she in the lead?"

"No. She made the others go first, in case I slapped one down," I said.

"She's smart, Joe, wicked smart."

Joe didn't answer. He slumped in his chair, staring into space. All the lines in his face drooped, so he looked like a sad bloodhound. I wanted to tell him how I pointed the pox-boss out and scared her, and how she winked out and left those poor little birds healthy again. But I didn't think Joe could take it. He was happier when he thought I'd gone crazy.

I left Joe sitting with Dakota and took the kids outside to play. We couldn't go far, only partway down the alley, but at least they got some afternoon sun. It might have been neurotic of me, but I walked around with a shotgun over my shoulder. Anything that tried to bite my babies was gonna get vaporized.

I spotted one normal rat, a couple of healthy squirrels, and a mixed flock of poxy and clean pigeons. None of them tried to go after me. They probably didn't know I only had two shotgun shells.

"Pwetty bird." Tito pointed at a pigeon.

I whipped my head around and checked it. *Whew. Normal.*

"That one not okay," Tito said, pointing at a poxy one.

"That's right, Tito! This pigeon is healthy," I said, pointing, "and that one there has pox. Never let a poxy one bite you. You'll get sick."

"Pox is yucky." Tito ran around, pointing out all the poxy animals he saw. "That one is yuck. That one not." He was right every single time.

"Do you know that you're the only boy in our crew who can tell the difference? I've tried to teach the big boys, but they can't see it. Not until the animal falls down sick."

"Look at da eyes," Tito said.

"I know, I told them that. You're such a smart boy."

Keenan burst out the back door of the bar and sprinted to me. I just about panicked until I realized he was only delivering a message. "Dakota sent me to get you guys in. Joe's got a visitor coming."

"Thanks, Keenan."

"Sure Jack, anytime, let me know if I can do anything for you. I've gotta go tell the sentries now." Keenan practically bowed before he ran off.

Honestly, I liked him better before. The groveling made me want to slap him. Plus, his whole suck-up act was fake as hell. Anybody could see it. Once Keenan quit worrying about being shot, he'd go right back to trying to run the crew.

I gathered my kids and went inside. "Somebody's coming over?" I asked Joe.

"Delivery," Joe said. "You got another one o' those hundred dollar bills? Or a ring?"

"Sure. Which one do you want?"

"I'll give 'im paper if he'll take it. Better have both on me, just in case."

I brought out the trade goods, hoping Joe would tell me on his own what the deal was. He didn't. That was irritating. Joe refused to be chief, even though he'd be a better one than me, but he wasn't much of a follower either. He let me make my own decisions unless I was about to screw up. Then he stepped in. I wondered what I was doing wrong this time, besides losing my mind over pigeons.

Joe reached out his thick fingers for the bills.

"So? What are we buying?" I stubbornly hung on to the money until he answered me.

"Shotgun shells. Show them birds who's boss," Joe said with a grin.

I laughed out loud for the first time that day.

The next couple of hours sucked. I had to hide while Joe and Dakota met with Viktor, our local small-arms dealer. I got one quick peek through the window as Viktor came down the alley, flanked by two muscular bodyguards. He was a tiny man, super-skinny and all shriveled up, like somebody left him out to dry in the sun. Viktor didn't look dangerous to me.

Joe knew better. He grabbed my arm and dragged me out of the kitchen before Viktor's team got anywhere near the door. "The whole world don't need t' know we got a girl, here, Jack. Viktor mostly sells weapons, but he might sell girls, too. If he don't, his brother does."

I got shoved into a dark closet. Dakota tossed me a blanket, and they locked me in. Joe wouldn't let me have the light on in there, since it showed under the door. I couldn't even eat, in case crunching noises or the smell of food gave me away. I sat on the floor and pressed my ear against the door. Outside, a sentry beat on a metal trash can lid. Boys howled from the rooftop.

Kids' footsteps danced down the hall. Even the smallest boys got to see the visitor, but I had to listen through the door.

"Joseph, my old friend. How are you?" Viktor boomed. He had an accent I couldn't place, Eastern European or Russian or something.

When the pox broke out, lots of foreigners got trapped here by quarantines. Soldiers on the borders didn't let anybody in or out. Quarantines didn't stop the spread of pox, and by the time people knew that, the air travel system was pretty well shot anyhow. So America got landed with Viktor, and his nasty slave-trader brother too. For them, it was a stroke of luck. Their kind thrived on chaos.

"Come on guys, into the diner," Dakota called. Quick little footsteps followed him. "Stay in here until I come get you. If you have a duty shift, go on out through the front door, not the kitchen. Caleb, if you want to listen in you can. You're old enough. Just keep your mouth shut."

"Awesome," Caleb said as he passed my closet. "Thanks, Dakota."

"Ah, teaching the children. Very good," Viktor rumbled. "This is your young chief?"

"Yep. This is Dakota Griffin. He does a hell of a job." Joe said. "Dakota, Viktor."

"Nice to meet you, sir," Dakota said.

I'd never been so mad in my life. I had to clap my hand over my mouth to keep from screaming.

"Still refusing the position you deserve, eh, Joseph?" Viktor said cheerily.

"I'm too old," Joe said. "That's a job for a young man."

A job for a man, I fumed. *After I fed them all these years!*

When the conversation switched to business the men lowered their voices. That pissed me off too. Only a few sounds carried, like the clicks of dry-fired weapons and the occasional impressed noise from Dakota.

Finally, the men must have sealed the deal, because Viktor switched to his loud-and-congenial voice again. "So good doing business with you, Joseph, and you too, young Dakota. Call me if you need anything, anything you can possibly imagine."

Dakota muttered something, and the men all laughed.

"Oh, I can help you with that, for a price," Viktor said. "But I hear you may already have a start on a very nice harem of your own. Little slip of a girl, dark hair?"

"Oh, you mean Sophia Arabola," Dakota said. "She's not ours. She lives in the next territory over, with the Zunos. That girl is smokin' hot!"

"Let me equip you with the right weaponry, and she will soon live with you," Viktor promised.

I thought I might vomit right there on the closet floor.

"Prob'ly out of our price range," Joe grunted. "But we'll talk about it."

They'll talk about it? Talk about kidnapping Sophia? Maybe they'll lock us both in the closet, or sell me and keep her, since she's so damn hot.

Viktor finally left, and Dakota unlocked the closet door for me. The instant I got an opening I took a swing at his jaw. It connected, and pain exploded through my hand. I thought my finger bones had shattered. Me and Dakota both yelled at once.

Dakota grabbed my wrist and twisted it. "What the hell, Jackie!"

I screamed. Keenan came flying out of the back room. A couple of seconds later, Ash showed up too. He looked mad enough to fight. When Dakota saw them coming, he let go of me quick.

"What's going on? Jackie, are you okay?" Keenan asked, his hands already balling into fists. "Did he hit you? I'll kill him!"

I shoved past all of them without answering and ran to the back door.

Joe tried to block me from leaving. "Don't you run off now, the sun's gone down."

I gave him a sharp kick on the shin. I got his wooden leg by accident, though, and it hurt my toe. Slamming the door open with my one good hand, I ran downstairs and into the dark alley.

Goosebumps tingled up my arms and set the back of my neck buzzing. I swept my gaze along the line where rooftops met sky, alert for stalkers. A white moon and one bright golden star sailed overhead. Of course I was being stupid, out there alone in the dark. At least I hoped I was alone. The Zunos had good reason to be mad at me, since I stole their Jeep. Sophia was probably madder about the rat I threw in her face. Either way, I was worth a lot of money. Enough to buy three or four new cars. Rico would think that was fair.

The Zunos must have told Viktor about me. They even gave him my description. *Little slip of a girl* didn't describe Sophia. She was too tall, and too voluptuous. They'd seen me, all right, and they knew exactly where I lived. Viktor was probably at the Zunos' house before he came to ours, selling weapons to Benny and Chubby and Big Angry Man. I imagined his accented voice, telling them, "Let me equip you with the right weaponry, and she will soon live with you." That was probably his favorite line. I bet it sold loads of guns for him.

Maybe they made a deal. That thought got me turned around, back down the alley to the bar. I climbed the stairs onto the porch and sat out there alone, wondering if Dakota really hoped to start his own harem someday. I imagined that most guys dreamed about it, even if they didn't talk about it in front of me. The crew had to want more girls. What if they brought one home someday? Would we become friends, or would I hate her? Honestly, I missed having girlfriends. But that didn't mean I wanted to be locked in some vile basement harem with a bunch of them, either.

Wind got funneled down the alley, making the porch miserable. That night I gutted it out, shivering in the shadows. I couldn't stand the thought of going inside, where Dakota and Joe were probably talking about kidnapping Sophia Arabola. Sophia didn't let her men hurt me. Even though she probably hated me, I didn't plan on letting mine hurt her either.

Chapter 10

The back door opened and Ash stepped quietly onto the porch, carrying a big blanket and a coat over one arm.

"Hey, Jackie. You cold?"

"Freezing."

Ash handed me the coat, which turned out to be mine. I put it on gratefully. He sat down beside me and spread the blanket over us both. Faint light from the kitchen window lit his handsome profile.

Heat radiated off Ash's shoulder, and I couldn't help pressing against it. "Thanks. That was nice of you," I told him.

"Sure. I'm that kind of guy. Not that it does me any good."

"Yeah, it does," I murmured.

He shook his head, the trace of a smile on his full lips. "Bullshit."

After that, neither of us said anything for a while. I stared up at the stars, twinkling in the narrow strip of sky between buildings. I glanced sideways to see Ash staring at me.

"You're so beautiful, Jackie," he whispered.

"You only think so 'cause I'm the last woman on earth," I said with a smile. "You have nothing to compare me to."

"But I do. Some of the shops still have old magazines."

"Eeuw. Too much information." I giggled.

"I didn't mean *those* kinds of magazines. There are lots of women's magazines around too."

"Sure there are. And you read them all. Good save," I smirked. We both ended up giggling.

I leaned in to whisper. "Ash, I'll tell you a secret, if you promise not to tell anybody."

"Promise."

"If you were a couple years older, you would rock my world."

"Really?" Ash turned toward me, and his dark face disappeared into shadow. "So, what's wrong with me now?"

"Nothing. Except you're fourteen, and I'm sixteen."

"I told Keenan we shoulda waited 'til we were older. He said it would be too late. You'd be settled down with Dakota or somebody, havin' his babies. I didn't want to wait. I didn't want to share you, either, but I needed Keenan with me to even have a chance."

I nodded. Part of me felt like I shouldn't be hearing this. It was too close to the heart. Ash should be crushing on some cute eighth grade girl, not me. But the world went to hell with the pox, and all I could do was try and be kind.

But leading him on wasn't kind, even if it kind of happened by accident. As much as I loved Ash, he was a brother, not a boyfriend. Dakota was the only guy I wanted. I scooted a few inches away and shivered as the cold air rushed in.

"I'm sorry, Ash. There's nothing in the world wrong with you. But I've got my heart set on Dakota."

He answered without looking at me. His voice sounded husky with sorrow. "I know. I've known it since we were kids. You two were always partners."

We stared up at the stars. I thought about those beautiful houses behind the fence at the Center. People lived all together there, and from the looks of the place, they had plenty of food too. I pictured my crew living there, with soldiers to protect us, and sighed out loud.

"What?" Ash murmured.

"Sometimes I just get tired, you know? Tired of being Chief. Tired of being responsible when things go wrong. If the pox hadn't hit, I'd be in high school right now. Playing sports. Hanging out with my friends. Prob'ly hoping some hot guy would ask me out."

Ash nodded. "I think about that sometimes. How life would be different, if the pox never happened. I'd still have my parents, and my sisters. Just about every girl I knew is gone now. Dead, or locked up someplace where she never sees the sky. Kind of breaks my heart."

Mine too. Because I couldn't admit it, couldn't say the words out loud, I just squeezed his hand. I never knew Ash had sisters. Pox took them, just like she took my mother. Like I told Joe, it felt personal. I knew it was crazy, but I was honestly starting to believe the pox was real. Like a real person. I didn't care who believed me. I saw a person in that bat. In the pigeon, too. And in Mom, five years ago. Whoever was running her body, there at the end, it sure wasn't her. I pushed that last thought away. That one always made me break down.

The bird, and the bat. Could it be the same person inside? Something that moves like a demon, or a ghost? She winks in and winks out, takes someone over and then disappears, kills and leave the bodies behind.

Anger rose up inside me, and Ash's comforting shoulder didn't help near enough. I stretched both hands down by my sides, fingers splayed against the weathered wooden planks of the deck, trying to ground that wild energy. Between the stress and my crazy delusions, it felt like I was coming unglued. Punching Dakota like that? He could've knocked me cold. If I didn't tone down the crazy, I was gonna lose my crew. Nobody wanted a nutcase as Chief, PMS-ing with a shotgun in her hands. Dakota would take over, and they'd find a dark closet just for me.

The pox. This is all her fault. Her fault women aren't free anymore. Her fault perfectly normal guys like Dakota plot with arms dealers to kidnap girls.

The thought made me mad all over again. I wanted revenge so bad I could taste it. But my enemy was invisible, and no one believed in her but me.

"Ready to go inside now?" Ash stood up. He offered me a hand, and I took it.

Ash pulled me to my feet. I stood up, and he didn't let go of my hand right away. Our eyes met. I could tell he wanted to kiss me. If he had, I didn't know if I would have kissed him back or punched him. All my rage wanted to turn into something else, something primal. Ash seemed to sense it, and his hand wrapped closer around mine.

I pulled away. That wouldn't do him any good. Not when he didn't have a chance. I only wanted Dakota, even if he could be a dick sometimes. I gave Ash a sad smile and went inside.

In the diner, Dakota and Joe sat together in a corner booth, with Caleb on the other side. A brand-new rifle and a couple of used shotguns lay on the table between them, along with two whole cases of ammo. Loose shotgun shells were scattered all over. They had to be planning a raid.

I marched over there, all pissed off, and whipped my coat in a big arc. It hit the middle of the table with a snap. Shotgun shells skidded across the floor. Joe and Caleb recoiled. Dakota just stared at me, his blue eyes narrowed.

I took a deep breath and let loose. "Planning on using *these* to kidnap Sophia? Well I'm not gonna let you! Sophia doesn't deserve to be treated like that, no woman does, and so help me, if you bring her here I'll help her get away, even if none of you ever speak to me again!"

Joe and Dakota looked up at me with identical shocked expressions, and then they both busted up laughing. I didn't actually expect them to shake with terror, just 'cause I yelled at them. But laughing? With tears running down their faces? I did not expect that. Not at all. I took a step back, and then another, unsure what to do.

Dakota tried to say something, but he couldn't stop laughing. "You . . . you thought . . . we . . ."

"Just so ya know, Jack. We ain't planning on kidnapping anybody," Joe grinned.

"Don't treat me like I'm stupid," I snapped. "I heard you talking about it!" I mimicked Joe's deep voice, adding a thick layer of stupid. "Prob'ly out of our price range. But we'll talk about it."

"That was *acting*, Jackie," Dakota said loudly. "Ever heard of acting? Like they used to do on TV?"

I turned on him. "So, what you're saying is, even if you guys are the decent sort who won't kidnap girls and rape them, you don't want creeps like Viktor knowing it. That would be embarrassing. Being a criminal is so much cooler. Kids like Caleb watch you, and they think harem building is exactly what a *real* man ought to be doing."

Twelve-year-old Caleb slid deeper into his seat, like he wanted to hide under the table.

I didn't give the kid any breaks. "You know, Caleb, it might seem really awesome to have a harem, but those women are prisoners. They're miserable victims who get raped and beaten every day of their lives."

Caleb didn't answer, not that I expected him to. I felt a soft touch on my elbow and turned. Marc stood there.

"She's right," Marc said, loud enough to be heard across the room. "I know, because I've seen a harem—from the inside. Two of them, actually. I get that we're not supposed to talk about our lives before we came here, but I have to tell you, Jackie's right. I know, because some crews don't just keep girls. They keep boys, too."

Everyone in the place went silent. I've seen a lot of traumatized kids in my life, but none of them had eyes as haunted as Marc's. That just about brought me to tears. But Marc didn't cry, so I didn't either.

"I would have respected you both a whole lot more if you'd told Viktor you didn't do that kind of thing," I told Joe and Dakota, who weren't laughing any more. Then I turned around and walked away.

Behind my back, I heard Joe mutter, "She's got a point, guys."

***

I huddled in my booth alone, wrapped in my blanket. Hours passed. I ate the food Joe put in front of me, but I hardly tasted it. Eventually people crawled into their beds and the room got quiet. Dakota never showed up. I didn't know where he was, and I didn't want to search the rooftops for him, either. With Flint's Army hanging around, he probably decided to take an extra shift on sentry duty. I had trouble falling asleep without him, so I shivered on my bench, listening to nighttime sounds. Everything seemed quiet except for some crunching noises from the kitchen. Somebody must have snuck in there to eat crackers in the dark. Whoever it was could have them, if they were that desperate.

Dakota came in at shift change and sent the next wave of sentries out. Then he slid into his side of the booth, which had been unoccupied lately.

Instead of lying down, he hunched there with his elbows on the table and his head in his hands. I crawled around to the back of the horseshoe-shaped bench. "Meet you halfway," I whispered.

Dakota scooted around the corner of the table to sit by me. "I didn't know if you wanted me here, after all that."

I reached out and took his hand. "Of course I want you here," I said, keeping my voice low. "I have no idea how to be a girlfriend, but I'm not gonna kick you out every time we argue. That seems like one of the basics."

"Well, here's another one of the basics, then. We don't hit each other. Trust me, you don't want to start that. I hit a lot harder than you do." Dakota sounded pissed. He rubbed his jaw where I punched him.

"Would this be a bad time for me to tell you how much your rock-hard jawbone hurt my hand?" I asked, a little smile on my face.

"Yes, it would," Dakota said. He tried to return my smile, but it wavered. "It's just that . . . my dad . . ."

I stiffened, pretty sure I knew where that story was going.

"It's okay, Jack, I want to tell you this. My dad was a big guy. Firefighter."

"Uh-oh," I muttered.

"No, it wasn't like that," Dakota said. "My father could have picked my mom up with one hand, but he never even raised his voice to us. He's gone now, but I like to think he'd be proud of me. So don't bring the war in here, okay? I'm on your side."

"Aw, Dakota," I whispered. "I should have known that."

He kissed me once, lightly, on the lips. The tightness around my heart let loose, and it took me a moment to realize that I cared if he was mad at me. I cared a lot. That wasn't my style. As chief, I sometimes had to use the iron fist whether it pissed people off or not. Survival mattered more than popularity. But with Dakota, it was different.

My eyelids got heavy. Dakota looked wiped out, too. We stretched out together, under our blankets, with my head pillowed on his shoulder.

***

I dreamed of pigeons. Somehow, pigeons got into the diner. They walked on the tables and perched on my arm as I slept. They all had pox, and they wanted me to have it, too. One of them walked up my chest, close to my face, and started pecking at my lower lip. The third peck drew blood. I gasped and woke up.

"Whoa, Jackie, you okay?" Dakota murmured sleepily. He pulled me closer.

I rubbed my lip. "Just a bad dream. Sorry."

Dakota rolled over and fell asleep again almost immediately. I got comfortable, but I couldn't relax. That boy was still eating crackers in the kitchen.

My sleepy brain put it all together. I lurched upright. "Oh my God! Wake up! Everybody up," I screamed.

I threw off the blanket and ran for the kitchen, with Dakota right behind me. Nobody was in there.

Keenan ran in a few seconds later. "What's going on?" He flicked on the light and grabbed the spare shotgun off the wall.

My eyes swept the room. I expected pigeons or something, but the place looked normal. The crunching noise had stopped. "I…I don't know. I thought I heard something in here."

Lights blazed in the diner. Tito whimpered. Boys prowled around, peeking out windows.

Joe hurried down the hall, pulling on a shirt. "Cut the lights, you guys."

Everything seemed scarier in the dark. Dakota cracked the back door, peered out, and then slipped outside onto the porch. Keenan followed him, gripping his shotgun. I tiptoed after them, barefoot on the cold planks, arms folded over my stomach for warmth. We all stood still, listening. None of the city's noises sounded unusual. Dakota grabbed the metal spoon and pan we used as a bell and banged out a triple pattern that told sentries to check in. The two note all-clear whistle came back from the first sentry, and then the second. I opened my mouth to apologize.

A shotgun blast came from the third sentry's position. All three of us jumped.

"That came from the east side," Keenan cried. "Ash is up there! Who's on duty with him? Caleb? Isn't it Caleb?"

"Keenan, go!" Dakota snapped.

Keenan leaped off the porch, shotgun in one hand, and disappeared in the dark. Dakota grabbed my arm and dragged me into the kitchen, cursing the whole way.

I shook him off and raced into the diner. Kids ran everywhere, half of them in tears.

"Listen up," I yelled. "Everybody away from the windows. Little ones, behind the bar, now. The rest of you, grab your weapons and get to your places. Just like we practiced."

Scared-looking boys obeyed. At least they quit crying, except for Tito. Paco had hold of him, behind the bar.

"Joe, what do we have for guns in here?" I called.

"Just my pistol," he grunted from his spot by the front door.

"Crap! That's it?"

Dakota nodded, jaw tight. "My fault, I sent Keenan out with the last shotgun. Bad call."

I grabbed my street pack from the closet and dumped out the contents on the diner floor. Dakota grabbed his cudgel out of the pile. I picked up the scrap-metal weapon I made when I was twelve. It was only a crude chunk of metal, filed to a dull edge. The thing didn't deserve to be called a sword. Outside, rifles cracked. I clung to my pathetic little weapon, feeling ridiculous.

Marc pointed to my slingshot. "Can I use that?"

"Sure," I said, and then really looked at him. Marc was no bigger than Paco. He should be hiding. Before I could say that, Marc snatched up my slingshot and ran for the kitchen, yelling, "Ammo! I need ammo!"

Paco pushed Tito into a cabinet under the bar. "Bad guys are coming. Hide." He looked up at me. "Jack, I gotta go help. Yell if Tito comes out." Paco took off down the hall. I let him go.

I crouched near the end of the bar, where I could see both entrances at once. My breath came fast and shallow, high in my throat. Every little movement made me jump. Dakota and Joe flanked the front door, ready to hit anybody who tried to break in.

"What do we do now?" yelled Paco from the kitchen.

"Sit tight," I called, trying to sound calm. "Remember the rules. Stay low, out of sight of the windows. We can't have unarmed people running around in the dark. That won't help our friends."

An eerie quiet settled over the diner. My boys looked sick in the neon glow from the orange and white Budweiser sign over the bar. I barely breathed. The unmistakable swish-click of a pump action shotgun came from just beyond the front door. The sound set my nerves screaming.

"That's one of ours," Joe muttered.

Our boy pulled the trigger. Up close, it was loud, painfully loud. I flinched hard. Around me, kids cried out. My shaking hands clenched into fists. Feet pounded down the sidewalk, right outside the front window. Men shouted. The shotgun blasted again, and nearby gunmen returned fire. Someone gave a strangled scream. I couldn't tell who it was, but the kid sounded hurt. Dakota lunged for the doorknob, but Joe yanked him back. With a huge crash, the front window of the diner shattered.

Glass flew everywhere. Boys shrieked. The dark outline of a man appeared outside the broken window. He kicked out the last shards of glass and then leaped on top of a table. A flashlight beam swept the room and caught me, glaring into my eyes. The intruder barked a laugh when he saw me. I recognized him, too. Big Angry Man, from the Zunos. Come to get himself a girl. I froze, eyes wide, like a cornered doe.

The intruder jumped off the table. His boots hit the floor with a thump. Behind my shoulder, Marc let loose with the slingshot and nailed the guy right in the face. The man spat a curse, swatted at the side of his head, and took a few big strides toward me. One of Paco's marbles rolled across the floor. Joe's pistol went off twice, but I couldn't tell if he hit his target. The big man didn't even slow down. I rose to meet him, hiding my sad little wanna-be sword behind my right leg. Then my boys were on him, all at once, like a pack of dogs.

Big Angry Man went down on his back under them, arms and legs thrashing. His long-handled flashlight struck Paco's head with a sickening crack. Marc got kicked in the stomach, went airborne, and hit the floor hard. Even with boys all over him, the man struggled to a sitting position. His fists swung left and right, smashing children aside. Some of my boys came right back. Others went down and didn't move again. Shrieking, I leaped in to protect them.

"Jackie, no! Stay back!" Dakota shouted. Joe's boot knife gleamed in his hand.

In the split second I took my eyes off him, the intruder seized my left wrist and yanked me forward. I let him do it. With all my strength, I stabbed him under the solar plexus. The man bellowed, then trembled and went still. Warm blood poured over my hands. I let go of the scrap-metal sword, staring at its handle in shock. Somehow, I hadn't thought it could do that to a man.

Chest heaving, I staggered to my feet. A wave of nausea churned my stomach, but I refused to give in to it. Boys writhed on the floor, moaning. In the dark, I couldn't tell which ones needed me worst. Freezing winter wind poured in through the broken window. My whole body shook with cold and adrenaline.

Dakota stood, bent over, arms wrapped around his stomach. I touched his arm. "Are you okay?"

He straightened and gave me a quick hug. "More or less. You?"

"I'm fine, but I don't think everyone is."

I moved from one kid to another. Most of them only had bruises. Paco lay still, blood seeping from an egg-sized lump on his head. I didn't know what to do, so I covered him with a blanket and left him there. He looked so small, and so close to death. It was my fault. I should have made the kid hide, but I needed him.

I found Joe on the floor, his knee twisted under him in an impossible position, toes pointed backward. Looking at it made me feel like barfing. Joe's big, gnarled hand still clutched his pistol. Beside him lay another body, a second intruder I hadn't even seen—Chubby.

"Joe, your leg looks really bad," I blurted. "It must hurt like hell."

Joe just shook his head. He reached down with one hand, grabbed his calf, and spun his fake foot around. "Straps came loose."

Nobody laughed. Dakota and I helped Joe to a seat, where he fixed his wooden leg back on.

"Keep the overhead lights off," Joe ordered. "Dakota, switch on that little yellow lamp by the bar. We gotta have light t' tend the wounded."

While I counted boys, Ash came in from the perimeter. Blood soaked the sleeve of his jacket, but he didn't seem hurt. Caleb followed him, walking like a winner. They must have gotten the better of somebody out there. The boys scooted into a booth, side by side, and stared at the broken window.

I hurried over to them. "Ash, Keenan hasn't come back yet. Have you seen him?"

"No." Ash hauled himself to his feet. Blood from his jacket smeared the table. "He went outside? Alone?"

"I'll find him. I need you guys to guard that open window. Get something to block it up with," I said. The intruder's long-handled flashlight glowed from under a table. I grabbed it, took Ash's shotgun and a pocket full of shells, and went out the back door alone.

I hesitated on the dark back porch, listening for the breathing of hidden men. Down the alley, the Zunos' bell clanged, calling their people in. The raid was over.

"Keenan?" I called, flashing the light around. "Keenan!" Nothing moved except rats in the alley. I tiptoed down the sagging deck stairs, into the dark.

Chapter 11

Keenan had to be hurt, or he would have come back with the others. Last I saw him, he was running down the alley toward the Zunos' parking lot. I really didn't want to go that way, but I couldn't leave him alone out there, either. I chickened out and circled the diner first. Blood spattered the sidewalk outside our front door. A big chunk of scrap metal lay partway inside the broken window, where the Zunos had thrown it. Shards of glass littered the ground.

"Keenan?"

"Over here." That didn't sound like him. The voice seemed too deep, too mature.

I crept closer, alert for ambush. The flashlight beam lit a patch of sandy hair, and I let out a relieved breath. Keenan sat against the wall, head tilted back, his shotgun on the pavement beside him. I dropped to my knees in front of him and laid down my weapon beside his.

Keenan squinted against the bright light. "Shut it off, Jack. Makes us too easy to see out here."

I switched off the light. "You hurt?"

Keenan didn't answer. Knowing him, that almost certainly meant he was. I couldn't see much by the red and blue neon glow of the bar lights. Heat radiated off Keenan's body, and his t-shirt felt damp under my fingers. He'd been running hard before they hit him.

"Easy. I'm gonna get you some help," I said. "Can I take a look?"

He barely nodded.

"How bad is it?" As gently as I could, I tugged his t-shirt up. "Damn, I could really use some light here."

"Don't do it, Jack," Keenan muttered. "They've got snipers."

The thought made my skin crawl. "Okay," I whispered. "I'd better bandage this before I get the boys out here to move you. You got shot? Where?"

He didn't respond.

My heart started to pound. Tears stung my eyes. "I need to pack it and stop the bleeding right away," I whispered to myself, trying to stay focused.

I ran my fingertips lightly across his chest, dreading the moment when they'd contact the bullet wound. "Keenan? Can you hear me? Say something."

Keenan's eyelids flickered a little. He didn't answer.

"Oh God, please don't let it be a gut wound," I breathed. Joe taught me about those. Keenan would die a lingering, painful death from infection. Wincing, I traced my fingers across his stomach. Like the rest of us, Keenan never got enough food to put on any fat. The hard sections of his abdominal muscles felt warm and perfect under my fingers, right down to the waistband of his low-rise jeans. I stopped there, mystified.

Keenan's eyes blazed open. He leaned forward and kissed me, wild and sweet, on the lips. It caught me completely off guard. I didn't even have time to pull away. My terror gave way to relief, and I laughed. I couldn't help it. I knew I should have been mad at him, but I wasn't.

I put a hand on his chest and pushed. "Stop that! You bastard, you were faking."

Keenan's golden eyes sparkled with mischief. A tiny smile danced around the corners of his lips. "You totally bought it, too. But seriously, keep it down. Flint's here."

A sick lump of fear dropped into my stomach. I crawled into the shadows beside him and sat still. "Flint? You sure?"

Keenan nodded. He bent his head, whispering low in my ear. "Yeah, they all wear the same green jackets. I killed four of 'em. Wounded a couple more. I doubt Flint cares much. He's got a lot of men."

I looked over my shoulder into the dark parking lot. "Shit. What're we gonna do?"

"They want you, Jack."

I nodded, feeling sick to my stomach. "I should give myself up. I can't let you guys die for me."

Keenan put a hand on my shoulder. "Don't you dare. Remember, they want you alive. If they take you, just hang on. I'll come get you back."

I knew he'd try, and it broke my heart. Keenan was just a kid, all balls and no brains. Flint's men would tear him apart. We could fight the Zunos, but that new crew changed everything. I knew I wouldn't be free much longer. I scrubbed my mouth with the back of a hand, fighting for control.

Keenan stroked my hair. "It's all right, Jack," he whispered, his voice husky. "You don't have to hold it together for me. I'm way too far gone to judge anybody."

That snapped my last shred of self-control. Sobs wracked my body. Keenan wrapped me in his arms and held me while I cried. I ended up half across his lap, like a child, my face buried against his shoulder. I hadn't cried like that in years, not with a bunch of boys watching me every second. If anybody else had seen me, I would've been mortified.

After a while, the sobs passed. I took a shuddering breath, feeling hollow and vulnerable. “Keenan? If you take on Flint, he’ll kill you for sure.”

“I never expected to live a long life. Not after all this shit went down, with the epidemic,” Keenan said. The calm certainty in his voice chilled me.

“Guess I never did either. I try not to think about it.” I tipped my chin up to give him a smile, but my lower lip trembled.

“I know, baby. I know.” Keenan lifted me a little and rocked my body against his. I felt his lips against the top of my head. The tension in them told me he was crying, without making a sound. Tears streamed from my eyes, soaking into his shirt. My shirt, actually. He’d stolen another one.

“We’d better go in,” I whispered. “Feels like we’ve been out here a long time.”

“If you insist.” Keenan cupped my cheek and looked into my eyes. One of my hands lay across his chest. His breathing quickened, and I pulled away.

I slid off his lap and stood up. My love for him felt heavy in my heart. Keenan really was crazy. Completely, bat-shit crazy. He’d been that way since the first day I laid eyes on him, crying on the porch of his old house, covered in his sister’s blood. I didn’t care. I loved him anyway.

I loved them all. Those boys were my brothers—except for Dakota. He was different. I hadn’t figured me and him out yet, and the extra attention from other guys just messed me up inside. But that night, in the dark, with an army around us, Keenan was my lifeline. Eventually he’d accept the fact that I loved him like a brother, not a boyfriend. Somehow, that would turn out okay. It had to, because I couldn’t give him up. Even if I did hate him sometimes.

I shoved the flashlight in my back pocket and shouldered my shotgun. Keenan led me through the shadows, his hand warm around mine. Glass from the shattered front window crackled under our feet. In unspoken agreement, we passed the front door with its flickering *Budweiser* sign. We both needed a minute, I guess. A minute, with nobody judging us. We went around to the back porch and stopped in a patch of shadow near the base of the stairs. Keenan stared down at me, his lips parted. I didn’t know if he was about to kiss me or say something horrible he could never take back. Either way, the look in his eye scared me.

Crunching noises came out of the dark alley, low and off to the right of the porch. I tensed. “Keenan, I need the light here. Go inside if you want.”

Instead of answering, Keenan leveled his shotgun in the direction of the strange sounds. I pulled out the flashlight and switched it on.

Thousands of rats massed against the concrete foundation of the building, chewing. Making a way in. The pox-boss had to be among them, in a rat body this time. I wanted to scream, but I couldn't. Not in front of her. She'd picked her moment well. The Zunos were only a distraction.

"Well, come on out, bitch," I told her. "Which one are you?"

Keenan didn't say a word. He shot me a panicky look and stood his ground, shotgun pointed at the rats. I knew he wouldn't fire unless I told him to. The thing I loved about Keenan was that just about anything I did seemed fine to him, including talking to rats.

"She's in there, somewhere," I whispered to him. "Probably in a female."

Keenan didn't scoff. He barely moved, except to give me a short nod. Rats kept on gnawing at the foundation. Gray concrete dust blew along the wall.

"Enough chewing," I snapped. With a sudden motion, I chambered a round, but I couldn't handle the shotgun and the flashlight all at once. The light hit the dirt, still aimed toward the damaged foundation.

Every single rat instantly stopped gnawing. They turned toward me, whiskers twitching. Some of them sat upright to get a better look, little front paws in the air.

I spoke slow and clear. "There will be no more chewing. Pox-boss, step up, or we start shooting. Maybe I'll hit you."

Keenan lunged for the light, snatched it off the ground, and held it over his shotgun. He swept the muzzle left to right, across the wriggling mass of rodents. All the tiny rat noses pointed the same direction. I followed their gaze and spotted their leader coming toward me. The slender female wove between the other rats, sometimes stepping on their backs or heads. Every one of them submitted quietly. I pointed. Keenan got the light right on her.

The pox-boss slipped behind a wrecked engine and peeked out, her bulging black eyes on mine.

"Here's the deal," I told her. "If your people don't bite us or chew our house, we won't shoot. You and me, we need to talk. So come out."

The female leaped lightly out from behind the engine, sprang to the porch, and scurried up onto the wooden railing, eye level to me. Keenan kept her in his sights.

"As you probably know, we're under siege," I said to the rat, feeling insane for talking to her like a person. "There are men on our borders, and they want me. I don't intend to let them take me alive."

Keenan and the rat both flinched at that. The rat spun nervously, tail out for balance, then stopped and stared at me.

"If I die, you'll never get me," I told her. "Not that I want you to, but we can fight that out later. Right now, you've got a decision to make. Are you gonna let those men kill me or not?"

I took a step back to show her I was done. The rat sat up on her haunches, gave a squeak, and leaped off into the mass of rodents below. All at once, the swarm moved down the alley, toward Zunos' territory. Keenan and I raced up the stairs. Dakota, Ash, and Joe stood on the porch, horrified expressions on their faces. I cringed on the inside when I saw them. *They'll never understand.*

"Jackie?" Dakota asked. "Who were you talking to?"

"The pox," I whispered. "Wait. Listen."

We stood out there for ten or fifteen minutes. Wind blasted down the alley, freezing my face and numbing my fingers and toes. Keenan swept the light around. Not a single rat stayed behind. Silently, he played the beam up and down the foundation, showing Joe what happened.

"First light, we need to—" Joe started.

From all around our borders, men began to scream. Gunfire rattled the windows as panicked men fired into the dark. I hadn't known there were half that many people stationed around us. The pox knew. She found every one of them in the dark. I saw it all in my mind's eye. Poxy rats swarmed up men's legs, biting and scratching, infecting them.

"Oh, my fucking God," Dakota muttered. "It's true. It's all true, just like she said."

"Inside," Joe ordered.

We stampeded into the diner. Someone had already hauled out the dead bodies, and a few of the bigger boys were busy boarding up the broken window. Younger kids pushed brooms around the floor.

"Gimme that flashlight," Dakota said. "I'm gonna check the walls to see if any rats got in."

I handed it over and hurried across the freezing room. "Oh, no, I forgot Tito in the cabinet under the bar."

Joe stopped me. "Tito's sleepin' in there. He's fine, I checked. But you'll scare the hell out of 'im if you wake him up lookin' like that."

I twisted to look at my reflection in the foggy mirror over the bar. Dried blood spattered my face and hands. "Oh, yuck."

Keenan grinned and blew me a kiss. He obviously didn't care if I was covered with gore or not. I made a face at him and said, "Not my blood." He disappeared down the hallway, throwing punches at his shadow on the wall.

I went around checking on the boys. Paco lay in his booth, a comic book open on his chest. He seemed dazed, and a bandage wrapped his head. I sat down beside him and took his hand.

"Ow!" Paco yanked his hand back.

"Sorry," I whispered. "I saw you get hit in the head, but I didn't know he got your hand, too."

"He didn't," Paco said, tucking his fingers away where I couldn't see them.

"Show me," I insisted. When he held his hand up, I gasped. The fingers were puffy, and angry red lines streaked his wrist. "It's infected. This didn't just happen."

Paco looked down. "The day we made that trap on the roof, with the water tank. When Keenan rolled the tank at Dakota, and we grabbed it. The broken pipe on the bottom was sharp."

"You never cleaned the wound, and I totally forgot to make you do it." I pressed my lips together to hold back a furious outburst. *This is Keenan's fault.*

Joe and Dakota gathered around. Joe didn't say much, just shined his flashlight over Paco's inflamed hand and shook his head. I stroked a strand of black hair off the kid's forehead. "He's burning up," I muttered.

Joe cleaned the wound with bleach water, which was all we had. "It ain't gonna do much good," he said. "The infection's on the inside."

Then he heated some water on the stove and sent me into the closet to wash. I stood in the shallow basin of warm water and shivered through a sponge bath. Afterward, I tossed my bloodstained clothes out onto the hall floor. As I closed the door, I glimpsed Dakota scooping them up for me and carrying them into the kitchen. That touched my heart. Dakota never cleaned anything.

I pulled on the white cashmere dress and went out into the diner. To my surprise, Keenan and Dakota sat together in our booth, talking. The boarded-up window loomed over their heads. That made me wonder if Big Angry Man had known where I slept at night. I tugged the curtains tight over the remaining windows, but the scavenged scraps of cloth weren't quite big enough. Dark cracks showed at the edges, and a two foot wide gap showed along the top too. That made me nervous.

Keenan smiled at me. "Good, you're wearing your wedding dress."

I looked away uncomfortably. "Don't call it that."

"Okay," Keenan said, like nothing was weird.

Dakota stood up and came around to join me on the other side of the table. He'd scrubbed and changed clothes too. Not that my boys cared that much about hygiene. We were all just scared of the pox.

"You did an outstanding job tonight, Keenan," Dakota said. "Now go get some rest."

Keenan fidgeted on his chair, but he didn't leave. "Um, no offense, dude, but…" He glanced up at the boarded window, and then at me. "I'm not tryin' to start a fight here. I just can't help it."

Sometimes I really missed having other women to talk to. Maybe Sophia Arabola knew why fights made boys horny. I sure didn't. It was true, though. I could tell. Keenan and Dakota were both on edge, hackles raised, eyeing me and each other.

I felt sorry for Keenan, even if Dakota didn't. "You wanna take the booth behind ours, just for tonight?" I asked.

Keenan didn't move until Dakota jerked a thumb at him. Then he rolled over the partition into the next booth, laid down, and disappeared. Dakota flashed me an annoyed look. I guess I shouldn't have invited Keenan to stay anywhere near us, but I couldn't help it either—I felt safer with him guarding a window.

I stretched out, comfortable against the familiar cushions. A scrap of winter moon arced toward the horizon. Sunrise wasn't far off, but Dakota couldn't relax. He left our booth and padded around the room, checking on each of the boys. After a minute, I got up and went around with him, whispering to my little ones and tucking their blankets close around them. Joe had moved Tito into his usual booth and covered him with an old coat. By the faint, white light of the moon, I memorized every line of that little boy's face. I stroked his black hair and then pressed my fingers against my mouth, tears in my eyes. I loved him so much it made my heart ache. Outside, the metallic clang of Flint's drums echoed through our alley. Soon, he would come and take me away.

Dakota put his arms around me from behind and hugged me. "That was a close one," he whispered. "I'm so glad you're still here with me."

I choked up and couldn't answer for a minute. "The pox won't protect me forever. She wants me for herself."

"I have no idea what that means," Dakota murmured. "But try not to worry about it. You haven't gotten sick yet. Maybe you're immune."

Somehow I didn't think so. I changed the subject before we had to talk about my crazy conversation with the rat. "Rico probably promised me to Flint in exchange for his help."

"Yep. Flint gets you, and Rico gets our territory. Betcha that's their deal," Dakota said. "But now a bunch of them are infected. All we have to do is hold 'em off another day or two, and they'll start getting sick."

Then we'll be surrounded by hunters instead, I thought, but I refused to say it out loud. That would make it too real. I leaned back with my head under Dakota's chin.

Dakota hugged me even closer. "You'll be okay. I'll make sure of it."

He pressed his body hard against mine, and I forgot my worries over Flint, or the pox, or anything. I tipped my head back, lips parted, my hands wrapped around the outsides of his thighs. Dakota's fingers traced the low-cut neckline of my dress. He kissed the soft hollow between my neck and shoulder. "I love you, Jackie."

A thrill went through me. "I guess I accidentally told you, the night we thought the pox got me, but . . . " I couldn't say it. Even though it was true. I couldn't tell him I loved him. I didn't know why. Maybe it was all tangled up in my mind with begging him to shoot me.

If I succumbed, and gave him my heart, would I become a girlie-girl, giggling and flipping my hair? I doubted it. I'd rather be a mythical outlaw, going into combat by my lover's side. Sadly, I suspected that my future would be a lot less epic, and a lot more about diapers and dirty dishes. Was I ready for that? Was he?

Dakota gently turned me to face him. I couldn't even speak. He was everything I ever wanted. My doubts faded. I stood on tiptoe and kissed him, his dark, wavy hair soft between my fingers.

"That night, when you stole the Jeep, and I thought you'd been infected," Dakota whispered. "That's when I knew I loved you. That could have been the worst day of my life, but it turned out all right."

He reached out and opened our ragged curtains a little. Only a few scattered lights dotted the dark city. On the other side of the diner, Keenan rolled over in his booth. I hoped he was asleep. It wouldn't be past him to come out and make trouble, especially if he saw me and Dakota kissing.

"So, I've been thinking about you and me, pretty much nonstop." Dakota laughed softly. "And I had this idea. Can I show you?"

I smiled. "Sure."

Dakota took me over to the bar. "See how there's already kind of an enclosed space here? With a little work, we could build ourselves a room. I know it smells like stale beer in there now, but…"

"I don't mind, as long as you're in there with me," I whispered.

We moved behind the bar and kissed until I thought we'd both lose control. Dakota slid his hands under my dress and touched me in places no boy ever had. His whole body felt tight with pent-up tension. "Oh, Jackie, I want you so bad," he whispered.

I twined my arms around his neck, stood on tiptoe, and touched his ear lightly with the tip of my tongue, enjoying the shiver it sent through him. I whispered one word. "Yes."

Dakota took a quick breath. He pulled back a little to look at me. "Are you sure?"

"Completely." I looked down in case he saw the truth in my eyes. I did want Dakota, more than anything, and I couldn't wait. Not just because I loved him. Not just because he drove me out of my mind with desire. I couldn't afford to wait. Flint's Army was right outside, and I wanted my first time to be with Dakota. That gift was for him. Not for Flint, or one of Rico's men.

After a while, I sat on the bar, legs dangling. Dakota stood in front of me, and I cradled his ribs between my thighs. His head rested on my chest. Joy radiated off him. So much love filled me that I thought it could fly out and heal the whole world. Then Flint's drums pounded from outside. Our sentries howled their defiance.

"Build this room soon, Dakota," I whispered, stroking his dark hair. "Really soon."

"I'll have it ready by tonight."

"Tonight?" I glanced out the window. Gray light gleamed through the crack in the curtains.

"Yeah, its morning already. Come on, let's get some sleep. Our watch doesn't start 'til noon." Dakota took me by the hand, and together, we walked to our booth.

***

An argument among the boys woke us way earlier than we needed to be up. Dakota cracked an eye at the clock behind the bar. "Damn. It's not even eleven yet. They're fightin' over food again."

"Go back to sleep. I'll deal with it." I kissed his cheek and crawled out from under our blankets. Dakota rolled over and passed out again.

I picked my way barefoot across the cold wooden floor, avoiding a few missed shards of glass from the broken window. A trail of torn cardboard littered the diner all the way to the hall closet. Angry boys crowded around the battered kitchen table, all yelling at once.

Keenan kicked an empty box across the room. "Who the hell ate the last of it? We're supposed to share!"

Caleb had his tongue inside a can of Spaghetti O's. The sharp-edged lid angled off dangerously close to his eye. He twisted and weaved, trying to eat and fend off thieves all at once. "Jackie, Jackie, make 'em stop," he said with his mouth full. "This is mine, Joe said so. I couldn't eat last night."

"Not fair," the other boys cried. "He got extra. Make 'im share!"

"Stop this right now!" I yelled. "Caleb, how many times do I have to tell you, use a spoon! You're going to cut your tongue off."

The boys laughed. Keenan made a mock grab at Caleb's food.

"Stop teasing him. That's his dinner from last night," I snapped. My hand reflexively went to my back pocket, where my car-antennae whip rode, but I only touched cashmere. I made an aggravated noise.

Keenan smirked. "Nobody takes you seriously when you wear that dress, *Jacqueline*."

I wanted to slap him for calling me that, but I only said, "So, we're at war, and your only advice is about ladies' fashions. That sure helps."

Keenan folded his arms. "Here's my advice. Man up. We're fuckin' starving around here."

"Fine. I can do that. Just don't whine about it later," I muttered, and went off to change. I put on jeans, a tank top, and the plainest of my new sweaters, a navy blue one. Then I went to check on Paco.

I found the kid in his booth, half awake and feverish. Gently, I picked up his arm and turned it over. The infection was spreading. Wispy red streaks crept up his arm, closer to his heart. Ash caught my eye and shook his head. I could tell he expected Paco to die.

Tears threatened, so I hurried outside into the bright, cold day. I hunched on the back steps, worrying. Paco needed antibiotics, but pharmacies were always crawling with hunters. Nobody went into drug stores anymore, no matter how desperate they were. That would be suicide.

Should we risk it so soon after losing Zachary? If I do go, who should I bring with me besides Keenan? He'll be going for sure. Maybe I oughta send him out alone. That would serve him right.

I got to my feet and climbed the rusty ladder to the roof. Joe sat on the far side of the first building, the best he could do with only one leg. He was looking out over our territory through binoculars. Our land included the diner, an almost-deserted trailer park nobody else wanted, and the two red brick buildings between us and the Zunos. Technically, the creepy abandoned office building on the other side of the alley was ours, too, but nobody in my crew ever went there.

Nothing moved in the garbage maze below, but men paced the Zunos' parking lot and leaned on Rico's black Camaro. Behind their parking lot stood the tall wooden building they called home. I used to wonder what it looked like inside. That day, I was afraid I'd find out.

"How bad is it?" I asked from behind Joe's back.

He jumped. "Jesus! Get down, Jackie."

"Afraid they're gonna shoot me?" I asked sarcastically, rolling my eyes.

Joe only grunted. He handed me the binocs, and I dropped onto my butt to take a closer look at the guys around the Camaro. Flint's face jumped into focus. His long, arched nose pointed right at me. I shrank lower, as though those piercing black eyes could pick me out a block away. Rico was glued to Flint's elbow, gazing up at him like an overeager lackey.

Damn. They made a deal, all right.

I panned the binoculars from left to right. Flint's men stood about ten paces apart, all around our borders. I had no idea he had so many of them. They wore matching army surplus jackets and decent jeans. Most of them were young, strong adults, all male, with a few old men and teenage boys.

Their weapons ranged from sturdy sticks to rifles.

Joe's binoculars suddenly felt too heavy for my small hands. *No way can my crew compete with that. If I ask them to fight, every one of them will die.* I set the binoculars down, tucked my knees up to my chest and bit my lower lip. "What should I do, Joe? Run or give myself up? I can't stay here."

Joe used both hands to stretch out his fake leg. "I ain't gonna hand you over to 'em, Jack. You didn't give up on me."

"I only pulled you from a car wreck," I sighed. "It wasn't an act of heroism. I don't remember an army breathing down my neck that day, either."

Joe wouldn't look at me. "Just demonstrators fightin' cops in the streets. That was enough."

"I'm trying to make a decision, here. And you're not helping," I huffed, tucking my cold hands into my sleeves. "By the way, we ran out of food while I wasn't paying attention. I had no idea the boys would go through all those cans so fast."

Joe said nothing, which annoyed me. The kid in me wanted him to have all the answers, and he didn't. Some days I hated him for refusing to be Chief.

I focused the binoculars on Flint's men. Red, scabby bites and scratches marked their faces and hands. Only a few guys had no visible injuries.

"You know," I said thoughtfully. "Most of those guys got bit by poxy rats. And that happened, what, seven or eight hours ago?"

Joe instantly saw where I was going with that. His brows drew together. "It didn't take near that long fer Zach to turn."

"Maybe they already turned," I breathed. "Flint might think those men are working for him. But they could belong to the pox by now. What if she's using them to trap me?"

Joe put a gnarled hand on my shoulder. "Settle down, girl. We got enough problems without you makin' shit up."

I gave up on convincing Joe and fell silent, scheming. *We can't beat an army. I have to run. And Paco's out of time. Without medicine he'll die.*

I got an idea. A crazy, dangerous idea. The kind that made my heart race just thinking about it. Later I'd realize it how desperate and stupid it was. At the time, I thought it was inspired.

"Joe, I think I have a way to solve two problems at once, but…you and me oughta keep it to ourselves."

Joe slowly turned. The wrinkles around his eyes seemed deeper than I remembered. "What?"

"I run over to the Tech Center. Show up at their gate. Ash says they'll let me in just ’cause I’m a girl. I can get Paco medicine there! While I’m gone, call a meeting. Tell Flint and Rico how you kicked me out. One girl wasn’t worth it. Let ’em search the place. Tell our boys that, too, so if Flint’s men interrogate ’em, they have their story straight. When Flint goes away, I come back. With antibiotics.” I squinted at the sun. From its position, I’d have time to get over there before sunset, if I was lucky.

The hound-dog folds of Joe’s face drooped. “You want me to lie to the crew.”

“Only to protect them,” I said, squirming a little.

“If I tell ’em I kicked you out, you know what’ll happen? They’ll go off on me. I guarantee, Keenan’ll shoot me dead. The others won’t stop him.”

I thought about it. Joe was right. Keenan and I hated each other half the time, but we had our own weird bond. He’d kill anyone who threatened me. “What if you say I saw the size of Flint’s crew and ran off, just to protect them? That’s true enough.”

Joe turned to face me. “Goddamn it, Jackie. You’ll get yerself caught.”

“Like that won’t happen if I stay here,” I spat. “And without medicine, Paco will probably die.”

Joe shook his head. “Ya ain’t gonna get past Flint. ’Specially not in Rico’s Jeep. They’ll see that a mile away. They got this place sewed up tight.”

“I bet I could get out on foot, if you distract ’em for me.” I stared until Joe dropped his gaze, and then resented him for it. I needed a hero, and the sweet old guy didn’t have it in him.

“Who you takin’ with you?” Joe grunted, and I knew I’d won.

“Nobody. If I’m spotted from a distance, all alone, nobody’ll figure me for a girl.”

“That’s plain stupid.”

I shrugged. “I do it all the time. It’s been workin’, if you don’t count the night the Zunos grabbed me. So, are you gonna help or not?”

Joe sat in silence, staring away across the rooftops. Finally he muttered, “Okay. Go get ready.”

I ran to the diner. Dakota was still asleep. I wanted to take one last look at him, but I didn’t trust myself not to start sniveling and wake him up. He’d try and stop me for sure. I stole his black and purple Colorado Rockies cap off the table, since I’d lost mine. That would piss him off big time, but I needed it worse than he did. My street pack was already loaded with weapons, an old juice bottle full of tepid water, and all the trade goods the crew could spare—two of the hundred-dollar bills and one diamond ring.

I found Joe crouched in the alley, pouring gasoline into old wine bottles and stuffing oily rags in the tops. Bent over like that, his shoulders looked huge. He'd been a powerful man in his youth.

Joe looked at me sideways and grinned. "Never did like that fancy car of Rico's."

"Me neither." I laughed nervously and pretended not to notice the damp streak on his weathered cheek. Maybe the gas fumes made his eyes water. "Don't get shot, okay?"

"Oh, I won't. I know right where to hide." Joe carefully arranged the bottles in a crate and straightened with a groan, one hand on the small of his back. "These're Molotov cocktails. Old-school firebombs. When you hear 'em go up, run through there." He twitched his jowly chin at a doorway in the abandoned building across the alley.

"Through there?" A chill went through me at the thought of the hollow-eyed freaks who occupied that rotting building. "No way! You know who lives in there?"

"Druggies." Joe spit on the cracked asphalt.

"Keenan says they're cannibals. When the high wears off, after a week or so, they get hungry." I felt stupid telling Joe the crazy stuff that kids whispered after the lights went out.

"He's right," Joe said. "But they're only half alive, and you're faster. Got your knife?"

I patted my back pocket. "Yeah."

"Okay. I better get moving. Good luck, Jack. See ya soon." Joe hefted the crate and started limping down the alley.

I tagged along. "Joe? Want some help carrying that?"

"No, Jackie." He kept moving, a long step and a short one, over and over, farther and farther from home.

I fell in step with him. "Um, Joe? When you get a chance, tell Dakota . . . I'm sorry. And tell him I'm coming back, I promise, so . . . keep building."

"Building what?"

"He'll know," I whispered, blinking back tears. I stopped, suddenly aware of how far I'd come down the alley, in broad daylight.

Joe limped on toward the Zunos, with a crate of homemade firebombs on one thick shoulder. I stood among wrecked cars and piles of old tires, watching him go.

Chapter 12

Tiny hairs stood up on the back of my neck. I jogged down the alley toward the back door of the diner, swiveling my head at every sound. A few pigeons took flight, circled me once, and angled away over the silent city. At the foot of the porch stairs, I relaxed my grip on the knife. On the far end of the alley, Joe looked tiny, but still recognizable by his wide shoulders and his limp. A shorter, thinner figure appeared beside him. The pair moved to a side door—one that wasn't ours. The slender one bent down, and a ray of sunlight touched his tawny hair.

I blinked in surprise. Keenan. Of all our boys, Joe trusted him? I couldn't get my head around that. The old man needed somebody fast to help him out. Still, Keenan? Maybe not such a bad choice. He was the best liar in the crew. Rico would get nothing out of him.

Keenan stood, pocketed his lock picks, and pulled the door open. Joe lifted the crate in that awkward, straight-legged way of his, and the pair disappeared into the service entrance of the old hotel. If they were lucky, none of our enemies saw them go.

I craned my neck to check the rooftops. Clouds rolled in, covering the sun. From my spot at the foot of the stairs, the alley felt gray, eerie, and far too quiet. Nerves made me a little bit sick to my stomach. Laughter spilled out of the diner, making me desperate to join in. I felt more alone than I'd ever been in my life, but I had to go. I had to get medicine for Paco. And when Joe called a truce, and parlayed with Flint, his army would come in and find me gone. Sooner or later, they'd figure it out. But at least it would give us a little breathing room. Time to make a plan, maybe try and get out of town. Maybe things were better in the mountains. Fewer people had to mean fewer hunters.

I tightened the belly strap on my backpack and edged toward the abandoned building. The scratched door hung tilted on its hinges, a square of blackened glass across the top. A block away, the first Molotov cocktails went off with a great whooshing roar. Flint's men shouted, and our sentries howled. The deep boom of automatic weapons fire shook the old diner. I gaped for a second, knees locked, paralyzed with fear for my friends. Choking, gas-tinged smoke poured down the alley, making me cough. I forced my feet toward the abandoned building.

Two poxy rats watched me open the battered door and step inside, still clutching the knife. I tried to tug the warped door closed so they couldn't follow me, but it didn't quite latch. Inside, the dingy hall smelled like rotting meat, stale beer, and cigarette smoke. My stomach constricted. Goosebumps tingled up my spine. A few oversized flies buzzed at the window, even in winter. The only light came from two dirty windows, one in the door behind me, and its twin on the far side of the endless hallway. Moving as quietly as I could, I paced into the darkness, stepping in an occasional squishy spot where something had soaked into the gray carpet and rotted there.

On either side of the hall, overturned office furniture and dusty computers sat in darkened offices. The hall got dimmer as I went along. I caught a whiff of feces. My legs itched to run, but slurred mutters came from inside some of the open doors. Like headlights in the garbage maze, running would attract attention. The addicts who lived here probably couldn't run much anymore. Closing in on the other door, I quickened my pace. Outside, a black shape flitted past the dirty window. A moment later, it came back again, caught the wind, and blew away. I slowed, keeping a suspicious eye on it. With a garbled cry, a skeletal woman stumbled out of a doorway and grabbed my wrist.

I yanked my arm out of her grip, brandishing my knife. With an effort, I swallowed the scream that wanted to tear from my throat. That would just bring her twisted friends. The woman shuffled toward me, showing no sign that her mind even registered the knife as a weapon. I backed up, unwilling to stab her for no reason. I'd never seen a person so thin. The poor woman's hipbones showed through her stained gray polyester slacks, and her knobby knees were bigger than her thighs. I tried to dodge around her and race for the door, but she sidestepped to block me, hands outstretched. I dreaded her touch.

"You. It is you," she whispered.

I stood still, trapped, my chest heaving. I'd never seen her before. Did she know me?

She blew a foul breath across my face. "You are . . . the only . . . safe harbor."

The woman stared me down with her own watery baby-blues. I focused on her glazed eyes. She was high, but she didn't have the pox. The smooth metal handle of the knife slipped in my damp palm. I squeezed it harder.

"Shelter is all she wants. An act of kindness," the woman said. Her soft southern accent reminded me of my mother. Then she suddenly shrieked, waving her arms. "Don't do it! Don't give in!"

I frantically shuffled sideways, holding the knife between us with both hands. Twice, the woman slashed her fingers on my blade, but she didn't react as if it hurt at all. My shoulder blades ground against the gritty wall. Another step, and I was free. I bolted for the door.

"Wait. Careful," the ragged woman cried, pointing to the sky. Blood ran down her arm. The dark thing flew past again.

I stopped with one hand on the door, tried to peer through the glass, and saw nothing. "What is it?"

"Let me..." the woman rasped. She tried to moisten her cracked lips with a dry tongue. "Let me go first. I am . . . an unacceptable sacrifice."

Her words made no sense. I trembled, heart hammering, feeling insane for not running from her, from this horrible place. The woman's sour body odor filled the narrow space as she pushed past me. I stepped aside. The knife fell to my side, but I didn't drop it.

At the window, the skeletal woman bent her knees to look out at the sky. Bloody fingerprints soaked into the parched wood of the door. Sunlight turned her greasy blonde hair into a halo around her face. I realized she was much younger than she looked.

The addict gave me a ghastly smile that exposed blackened, rotting teeth. "Which way you goin', baby?"

I pointed right.

She kicked the door open, dashed outside, and took a sharp left turn. Once-elegant stucco homes rose on either side of the deserted parkway, their windows dark. The woman cut across the nearest front yard, looking up at the sky as she ran, and stumbled on a rusted tricycle tangled in last summer's weeds. Ravens folded their wings and fell like falcons from the sky, beaks pointed straight down. One bird stabbed her shoulder and fell broken to the sidewalk. She let out a heart-rending scream and picked it up, cradling the limp, black body in her hands. I should have run, but I stood in the doorway, mouth open, staring.

The woman collapsed to her haunches on the frozen ground, still holding the dead bird. She gently stroked its tousled feathers back into place. A cloud of ravens flapped around her head, but she seemed oddly unconcerned. Blood stained the shoulder of her yellowed blouse, but no other bites or scratches marked her pale skin. She held the little corpse close to her face and began to sing to it in a soft, rich voice. I hadn't expected this wreck of a human being to sing so beautifully. Ravens gathered around her, strutting across the dead grass and perching on her bony thighs. Their shiny black bodies wove from side to side in time to her song. Every one of those birds had the pox. She didn't.

The addict sang and swayed, lightly petting the dead bird. Something silver started to gleam on the raven's feathers, like mercury from a broken thermometer, whipped into foam with sunlight and air. Tiny globules of it slowly joined into one marble-sized sphere that shimmered like the heat wave over a candle. I gaped, spellbound. She tossed the bird body aside and held the sphere at eye level on her palm, whispering to it. After long minutes, her shoulders slumped and she let the weird marble roll off her hand. Black swirls overtook it, and it crumbled into ash. The woman sobbed. Then I knew. Her sacrifice had been refused. The pox wouldn't take her. Why she wanted it to, I couldn't imagine.

I remembered the shiny button eyes of the infected rats in our alley. They watched me go into the abandoned building where the addicts camped. Was it a coincidence that poxy ravens haunted the exit? I doubted it. Somehow, the infected animals had communicated. Cooperated. To catch me. Maybe, before long, thousands of poxy pigeons, rats, and cockroaches would swarm after me. The thought made me feel sick, and I clung to the door frame. Old paint flaked off under my fingernails and fell to the carpet like snow.

The flock of ravens still bobbed their heads in unison, mesmerized by the woman's song. Behind me, inside the abandoned building, one of the addicts let out a hoarse cry. Agony or ecstasy, I couldn't tell which, but the voice was definitely male. Not someone I wanted to meet, especially there. I had to get out of that place. Pushing off with my hands, I ran down the sidewalk, shoulders hunched, ready to duck if the ravens swooped after me. Overturned trash cans and broken tree branches littered the sidewalk. I leaped them without slowing down.

Abandoned office buildings were bad enough, but empty houses made my skin crawl, especially when they had old toys or rusty swing sets in their yards. Just to get some distance, I veered into the middle of the street. A few derelict cars sat in the road on flat tires. No other travelers dared come this way. To the west, smoke billowed over the rooftops, turning the sun red. I coughed, wiped my stinging eyes, and pushed on.

At the next intersection, I slowed. At the end of the block to my right, orange flames licked the wall of Rico's clubhouse. Keenan and Joe had done a hell of a job with those Molotov cocktails. Men raced back and forth, throwing buckets of water on the fire. Benny's bald head gleamed with sweat as he sprayed the burning black Camaro with a hose. Flint's men watched the Zunos from their posts around our perimeter, but didn't move to help them.

I ran two more blocks and dropped to a walk in a business district full of smashed storefronts. Broken glass crunched under the soles of my tennis shoes. I cut through a strip mall parking lot and worked my way along the row of giant concrete blocks that store owners had put in front of their windows four or five years ago, during the riots. The blocks kept cars from crashing through the storefronts, but they didn't do shit about guys with sledgehammers.

The sun moved slowly overhead and sank to the west. As I passed the last store in the shopping district, an abandoned Dunkin Donuts, my stomach growled. Their cheery pink and orange coffee cup logo made me crave a hot cup, but coffee wasn't something we found very often anymore. I looked longingly into the building, but didn't risk the side trip. Broken windows told me scavengers had been there before, so the place was probably picked clean anyway. I forced my aching legs on.

Afternoon gave way to evening as I entered the historical district, with red brick buildings, arched windows, and those funny Western false fronts that made the buildings look bigger than they really were. Roofs tended to be flat, except for the occasional peaky-roofed church, and close enough together that an athletic kid could run down the block without ever touching the ground.

I turned down the narrow, two-lane street that ended at the Center's imposing fence. *Almost there. Maybe another mile to the gate.* Buildings five or six stories high lined the road, casting it into shadow. The strip of sky overhead turned a gorgeous royal blue, but I was past appreciating it. Fear had me on edge. My eyes flicked from side to side, alert for movement. A flock of pigeons whirred over my head and landed in their nighttime roost, a burned-out neon sign. I bent my neck and peered up, but I didn't see the pox looking back at me. *Good. Regular old pigeons.*

As twilight fell, walking over the shattered asphalt got scarier. A sprained ankle could strand me out there. Faint, faraway sounds nagged at my nerves, rhythmic thuds and clanks that couldn't be natural. Slowly, the thuds resolved into footfalls, hundreds of them. Coming my way. *Oh my God.* I ducked into a shadowy alley and peeked out, eyes wide, pulse pounding in my throat. Three blocks back, a column of men rounded the corner, a ragtag army in jeans. Weak crews like mine posted sentries and hoped nobody invaded. Big ones patrolled their territory, flushing the scum from the streets. This crew was the biggest I'd ever seen, over a hundred adult males, all marching in step. Most guys had flashlights, and a couple of them held sections of pipe that they used to beat out a rhythm on hubcap drums. Hollow, irritating clangs bounced off the walls.

I retreated farther down the alley and froze. Soft scuttling noises came from all around me. *Oh, shit. Rats.*

In the dark, I couldn't see their eyes, so there was no way to tell if they were poxy or not. They scurried toward me, and that tied it. Normal animals didn't do that. The swarm pushed me out of the alley, back into the street. I stuck close to the building and walked as fast as I could, cap pulled low, resisting a powerful impulse to run. That would just make me look like prey.

They spotted me at the next intersection.

A huge collective shout went up, and the drummers went wild. I took a few steps, right into the empty street, and turned to face them. My breath made scared little wheezing sounds I hoped they couldn't hear. Their leader raised a hand, and his men halted. Every voice fell silent at once. My knees trembled in a tiny vibration that wouldn't quit.

My head swiveled, but I saw no way out. I couldn't outrun them. A couple of flashlight beams crossed the chief's face, revealing a fiercely handsome face with straight black hair and an Arabic nose. *Flint.*

No rat bites marked his smooth, olive skin.

Does he know his people are infected? Can he even tell?

While Flint clustered with his lieutenants, the pox-infected men stared at me hungrily. I wondered if they'd hurt me just for fun. The thought made me dizzy and sick. I swallowed over and over, trying not to puke.

I paced nervously away, down the middle of the street, cutting fast glances over my shoulder. No one followed. I stopped when I realized why they weren't closing in. I looked like bait, and a really bad, overdone job of it, too. One girl scavenging with four or five boys? A few years ago, that would have looked real. But real girls didn't go out anymore. Not alone. Not at all—except for me.

Then, all of a sudden, a young, cute one shows up, all alone, carrying a fat pack. Under other circumstances, I could have laughed.

Bait. Obvious bait.

I faked a smirk, posed with a hand on my hip, and blew Flint a kiss. Only a few of his guys whistled and hooted back. The rest stared in perfectly focused silence. I had a pretty good idea why. *Most of 'em are infected.*

I took off again, looking from side to side as though checking on hidden friends. Flint's main force waited in a rectangular formation while long-legged boys scrambled up fire escapes to the roofs of buildings. It wouldn't be long before they figured out there was no ambush.

A low whistle came from the roof of the building on my left. Their scout came even with me, his outline black against the sky. Another one watched me from a rooftop on the far side of the street. I gave in to panic and started to run, my loaded daypack bouncing. Behind me, eerily unified footfalls pounded the asphalt.

"Now!" I screamed. "Let 'em have it!" I didn't look back to see if that trick worked.

Flint's cry echoed from the high walls on the sides of the road. "Halt. Company, halt." The infected men kept chasing me, ignoring their commander's shouted threats.

I pushed my exhausted body to its limit. The ache in my legs turned to fire, but I couldn't slow down. A hidden pothole caught my foot. I crashed to the pavement, grunting in pain. In a flash I was up and running again, knees and palms stinging. My own sweat filled my nostrils, sour with terror. Ahead, the Center's fence gleamed silver by starlight. I made it to the intersection, veered left, and sprinted for their gate. Above the sleek, white-painted guard house, a rare working streetlight feebly illuminated an American flag. The place felt empty. Had the guards gone home for the night?

Twenty-foot tall chainlink loomed ahead. A thinner mesh overlaid it, a faintly metallic net, almost invisible in the dim light. Darkened buildings squatted beyond, connected by tubes. At the Center, people never had to go outside.

"Help me! Let me in," I shrieked.

No one answered.

Trapped with my back to the gate, I turned to face the mob. They strode toward me, exactly in step, machine become flesh. Somewhere in back, an unseen drummer tapped out a rapid rhythm on a hubcap. Every hunter wore the same intense, predatory expression. Tiny, frightened whimpers came from my throat. I drew my homemade sword, determined to take down a couple of the bastards before I died. I raised the scrap of metal over one shoulder and gripped it hard with both hands.

The pointed tip brushed the fence. An electric shock blasted through my body. It felt like I'd been hit by a truck. I don't think I even had time to scream.

***

I woke, aching and nauseous, on cold concrete. Helmeted figures bent over me. Their breath hummed in and hissed out, like some mechanical lung kept them alive.

"Excellent. Good steady heartbeat. She's going to make it," one of the aliens said, only his voice didn't come out of his mouth. It got relayed through a speaker mounted on his helmet. I could barely see the face behind the reflective faceplate.

Chilly air wafted past my nipples as the suited figure peeled two flat, sticky pads off my skin. He set the pads aside, trailing wires behind them. Underneath, my chest felt bruised to the bone. Gloved fingers tugged my shirt down, covering me. I didn't care. I wasn't coherent enough to be embarrassed.

It was still dawning on me that those protective orange suits had people inside. People who were afraid I had the pox. That meant they weren't infected themselves. So Flint didn't have me, the Center did.

Someone handed the orange-suited man a sheet of paper, and he held it to his faceplate. A slightly distorted voice crackled from his helmet speaker. "Bloodwork's in. She's clean. What a find, a healthy female!"

A young male voice came from a different helmet. "She's a cutie, isn't she?"

"This could be your lucky day, Adam," another suit answered. "You could finally get laid." Men laughed. Their filtered breath hummed and wheezed.

"Flint's Army…they all got pox," I tried to say, but my tongue tingled, numb in places and sore where I bit it, so the words came out garbled.

"Zip it, you guys, she's awake," the first man said. He pulled off his helmet, so his thinning red hair stood on end. I strained to focus on the man's watery blue eyes and jowly, middle-aged face. Tight orange material hugged his thin arms and flabby belly.

From the looks of him, life was easy at the Tech Center. *And I just made it inside. Hot damn. Too bad I feel like shit.*

"Keep your helmet on, Graham," another faceless guy said. This one looked different, mainly because he was teeny, almost child-sized. His suit stretched tight over a little round gut and wrinkled over skinny, bowed legs, but the voice from his speaker rang with authority. Graham immediately obeyed.

Men lifted me onto a wheely stretcher and rolled it through the door of the guard shack. We were still outside the fence. I tried to look around, but someone stuck a rubbery oxygen mask over my mouth and nose, and the stiff tube made it hard to turn my head. A high, continuous whooshing sound came from somewhere out in the street. As they took me through the gate I slapped aside the mask and pushed myself up on an elbow.

"No, no, lie down, Miss. Keep your respirator on, for your own safety," someone said, trying to hold the rubbery mask against my face. Plastic-tainted air blew out of it.

I didn't even look at him. Because the pavement was covered in dead bodies.

Space-suited people on tractors were loading the corpses into a dump truck. Giant yellow scoops tipped. Corpses fell out, limbs tangling, skulls striking each another with dull thuds. An air compressor hummed, forcing whitish foam out a nozzle that arced over the bed of the truck. Foam hissed against the bodies, coated them, and quickly dried. Sealing in the pox, no doubt.

"Good. Least you guys got sense," I slurred, but nobody understood me.

The short man put a gentle hand on my shoulder. "Oh honey, don't look."

I snorted through my mask. He had no idea. That was the coolest thing I'd seen all year.

Flint's Army, wiped out to the last man. Hell, yeah!

The gate snapped closed behind me. I twisted to look up at the roll of razor wire on top. True, I'd gotten rid of Flint. But I still had to steal the antibiotics, get past the Center's enormous fence, and run home. Paco didn't have much more time.

Chapter 13

Faceless men pushed my stretcher into a weird plastic tube. Aboveground tunnels connected all the buildings at the Center, like a hamster habitat I had as a kid. I rolled along, drifting in and out of consciousness. A distorted image of the full moon glimmered through the arched ceiling. The wheels bumped over a threshold, and I woke with a start.

A clear glass chamber blocked the tube. We had to go through it to get to the other side. A keypad with multicolored buttons glowed from beside the door. Anxiety rose, tightening my throat. I wanted to run away, but wasn't sure I could even sit up.

One of my jailers pulled the mask off my face, but kept his own on. "Up you go, Miss. Into the decontamination chamber." He picked me up in his arms, carried me a few steps, and dumped me on the floor of the big shower stall, clothes and all. The door slid closed, leaving me trapped in there alone. The man touched a button on the wall.

Nasty, medicinal water hissed from nozzles all over the walls. The tepid liquid soaked through my clothes and stung my skin. My eyes burned. I coughed and gasped, and the slimy liquid got between my lips. It tasted like chlorine, soap, and bug spray. I thrashed to my feet, slipping on the slick, soapy floor, and ran my hands along the walls. They were completely smooth. The only latch was on the outside.

"Let me out!" I beat my fists against the thick-paned glass. Cold, oily droplets of poison bounced off and flew into my face. The glass didn't even crack, so I started throwing elbows. The chamber rocked under my blows.

A blurry orange figure stepped up and pressed a button on the keypad. A punishing jet of steam flashed out and scalded my hands. I yelped and jerked back.

The deluge went on until I gave up and slumped to the floor in a shivering heap, trying to shield my raw, burned hands from the stinging chemicals. Finally the spray slackened and stopped. Then it switched on again, this time as warm, soapy water. I gratefully rinsed my eyes and hair, letting the stream go down my neck, under my sodden hoodie. One more quick, ice-cold blast, and the pumps switched off. My ragged breathing sounded loud in the sudden silence.

Doors on the far side slid open automatically. I stumbled out and the doors zipped shut behind me. Four orange-suited people took my place in the decontamination chamber. Chemical fumes rose from my dripping clothes, making my eyes water. I shook with cold. Mad as I was, I couldn't resist the lure of the fluffy white towels on a shelf against the wall. I limped that way. With soft mechanical hums, cameras in the corners panned to follow me. I spun in place, flipping them the double bird with style.

I hid from the perv-cameras in a curtained changing area, where I left my soaked clothes on their upholstered chair. Dakota's Rockies cap was gone. *He's gonna be mad. I never should have taken it.*

A stack of gray flannel jumpsuits waited on a shelf. I stepped into one, zipped it up, and took a look in the mirror. Spiky cinnamon hair stood up above my burned, pink face, and I looked pissed. The oversized jumpsuit was ridiculous on me, too. I came out from behind the curtain, rolling up the sleeves.

I was the only person already on the other side. A closed wooden door tempted me to break on through, into the unknown. *They're busy. Here's my chance.* I moved toward the door. Reached out a hand. Someone behind it knocked, startling me.

I whipped open the door, picturing the creeper who'd been spying on me by camera. "What!"

A nerdy boy about my age stood in the doorway. He gave me a shy smile, and the anger rushed out of me. The Center was run by adults, not teens. This guy wasn't responsible for my torture-shower.

The gangly teen stuck out a hand. "Hi, I'm Adam."

I'd never seen anyone so pale. Even blond kids had some color. Not this guy. Everything about him was bleached, even his teeth. They looked like something out of a toothpaste commercial. Limp strands of blond hair fell across his broad, white forehead. With his thin arms and baby skin, Adam hardly seemed like a real boy.

I quit staring and remembered to shake his limp hand. "You can call me Jackie. But not Jacqueline, unless you want your nose broken."

Toothpaste Boy recoiled. I almost laughed in his face. Back home that would have been a good opening line—friendly enough, but with some backbone.

Adam edged out of reach. "Okay, sure. Jackie. Yeah, Jackie. Not Jacqueline. Got it. I…I'm on the greeting committee, um, except you're our first ever, and I don't really know how to welcome someone who just offered to break my nose."

That made me laugh. "Relax, Adam, I was only kidding. Actually, I was hoping you could help me."

He squared his shoulders and stepped right up. "That's what I'm here for. What do you need?"

"Antibiotics."

"Oh, are you sick? Don't worry, the doctors were going to see you anyway. Routine check, you know. They'll send for you any minute now. When they do, I could walk you over there." The overeager way he said it told me girls were in short supply inside the Center, too.

I shrugged. "Okay, I guess."

I just wanted to get Paco's medicine and go home. But after getting electrocuted, shocked back to life, and freezing my ass off in a poison shower, I wasn't in much shape for an escape.

Act nice. Make friends. Get them to believe I want to stay. I looked up at him and pasted on a smile. "So, what do you do around here, Adam?"

"I'm in training," he said proudly.

What a dork. I suppressed the impulse to roll my eyes. "And when you're done?"

"Well, the same as anybody. You too, I expect. Aren't you going to put your name in?"

I said nothing. He didn't give me much to go on there.

"Oh, you're a bit nervous about the launch, aren't you? That's understandable. It's very safe, I'm told." Adam showed his white, even teeth.

I had no idea what launch Toothpaste Boy was talking about, and I didn't care about boats. Apparently all that showed on my face.

"Oh…you haven't heard! It's like a small town here, everyone knows everything." Adam pressed a button on the wall. An intercom crackled to life. He gazed through the wet glass at the men waiting their turn for the poison shower. "Doctor Stuart, I want to take Jackie up to the observation lounge. Ping me when they're ready for her?"

The short, bowlegged man nodded from behind his faceplate. He gave us a wave, and we walked out into the hospital corridor.

"I can't wait to show you this. It's so awesome," Adam said with a wheezy laugh.

"What is?" I wasn't paying much attention. My head swiveled, scanning for a pharmacy or medicine cabinet where I could get my hands on some antibiotics. No luck.

"It's a surprise." Adam led me into an elevator and touched number ten, the top floor.

The doors opened into a break room with wooden tables and squishy beige chairs. The smell of fresh-brewed coffee took me back to childhood, and I had to swallow back a wave of emotion. Then I glanced out the window and gasped.

An enormous white rocket gleamed under spotlights, its nose pointed at the sky. Some weird frame stood beside it, probably so it didn't tip over. It took me a minute to grasp the scale of the thing. Those little specks running between the rocket and the scaffold beside it were people.

"Whoa," I breathed, pressing my hands to the glass. "That's the launch you were talking about. You're seriously going into space?"

"I hope so. If I make the team. And now you want to go, too." Adam laughed out loud. "I can see it in your eyes."

"I kind of do. Well, not really, because I have lots of little brothers. But it's still the most beautiful thing I've ever seen." For the first time, I gave him a real smile. "That's the coolest dream. I hope you get to go."

"What's your dream, Jackie?"

"To keep my boys fed," I blurted, 'cause I didn't have the sense to say *college*, or another good lie.

Adam looked serious, and I thought I'd blown it. "I guess it's rough, being a big sister. Sort of like being the third parent, I imagine."

He probably thought I was put out 'cause my mom made me do the dishes. "Third parent? Oh, yeah," I snorted. "Story of my life."

That made me think of Dakota and Joe. Together, the three of us were the closest thing to parents our boys had. I missed both of them already.

Something in Adam's pocket chimed. He pulled out a cell phone and glanced at the screen. "Room three. I'll walk you down."

We rode down in the elevator, and he left me outside the exam room. "I'll come see you tomorrow, okay?"

"Yeah, sure." *Whatever.* I hardly noticed him go. My mind had switched back to my one obsessive thought. *Antibiotics. Find the antibiotics.*

The second the door closed, I dropped the paper poncho I was supposed to put on and started ransacking the room. They had shitloads of useless stuff, like tongue depressors and long-handled cotton swabs, but nothing that looked like antibiotic pills. Someone gave a quick knock on the door and immediately opened it. I dove for a chair, trying to look innocent. The cabinet door hung open behind me.

That same paunchy red-haired doctor came in. His pasty skin belonged on a blind cave fish. I owed him my life, so I didn't point that out.

In return, he ignored the open cabinet and the handful of tongue depressors I'd accidentally scattered on the floor. "Hello, Jacqueline. I'm Doctor Graham. Do you remember me?"

"Yeah, I remember you. You're the dude who got my heart going again after I knocked myself out on your electric fence."

"I'm surprised you know that, since you were unconscious at the time.

Did Adam tell you?"

I shook my head. "I put it together, after."

"Hmm. Clever girl," he murmured, motioning me to climb up on the paper-covered exam table. In between poking me and looking farther up my nose than a normal person oughta want to, he asked a string of questions. "How old are you?"

"Sixteen."

"Really? You're sure?" The doctor's eyebrows rose. He glanced down at my flat chest.

I flashed him an irritated look. "Yes, of course I'm sure!"

"Okay. Where did you live, before you came here?"

"Outside the fence," I said shortly.

Graham let that one go. "Who was taking care of you? Feeding you?"

"Feeding *me*?" I barked a laugh. "I wish."

The doctor looked annoyed at my bullshit answers, but I wasn't gonna give him directions to Joe's diner. He tried another angle. "You're quite small for your age. You appear to suffer from chronic malnutrition."

"Figures. Got any food?"

The doctor typed some notes on his electronic pad. "You'll be well fed. I'm going to keep you in the hospital overnight for observation."

Observation? That reminded me of their perv-cameras. I bit back a snide comment. Doctor Graham made a few more notes and turned to go.

"Hey, wait," I cried. "I need antibiotics!"

"You have vitamin and mineral deficiencies, but no signs of infection. I'll prescribe some supplements." Graham bent over his pad, typing with one hand.

My fists clenched against the exam table, shredding its paper cover under my nails. "I *need* antibiotics. Right. Fucking. Now!"

The doctor's watery blue eyes turned to ice. "You don't give the orders here, my dear. I'm sure you'll adjust, once you've been adopted into a good family."

"Adopted? But I already have a family," I blurted.

Graham stopped in the doorway.

I had to trust him. "Look, my little brother's real sick. He cut his hand on a slimy pipe. He's got a high fever, and red streaks are spreading up his arm, all the way to here." I traced my fingertips up my own arm to demonstrate.

From the look on the doctor's face, Paco was in bad shape. But I already knew that. "Please help him," I begged. "He's only ten years old."

"That's why you came here? To get medicine for your brother?"

I nodded, tears in my eyes.

Graham leaned forward, shoulders tense, holding me in his intense gaze. "Do you have any sisters back home? Any other girls? Any that you know of?"

Sophia Arabola popped into my mind. *They want her, too.*

"No. Just brothers." My gaze dropped, and I forced it level. "Paco's the sick one. He got cut a couple days ago, and…" I started, but the doctor's red head bent over his notepad. He had lost interest.

Graham finished typing and looked up. "I'm sorry about your brother," he said. New hope flared inside me. I pictured gifts of food and medicine, maybe a ride home. Then he added, "But you are my main concern. Your recruitment process has already begun. If you cooperate, the Committee will give you anything you want."

"I *want* antibiotics for Paco."

"Patience. Show the Committee you can cooperate, Jacqueline," the doctor said. "Show them." He opened the door and strode off down the hall.

I jumped off the exam table and stuck my head out of the exam room. "I can cooperate!" I shouted after Graham's retreating back. "I can, I swear. But my brother can't wait, don't you see?"

I knew he heard me. I knew it! But he never looked back. I fumed.

Two male nurses took me to my hospital room. The promised food showed up, an enormous portion of beef stew, fresh-baked bread, and a tall glass of milk.

When I finished eating, one of the men brought me a round, white pill. "Here's your vitamin." The faintest smirk flashed across his face, gone before I was even sure I saw it.

I almost refused the pill. *Show them you can cooperate,* Graham had said. I set the pill on my tray. "Okay."

The nurse picked it back up and pushed it in my face. "Take it now."

I obediently put the pill in my mouth, jammed it under my tongue, and took a sip of milk. The pill began to dissolve, filling my mouth with its bitter taste. I used all my control to keep my lips from twisting into a disgusted grimace. "Thank you all for taking me in," I told the nurses. "It was awful scary out there."

That got the expected round of smiles all around. "We'll relay your thanks to the Committee," the pill-pusher said.

"Please do." Hand over my mouth, I faked a yawn.

"Get some rest. You've got a big day tomorrow. Lots of prospective parents want to meet you." The nurses switched off the light as they left, leaving the room lit only by the soft glow of the computer screen

I spit the remains of the damp pill into my hand. Part of it had already dissolved into a nasty film under my tongue. I hid the gushy crumbs deep in my pillowcase, rinsed out my mouth, and lay down to wait. I didn't count on the powerful wave of sleepiness that swept me away.

Hours later I woke, disoriented and groggy. Even a small dose of that drug packed a punch. I pushed back the covers and crept to the window. It didn't open, and besides, my room was on the fifth floor. There'd be no jumping out. Judging by the sinking moon, it was late, three or four in the morning. I swore under my breath. I'd lost hours.

A peek out the door revealed a crowd of men in scrubs hanging around a pretty young Hispanic woman at the nurses' station. She giggled and flipped her glossy hair, and the guys were eating it up. The scene made me miss Dakota like crazy. He must have already found me gone. He'd be angry and hurt for sure.

When I come home with medicine, he'll understand. That'll make everything okay. I hope.

I slipped out of my hospital room, the sanitized tiles slick and cool under my bare feet. Behind me, laughter and conversation continued from the nurses' station. I took the first left turn I came to, just to get out of sight, and followed signs to the elevators. On the trip down to the ground floor, I struggled to come up with a plan. I had to find the hospital pharmacy, steal Paco's medicine, and run for it. But how would I get past the electric fence? Plus, I'd never make it home barefoot. Not with ice and broken glass all over the streets.

My drug-addled brain fixated on the missing shoes. *Back to the decontamination chamber.* The elevator opened, and I stepped out into a deserted waiting room. On my right, a young male receptionist sat behind a long counter, staring at a computer. Just past his work station, a circular doorway opened into one of those plastic hamster tunnels. I'd have to walk right past the receptionist to get inside it. Across the room, a second round portal yawned open. I didn't remember which one led back the way I'd come, so I picked the far one, shoved my hands in the pockets of my gray Center jumpsuit, and strolled that way, casual as hell. The receptionist never glanced up. I practically danced into the tunnel, all proud of myself.

Oh, yeah, I'm a ninja. That's right.

Narrow, sunken tracks ran the length of the tunnel, but no train appeared, so I kept going. My feet were freezing, and the plastic floor only got colder as I moved farther from the hospital building. On the stretcher I'd been half-conscious, and I had no idea how far I'd really come. I walked about a quarter mile into darkness, arms folded across my body for warmth. Glowing yellow LEDs lined the path without really lighting the space. That creeped me out, but I kept going anyway. The tunnel curved, and I came to an odd portal, where strips of heavy, flexible plastic hung from above. They overlapped, making a kind of seal. A weird whooshing noise came from inside. I didn't remember that place. Had to be in the wrong tunnel. Curiosity egged me on.

I pulled on one of the plastic rectangles and warm, fragrant air swirled out. With both hands, I separated two of the strips. When I let go, air pressure sucked them back together. I broke the seal and stepped into an enormous dome full of plants. A giant spiral of pink flower petals swirled down from above, dove at me in a current of wind and streamed past my face, out the crack in the door. When I let go of the plastic, the rain of flowers stopped. I pulled a few from my hair and breathed in the unmistakable scent of cherry blossoms. I tipped my head back, mouth gaping, and gazed up. The dome must have been ten stories tall. Trees and plants grew everywhere, with old giants in the middle and flowering vines hanging off balconies on the walls. Birdsong and the sound of trickling water filled the humid air.

As far as I could tell, nobody was there but me. I sat on my butt in a patch of lawn, green in its indoor summer. Giant glowing panels lined the ceiling, putting off a comforting warmth. It brought back memories I didn't want to think about, memories of my backyard in summer, playing on the swing set while Dad cooked burgers on the grill.

Dad. One day, right after the riots started, he didn't come home from work. I never saw him again. I used to daydream that he was still alive, living with a crew, doing alright. I couldn't think like that about Mom. I'd found her myself, sitting up in bed with the pox looking out of her eyes. It smiled at me with her mouth, and I ran. I didn't even try to help her. I just ran.

I never forgave myself for that.

I licked my dry lips and went off following the sound of water. A tiny stream bubbled over rocks. The electric pump sat half hidden under a shelf of rock, but its mechanical hum gave it away. Face down on the moss, I slurped 'til my belly felt tight, then rolled over. Pears hung from a tree over my head. I jumped up and got one. Sweet flavor exploded in my mouth, and juice ran down my chin. After I finished it, I buried the core under a plant so nobody would know I'd been there.

I washed my sticky hands in the little fake stream and set off to explore, picking my way barefoot along stepping stones to a spiral staircase that coiled around the central tree. The tree, a giant walnut, must have come out of some crazy laboratory. It grew ten stories tall, and the trunk was as wide as a bus. Instead of climbing the stairs, I took the little two-man cage lift that waited on one curved wall. It hummed up, making my stomach lurch, and opened onto a balcony that ringed the dome.

I padded along a curved hallway, the steel guard rail gliding under my right hand. The open air was filled with walnut leaves, reaching high for the artificial sun. Fat clusters of nuts hung just out of reach, but I didn't dare lean out over the hundred-foot drop to grab them.

On the left, more of those weird, plastic-strip doors sealed off labeled rooms. I stuck my head into the one called *Taiga* and got a blast of cold air in the face. Pine trees grew inside, and there was real snow on the ground. I spotted a big brown weasel and sealed the strips quick so he wouldn't get out. *Desert* felt hot and dry, of course, and I couldn't stand it for long. Inside *Temperate Deciduous Forest*, bright red songbirds chirped from maple trees. The dome held at least a hundred of those little worlds.

Then it hit me. *They're lifeboats, setting sail to escape the pox.* I knew the world was fucked up, but if this was happening, things were worse than I realized. Way worse.

I rode the lift back down and wandered around, feasting on the first fresh fruits and vegetables I'd had in months. Back on the main floor, I got a surprise. Up against the far wall, a herd of goats chewed hay in a pen. They had weird light-brown eyes with rectangular pupils, so it took me a while to decide they didn't have pox. Neither did the hens that clucked from nests on the walls.

I sat on the fence with the goats and tried to decide what to do. As the last traces of the sleeping drug wore off, my anxiety grew. *I'm trapped, while Paco gets sicker. They think I'm just gonna let myself get adopted into some cushy home while the rest of the crew starves? Like hell. I need to get moving again, find the pharmacy.*

The back of my neck prickled. I whipped my head around, eyes wide. Nobody was behind me. The nagging feeling didn't let up. I slid off the fence and hid between some big-leaved plants and the wall.

Faint voices whispered from a ventilation shaft, sending tingles of fear down my arms. "Tell me the truth, Bill," a woman said. "It's not being contained, is it?"

Someone's here! I ducked lower, pressed my head against the grate, and listened.

A man's faint voice came from above. "No, Clara. It's not. I am so sorry. It's all my fault. I never should have involved myself with the CIA. I was a true believer. God and country." He snorted. "Look where that brought us. All to ruin."

"It's too late for that," the woman said impatiently. "Quickly, tell me, before she comes back. It's jumped species? How many are compromised?"

"Every bird and mammal population is affected to some degree," the man said. "In laboratory tests, every mammal is susceptible."

"How did that happen? It wasn't designed for that! It . . . it's changing. *She's* changing. I told you not to use Bianca as the imprint. I never trusted that woman." The woman began to sob. "Bill, you have got to get my son on that ship. The planet is lost. The colony is his only hope."

"I'll do my best, I swear. Don't lose heart."

They're talking about the pox. That man created it! Let it loose. And he can't stop it. The rocket ship is their ride out. They're leaving us to deal with it alone.

Chapter 14

My whole body grew hot with anger. I burst from my hiding place and ran for the upper deck, ready to confront the people who killed my parents. Make them pay.

The cage lift suddenly looked too much like a trap, so I leaped onto the spiral staircase, taking steps two at a time. Three or four stories up, the foliage grew denser. I ducked under branches, slapped leaves aside, and finally dropped to a walk, gasping for air. Laughter tinkled through the foliage. The sound reminded me of a fairy tale I read as a child, an old story about the Fair Folk teasing travelers in the woods.

"You'd better watch out, Doctor Stuart," the woman taunted. Her voice sounded the same, but the warmth was gone. "I think I might know this one. She's a tough little thing. Dangerous when she's angry."

They're watching me. That woman knows me? Who could she be?

"Oh, it's *you* again. I was talking to Clara. Get out," the man said. For a second, I thought he meant me.

The woman answered. "No. This is interesting." There was no more laughter.

Hauling on the handrail, I pulled myself onto the top deck of the biosphere, a mechanical area full of computers and equipment. No one was there but me. I sank to the gritty floor. My chest heaved, and I felt sick to my stomach. Weird tingles began in my lips and spread to the tips of my fingers. Irrational thoughts filled my mind. *Could it be poison gas? Is someone trying to kill me?*

That was a whole new level of fear. As a girl, I'd never been targeted, even by our enemies. But that didn't make sense. If I wanted to kill someone, I wouldn't give her access to a room humming with electronics. A determined enemy could do a lot of damage before she died.

After a few minutes of rest, I felt well enough to get to my feet. "All right, game's over," I yelled. "Come on out."

Nothing moved. No mad scientists appeared.

"Bastards," I muttered, wondering what to do. Roaming the mechanical room, I saw a switch labeled *Manual Control: Fire Suppressor System.* "Oh, look, the fire suppressor system," I said, reaching for the labeled switch. "Wonder what'll happen if I switch it on, and water pours all over these nice computers?"

"Don't do that! You could get electrocuted." The man's voice came through speakers all around the walls, deep and loud, so I felt the vibrations in my body.

I grinned. "Maybe I'm crazy, and I just don't care."

The woman's amplified laugh sounded high and wild. "Control. It's all about gaining control."

"That's right. So get some, you crazy bitch," I told her. "What the hell did you do to the air?"

The man's chuckle filled the room. I kept my finger over the button, but I didn't push it. Part of me kind of wanted to, but I wasn't gonna fry myself just to piss somebody off.

The man's voice came through the speakers again. "All right, Jacqueline, you win."

I let my hand drop to my side. *He knows my name.* "Don't call me that."

No one answered. The speakers went dead.

On the other side of the room, an automated door swished open. I whirled, nerves crackling, ready to run or fight. The oldest man I'd ever seen stood in the doorway, smiling. He was even shorter than me, with wispy white hair that stood up in all directions over his little round head. Fat cheeks and bright blue eyes gave him a friendly, harmless expression. He reminded me of those gnome statues people used to put in their yards, minus the pointy hat.

The gnome-man beckoned me. "Welcome, my dear. Please come in."

I folded my arms and stood still, staring him down. "Who are you?"

He gave me a serene smile. "Doctor William Stuart. We met at the gate, if you recall."

"Yeah, I remember you. Thanks a lot for the *decontamination.* Bet you never tried going in there without a suit, huh? Burned like a sonofabitch." I looked past him, into the empty corridor. "Where's the woman who was in here with you? The one who said she knows me."

"What woman?" Stuart asked innocently.

I took a step closer. "Don't bullshit me, I heard you talking. I heard you admit you started the plague!"

Stuart took a timid step back. "Come inside. I . . . I'll try to explain."

The old man hobbled away. If I wanted to keep on arguing—and, as mad as I was, I did—I had no choice. I followed. Stuart led me down a blue-carpeted hall and into the most beautiful room I'd ever seen. Instead of walls, an enormous curved aquarium enclosed the room. I circled the place, gazing in wonder as schools of silvery fish flashed past. Blue-green light filled the air.

No woman was in sight.

A small kitchen took up one side of the space, separated from the living area by a stainless-steel bar. The little white-haired man opened a refrigerator, bent his back with a grunt, and started pulling out food.

He spoke to me without turning. "The tank is not the simple luxury that it appears. It is a closed ecosystem. Nothing is added but sunlight to feed the algae, and we get a fine harvest of fish every six weeks. It's considerably more successful than our terrestrial effort. We're having problems with the gas balance, as you probably noticed."

Two semi-circular couches faced each other in the middle of the aquarium room, with a round wooden table between them. I sat down, bracing my dirty toes on the table. A potted orchid rocked dangerously. "I noticed, all right. I felt okay until I started to run. There's not enough air in here."

"Not enough oxygen," Stuart corrected, setting a bowl of fruit on the table. "Air is a mixture of gases. Still, clever of you to grasp the concept."

"It doesn't take a lot of brains to notice when you're suffocating." I bit into an apple and talked with my mouth full. "Whyncha man up an' barbeque some goats?"

The old man lowered himself onto the couch opposite mine. "Removing surplus goats is, of course, the correct answer. But politically speaking, I can't get rid of a single one of them. At this stage of the experiment, the goats stand in, metabolically, for the eventual human inhabitants of the biosphere."

"This thing, this . . . biosphere. It's going into space?"

He nodded, blue eyes twinkling with enthusiasm.

I chewed thoughtfully. "You're saying those twenty goats breathe as much as however many humans are going on the rocket. At some point they'll get swapped out for people."

"Yes, yes! Very good, Jacqueline." Stuart bobbed his head like a proud teacher. "Today, the Committee insisted we seal the dome for a trial. I knew it wouldn't work, but I couldn't say anything. Do you see my dilemma?"

I laughed. "Oh, I get it. Everybody wants to go on the boat. The list is too long, and you don't have the clout to trim it. That's why you've got too many goats."

"Right." Stuart nodded again. He was starting to remind me of one of those bobble-head toys. "Each committee member backs a few of our most gifted youngsters, lobbying for their inclusion on the launch team. The list continues to grow, and no one listens to reason."

I shook my head, smiling bitterly. "That's your goal, isn't it? Fly away and leave your problems behind. The rest of us can just die. Who cares?"

Stuart pursed his lips. "You are distressingly direct, Jacqueline."

"Want direct? Here's direct," I snapped. "The ship's taking less kids than you promised. Parents are gonna be homicidal. You'd better get your ass onboard, or somebody's gonna lynch you."

The scientist shook his white head. "I'm afraid I don't qualify for the astronaut program. I'm too old, and I have physical problems."

"You have mental problems, if you really created the pox." I leaned forward, watching his face.

Stuart sighed. His chin sank, and I knew he did it. He killed my mother, my grandmother. And practically every other woman on earth. Hate boiled up inside me. I could have punched him, but he was so old and frail, I didn't have it in me.

"I'm not surprised that you mistook the outbreak for an organic disease," Stuart finally said. "In fact, what you call pox is actually a swarm off self-replicating nanobots— infinitesimally small machines, programmed with state-of-the-art artificial intelligence. We once had control of them. Now, they have an agenda of their own."

"So shut 'em off," I cried.

"We can't. The imprinted personality, the artificial intelligence . . . it is driven to gather information. Its intellect is beyond ours. Jacqueline, the planet is doomed."

"No!" I leaped to my feet, rocking the table. Fruit rolled, and the delicate orchid crashed to the floor. "Go ahead and leave. We don't need you anyway. I know her. I can spot her, whatever body she takes."

I crushed a few strawberries into the plushy blue carpet on my way out. I didn't care. The whole way down the hall to the door, I willed myself not to cry. I didn't believe him. Didn't want to believe him. Stuart and his scientist friends could beat the pox, if they really wanted to. If they cared enough about the rest of us to bother. But they didn't. Running away was easier.

The automatic door refused to open, even when I pushed the button. A tiny light on it glowed red. I lost my temper and kicked the door hard. It hurt a lot. My foot, not the door. It wasn't even dented.

Stuart appeared at the end of the hall, wheezing. "Jacqueline, please. We need you."

I shook my head. "No you don't. Open up, I'm done here."

One hand on the wall, Stuart labored for breath. When he was finally able to speak, his voice sounded kind, even sympathetic. "Healthy, fertile females are one in a hundred, even here. Outside, maybe one in ten thousand, if that. You will live like a princess, I assure you. But you're far too valuable for us to let you go."

My control snapped. “Get away from me. You can’t keep me here!” I pushed off the locked door and dashed down another hall.

The old man hobbled after me, wheezing louder. “No, not that way. You don’t want to let her see—”

I rounded a corner and hip-slammed the next door I saw, expecting it to be locked. It burst open, and I almost fell on my face. An armored glass wall enclosed most of the room. Inside the jail cell stood a middle-aged woman wearing a loose cotton hospital gown. Our eyes locked, and I instantly knew she had the pox. She had been pretty once, with a slim figure and curly dark hair, but her face looked haggard. Sharp-edged cheekbones stuck out from under peeling, ashen skin. The prisoner’s faded green eyes were sunken, and streaks of gray shot through her matted hair. When she saw me, the woman let out a wail, surged forward and pressed her body against the transparent wall. The barrier flexed and released under the pressure with a dull popping sound.

I recoiled, stumbling over one of the two empty visitors’ chairs that waited outside the jail cell. The infected woman began licking the glass, making hungry, desperate noises. My stomach twisted in revulsion. Stuart was keeping her here. Keeping her alive, even though her mind was gone. It would have been a thousand times kinder to let her die.

The woman stopped licking the window and stood there, head cocked, watching me through the smeared spot. The saliva grossed me out, but my sick fascination pulled me a step closer.

“Occasionally a bacterium or a dead skin cell gets through,” the woman said, in the same detached voice I heard through the air vent.

I blinked and forced my mouth closed. She sounded awfully lucid for a window licker.

“Through the air filter, I mean,” the woman added. She pointed to a slender, waist-high cylinder mounted to the wall beside me. A segmented metallic tube arced from it to the clear ceiling of her pen.

“Um, okay,” I said uncertainly. “And then what happens?”

“Come inside, and I’ll show you.” She raised a torn fingernail to point at a keypad on the wall. “Today’s code is six, seven, seven, nine.”

I folded my arms and pressed my lips together. “I bet you’re not supposed to know that.”

She flashed me a self-satisfied smiled and didn’t answer.

“I’m not opening it. Show me from here.” I only said that to fill the silence, so I wouldn’t look scared.

The pox-woman nodded. “As you wish.”

Harsh florescent light glinted off the prisoner’s skin, which gradually became shinier until a thin layer of light enveloped her. Droplets of a silvery substance sweated from her pores, and she glowed like an angel.

The infected woman steepled her fingers and then, ever so slowly, lowered her hands. Gleaming rivulets ran down her thin arms, pooling into teardrops at her fingertips.

I shivered. That same silvery stuff came out of the infected raven. It had to be the pox itself, naked, without a stolen body to disguise it. The globules grew to the size of golf balls that hung heavily from the host's fragile bones. Horrifically distorted versions of my face reflected off each of their mirrored surfaces. With a rapid flick, the pox-woman swept all the spinning silver globes into one. The ball trembled and writhed, reshaping itself. I looked into it and screamed.

My shrunken head hung from her hands as if suspended by tendrils of flowing mercury. The head was about the size of a newborn's, but it looked like me when I was about ten, with wide eyes in a heart-shaped face. Long, straight hair swished below.

"We've been looking for you, child," the pox-woman said. Her cold, impersonal smile seemed familiar.

I knew her, not as the stranger that she inhabited, but as my oldest enemy, the being that killed my family. The pox. My lips didn't want to move, but I had to ask the question that kept me up at night. "Why me?"

"You are . . . the only . . . safe harbor," the pox-woman whispered.

I bit my lip so hard it drew blood.

The woman's eyes were drawn to it, so I licked it away. She raised the Jackie-doll head. The thing vibrated, and its features melted into those of my mother. My mom's laugh lines still showed, even though her eyes were empty. I clenched my jaw and wrapped my arms around a sudden ache in my stomach. I didn't even have a picture of my mother. When I left home, the day she died, I took nothing with me. I never had the heart to go back. Not with her body still in that bed.

The pox-woman bent her neck to peer into my mother's face. "We had hopes for this one, but she failed, like so many others. You . . . will not."

Hot tears welled, but they didn't spill. My fear and grief crystallized into fury. "I will not fail," I repeated, biting off the words.

The pox-woman nodded eagerly.

"I will not fail to kill you, wherever you hide," I screamed.

Rage contorted her features. The shrunken head suddenly became mine again, and she smashed it against the wall. The thing splattered right in front of my face. Mucus globules slid down the glass. I flinched backward and stepped on Stuart's feet. I'd forgotten all about him.

The old man wore a weird tinted face shield attached to his head by a plastic loop, and he held a long, boxy flashlight in one blue-veined hand. "Hide your eyes, hide your eyes," Stuart bellowed. "Don't look!"

I couldn't look away.

Stuart switched on the light, and a purple beam blazed through the glass, onto the glistening remains of the shrunken head. Wherever the light touched it, pox blackened and turned to ash. The prisoner dropped to her knees. She held out her hands, palms up, while silver trickles struggled toward her. When Stuart incinerated them, she howled in agony. Her high-pitched keening couldn't possibly have come from a human throat.

"Kill it, kill it right now," I shrieked, jumping and punching the air. "Do it!"

Stuart elbowed me aside. "Ultraviolet, don't look. Eye damage!" He raged up and down the barrier like a much younger man, sweeping the pale purple light before him.

Someone grabbed me from behind. I dropped a heel on the attacker's instep, swung an elbow, and felt a visceral thrill when both strikes connected. I spun around to face my enemy and only saw that tall, nerdy kid from the greeting committee, wearing a dark visor like Stuart's. He staggered back, one hand clutching his bruised ribs. The other held an extra visor. For me, obviously.

"Crap," I muttered, snatching the plastic ring out of his hand. "Sorry, Adam. What are you doing here?"

The visor was too big. Adam wasn't about to help me with it, either. I got the face shield on by myself. The ring part squeezed closed around my head with a series of clicks.

By then, the pox-woman had retreated to the far side of her cell. She looked heartbreakingly human huddled on the floor, with her arms wrapped around her knees. I tried not to feel sorry for her. She wasn't any more real than the remnants of the shrunken head spattered on the armored glass wall. I reached under the visor and wiped my stinging lip with the back of a hand. The woman's chin snapped up, eyes fixed on the blood like a vampire. I held out my hand, letting her stare at the red smear.

Stuart stood still, watching her intently. He switched off the ultraviolet light. Moving fast so I wouldn't chicken out, I grabbed my knife and slashed the palm of my left hand. Drops of blood marked my path across the room to the air filter. A faint current of air got sucked in and blown into the prison cell. I wasn't sure why the place didn't pop. As long as air went in, that was all that mattered to me. Hissing with pain, I rubbed my cut hand across the spongy surface of the filter. Stuart stepped up and stood beside me. We held our breath and waited to see what would happen.

In a moment, the pox-woman lost interest in us. She got to her feet and began sniffing at the air intake vent on the ceiling.

"It's not big enough for her to get through, even if she climbs up there somehow," I muttered to Stuart. Then I noticed something odd. "There's nothing in the cell to stand on. No bed, not even a toilet. Does she stay there all the time? How—"

Stuart made a sharp slashing motion with his hand to shut me up. The pox-woman was changing. Foamed mercury melted out of her, dripping off her hands, her face, her hair. Afterwards, she looked visibly thinner. The pox began its slow self-propelled flow across the floor.

"That's why she doesn't need a sink or a toilet, she's not human," I said.

"She is, partially," Stuart said softly. His longing gaze never left the woman's face. "She has her moments. Less and less often, these days."

The pox-woman said something, but her voice sounded choked and garbled. It took me a moment to understand. "It's all about gaining control," she said, and then bent over at the waist. At first I thought she was vomiting. I looked over at Stuart so I wouldn't have to watch.

"She says that a lot," he said. "Certain phrases seem to be diagnostic—"

He stopped talking. A thick silver stream erupted from the woman's nose and mouth and flowed across the floor, pushing the smaller stream of pox onward. Rivulets split, spread out, and began climbing the wall, toward the vent.

I edged backward. "Uh-oh. That blood thing was a mistake. Can we seal off this room?"

Stuart shook his head, his eyes never leaving the silver stream. His thumb rested on the switch of his ultraviolet light, but he didn't turn it on.

"How does it climb?" I hissed. "That wall looks slicker than shit."

Stuart shot me a sharp sideways look, clearly meant as a rebuke, and then said, "Amoeboid motion."

I didn't know what that meant, but I had bigger problems. The stream of pox had reached the air vent. Small flakes of what looked like snow began to fall.

Then I understood. I grabbed Stuart's arm. "She's eating through the filter. Shoot! Shoot it!"

He held the UV wand out of reach. "Wait. This could be the first cure."

"A cure?"

Then I understood. Stuart knew the pox wanted me. It would abandon its old host for me, possibly completely. Leaving that poor woman clean. Healed. Stuart's eyes glowed with hope, and something more. The pathetic way he stared into that chamber reminded me of Ash. *Love, from afar. That's why he's keeping her here. The old man's in love.*

I stood on tiptoe and blew into the filter. It inhaled my breath and fed it to the pox. The silver stream picked up speed. The doctor wasn't watching the front of the tendril, but the rear, where it came out the woman's mouth. The stream narrowed there, by her lips, until only a pencil-thick line emerged. The prisoner sank onto her stomach, only half conscious.

"Wait, Doctor," I whispered. "Patience. Don't shoot too soon."

The stream thinned to a thread. Stuart's finger tightened on the button. He practically trembled with eagerness. We waited forever as the thread flowed like spider silk from the woman's lips. It showed no sign of ending.

"The construct is moving forward as a pseudopod, while attempting to remain attached to the host," Stuart mouthed at me.

I was about to ask what the hell a pseudopod was, but inside the cylindrical air intake filter, a rhythmic thumping began.

"Oh my God," Adam shouted. "It's breaking out!"

Stuart shoved me behind him and aimed the light.

"Not yet," I hissed. "That silver stuff is still coming out of her. If you shoot it now, that woman won't be cured. Let me take the light, doctor. It'll follow me."

"No, Jackie, that's too dangerous," Adam moaned. "You could be infected."

"I've been around poxy animals lots of times," I said. "As long as you don't eat them, and they don't bite you . . ." I looked down at my cut hand. The pox had another way in.

I yanked my sweater off over my head, taking the visor with it, and used it to wrap my hand. In a minute, I peeked. Blood already soaked the inner layer of wool. I'd cut myself deeper than I meant to. The wound ached and burned.

The hammering from inside the filter got louder and faster. Bits of confetti rained down from inside the cylindrical housing. "Gimme the light," I screamed. "Get out of here!"

"Put your visor back on," Stuart said. Then he slapped the UV light into my hand, grabbed Adam by the shoulder, and scurried out, leaving the door wide open.

I pulled the shield over my face, backed up a few steps and waited, heart pounding. "Perfect. Stretch her out," I breathed, trying to feed my courage. It wasn't working. Sweat soaked my tank top, and my hands shook. I faded back another step. The pox punched into the room in an explosion of papery filter. I leaped back with a squeal and trapped myself in the corner. The snakelike thing that came after me was a pale, creamy white color, like something that lived underground, and twice as wide as my hips.

"Not fair! How'd you grow like that?" I yelled, sidestepping fast.

The eyeless head rose up to the ceiling and then struck at me like a viper. I rolled sideways, behind a chair, and tried to crawl away. My hot breath steamed up the visor, making it hard to see the snakelike coils that blocked my path to the hall. The construct's conical head swung from side to side, seeking me. The thing lacked detail, but its snapping mouth was still lethal as hell. I grabbed a chair and swung it, but my target stretched out into a sheet and fell on me like a great, suffocating blanket. I hit the floor with a grunt. Only the chair overhead kept the nasty thing from wrapping around my face. Inside the semi-transparent tent it made, the air smelled yeasty and sickening, like rotting bread dough.

A claustrophobic panic hit me. Rapid, shallow breaths panted from my open mouth. I fumbled for the UV light switch, but couldn't switch it on with only one hand. A frilled skirt of living tissue hung down around me, not quite touching the floor. Eyeless tendrils grew from it and began feeling around. Using the chair, I pushed the sheet up, ducked under its heavy, pulsing edge, and ran.

Halfway down the hall I chanced a look over my shoulder. In a trail of slime, the tail end left the woman's mouth. I almost gagged. The tail snapped forward and joined the front with a crack. I screamed. The thing got a whole lot thicker, waist height in most places. The front end shot out strands that caught the blue carpet and clung, and then sucked the back half forward again. The construct rolled forward faster than I could run, ready to engulf me.

I whirled to face it. The fake, toothless mouth rose out of the mass, snapping at my injured hand. It caught the sweater and jerked me off my feet. I fell on my face, carpet-burned my bare arms, and panicked. Sobbing and kicking, I struggled with the UV light, trying to switch it on. Damp tendrils pinned me against the floor, chewing through the wool to get at the cut on my hand. I cringed at their cool, slimy touch. The pox shook me like a dog with a toy, and I managed to hook the switch against a doorframe. The light blazed on! Howling a war cry, I let that bitch have it.

The big flashlight buzzed in my hands, bathing the white-painted hall in a lavender glow. The pox spasmed, yanking on my arm. I lost my grip on the light and it tumbled away, still on. I dove after it, snatched it up, and let out a triumphant whoop as I swept the beam over off-white flesh. Tissue fried with a smell like burning hair. In the narrow hallway, the stench almost brought my lunch back up. I retreated around a corner, coughing and gagging. The construct exploded with a hollow boom.

Goo coated the walls and floor. Apparently the inside of the giant blob was mostly hollow. If its size was a trick, designed to terrify me, it worked. I swept the ultraviolet light over the hallway. Little hissing pops went off whenever the beam struck pox flesh. I kept at it until the last of the sizzling died down. Then I retraced my steps back to the visitor's room and lit that up too.

I didn't know what to do about the transparent chamber. Even though the filter was destroyed, the prisoner was still trapped inside. She seemed to be sleeping. Her bony ribcage rose and fell with calm, even breaths. I played the light over her, and all around the room, making sure to get the slime track on the wall. The vent was a problem. If stray nanobots were hiding anywhere, they'd be inside that long, metal tube, where light couldn't reach.

Alone, I was too afraid to switch off the UV light, so I cleaned myself from head to toe, then the ruined filter and as much of the ventilation shaft as I could get. No one came in to see if I was okay. I missed Dakota so bad it made my chest ache. After anything scary, he always hugged me and made sure I wasn't hurt too bad. When I had no more work to do, I made myself switch off the light. Righting one of the padded visitor's chairs, I crawled into it and pulled off my cracked visor. I kind of expected to have a meltdown then, but instead, I started to laugh.

For the first time since the epidemic began, I had hope. Humanity had hope. I gripped the UV light tight in my bloody fist. The last traces of adrenaline still rushed through my veins. I finally had something that hurt the pox! I was gonna hunt her down.

I reconsidered that. No . . . traps would be better. With a bunch of those lights, I could set up traps and bait the pox out of every living thing in the city. Maybe, if I got the pox-boss out of whatever body she was in, the whole epidemic would end. I leaned back in my chair and tried to ignore the dread churning in my stomach.

Because the only bait the pox wanted was me.

Chapter 15

A camera in the corner of the jail panned over to focus on me. "Hey, Doctor Stuart," I called to it. "I think it's safe for you to come back in now."

Nobody answered. I dragged my exhausted body out of the chair. The camera pivoted to watch me walk a few steps to the door. "Should I come back to the aquarium now?" I asked it out loud. "Or are you coming in?"

No response from the speakers. I made an aggravated sound deep in my throat. They could at least say something, after what I'd been through. I tilted my head to peer up at the camera, as though I'd get a glimpse of the gnome-man inside. A shoe whispered on carpet. I spun around.

Adam stood in the doorway, aiming a gun at me.

"Oh, for God's sake," I burst out. "You can't be serious. Put that thing down. What kind of gun is that, anyway?" I'd never seen anything like it.

The business end was a perforated metal nozzle, and a bendy tube connected it to a backpack tank. Adam wore thick elbow-length gloves and a stiff coat that would have looked at home on a fireman. He made no move to shoot me, but he didn't lower the nozzle either. It slowly dawned on me what that weapon was. A flamethrower.

Adam meant to incinerate me, in case I got the pox.

"I'm not infected, Adam," I insisted. "I won that fight. Didn't you watch from the safety of your living room?" Some tiny, logical voice in my brain told me not to provoke the boy with the flamethrower, but I ignored it.

"We watched," Adam said shortly. He stood his ground, lower lip caught between his teeth. The nozzle wavered.

"Take your finger off the trigger," I said. "You'll feel stupid if you set me on fire by accident."

Stuart shuffled in, looking about as close to collapse as I felt.

Adam lowered his gun and stood aside. "It's still her. No AI could replicate that personality." He didn't exactly say *annoying*, but I heard it in his voice.

"Thanks a lot," I told the old man. "I save your asses, and Nozzlehead there wants to cremate me."

"Cremation is burning people after they're dead, not before. And I was only going to do it if you were compromised. Doctor Stuart's orders," Adam interrupted. He cradled the scary metal fire-sprayer in the crook of his elbow, like it was a baby or something.

"Compromised?" I repeated. "You mean infected? I'm not that easy to catch. The pox has been after me for a long time, and I'm still clean."

Stuart stepped between us. "Adam, go depressurize the fuel canister and secure the equipment in the locker. Then come back here in case your mother awakens."

"That's your mother?" I gasped, forgetting my exasperation. "Oh, Adam, I am so sorry."

Adam looked stricken. He barely nodded.

"Do not enter the chamber under any circumstances," Stuart ordered. "Come with me, Jacqueline."

Demoted. From warrior to child, just like that. I was too tired to argue, so I followed Stuart down the hall. He took me through the aquarium room, into another, cozier room, with bookshelves and reclining armchairs in front of a big-screen TV. The chairs made me miss my dad all over again. He used to have one, in brown leather, and I'd completely forgotten it. All that showed on Stuart's TV screen was an image of the sleeping woman in jail. While we watched, Adam came into the visitors' area and sat cross-legged on the floor, knees against the armored glass wall. He tried to talk to his mother, but she didn't wake up. When tears started coursing down his cheeks, I had to look away.

Stuart came over wearing latex gloves. He opened a first aid kit and started soaking a gauze pad with disinfectant. "We need to get this hand patched up. I'll get you some more food as soon as that's done. Are you aware that you suffer from chronic malnutrition?"

I didn't answer. My head felt too heavy for my neck, and every muscle in my body ached. I leaned back and submitted to Stuart's meticulous scrubbing. The rough gauze scraped and burned, so I handled the pain the way Joe taught me to, by taking my mind someplace else. Unfortunately, my thoughts went straight to Dakota, who deserved better than the way I treated him.

Stuart finished with the bandaging and prodded my arm. "Jacqueline, listen. You should never have left the hospital without permission. The Committee will not approve."

Lots of things shook me up, like the nanobot construct. And Adam's flamethrower. That thing made me want to pee my pants. But after the shit I'd been through, the disapproval of a bunch of old men didn't rate. "Fuck 'em," I muttered.

"Never say anything disrespectful about the Committee," the little doctor hissed. "Their antennae are everywhere."

I squinted an eye at him. "Good. Then maybe they'll overhear this. I can cure the pox. What I want in return is medical care for my brother."

"Yes, I heard that's why you came here." Stuart said. He pulled up a straight-backed chair and sat in it, facing me. "All right. I could provide medicine for this boy."

Excitement tingled through my body. "Really?"

"In return, I want you to choose me as your adoptive parent."

I sat bolt upright, both hands up, warding him off. "Creeper! Don't touch me."

Stuart flushed pink and folded his hands prissily in his lap. "I assure you, I haven't the slightest interest in such perversions."

"Then why, creeper?"

"Jacqueline, stop it! You're in more trouble than you realize, sneaking out of the hospital like that. The Committee won't turn you out on the streets. You have too much value as a potential mother. But we happen to have an empty armored glass chamber now."

"Oh, fuck off!" I struggled to get out of the tipped recliner. "You're nothing but a kidnapper."

"Wait." Stuart reached out a small, pudgy hand. I slapped it off.

The old man recoiled, and those weird wheezing noises started coming out of his chest again. "Jackie, calm down. Let me explain. Together, you and I could combat the nanobot threat. Politically speaking, that would be easier if you were my adopted daughter."

I scowled and said nothing.

"You are a minor," Stuart reminded me. "The Committee will adopt you out, whether you like it or not. Perhaps to a good conservative couple, bent on discipline."

I swore. Stuart said nothing and waited. I looked over his wispy white hair, little round belly, and tiny, thin legs. *Could be worse. At least he'd be easy to outrun.*

"Okay. Put me in the will, Dad."

"I'm touched," Stuart said acidly. He stood. "I'll go ping the hospital and inform them that my dear daughter has been discharged."

"You do that. I'll be right here, making my Christmas list. How do you spell Ferrari?"

The doctor went into the aquarium room, leaving me alone. I put my head in my hands. *Aw, hell. My new father is a gnome. What now?*

Tipping the recliner back, I gazed out the small, round portholes that lined the wall. They showed nothing but clouds in a darkening sky. *Sunset . . . Dakota's getting ready for sentry duty. Having dinner, if there is any.* I couldn't wait for Stuart to bring me that medicine. He'd have to let me out to deliver it. Then I'd fly back home and never come near the Center again.

I dozed off, but woke up when Stuart and Adam tiptoed in. Where I came from, heavy sleepers died young.

"She looks okay," Adam murmured. "When will we know for sure if the construct infected her?"

I laid still, eyes closed, listening.

"I sent some of that bloody gauze to the lab. Results should be in any time now." Stuart whispered. He crossed the room while I peeked at him from under my eyelashes. Against the far wall, a computer sat on a dark-stained wooden desk. Stuart sat down and tapped quietly at the keyboard. "Good news—she has not been compromised. That's a miracle. Come on, Adam, we'll let her sleep."

The pair left the room, leaving the door ajar. Adam's relieved sigh carried all the way from the kitchen. "Not compromised. That's a relief. What about the genetic tests?"

"Confirmed. They are related, although distantly," Stuart said. "A common ancestor, four or five generations ago. Apparently Jacqueline inherited the very cell-surface markers the system was set to recognize."

"The exact set," Adam exclaimed. "Well, that explains it."

That explained nothing to me. *Who am I related to? What genetic tests?* I craned my neck, trying to make out Stuart's muffled voice.

"Adam, this is serious. If Jacqueline gets infected, she won't be anything like your mother, or any of the other victims. She'll never become ill. That girl will possess all the information the nanobots have gleaned from their hosts since the outbreak began."

"So? What can she do with that?"

"Gain control," Stuart said. "That was the gist of the original programming. To gain and maintain control, politically and militarily."

"Lucky she's just a girl," Adam said.

Just a girl? That was irritating. I quit pretending to be asleep and sat up. The recliner faced away from the door anyway, and its high back hid me. I had to hear what they were saying. Stuart knew why the pox wanted me.

"It doesn't matter who she is," Stuart said bitterly. "The AI will take over Jacqueline's personality. It'll use her, just like it used President Mason. This is all my fault. I never saw it coming. Initially, the system worked as intended. On several occasions, 'bots successfully left the president's body during meetings, invaded the minds of world leaders, and returned to her with their secrets."

"Why'd they start taking people over, then?" Adam asked.

"No one knows for sure. I suspect the source of the personality imprint. Bianca had undiagnosed mental issues." The doctor fell silent for a long moment. "This news is a terrible blow. A second primary host?

After what it cost us to deal with the first? The odds were a million to one against another person carrying those same cell-surface markers. We dismissed the possibility."

I flinched. He said *we*. That reminded me that Stuart helped create the pox. *My new father killed my old one.*

"What are we going to do, Doctor?" Adam asked.

"We can't just leave the planet and wait for the epidemic to burn itself out. If the nanobots compromise Jacqueline, it will never end. Adam, I know you like her. I do too. But the girl is dangerous. Her very existence puts the planet in peril. We could send her to the space station, but if she won't go . . ."

"Don't ask me to do it, Doctor Stuart. You want her dead, do it yourself."

My hands flew to my mouth, stifling the cry. I wanted to run in there and confront them, or maybe run away. I didn't have guts enough for either, so I just sat there, my nails digging into the arms of the leather recliner.

"No, no, I didn't mean that. I should. I know I should! But I can't bear the thought. I've done so much damage already." Stuart blew his nose. "I was only trying to help my country."

"I know you were, sir," Adam said. "Does the rest of the Committee know about her relationship to the president yet?"

"No, I used a trusted lab technician, one of my former students. Still, it won't take my enemies long to draw the same conclusions I did. But we still have hope. On the orbiting colony, she'd be safe."

"And the world would be safe from her," Adam finished. "I doubt she'll go willingly, though. All she talks about is those street kids. She's not going to leave them. Not as long as they're alive."

"There's a horrible thought," Stuart muttered. "The Committee is bound to leverage them, if she doesn't cooperate."

Leverage them? I knew what that meant. Someone was threatening my crew.

I curled in my chair, knees pulled up. I couldn't believe it. Stuart's people gave pox to the president, on purpose. And then it backfired. If I got infected, it wouldn't kill me. It would make me into some kind of monster. Then I wouldn't be me anymore. My body would go on, hurting the people I loved.

Adam was right to aim that flame gun at me. He should have pulled the trigger.

Voices from the kitchen stopped. Hours passed while I dozed, on and off, then woke up to worry about Paco all over again. No one came to check on me. I wondered if they planned on letting me sleep in the chair all night. Even the curved vinyl bench at the diner was more comfortable. Dakota was there, all alone in our booth. I wondered if he could sleep without me. I pictured myself in his arms, his lips on mine, hands moving over each other's bodies, until my heart raced. Damn. I was a mess on a lot of different levels.

After a while I fell asleep again, but that didn't last long. My aching back woke me, and then my stomach growled. I got up and stretched, fixing to raid Stuart's refrigerator.

A crack of light still showed at the door. I pushed it open and went into the modern kitchen. Blue-green light from the aquarium reflected weirdly off the stainless steel countertop. Adam sat slumped at the table, his head on his arms. He looked up, his face puffy, tear-streaked, and angry all at once.

I almost backed out of the room. "Sorry," I whispered.

Adam's voice was husky. "You've got nothing to apologize for."

He reminded me of my own boys, when they tried to be tough and failed. It melted my heart. I squeezed his shoulder. "Actually, I kind of do. Can we talk?"

Adam pushed a lock of limp blond hair out of his eyes and shifted in his chair to face me. I took that as a yes, so I dropped into a chair. "It's about the flamethrower."

Adam didn't answer, but his jaw went tense.

"I know you feel bad about aiming that gun at me. But don't. You did the right thing." I struggled to explain. "Where I come from, that's a really big deal. It means a lot."

Adam rubbed his eyes tiredly. "You're not making sense."

"Just listen, please? In my crew, our tradition is . . . if somebody gets infected, and they know it, before they completely lose their mind, they ask the person they care about most to do the honors. To pull the trigger, I mean. I asked Dakota, but he's not here. So you took on his job, and I appreciate that. Because if the pox gets me, I . . . I don't want to live." I choked up for a second and wiped my teary face with a sleeve.

"You people kill your friends if they're compromised?" Adam's mouth twisted in disgust. "That's . . . horrible."

"It is horrible, Adam. But not as horrible as seeing someone else looking out of your mother's eyes."

He flinched. "That was a low blow."

"It wasn't meant to be. I was trying to thank you. I'm just not very good at this." I pushed myself out of my chair, walked to the aquarium, and stood there, staring into the tank. An octopus unfurled its tentacles and glided past with alien grace. I crossed my arms over my stomach and hugged myself, aching with loneliness.

I felt a soft touch on my shoulder. I turned and let Adam hug me. His arm felt secure and reassuring across my back. "I get it," he whispered. "You guys don't have medical care, or isolation chambers. You have no choice."

I nodded, unable to meet his eyes. "I know I'm different, Adam. The pox knows it, too. We absolutely cannot let her get me. The isolation chamber probably wouldn't work on me. I might get loose and . . ." My throat tightened, and I couldn't talk.

Adam looked shattered. The pain in his eyes flashed me back to the worst moments in my life. Keenan, crying on his front porch, right after his sister died. Ten-year-old Dakota, clinging to his pox-infected mother, while I tugged on his arm . . .

I felt my body start to shake. We were all broken in one way or another.

Adam put two fingers under my chin and forced my gaze up. His blue eyes looked clear and determined. "I promise."

I let that sink in. "On fire. Damn, that would be a hard-core way to go." My knees sagged, and I swayed a little. Adam's shoulder steadied me. "If you had time, I'd appreciate if you'd send for Dakota and have him shoot me first. Because, frankly, your flamethrower scares the shit out of me." I giggled nervously.

"It scares me, too," Adam admitted, giving me a shaky smile. "We won't need to go there. You've avoided her for a long time. You'll do okay."

"Her. So you know the pox is female. She's like a person, kind of."

Adam nodded. "I talked to her a lot, when she was in my mother. Doc Stuart still wants to believe she's a computer program. But she's not. Not anymore. She's logical, but she can be emotional, too. She believes that the people she infects become her family."

"That's fucked up," I muttered.

Adam and I sat on the couch, watching fish circle the giant tank. They were trapped, just like me.

***

I spent a restless night in their luxurious guest room. In the morning, I limped to the kitchen on sore legs, wincing at pangs from my wrenched back. The pox construct had shaken me hard. Stuart hummed around the kitchen, mixing up something green and disgusting in a blender. He offered me a glass.

I backed away, shaking my head. "No way. I'm not drinking that. Not that I wouldn't, if there was no other food around. I've eaten stuff you wouldn't believe. But right now I have options."

Stuart chuckled. "I actually made it for Clara—Adam's mother. She's recovering."

"That's great," I exclaimed. "She's really cured, for sure? Has her bloodwork come back yet?" I got quiet all of a sudden, mentally kicking myself for making it obvious I'd been eavesdropping.

Stuart looked at me knowingly. "You are remarkably well informed."

"You'd be surprised," I said, giving him a sheepish smile.

Stuart sighed dramatically, his eyes twinkling with good humor. "I should have known. And yes, Clara's bloodwork is in, and it came back clean."

"Whoohoo!" I spun a happy circle on the slick tile floor. "Cough up those antibiotics. I'm goin' home."

Stuart raised a wispy, white eyebrow. "You signed the papers, remember? This is your home now."

"Oh, yeah. Right. But we have to deliver the medicine to my brother first, or no deal."

"I'll keep my end of the bargain, if you still intend to help me counter the nanobot threat," Stuart said.

"You bet I will. I'm out to get that bitch, and it's personal," I said, and I meant every word. What I didn't mean was the part where I promised to be his daughter. But Stuart didn't need to know that.

The gnome-man gave me a smile, so his little round cheeks puffed out. "You persist in referring to the nanobots as though they are a single, feminine individual. Actually, there are billions of them, all submicroscopic."

"Sure, but a single animal always hosts the pox-boss," I told him. "She can move from body to body, and I think she learns from each one. She makes the decisions. Sets overall strategy." I cut myself off before mentioning the rats. I was losing track of what I was supposed to know.

Stuart spoke between coughs. "Yes, but I . . . must . . . warn you. What you faced yesterday was derived from only one patient. Bianca will be different."

"Bianca?"

"That's our name for her. For the AI. Bianca was the woman we used to imprint the artificial intelligence with personality," Stuart said. "An AI without an imprint lacks ambition. Of course, her goals should have been those of the Monroe Administration."

A rush of weakness passed through my body. "But they're not. Bianca wants me. That's her goal. That's why I've gotta do this. I'm the only one who can. She won't leave her host body for anyone else."

The old man inclined his head to me in an old-fashioned gesture of respect. "I understand. But win or lose, you owe me for saving your brother."

"After I bait in the pox-boss, you still think I owe you?" I looked at him in disbelief. "Owe you what?"

"When that rocket launches, you will be onboard."

I stood there in shocked silence. Then I looked the guy right in the eye, like I always did whenever I wanted to tell a really convincing lie. "If I help you against Bianca, you'll fly me away, somewhere safe? You swear."

He nodded.

"Okay. As long as I get to go home first and give my brother his medicine."

"But that's an infection risk," Stuart protested. "We can have the prescription delivered."

I folded my arms. "No way. I get to say goodbye."

"At least consider donning one of our protective suits for the trip," Stuart said.

"I'm not going home in an astronaut suit. Some kid would panic and shoot me. Besides, I've lived out there for years. What difference is one more day going to make?"

"All right, Jacqueline. But be careful, please."

"I always am."

I turned away, already working on my problem. *How do I kill Bianca, and avoid a one-way trip into space?*

Chapter 16

An hour later, I was perched on the bench seat of an armored truck, heading home after only one night away from Dakota. I had my own freshly laundered clothes on again, and a fat bottle of antibiotic pills rattled around in my bag. I was feeling pretty proud of myself.

Adam rode along just for fun. We sat together in the back seat as the truck bounced and swayed through potholes and around abandoned cars. Using their satellite maps, the Security dudes plotted a course right to my door. Our convoy would approach the Bar and Grill from the west, on the highway side, opposite our border with the Zunos.

"Don't take me all the way," I yelled to the driver over the engine noise. "I don't want to be spotted coming in."

"Okay, Miss. I understand. We'll see what we can do."

As we rumbled down the highway, I looked out the window, navigating by gang graffiti on walls and buildings. A few underfed minions still skulked around in Flint's territory. No doubt, word had gotten back about the massacre at the gate, and they were scared. Adam tapped my arm. I ignored him, concentrating on the view out the window. I didn't entirely trust Stuart's promise about bulletproof glass. If someone shot at us, I wanted to be ready to hit the floor.

Adam scooted closer, until he sat like three inches away. I gave him a level stare, flicked the blade out of my folding knife, and twirled it.

"Put that away. Listen, I need to ask you something," he hissed. The low rumble of the engine almost drowned out his voice.

"What?"

Adam glanced at the soldiers in the front seats, seemed satisfied that they were ignoring us, and leaned close to whisper. "About the rats."

My eyes flew wide, and I refused to answer.

"I'd get in trouble for telling you, but night before last, the computer pinged the Committee," Adam said. "I heard my dad's phone go off. There's a special tone for emergencies."

I tilted my head. "Oh, the Center had a super-scary rat emergency? What happened? Somebody saw one and called out the Army?"

Adam scowled. "This is not a joke. Using a signal the designers inserted, scientists can track the nanobots. An unusual concentration of them gathered in one location. The Committee took a look by satellite, and saw compromised rodents swarm around a couple of kids. Didn't hurt 'em. Then the rats ran off and attacked a bunch of people! Jackie, they identified the girl as you. What the hell happened?"

I elbowed him hard. "None of your business. You people are a bunch of perverts, spying on me like that."

"I wasn't spying on you! I only heard about it because my dad's on the Committee. The point is, it looked like you controlled the nanobots. You sent those rats against your enemies."

"Our territory was under siege. I negotiated with the pox. She doesn't take orders from me."

"All right, all right. Keep your voice down." Adam glanced toward the front. "I'm not saying you did anything wrong. But never forget the eye in the sky, Jackie. Half the times I've been grounded, that was why."

"Your parents watch you by satellite? Seriously? That's beyond weird."

Adam shrugged in a good-natured way. "When the epidemic struck, satellites just kept on going, so the space program uses them. There's a lot of spare capacity, now that international espionage isn't a thing anymore."

He pulled a little package out of his pocket and handed it to me with a shy smile. "Here's a present for you. It's from me and Doc Stuart, but, uh, mostly from me. Go ahead, open it."

I opened the box and pulled out a new cell phone, already set up with Adam's number, and Stuart's too. "Wow, thanks."

"Call me if you have any problems. Any time, even late at night." Adam touched the map icon on the phone's little screen. "See? It shows us exactly where you are, so if you call for help, we can send Security to the right place."

"That's, uh, great," I said. Inside I was, like, *whoa, an invisible leash. Maybe I should lose this thing in the river.*

"Miss," a soldier called. "This is about as close as we can get, if you don't want to be seen from the east."

"Okay. It'll do," I said as casually as I could.

The truck jolted to a halt by a gap in the wall that I didn't know about. I pocketed the phone and strapped on my daypack, already tingling with adrenaline. *This is it. From here, I have to go on alone.*

It would be a mad sprint to the diner across a no-man's land of burned out houses. Nobody I knew had been in there since the neighborhood got torched during the riots, five years ago. Some crew might have taken over the territory, but I didn't see why they'd bother. The place was probably just a breeding ground for rats.

"Masks on," the captain yelled. "Keep 'em on all the way home, until you're decontaminated."

They all put on astronaut helmets and started sucking air from pressurized tanks. One of the guards touched a button, and the door seal broke with a hiss of air. A side door slid open. Outside, the air smelled like oil and old soot. I stood up in the aisle, stomach tight, and hunched to look outside.

"Hey, don't leave without saying goodbye," Adam said through his helmet speaker.

"I wouldn't do that." I spoke without looking at him. Actually, Adam was right. I really had been about to walk away without a word. Not that I meant to be mean. My mind had already switched gears, searching for signs of danger. Getting home wouldn't be a sure thing, even with this much of a head start.

"Hold up a minute, Miss," the big orange-suited security boss said. He waved his men into position along the wall. "We'll cover you as far as we can."

"Cool. Thanks," I said. Privately, I brushed it off as nothing but a polite gesture. Unless they planned on holding my hand all the way to the door of Joe's diner, it probably wouldn't make any difference. "Bye, Adam. Say hi to your mom for me. I never got to talk to her, you know, after."

"I will. Call me! Just touch my picture, then the green button. And don't forget to charge the phone."

"Okay." I doubted I'd call. That would be awkward, with Dakota sitting right there.

I felt lost as soon as my feet touched the ground. Nothing looked familiar, even though I couldn't have been more than a quarter mile from home. Saplings as tall as I was grew from cracks in the asphalt, bare branches reaching for the sullen, gray sky. A cold wind blew, ruffling my spiky hair and finding its way through the holes the pox chewed in my brand-new sweater. My eyes flicked from side to side, drawn by every dead leaf and bit of trash that blew by. I had a bad feeling about the route. If I'd been alone, I would have turned back, gone another way.

I swept my gaze around the road, forcing myself to check inside the wrecked cars. I hated the ones with dog skeletons inside, but minivans with baby seats in back were the worst. Nobody wanted to look too close, and sometimes hunters took advantage of that.

The Security guy motioned me forward, toward a gap in the roadside barrier. His voice crackled through his helmet speaker. "Good luck."

I barely nodded, my eyes locked on the jagged slit in the concrete wall. Without my ball cap I felt naked, obviously female at a glance. My legs twitched to run. The soldier bent his back, offering me one big hand as a step. I put my left foot in his palm and he boosted me lightly into the gap. I grabbed the pebbly sides, pressed my hands and feet outward, and stuck there, four or five feet off the ground. The burnt remains of a poor neighborhood crowded against the old highway, charred brick chimneys jutting out above the ruins. A narrow lane down the middle shot arrow-straight for home. I hopped down and ran, my lumpy backpack bouncing against my shoulders.

Gritty soot swirled around my feet and tickled the inside of my nose. The treacherous footing demanded all my attention. Sunken foundations yawned all around, heaped with burned rubble. Strange shuffling sounds came from the nearest basement, on my right, so I faded left and kept moving. The dull clanking noises got louder. Whatever was in there was big enough to kick through piles of heat-twisted metal. My nerves screamed at me to run faster, but a fall could be deadly.

A raccoon scrambled out of the basement, its long claws scraping on concrete. The coon was a big one, almost three feet long, not counting the ringed tail. His shiny black eyes were surrounded by black fur, making them hard to see. I squinted, trying to decide if he had pox. He pulled a lip back, revealing fangs fit for a Rottweiler.

Infected! I turned a frantic circle, but there was nowhere to hide among the ruins. A few scarred old trees had survived the blaze, but coons could climb, couldn't they?

The raccoon balanced on its hindquarters, sniffed the air, then dropped to all fours and came galloping after me, faster than that chubby furball should have been able to move. I gave in to my panic and fled.

I hadn't made it twenty feet when shots rang out behind me. I whirled. The poor, infected coon was down in a puddle of blood. A silver sheen was already spreading across the animal's black mask. Stupid security guards kept pumping bullets into him, making exit holes for the pox. I gaped for a second and took off again, flinching with each shot that rang out. A gust of wind came up behind me, lifting soot into the air. I squinted my eyes, trying to run and hold my breath all at once. Were nanobots riding on flecks of dust, catching in my hair, crawling across my skin?

In seconds, a tearing sensation in my chest forced me to inhale. I sucked in talc-fine ash, scorching my lungs. Fifty yards away, the charred neighborhood gave way to intact buildings. The roof of Joe's diner stuck up above a sagging wooden privacy fence that wrapped our back porch. Legs and lungs burning, I hurtled toward home, imagining poxy animals on my heels. My sentries howled.

The cries quickly turned glad, and someone started banging the all-clear rhythm on our scrap-metal bell. I stumbled onto the stretch of dirty white sidewalk right in front of the bar, almost weeping with relief.

Nothing pursued me. Thighs trembling, I sagged against the cool cinderblock wall. Boys burst outside and sprinted around the corner, shouting happily. They surrounded me, all trying to hug me at once. I reached out, squeezing every one of their hands, smiling into every familiar face. Ash lifted little Tito over the crowd and handed him to me. Tito glommed on to my neck and clung like a monkey. I closed my eyes and buried my nose in his black hair. When my strength gave out I sank to the sidewalk, still holding my youngest boy.

Ash supported me, or I might have collapsed under the combined weight of the child and my heavy backpack. He smiled, teeth white against chocolate skin. "Let me help you. What's in this thing, bricks?" He reached down to unclip the belly strap and lift the straps from my shoulders. For once, I didn't slap his hands off.

"Go ahead and open it," I said. "I brought you guys presents."

"What? What is it?" a chorus of voices demanded.

"Oranges." I slumped against Ash's shoulder, thrilled and worn out all at once. I'd never been so happy to be home.

Caleb grabbed my bag and handed out fruit, one piece per person. He dropped one in my lap, too, and that got a cheer. He held up the pill bottle. "What's this?"

"Medicine for Paco," I said proudly. "How is he?"

"Still alive, anyway," Caleb said. "He's in his bed."

Keenan showed up then, loping down the alley, sandy, shoulder-length hair blowing back like a lion's mane. Younger boys scattered, clearing a path for him. Maybe it was only because I was looking up from the ground, but he seemed bigger. Come to think of it, Ash's chest felt a little wider too. *Can boys really grow in one day?*

Keenan dropped to one knee, gave Ash's shoulder a friendly squeeze, and then cupped my cheek and kissed me, quick and casual, right on the lips. I was too tired to make anything of it, and people noticed. All the kids got quiet for a second.

"I am so glad you're home," Keenan told me, his eyes shining. "I'm on sentry duty, though, so I gotta go. See you in a couple hours, babe."

He turned his back and strode off through the crowd. I watched him go, realizing, too late, that I forgot to tell him not to call me that.

I didn't know how sore I was until I tried to stand up, and people had to practically drag me to my feet. Ash's brow furrowed in concern. For some reason that made him look older. For a second, I saw him as he'd be in his twenties—handsome and reliable, the perfect husband.

Ash put an arm around my waist and walked me toward the front door of the diner. I leaned on him, grateful for the help. He bent his head and breathed in the scent from my freshly shampooed hair. "What happened to you, Jackie? You smell great, but you look like hell. Um, no offense," he added, while the younger boys giggled.

Around us, kids imitated him, telling each other how they smelled great, or looked like hell—mostly the latter.

"I battled the pox," I said, grinning at my boys despite the pain in my legs and back. "And I won! They had this infected woman trapped in a glass cage, and the pox left her to attack me, and without a body it looked like this gross white blob, but it could change shape—"

We came through the door, and my voice died. Dakota stood there, arms folded across his chest. "Well, isn't she just full of fun stories," he said sarcastically.

I froze, lips parted, staring at him in disbelief. I didn't say it out loud, but Dakota looked like hell too. He had on a filthy shirt, and judging from his greasy hair, he hadn't bathed since before I left.

Ash gently tugged me forward. "Hey Dakota, Jackie's not doin' so good, wanna give me a hand here?" Not that he needed any help, but it was a nice way to include my boyfriend and get out, all at once.

I envied Ash his instinctive tact. I was always saying the wrong thing, even when I meant to be nice. That day, I didn't dare say a word. I extended a hand to Dakota, aching to feel his arms around me. He didn't move. Didn't unfold his arms.

Ash tensed, but said nothing. He helped me to my booth and left me there. "You rest, Jackie. I'll take Paco his medicine."

Dakota stalked out of the room. I crawled dejectedly onto my red vinyl cushion and collapsed. Above my head, plywood still covered our broken window. After a while I fell asleep and dreamed of the pox, snapping at me with her snake mouth, chasing me, suffocating me under her disgusting umbrella of wrinkled skin. I startled myself awake a couple of different times by talking in my sleep, but exhaustion pulled me right back into the nightmare.

The pox sneered at me with my mother's voice, telling me I was a liar. I didn't deserve my crew's loyalty. She'd take every one of them, starting with Tito. I woke up thrashing and found my head pillowed in someone's lap. A boy's hand stroked my hair. It felt late, after midnight at least. The diner was dark and quiet except for the sounds of children's breathing, deep and even, in peaceful sleep.

My body went loose with relief. Dakota had forgiven me. My love for him was so intense that my chest ached. I rolled over on my side and wrapped my top arm around his hips, so my hand fit in the warm hollow behind the small of his back. "Dakota, I'm sorry I left without saying goodbye," I whispered sleepily, my lips muffled against the hem of his black fleece hoodie. "I love you so much."

"I know you do, babe. But you'll get over it. He's kind of an asshat, if you ask me."

"Keenan! Oh my God." I froze, acutely aware of exactly where my face was. My cheeks heated in a blush that, thankfully, was hidden in the darkness.

Ash laughed softly, from right beside Keenan. The two boys sat hip to hip, taking care of me together. I edged my arm out from behind Keenan and turned onto my back again. I moved to sit up, but my whole body ached, and Ash stroked my hair softly with the tips of his fingers. I relaxed into the delicious sensations and almost forgot how weird it was to be there, with both of them at once.

Keenan even try to didn't take advantage, which surprised me a little. His hand stroked my shoulder in a soothing rhythm. "Go back to sleep, Jack," he murmured. "You're safe now."

I knew I wasn't, not really. None of us were. But I planned to do something about that.

***

I passed out again and woke up when my phone rang. It was still dark in the diner. Keenan answered the call before I could sit up. I snatched for my phone, but he switched ears with it and refused to hand it over. Adam's voice sounded faint, asking for me. I didn't catch everything he said. The whole diner got Keenan's side of the conversation.

"Nope. She's sleeping. Who the hell is this?"

"Keenan," I hissed, even though my ringing phone already woke the whole crew. "Give me the phone!"

He ignored me.

A shadow loomed over our table. Dakota stood there, looking serious. I couldn't tell if he was angry or not.

"Jackie's fine," Keenan said, holding the phone with his right hand and blocking my grabs with his left. "We plan on keeping it that way, so if you want to see her, you'd better talk to us first. Right, Dakota?" He pinned my wrist for a second and held the phone up in Dakota's general direction.

"Right," Dakota said, deep and loud.

"Oh, and Adam? Thanks for the cell phone." Keenan had this huge shit-eating grin on his face. "I'm sure Jackie would appreciate it if you bought one for me, too."

He hung up the phone and busted up laughing. Even Dakota cracked a smile.

"Keenan, what are you doing?" I squealed. "You are not my father! You can't dictate who I see. Not that I'm wild to see Adam or anything, but we're going pox hunting together." I shut up, instantly regretting my choice of words.

Yeah. Wild to see Adam. That was good.

"Pox hunting?" Dakota repeated dubiously.

"You should have listened better to my fun story," I snapped, imitating the voice he'd used to make the crack. "It's true. I have a way to kill the pox now. I bait her out of her host bodies, 'cause she, uh, wants me worse. And then I burn her up with these UV lamps they build at the Center. I know," I added, seeing the horrified look on his face. "Imagine how I feel about it! I'm the bait. But I'm still going." I swiveled to check with each of the boys. "Seriously, you guys. I am gunnin' for the pox-boss. Wanna help me kill that bitch?"

"Hell, yeah," Keenan said, way too loud, considering kids were sleeping all around us.

"I'm not even sure what this is about, but I got your back," Ash said.

That choked me up a little. I wanted to thank them, but then a picture popped into my mind—black marbles swirling around the bottom of a jar, one of them mine. I pushed the thought away.

"We'll hash out our plan tomorrow, okay? I'm not feeling too good right now. My back is wrecked. The pox construct picked me up and shook me. See the holes she ripped in my new sweater?" I stopped talking when their eyes went wide.

"Pox construct?" Ash mouthed to Keenan, who shrugged.

Dakota waved a hand. "Clear out, you two. Let her rest. The rest of you guys, go back to sleep." All around the diner, little heads sank down onto red vinyl cushions.

Ash started scooting around the booth the long way, so I didn't have to move. Keenan gave me a final squeeze on the shoulder and followed. They took their time at it. "I know, we're still on probation. Not breakin' any rules here," Ash said.

Dakota glowered and said nothing.

Ash stood up, looked Dakota in the eye, and flashed him an understanding smile. "Dude. Seriously. What did you think was gonna happen? You're doing us a favor, bein' a dick."

Ash and Keenan stood side by side, facing off against Dakota. They weren't that much shorter than him anymore. The partners shambled toward the door. "If you won't take care of her, we will. There's nothin' wrong with that," Keenan added.

Dakota slid into our booth, on his side.

I couldn't resist shooting off my mouth. "So, I noticed you didn't volunteer."

"For your pox hunt? Oh, I'm going, all right. But I still think you're nuts," he grumbled.

"You'll see," I said, stretching out on my familiar cushion. I figured I might as well not tell him the truth quite yet. He'd be happier that way.

***

I woke before dawn, probably because I went to sleep around dinner time, and crept over to Paco's booth. The pill bottle sat in the middle of his table, and he was sound asleep. I touched his forehead, and the worry inside me let go. *No fever. The medicine's working.*

Cool air flowed across my face. I looked up to see where it was coming from. Dakota quietly closed the front door and stood there, half in shadow. The hollows of his cheeks were deeper, his body thinner, but somehow, he'd grown taller on our starvation rations. He was a survivor.

I tiptoed across the room, hesitated at his elbow, and then slid under his arm, half expecting him to push me away. Together, we stared out at the starry sky. A narrow band of indigo on the horizon marked the coming dawn.

Dakota pulled me close and touched his lips to my hair. "Hey," he whispered. "Feelin' better?"

"Yeah."

I noticed that he'd cleaned up, but I didn't dare mention it. Joe had the whole crew convinced that washing reduced the chance of pox infection. I was pretty sure it didn't make any difference, but the story was working for us and I didn't want to mess that up. The diner stank bad enough as it was.

Dakota grabbed our blankets off the booth seats, took me by the hand, and pulled me out the front door. We whispered a greeting to Caleb, on sentry duty, and veered left, to the back porch. For once the wind came from the south, instead of east, down the alley. A softening of the chill told me winter would soon be giving way to spring. Every year, another victory. Every year, my boys grew bigger and tougher, our crew safer. Except not this year. This would be our last year—unless I beat the pox. The people who knew the most about her had no hope. They were abandoning the planet. A shiver went through me, thinking about all the desperate parents at the Center, battling to get their kids on the ship.

Dakota tossed a blanket over my shoulders and we sat together on the deck, up against the outer wall of the kitchen. Inside, low-pressure water trickled into a big bucket in the sink. It took half the night to fill. Water didn't run as well as it did when I was small, and it sure didn't run hot. If we saved enough, we could pour it into the toilet tank and get the thing to flush.

I stared up at the strip of black sky between the buildings, trying to figure out what to say. "Dakota?" I murmured. "I . . . I'm sorry I didn't talk to you before I took off."

"Yeah. I had to hear about it from Keenan," Dakota said. "Lemme tell ya, he loved that." He imitated Keenan's taunting voice. "Oh, she didn't *tell* you?"

"I was afraid I wouldn't be able to do it," I muttered. "I just couldn't leave, if I saw you."

"Aw," Dakota breathed. He got it, I could tell. He understood. Or at least I thought so, until he said, "I did you a favor and didn't put a bullet through your boyfriend's head."

"Adam is not my boyfr—" I started, and then went, "wait a minute. When did you see him?"

"From the roof. Through the scope of my rifle. You think I wouldn't notice a frickin' military convoy comin' in?

"And you almost took a shot at 'em?" I didn't point out the bulletproof glass, or the fact they those soldiers would have vaporized him if he'd tried.

"Nah. Adam's no threat. You'd never dump me for a guy that soft," Dakota said.

"You're right, he's not," I said. Then I got a teasing smile on my face. "Funny how you can tell that from, like, a mile away."

There's this subtle way you move, when you're around a guy who interests you," Dakota whispered. "A guy who can light you up, like this." He wrapped a hand around my leg and ran his fingers up my inner thigh.

I gasped. Even through my jeans, it gave me a thrill. I couldn't talk for a minute. I breathed faster, my hand on Dakota's hipbone, squeezing, pulling him closer.

"I bet you don't react this way to Adam," Dakota said, his mouth inches from mine.

"No," I breathed, wishing he'd shut up and kiss me.

"But I sometimes see hints of it when you're near Keenan." Dakota's hand stopped moving. "And Ash too, lately."

"Uh," I stalled, not entirely certain I wanted to 'fess up about that.

"Relax. You don't have to hide it, Jackie. I expected some serious competition when I fell for the last woman on earth."

I loved how he said he fell for me. Plus, Dakota wasn't all that pissed about my embarrassingly obvious attraction to Ash and Keenan. That was good news. I wouldn't cheat on my boyfriend, but I couldn't help it if other guys were hot, too.

"I'm not the last woman on earth." I giggled. "Last woman. Funny, Ash calls me that, too."

"We all call you that."

I shook my head, smiling, and then tilted my face up for a kiss. Our lips met. I found the hem of Dakota's sweatshirt and gradually worked my fingers under it, up the broad muscles of his back. His hands wrapped my waist and started to slide up, achingly slowly, leaving tingles in their wake. A prickling on the back of my neck snapped my brain onto another channel.

Someone's watching us!

My back went rigid, and I swiveled my head, searching the shadows. I didn't have to say a word. Dakota already knew. He seized my hand and yanked me to my feet. Blanket flapping, we raced for the back door of the diner. The screen door slammed shut behind us with a bang. I felt silly for overreacting, but I wasn't the only one. Dakota paced the warm, well-lit kitchen, looking out the windows into the dark.

Ash came out of the back room, rubbing his eyes. "What's wrong?" He yawned. Something goin' on outside?"

"Um, no," I stammered. "At least I don't think so. I just got scared, you know, by the shadows, or, I don't know, something."

"Scared o' the dark? That's not like you." Ash peered through the crescent-shaped window in the diner's back door. "Okay, that is creepy," he muttered, and grabbed a dish towel off the counter.

I hoped he wasn't planning on running outside, whipping a towel at whatever frightened me. "What's creepy?"

"That bug." Ash twitched his chin at the little arc of a window. A lone wasp buzzed there. "In winter? That's not right." He twirled the towel in one dark hand, getting ready to whack the insect.

"Wait!" I put a hand on Ash's wiry forearm. "Don't smash it. That'll release pox all over, if it's infected."

"Oh. Right." Ash grabbed an empty jelly jar out of the cupboard, trapped the wasp, and set it on our battered wooden table. I cautiously stroked the glass. Antennae waving, the wasp walked around the inside, following my finger. I changed direction, and it did too.

"Oh, shit," I whispered. "Bugs are infected now. How are we gonna avoid bugs? Will mosquitoes be next? If that happens, we're done."

Ash turned on the porch light. I pressed my face to the window, expecting to see a cloud of wasps orbiting the light bulb or sinking, frozen, to the warped wooden deck.

Nothing was there.

I jumped when a sentry rang the all-clear bell from our rooftop. "Who's here?"

"Joe's back, finally," Ash said.

I felt bad. I hadn't noticed the old man wasn't around. "At this hour? Where was he?"

"Peace talks with the Zunos. Maybe with Flint too, if the bastard had the balls to show up. Haven't seen 'im in a while."

I opened my mouth to chew them both out for not reporting that the second I got home, but Joe limped in and I forgot all about it. Because Sophia Arabola was with him.

Joe saw me and quickly masked the dismayed look on his face. I felt sick to my stomach. He was keeping his side of the bargain, bringing the Zunos in to see I was gone. Only I came back early, like an idiot. What the hell was I thinking? Why didn't I ask someone? Had the pox scrambled my brain?

Even at five o'clock in the morning, Sophia Arabola looked stunning. Sable hair fell in windblown waves to her waist, and she had on a black leather jacket over her jeans. A pale pink blouse peeked out at the neck. I couldn't wear pink if I wanted to. If my boys saw me in that, they'd lose whatever shreds of respect they still had for me. Lately, I felt more like the crew mascot than their chief, anyway.

Sophia caught me looking at her and smiled back. I used to have kind of a fangirl crush on her, since she was older than me, and prettier, and she came from a crew of grown men instead of little boys. Not so long ago, I would have done just about anything to be friends with a woman like that. But that night, when Sophia walked into my kitchen, I had a crazy impulse to grab the shotgun off the wall and blow her in half. Of course I didn't do it. I stood there, awkwardly silent, as Joe ushered the visiting beauty into our old industrial kitchen and gallantly seated her at the table. The place looked run-down with her in it. My eye picked out dents on the old steel counters and dust on the blue cotton curtains that I made by hand when I was fourteen.

Joe looked me up and down with feigned distaste. "Well, look who's back," he sneered. "Come t' get yer gear before yer gone fer good?"

"Yeah," I said. "That, and say goodbye to a couple of people, who aren't assholes like you are."

Joe looked down, like he usually did when he tried not to laugh, and I wondered if I laid it on too thick.

"Now, now, Joseph, this isn't necessary." Sophia told Joe, and then turned her charm on me. "Jacqueline, isn't it? Can I call you Jackie?"

I refused to answer.

If that irritated Sophia, she hid it well. "Won't you have a seat and talk with me for a few minutes?"

Joe immediately took the wooden chair next to hers. I folded my arms and leaned on the wall next to the gun rack.

"Don't worry, Jackie," Sophia said. "I'm here to make peace, not hash out old arguments. We already knew you were here, anyway. My people saw you come across the burn zone."

The Zunos saw me, when I came in on the far side, opposite their territory? I wondered how. Maybe they'd salvaged a telescope.

"You are a very special girl," Sophia said. "You overcome the odds, time and again. I find that . . . impressive."

I wasn't sure I believed her. I tried to read her expression, but long black lashes, thick with mascara, half hid Sophia's eyes. When I took my crew on raids of abandoned department stores, we walked right past makeup counters. Comparing my plain face to her beautiful one, I had a twinge of regret over that. Sophia's black eyes had been artfully painted in a smoky palette, and lined in shimmering pewter. The effect was sultry and mysterious. Ash and Dakota practically drooled.

"I'm here to make peace. Things have been so awful lately, just terrifying." Sophia Arabola spoke directly to the men, who nodded sympathetically. A single silver tear rolled out of her eye. She tilted her head as though Joe might wipe it away for her. When he didn't, she pulled a tissue from her purse—a real Kleenex—and dabbed at her make-up. That was weird. Seriously, who had tissues anymore?

Sophia tossed the used tissue onto the table, startling the wasp trapped in the jelly jar. Delicate wings beat against the transparent walls. I got a flash of Adam's mother licking armored glass.

"Jacqueline, let me level with you, woman to woman," Sophia said. "The most important thing is our children."

That shocked a response out of me. "You have children?"

"In a manner of speaking, I do. Adopted ones. But they're so fragile! You understand, how quickly they . . . you know."

I didn't understand. My kids weren't that fragile. What was wrong with hers? Maybe they were sickly, and that was why we never saw them playing outside.

Sophia picked up the jelly jar and rotated it, examining the wasp inside. "What I propose is an alliance. Alone, we're powerless, imprisoned for our own safety. Together, we can build a safe harbor. For ourselves, for our children."

Joe grinned. "Yeah. Great idea."

"Safe harbor?" I repeated softly, numb with horror. "Oh my God, it's you!" I shrieked, seizing the shotgun off the wall. "Do you know who that is?" I screamed at Joe. "You let her in!"

"Hey, hey, settle down there!" Joe bellowed. He got out of the way pretty fast for a one-legged man, leaving my shotgun trained only on Sophia.

"Put down the gun, Jackie," Dakota snapped. "This is a negotiation, not a war."

Before I could stop her, Sophia twisted the lid off the jar and let the wasp out. It buzzed to her chin, walked across her lip and disappeared up her nostril, wings folded tightly. She shivered, like the tickley little feet felt good in there.

"Didn't anybody but me see that?" I howled.

The visitor shook her head slightly, let out a satisfied sigh, and then turned her attention back to me. For the first time, I saw the pox look out of her eyes. I kicked myself for not spotting it before. Was I distracted by Sophia's glamour, or were her irises so black it didn't show?

Keenan spoke from behind me. "I saw, I saw! That ain't human. What should I do, Jack? Kill her?" He drew a long knife from his belt sheath.

Dakota leaped between them. "Back off, you fucking lunatic!" He hard-blocked Keenan's arm, twisted it, and trapped him in an arm-bar, pushing the smaller boy's elbow backwards. Keenan bent over, crying out in pain. The knife hit the floor between them.

"Stop it, both of you," I shouted. Not that it did any good.

"Wake up, Dakota," Keenan snarled, his face white with pain. "She just let a wasp walk right up her nose, and she didn't even sneeze. What kind of girl does that? I'm telling you, she's infected."

Dakota cut a sidelong glance at Sophia, but he didn't let Keenan straighten up.

"Dude, I'm on your side. That's the enemy, not me," Keenan gasped.

Dakota eased up on Keenan's arm. He glanced a question at me.

I nodded grimly. "He's right, Dakota. She's got the pox. Let him go."

He did. Keenan staggered over to the stainless steel sink and leaned on it, rubbing his arm. On the other side of the room, Joe looked like a man who'd just run over his own dog.

Dakota returned to my side, jaw set. He leaned close and spoke low in my ear. "The pox . . . it's a disease, but it's really aware? Sentient?"

"Yeah. One personality controls all the infected bodies. Remember when the pigeons attacked us, up on the roof? I told you about the pox-boss then, and you didn't believe me."

Sophia, or the pox inside her, giggled.

Joe's jowls sagged. He believed me by then, I could tell. I bet he remembered saying I was nuts, too.

"Oh my God. That's really her, in Sophia," Dakota muttered. "What does she want?"

"Me."

I didn't have time to explain. A mob of sleepy kids poured into the kitchen. "Who's here?"

"What's all the yelling about?"

"Out," I ordered. "Everybody out." Only the younger ones listened.

Sophia's clear, girlish laugh rang through the room.

"Do what she says," Dakota thundered.

Our boys reluctantly moved down the hall, except for Tito. He toddled through the open archway into the kitchen, rubbing his eyes with his knuckles. "Jackie? Why is da pox-lady here?"

Every boy went still. Joe groaned like a man in pain. I chambered a round.

"Oh, such a small, drafty room. Pull the trigger, please," the pox-boss said with Sophia's mouth. She raised her voice in a sing-song imitation of a kindergarten teacher. "Children, come in here now."

People stirred in the hall. A few boys stuck their heads in.

I frantically waved them off. "Don't you dare, she's infected! Get out, go, all the way to the booths."

Tito peered curiously at the pretty new lady. He pushed past the bigger boys and headed for the stranger.

"Come here, little one," Sophia cooed.

"No, Tito, don't listen to her. Don't come in here." I grabbed for him as he went by, but his tiny hand turned to Jello and slipped out of mine.

In a flash, Sophia lunged for the child and seized his arm. The three-year-old bent his knees and hung, trying to pull free, but the pox-boss gripped his soft flesh with brutal force. "Jack, make her stop," Tito whimpered. "Hurts."

"Let go of him." The words came out before I knew what I was doing.

The pox smirked. She had something I wanted, and she knew it.

"What should we do, Jackie?" The whites of Ash's eyes showed, but he stood his ground, backing me up.

I kept my gun aimed right at Sophia. "I doubt it'll help to blow her head off. The construct will just get out of her body faster that way. And this construct won't be the same as the one I told you about, from Adam's mother. This one's the boss. I have no idea what it can do."

"Oh my God, Oh my God." Ash whispered. "We have to get her out of the house."

I swallowed the sour acid that rose in my throat. "I can run. She'll follow me."

"Yes, I certainly will." The pox eagerly licked Sophia's lips.

"No! Don't do it, Jackie," Dakota hissed. "She'll catch you out there."

I wondered if the real Sophia trapped somewhere inside her head, watching us and screaming. Or maybe not. Maybe her personality was gone, used up and blown away, like pox in the sun.

"Keenan, quick, grab my phone," I said, talking fast. "Call Adam. Tell him what's going on."

Keenan shot out of the room, slamming a hand on the wall to make the corner.

"You and me." I pointed at Sophia with the barrel of the shotgun. "Outside."

She dug her red-painted fingernails into Tito's shoulders, backing him up against her legs. "No. I like it right here."

"Fine." I shoved the gun into Dakota's hands. He took it, gaze jumping from Sophia to Tito and back again. If he shot her at that range, it would be a mess. Tito would get infected for sure. Maybe we all would.

I bit my lip, reached under the stainless steel counter, and set my wrist against the ragged metal edge of the rough-cut industrial counter in our old diner kitchen. I'd always hated that counter. Kids sometimes cut their fingers on it. Joe had promised to fix the thing for years, but he never got around to it. I drew my arm back, wincing against the sting. Then I made myself do it again, and again. Blood filled the wide, shallow scrape. It stood out, dark against my white skin.

"Jackie, what are you doing?" Dakota hissed.

"Going outside." I forced my voice even and steady. "You guys stay here. All of you. That's my last order as chief, so please, if you love me, follow it. Once I go out that door, Dakota's in command. Permanently."

"Jackie, please don't do this. We'll find another way," Dakota muttered.

I couldn't meet his eyes. My gaze slipped down to his long, strong hands. They gripped the shotgun so hard that wiry muscles stood out along his forearms.

Dakota would fight if I asked him to. So would the rest of my crew, but we couldn't win against the pox construct. Not there, in the predawn dark, surrounded by kids we were supposed to protect. I looked up into Dakota's face, memorizing every line. Blue eyes over high cheekbones, and that one long scar that arced across his left cheek. A scattering of freckles stood out against his waxen skin.

"*I love you*," I mouthed to him, silently, so the pox wouldn't hear.

Then I held up my left arm so Sophia saw the blood running down the inside of my wrist. Her nails went slack on Tito's shoulders. Black eyes locked on my bloody wrist. My wound burned.

"Ug, what is that, a frigin' vampire? I can't believe I ever thought she was hot," Keenan blurted.

Joe stood against the wall opposite me, wrinkled hands clutching the back of a chair. "She don't wanna drink the blood," he whispered. "That's her way in."

"Stop baitin' her, Jack! Wrap that arm." Keenan tossed me a dishrag, but I let the damp towel slide off my shoulder and fall to the floor. Sophia, or whatever was controlling her, still had Tito. The whole scene felt unreal, nightmarish. Stepping sideways, I floated toward the door, barely feeling the floor under my feet.

"Jackie, no!" Dakota shifted his gun and grabbed for my arm, but I yanked it out of reach.

"Stay out of this, Dakota. It's me she wants. I have to deal with her alone."

I slammed open the door as hard as I could. The tarnished brass doorknob broke through drywall with a crash and stuck there. A blast of winter wind instantly sucked all the heat from the room. Tito tore free and ran for the hall. I burst onto the porch into the cold, still air. The door yawned open behind me, a rectangle of golden light. Sophia followed me into the dark winter morning.

Chapter 17

Smoke from squatters' campfires hung around our deck like mist. I leaped off the short staircase and pounded down the lane, leading the pox away from home, away from my kids. The alley lay deep in shadow. Rooftops on either side loomed black against the brightening indigo sky. Overhead, sentries shouted and beat scrap-metal alarm bells.

Sophia prowled along the base of our deck, not even hurrying. She set off after me, sticking close to the wall the same way a rat would. A little flock of sparrows fluttered through the alley, flying just far enough to stay ahead of her, and then landing again.

I chickened out when I came to the alley that marked our border. Rico's men had to be watching. Sophia was farther behind than I thought she'd be, hard to see in her dark clothes. Someone else seemed to be with her, or was it just her shadow on the wall? In a minute, she emerged alone and started walking toward Zunos territory, glancing up occasionally at my sentries. Part of me hoped one of them would pick her off, but I wasn't ready to give that order. In the dim canyon between buildings, the construct would rule.

I made my stand in the mouth of the alley, where the first beam of morning sunshine splashed the dirty bricks with golden light. My knees shook, just the tiniest bit, enough to remind me I wasn't that tough. Standing still, I had time for reality to sink in. I couldn't win this one, not without Stuart's UV light. Sunshine wouldn't do it. Not when the pox was protected inside a host body. But it might stop the construct.

At least my boys hadn't followed me. That gave me some satisfaction. Sophia and I were the only humans in sight. On second thought, I guess I was the only one, since she wasn't really human anymore. I should have been terrified, but I only felt frozen inside. Numb. Half dead from days of fighting and fear. *All of this will probably be over soon.* The thought made me desperately sad. Our turf war was all my fault. Sophia was a survivor. She'd avoided the pox for years, until I threw that rat in her face, the same night I stole her car. She didn't do anything to deserve that.

Something scuffled in the shadows between a dumpster and a couple of stacks of weathered pallets. One of the Perkins' Chihuahuas pounced into view, seized a mouse in his tiny jaws, and fled with a pack-mate snapping at the wormy tail hanging out of his mouth. The other dogs surrounded me, their high-pitched yaps echoing off the sheer brick walls. I stomped my foot and the five-pound killers scattered, tails tucked between their fragile legs. Twenty yards away, Sophia raised a hand to me in a tentative wave. *Oh, please. How stupid does she think I am?*

Sophia moved closer. Something white hung limply from her hand. A tissue. She held it high overhead, showing my sentries a white flag of truce. I rolled my eyes bitterly. *That's no truce. She's trying to get close enough to strike.* I searched the rubble for a weapon. Something blunt, so the construct wouldn't get out too fast. I put my foot on a pallet, bent down, and wrenched a slat off. Too light, too brittle, and the old wood gave me splinters, but that didn't matter. It was all I had, and I wasn't giving up.

Sophia rounded the corner and stepped into the sunlight, looking lost. "Jackie? Is that you? What…what are we doing out here?"

I readied the wooden club over my shoulder, like the old-school baseball players my dad used to watch on TV.

Sophia stopped. She clutched her black leather purse in trembling hands. "I…I'm sorry. I didn't mean to trespass. I woke up inside your territory, just…walking. It was like I had some kind of blackout, but I don't even drink. I'm way over the border—Rico's going to be furious."

I sidestepped to block her from passing, club in my right hand.

Sophia cringed. "Jackie, please. What the hell is going on?" She took a step back, and the rising sun lit her face.

"Hold it," I snapped, pointing my wooden club at her jaw. "Tip your chin up. Look at the sun."

Sophia squinted, but not before I saw her eyes. She was clean.

I dropped my club. "Shit! She got away. You're not infected anymore."

"Infected?" Sophia repeated. Her glossy lip twisted in horror. "Why do you say that?"

"The pox talked to me, Sophia! With your mouth. Trust me, I could tell it wasn't you."

"How? You don't even know me."

"Um…I'm not gonna get into the gory details here, but you, uh, might want to blow your nose." I grimaced.

Sophia raised her sweat-damp tissue and blew. I had to look away.

In a moment, her strangled coughing stopped. "Ug! Disgusting! My God, what have I done?"

"Good question. What have you done?"

"I don't know! Jackie, I've had these disjointed memories, like, I'd be someplace, and then suddenly I'm somewhere else, hours or days later. Rico's sure I'm sneaking off, spying or something."

“She’s jumping in and out,” I muttered, putting it all together. “She knows if she stays in you too long, she’ll kill you.”

“She? Who?” Sophia’s voice rose high with frustration.

“The pox-boss.” I whipped my head around, looking for any living thing. Nothing moved except me and the beautiful, terrified woman with me. “What touched you last? Was it a sparrow? A rat?”

“I don’t remember. How can I stop it from coming back, taking me again?”

“Don’t let any animal get near you. Don’t eat meat unless it came out of a can. Outside a body, the pox looks kinda like mercury from a broken thermometer, only foamy. If you see that, especially on a dying animal, run like fucking hell. And, um, try and avoid bugs.”

“I do that anyway.” Sophia grimaced and wiped her nose self-consciously. “Jackie, your crew could have killed me. I have a feeling you stopped them. I don’t know how to thank you.”

“Maybe forgive me for stealing your car?” My voice broke. I kept on talking, desperate to unload my guilt, even if I hadn’t exactly protected her from my crew like she thought. “I know, that started everything, I never should have done it, and I am so sorry—” Something moved, up high. I barely saw it, out of the corner of my eye. *Sparrows?*

Sophia looked around nervously. “We’d better get back inside. But please call me. I could use a friend.” She reached in her purse and handed me a shiny square of paper with her name and a phone number on it.

I peered at it. “You seriously have business cards?”

“Handmade ones. How else am I supposed to keep from going insane? I talk to women all over the city, since I hardly ever get to go out. We have a whole network. Most of the survivors are secluded, either by choice or, uh, not…so we don’t meet in person very often. But you and I could hang out.”

“Sure! I really will call. I just got a phone.” I practically danced with enthusiasm. A girl friend to share stuff with, how cool was that? “Um, I don’t know my phone number yet.”

“It’ll pop up on my phone when you call. Hey, walk me part way? We can’t use the back door any more, since that wing of the house burned.”

“Oh.” A guilty flush warmed my cheeks, and hoped she didn’t notice. “Sure, I’ll walk you to the line. To the official border.” We shared a smile. I leaned in so she’d hear me when I lowered my voice. “I have loads of questions I can really only ask another woman.”

“Oh, is it romance?” Sophia grinned. “Tell me, what’s his name?”

Sophia and I took a right at the corner by their parking lot and walked down the alley together, elbows almost touching. “I really like this guy called Dakota, but a couple of other boys just won’t quit—” I began.

Her laughter almost drowned out the faint sounds. A low rumble, far away. Hissed whispers. The back of my neck prickled.

Sophia squeezed my hand. “I’m so glad we made friends. I’ve been really lonely, with only men around.”

“Me too,” I said automatically, my attention elsewhere. Sloshing water gurgled, high above. I looked up, but saw nothing but the edge of the building against sky.

“It’s got a hold of ’er! Now, now, now,” Dakota shouted, from high on the roof of the old hotel.

“No!” I shrieked. “Sophia, move!” I yanked her by the hand.

Our fingers slipped apart. The narrow strip of sky above us went dark. Boots skidding on gravel, I scrambled back the way we came, screaming gibberish. The enormous water tank bounced off the far wall, six stories up, showering us with rusty water. The trap came down fast, booming and splashing between the walls of the narrow alley. Hunched low, I ran for my life, took a dive, and thought I made it. Until the edge of the tank clipped the back of my leg.

Unbelievable force slammed me down as a flood of filthy water washed the alley of everything vile that ever shit or died there. My chin hit pavement and exploded in agony. Groaning, I tried to roll over, but failed. Pain shot from my ankle all the way to my hip. Freezing water soaked my clothes. I barely had the strength to lift my mouth out of the brown stream. The stale urine smell set my sinuses on fire.

I lay on cold concrete, in a rapidly draining puddle, screaming, “Sophia? Sophia!” She didn’t answer. Tears coursed down my wet, dirty face.

The cracked water tank loomed over my head, completely filling the alley. A bloom of dilute blood flowed out from beneath it, soaked my jeans, and puddled around my hands. My sobs turned to gurgling, hysterical screams.

A fawn-colored Chihuahua picked its way across the damp ally on delicate paws. Our eyes met. I fell abruptly silent. Shaking with cold, I pushed up on my arms and tried to crawl away, but my left foot was trapped. Pain lanced to the knee, worse when I twisted. I gritted my teeth and kept struggling. The cute little dog bent to sniff my wet hair and then spun a happy circle, prancing and wagging its tail like a pet whose owner had just come home. The pox-boss laughed at me from behind its eyes. She pulled the dog’s lips into a snarl, showing rows of white, needle-sharp teeth. I screamed and tried to lurch to my feet, but yanking on my pinned leg made the pain so bad I almost threw up. The rim of the huge water tank lay on top of my ankle, and I didn’t have a chance of lifting it. I balanced on one throbbing arm and waved the other, trying to fend off the

Chihuahua's flashing teeth. The pox danced her agile little dog-body out of the path of my clumsy fist and darted back in, snapping at my bare knuckles.

Boys shouted. Keenan's big knife bounced off the yellowed plastic of the tank. The pox-dog yelped, and a few drops of crimson blood fell from a small cut on its ear. Were nanobots swirling toward me, invisible in the dark water? I fought to raise my body out of the puddle before they could creep inside one of my cuts. My arms didn't have the strength. My head sank down. Icy water dulled the pain.

***

I woke up inside, lying on the diner floor, soaked with stinking water. Some idiot was peeling back my eyelid, shining a bright light into my eye.

"Is she infected?" *That's Ash,* I thought dimly.

"No. Not," Tito said. "I think. Do again."

Tito bent over my face. His small hands pressed on my chest, making it hard to breathe. Light stabbed like an ice pick to the brain. I pushed the light away. "Ouch! Enough with the flashlight, guys. It's still me."

Tito squealed with joy. His hard little head jammed under my jawbone as he hugged me, and my backbone grated on the wood floor. Everything hurt.

"Careful, there," Ash said, pulling Tito off. "Watch her leg."

I coughed. "Sophia? Did she make it?"

Dakota's warm, familiar scent filled my nostrils as he bent to whisper. "It's all right. You're safe now. She'll never hurt you again."

Tears leaked from the corners of my eyes, tracked across my temples, and disappeared into my hair. Sophia was dead, crushed under my trap. Dakota thought she'd infected me. He did his job, shutting me down, just like I begged him to do. That trap was meant for me, too. Only I was too quick for him. I got away. The pox-boss got away, too. Sophia didn't.

Sobs wracked my body, sending jolts of agony up my left leg. I took a breath and screamed. Then I did it again. My cries blended with the sounds of sirens, coming closer. I recognized the sound and bit my tongue to silence myself. Alarm bells rang from the roof. Then a pack of men kicked open the front door of the diner. Boys shouted. Dakota swore. I caught flashes of orange suits, assault rifles, and reflective faceplates. Masked soldiers marched Marc and Caleb in the front door at gunpoint. They'd been on sentry duty with Joe, who wasn't there. The kids looked so small to me. Their faces were rigid, but I saw the fear in their eyes.

"Don't shoot, I called 'em in from the Center," Keenan bellowed. "I called 'em! Jackie needs help."

"Not your decision," Dakota spat.

"Look at her leg, Dakota! The bone's stickin' out! If you ever want her to walk again—"

Five more space-suited guys with automatic rifles burst out of our hall and pushed the boys back. We were surrounded. Our tiny crew had rolled over without a shot being fired. All for the best. The Center could have crushed us easily.

Two orange-clad men knelt beside me, a young, dark-bearded one and his fatherly partner. Air hissed in and out of their helmets as they breathed.

Reassuring voices crackled from their speakers. "It's all right now. We're paramedics. Looks like you had quite the crash there. We'll get you patched up and off to the hospital."

Back to a glass cell at the Center, they mean.

One of the paramedics tried to stick a needle in my arm. I batted the syringe away. "No! I'm not leavin'." The motion twisted my busted ankle. The sudden flash of pain almost made me scream.

Tito rushed forward. "Get off her," he shrieked, his voice shrill. He whacked the paramedic once in the knee with his toy baseball bat before Ash dragged him away. The paramedic grabbed his leg, cursing, but saw who hit him and didn't retaliate.

"Good man," I rasped, but he probably couldn't hear me over Tito crying.

Keenan knelt beside me and squeezed my hand. "Keep on patching her up," he told the paramedics, like he was in charge. "Hey, wait a minute. What's in that syringe? You plannin' on puttin' her down like a dog? She's not infected, I'm tellin' you!"

The dark-bearded medic spoke quickly. "No, no, we wouldn't do that. It's only a painkiller. It'll probably make her sleep."

"You want that stuff, Jack?" Keenan growled.

I shook my head. As much as my ankle hurt, it was not a good time to be loopy.

"No painkillers," Keenan ordered. "Sorry. I don't trust that shit."

Neither did I.

The medic went to work, splinting my leg. "You're a lucky girl. You have some influential friends."

For a second I was bewildered, because I thought he meant Keenan. Then the paramedic glanced over his shoulder. Seven orange-suited figures came in the front door, all unarmed. Stuart was among them. I recognized him by his round belly and short, bowed legs. Space-suited soldiers clomped after them like faceless robots.

A distinguished, silver-haired black man looked me over from behind his sealed faceplate. "That must be her," he said.

"Yes," Stuart admitted. "But she's been cooperative, and she shows a great deal of promise, so please—"

"We need her, Bill," a sharp-faced woman interrupted. Light glinted off her little round glasses. "There's no other way. We're all very sorry, but she's only a street urchin, after all."

She didn't look sorry. Not really. I saw the apologetic look on Stuart's round, pale face, and I instantly knew who those people were. *The Committee.* In person, because they knew what would happen if the pox took me. She'd have her safe harbor, a host who wouldn't sicken and die. Together, we'd compromise every living thing on the planet. Some of the Center's kids might escape on the rocket, but they'd never be able to return to earth. Adam's descendants could cling to that orbiting space station for a couple of generations, maybe more. When it crumbled around them, they'd have to come down. The pox would be waiting.

I'd rather die now.

From her ice-cold expression, the Committee woman seemed to agree. Goosebumps tingled up my arms.

The hawk-nosed woman turned to the paramedics. "Stabilize the girl for immediate transport to the array."

"Directly to the array?" the older medic repeated, eyes wide. "Not the hospital?"

"Forcing an injured child into a combat situation? That's...that's barbaric," Stuart sputtered. "I won't allow it. She's my adopted daughter. The papers are signed."

The tall, silver-haired Committee chief stepped in. He and Stuart stared each other down through their faceplates.

"I have rights, under the law," Stuart reminded him. "And my *daughter* does, too."

The chief's exasperated sigh came through his helmet speaker. "Don't pretend the child means anything to you, Bill. This is just another of your liberal ploys. Harsh realities must be faced."

Stuart said nothing and stood his ground, looking small beside his opponent

The Committee chief glared down on him. "Fine. Take her to the hospital, if you insist. If we're too late, it'll be on your head."

"It's on my head already," Stuart muttered.

"Preparing for immediate transport," the older paramedic said. "We'll need to splint her broken ankle first."

The hawk-nosed woman rolled her hand impatiently. "Be quick about it. We're running out of time."

I didn't know what the hurry was, and I didn't ask. The paramedics readied their stretcher. They were taking me away. Away from everyone I loved. The pain in my leg couldn't compare to that.

Dakota got in the Committee chief's helmeted face. "You want to use her as bait, don't you? This array—I bet it's made of those ultraviolet lights that Jackie told us about. It's a trap, isn't it? Made to destroy nanobots."

I was a little surprised Dakota knew all that, since he never seemed to listen to anything I said unless we were in bed.

"See, I told you they weren't stupid," Stuart whispered. His helmet speaker picked up the faint sound and broadcasted it.

The hawk-nosed woman sneered. Her boss just looked irritated. "I thought you said they were *children*," the chief said to Stuart, out of the side of his mouth.

"They are children," Stuart said testily. "Resourceful, well-armed *children*. How did you think they survived on their own for this long?"

We weren't really on our own, but I wasn't about to tell the Committee that. Joe had been with us since I scorched my hands pulling him out of his burning car. I remembered the oily smoke, and the shouts of the demonstrators. Joe was fatter back then, and I had no hope of lifting him, but I helped him crawl the long, slow half mile back to his diner. Gave him water. Tried to figure out what to do about his crushed foot. Failed on that one. He lost his leg, but my crew moved into his restaurant and made sure he didn't lose that too. Without us, Rico would have taken it for sure. I rolled my head from side to side on the hardwood floor, but didn't see the old man anywhere. *Be okay, Joe, please, be okay, wherever you are.*

Soldiers pushed my boys to one side of the diner and made them sit on the floor.

"What's wrong with you people?" Dakota snapped, despite the gun pointed at his back. "Jackie would help you, if you only asked. If you kidnap her, you'll be sorry."

The hawk-nosed woman rolled her eyes. The Committee chief shook his head dismissively. The paramedics slid me onto a blanket and prepared to lift.

Then Dakota dropped the bomb. "Jackie can control the nanobots. Abuse her, and you'll be targeted for infection. Avoiding that is harder than you think. Tell 'em, Jackie."

Talking was the last thing I wanted to do. My leg ached so bad it made me sick to my stomach. I forced out a few words. "Insects are compromised now. Bianca told me so."

She hadn't told me anything, of course. I'd seen the infected wasp with my own eyes. Either way, Bianca's name had the expected effect. Committee members paled. Paramedics froze. Stuart shot me a microscopic nod of approval.

I pushed my advantage. “Bianca says you saw me by satellite, the night I sent the rats against our enemies. Imagine that happening at your own homes, to your own families. Might not be rats. Might be wasps. Or centipedes, crawling out of your drain while you’re in the shower.” I narrowed my eyes at the hawk-nosed woman. “You wanna wear that suit every minute for the rest of your life? Or do you want to make a deal?”

Chapter 18

Half an hour later, the paramedics rolled me out the front door of the diner on a stretcher. "Wait," I cried. "I don't see Joe. We can't leave him. What if he comes back and finds us all gone?" They wouldn't stop. Nobody listened to me.

My crew filed out the door, meager bundles of belongings clutched tight to their narrow chests. Their young faces were set in hard lines. Tough guys, trying not to cry. That tore at my heart. Paco left the diner last, under his own power, carrying his pill bottle in one pudgy hand. Tears streaked his brown face as he reached back and quietly closed the door. Red and blue neon beer signs flickered forlornly from the diner window. I couldn't bear to look.

No one said a word except Tito, who wouldn't shut up. "Why? Why we goin'? I don' wanna go. I'm hungwy. I only want bweakfast. Bweakfast! Wight now!"

Dakota had to scoop him up and carry him out. Tito kicked and screamed the whole way. I should have comforted him, but I was trapped on that stupid gurney, and the men wouldn't stop rolling it along. The paramedics refused to let a child in the ambulance with me, especially one screaming like that, so they made Dakota take him in the huge armored van with the Committee and the rest of our crew.

Without asking permission, Keenan climbed in the ambulance and took a seat next to one of the paramedics. Someone slammed the back doors, and we pulled out. I grimaced with pain. Everything hurt more once we started bouncing along.

"Jack…you sure 'bout this? I mean, we fought so hard to hang onto this place, and now we're just walking away. Shouldn't we leave some guys behind to hold the territory?"

"No. It doesn't matter anymore." I held his warm hand with my damp, dirty one. "The pox—" Going out of the junkyard that used to be the diner parking lot, the ambulance hit a pothole. I hissed in a breath, fighting a stomach-clenching urge to vomit.

The balding paramedic bent over me. "Change your mind about that painkiller?"

"No," I whispered, squeezing Keenan's hand hard. We hit another bump and I gasped out loud.

"We really ought to medicate her," one of the paramedics told the other.

"She said no, asshole," Keenan spat.

"All right, just an IV then. To keep her hydrated." The man tugged on my hand, straightening out my arm.

I felt a pinprick in the crook of my elbow as the needle went in. Then we jolted across another series of bumps. It took all my strength not to scream. One of the paramedics reached up, and I caught a flash of the syringe in his hand. With a quick squirt, he delivered the medicine into the IV line. I opened my mouth to bitch him out, but a flood of euphoria washed over me and I forgot to be mad. Keenan lit into the paramedics for me. His angry voice sounded far away, like something from a dream. After a while, the voices stopped. The only sound was the droning of the engine.

"Keenan?" I whispered. "Please don't leave me alone with these guys."

"Don't worry, babe. I'll stay with you the whole time."

The rest of the trip passed in a doped-up blur. Lights sped overhead, like they were on a conveyor belt, or maybe flying through space. It took me a moment to get that I was the one moving, not them. We glided down a white-painted hallway, painfully bright, and then I was surrounded by doctors and nurses in blue scrubs.

"We had a deal," I muttered. "The Committee agreed. We can leave whenever we want."

Someone pushed a rubber mask over my face. The last thing I heard was Keenan shouting when they dragged him out of the room.

***

I woke, nauseous and groggy, in a clean, white hospital bed. Wiggling my toes, I discovered a weird inflatable cast on my left leg. Lines connected it to a humming machine that squatted at my bedside, blue lights blinking like robot eyes. I half expected it to stand up on hydraulic legs and walk away. At intervals, pressure inside the cast dropped off and then increased again, like my leg was breathing. The squeezing sensation creeped me out. I had this wild impulse to crawl away, but my leg was pinned down under a tangle of wires and plastic tubing. My arms didn't move much either, but as sleepy as I was, it didn't matter. I gave into the drugs and floated, dimly aware of a conversation going on nearby. After a few minutes my mind started making sense of their words.

Gaily printed curtains on a curved rod separated my bed from the rest of the room. A woman's voice spoke from behind it. "I don't care what Doctor Stuart says, I don't believe that girl for a second. No one controls infected animals but Bianca."

"I agree. And the girl isn't even compromised," a man said. "We repeated the test to be sure. But the satellite feed certainly appears to show her influencing infected rodents. That's odd, because when President Monroe received the initial nanobot treatment, triggering the epidemic, Monroe herself displayed no control over any other compromised—"

"Oh, Graham, must you obsess over old news?" the woman interrupted. "At this point, it doesn't matter. Experiments conclusively show that the nanobots are chemotactically attracted to this patient. They even respond to isolated tissue samples. There's no doubt. She's a primary host, just like . . ." The woman's voice broke. "Just like . . ."

"Like the president was." Graham made a small, sick noise, deep in his throat. "Madeleine, I know she's not much more than a child, but…this girl is dangerous."

"I know, but what would you have me do, Graham?" Madeleine's voice rose higher. "What would you have me do?"

I was having trouble following the conversation. *I'm dangerous, why?*

Behind the curtain, a door clicked open. Rapid footsteps entered the room. A man spoke, words tumbling over each other in his haste. "This data just came in. Look at the growth curve!"

Graham swore. "Nanobots are spreading exponentially. But why this sudden acceleration, why now?"

"Doctor Stuart says *she* did it," the new guy said, his voice tight with fear, and for a second I thought he meant me. "He thinks the AI is making a strategic move, mobilizing all her resources at once in a bid to take the girl. Let me bring over a syringe of sodium pentothal, right now! That would be the smart thing to do. We can't let that kid get compromised. Sodium pentothal. That's the answer."

I blearily wondered what sodium-whatever was. Was that a cure for the pox? My eyelids slid shut, and I just wanted to drift off…sleep…but the people behind the curtain kept bothering me, nagging, like a fly at the window that wouldn't stop buzzing. My leg breathed, and that annoyed me too.

Short, shuffling footsteps approached, along with that familiar wheezing. My heart surged. *Oh, good, Doctor Stuart is here.* He sounded worse, though. A lot worse. Air made a low roaring sound as he forced it into his lungs. He coughed and spat before he spoke, low and furious, then rising to a scream. "I entrust you with the care of an innocent child, and return to find you discussing lethal injection? Doctors, remember the Hippocratic oath! We are not murderers!"

Lethal injection? I blinked, forcing myself out of the pit of sleep. Glowing red numbers on the monitor by my bed climbed as my heart beat faster.

"Calm down, Bill," the woman said. "Nobody's administering lethal injections, all right? But we can't wait much longer. We need to get her out to the array."

"You don't understand," Stuart spoke between wheezes. "She's not…going to sit up there…in a cage. The array was designed…for Jacqueline to operate. Actively."

"We know that," Graham said. "We've seen the schematics."

"She can't climb right now. She can't fight. You have to give her time." Stuart broke down coughing again.

"Oh, Bill. I wish I could do more for you," the woman murmured.

"I'm not important right now, Madeleine." Stuart wheezed. "Focus…on the issue. There is one thing we could do to speed Jacqueline's healing, although it would be a bit painful for her. We still have samples of the first-generation nanites, don't we? The ones designed for tissue repair?"

Nanites? Is that the same as pox nanobots? I held my breath. No one said a word.

Graham cleared his throat. "Uh, Bill, we made a decision on that. She, uh, already received the treatment. She'll be walking this evening. Running and jumping by tomorrow."

Stuart's wheeze became a gasp. "Tomorrow…that means…you didn't use Class One nanites. Did you? Did you!"

"No…no, Bill," Graham admitted. "Doctor Stafford and I consulted, and we agreed that the circumstances warranted Class Three."

"But…but nobody does that. Those things were banned for a reason." Stuart's voice faded. "Have you ever witnessed such a thing, Graham? I know you haven't, Madeleine, you're too young. This is cruelty of the worst kind. The biotechnologist that developed it—"

"I know, Bill," Madeleine's voice was soothing. "We all know what Doctor Samuelson did to herself. I attended her funeral."

I gulped, wide awake now. Looking for a way out. A dull thunking sound came from the bed frame whenever I moved my arms. Plastic zip ties held my wrists down. I struggled against the bonds, pressing my lips together to stay silent. Bastards had me pinned down good.

"In this case, we had no choice," Madeleine went on. "There simply isn't time to allow the patient to heal normally. Look at this." Paper rustled.

"I've seen it," Stuart snorted.

"Read the fine print. Forty-seven new species compromised in the last two days. The girl was right about one thing—they're all insects. Ants. Bees. Mosquitoes. The odd thing is, they're active in sub-zero temperatures. We've never seen organisms changed so fundamentally before. And then this."

Fingers pecked rapidly at a keyboard. I was dying to see the computer screen, but I held still, afraid to make a sound.

Stuart wheezed quietly, almost in time to my leg's mechanical breathing. "Lord God. They're coming. From all over Colorado."

"Over the plains, too, from the east," Graham said. "And south, out of Montana and Wyoming. These satellite images were taken about thirty minutes ago. See how all the highways look dark? Now we zoom in, and—"

"The roads are packed," Stuart exclaimed. "They're weaving between wrecked cars. Working their way along the shoulder. Even the medians are crowded."

With what? I wanted to scream, but I knew if they found me awake the conversation would end. I gritted my teeth and writhed.

"The array wasn't designed for this," Stuart moaned.

"And Bill, I should warn you, this is happening locally too." Madeleine's voice broke. She cleared her throat and went on. "We should have known. Bianca—I mean, the AI—is mobilizing all her resources. We believe she wants the girl. And if that child is compromised, with Level Three nanites in her system—"

"Why don't you just kill the kid, then?" Stuart snapped sarcastically. "Get it over with."

"We discussed the possibility," Madeline admitted, her voice calm and even. "But with that piece on the board, Bianca's strategy is clear. She'll launch an all-out assault. Which, of course, requires her presence to coordinate."

"Giving us the chance to incinerate her," Graham finished. "Or, uh, it, I should say. The AI."

When Stuart spoke again, he sounded defeated. "My friends, I apologize. For my part in creating this epidemic, and for being judgmental. In this case, Class Three nanites are warranted. May God forgive us for torturing that poor child."

On slow steps, the doctors retreated.

Torturing? I felt my eyes go wide in their sockets. *What's he talking about? I'm not feeling any pain.* Clenching my stomach muscles, I fought to sit up. A sturdy nylon strap over my chest held me to the bed. If I hadn't been so doped up, I probably would've lost my shit right there. I got a look at my bare arm before my head collapsed back onto the pillow. A needle was taped in the crook of my elbow, and a tube dripped clear liquid into my vein. That didn't bother me. But the huge scrapes on my forearms, from the water tank slamming me down—those were gone. Completely gone. Had I been asleep long enough for them to heal? Somehow, it didn't feel like it.

A tiny glass cylinder hung near my head, swaying gently as I struggled. Inside it, a rubbery valve flexed in time with the change in pressure around my leg. The seal trapped foamy, silver liquid in the bottom of the vial. A chill spread through my body as I recognized the spun-mercury shine of nanobots. Pressure increased around my ankle, then released. The rubber seal dropped a little. Eerily beautiful metallic liquid got forced down a clear plastic tube. The line disappeared under the gray plastic cast on my leg. My drugged brain took a moment to process this.

Nanobots. Going into my leg.

I started to scream. I thrashed, tearing at the zip ties until my wrists bled. In seconds, the skin closed again. Crimson spots of blood lay over new, pink skin. Then even the blood disappeared.

Two white-uniformed men whipped back the curtain and hurried to my bedside, making soothing noises. They checked my restraints first, like that was most important. Then they made a rapid sweep of the equipment, moving briskly from one machine to another. Their faces slipped out of focus, and back in again.

"Let me go," I begged. "Please don't do this." I couldn't tell if my words had any effect, because by then, the men had faded to hazy white blobs.

Then the pain began.

Heat built in my injured leg, slowly at first, then hotter and hotter, until I thought the plastic cast would melt. I screamed with every breath. Frantic white-coated people raced into my curtained enclosure, promising me painkilling drugs. I couldn't tell if I got the medicine or not. No painkiller could touch the fire that consumed my leg, charring bone, sadistically refusing to kill me. My broken ankle became the center of my universe. It erupted, sending blood-red splashes of color across the insides of my closed eyelids. Pain spread from the injury outward, rolling slowly like molten lava, engulfing me. I lost all sense of the passage of time. I lay there, burning, forever.

I think I remember begging them to make it stop. I know I remember begging Dakota to shut me down. Do it right this time. Get the job done. Only he wasn't there, so I pleaded with the doctors instead, begging for a shot of some poison to stop my heart. They refused.

I raged against Stuart and his misguided team of scientists, so sure his spy bots could give America the edge. I raged against the pox-boss. Why couldn't Bianca just do her damned job, and gather intelligence for President Monroe?

"*It's all about control,*" I heard her say, with the voice of Adam's infected mother. I wanted to burn her, like I was being burned. Behind my screams, I heard pounding. Forgot about it. Heard it again. I took a breath to scream, and in that heartbeat of relative silence I recognized them. My boys, in a panic, shouting and pounding on the door.

Something slammed, deep and loud. The splintering crack almost sounded like a gunshot. That penetrated my nightmare. *My crew just kicked down the door. They're here.* Instead of being glad, all I hoped was that one of them brought a pistol to put me down.

I couldn't make out their faces behind the red blur that had taken over my vision, but I knew their voices. Ash's groan, something between revulsion and pity. Keenan's furious shouts. Dakota's snapped questions. All of them were meaningless to my garbled mind. At least I knew Ash's touch when he took my hand. Pried my fingers open. Tugged my nails out of the bloody crescent-shaped gouges they'd left on my palms. He spread my hand flat, so I wouldn't hurt myself anymore, and held it. When he dropped it and recoiled, I knew he'd seen me heal.

I rolled my palm up and strained my eyes. The marks from my fingernails had faded to raw, inflamed skin. My boys muttered. I couldn't understand their speech, but I figured they knew I was infected. They sounded scared. I had faith. Dakota would do his duty. He'd stop my pain.

But he didn't. He let it go on and on. I hated him for that. My mind left my body and floated, so I no longer felt the bed beneath me or the zip ties cutting my wrists. Even my broken ankle went numb. I breathed, and I could have sworn I felt each individual molecule of air that streamed into my lungs. The slow cessation of pain was a drug all by itself.

"Found it."

That was Keenan's voice. What had he found? Joe's pistol?

Something tugged on my wrist, and then that arm was free. In a moment, the right one could move too. I pushed myself up on my elbows. Keenan stood over my bed, gripping the brilliant yellow handle of a pair of pliers. The whole world looked weird. Everything stood out in super-sharp focus. My eyes flicked from the scratches on Ash's arm to the blood on Dakota's knuckles. On the other side of the big laboratory, white-coats stood by the broken door, huddled in a terrified cluster. One sturdy young orderly had a bloodstained handkerchief pressed to his face. I felt this insane impulse to laugh.

Keenan traced his fingers lightly down the plastic tube that went into my leg. "What about this? Should I cut it?"

A white-coated man dashed across the room and skidded to a stop at my bedside. "No! Please don't release them! They're old technology, it might not really matter, but we can't risk it," he blubbered. I recognized him. *Doctor Graham.*

"Them? Who?" Keenan repeated. I knew that dangerous edge to his voice, and I hoped Graham wouldn't tell him the truth about the nanites. I was in no shape to head off one of Keenan's rages.

The gangly doctor shifted his weight from one knock-kneed leg to the other. He said nothing. Lank wisps of ginger hair stuck to his receding hairline, damp with perspiration.

"Am I compromised now?" I asked him. "Shouldn't I hear Bianca in my head?"

"Do you?" Doctor Graham asked. His pasty face went another shade paler.

I shook my head. "No. It's just me. Only different, somehow. Colors are brighter." I gazed around in wonder. "Wow, Dakota, your eyes are so blue. They're…amazing."

Keenan snorted dismissively. "She's high."

"You haven't been compromised," Doctor Graham assured me. "Level three nanites are old technology. No artificial intelligence, no imprinted personality."

"None that you know of, you mean," I sniped. The drugs had worn off. My mind was sharp. My body felt oddly rested, pain-free and ready to go. I couldn't wait to get the hell out of there. Dakota, Ash and Keenan hovered over me.

"Please stand back," Graham told them. "I'll release her."

The doctor took forever detaching me from the machines. He capped off the vial of nanites with latex-gloved hands, a worry line etched between his bushy red brows. A blue smock covered his clothes to the thigh, so he'd be damn sure none of the stuff they gave me got on him. *Nice.*

"Is she all right?" Dakota asked.

"Better than ever. Theoretically," Graham added. He helped me sit up, holding onto my upper arm like I might keel over. "Jacqueline, you may need a couple of days to regain your strength—"

I slapped his hand off. "Don't touch me. I haven't forgotten what you did to me. I'll never forget."

Graham flinched. "There's a lot at stake here. I don't expect you to understand." He looked down and away, refusing to meet my eyes.

"Oh, I understand plenty," I snapped. Then, just to fuck with him, I said, "Bianca told me all about you."

Graham gaped, his wide, soft mouth stretched into a horrified grimace. I know, it was a mean lie, and I probably shouldn't have said it. But I figured I had the right to be pissed.

I stood up, head held high, ready to sweep from the room like a queen, surrounded by her loyal men. A cool breeze up my backside made me squeal. I snatched for the flapping sides of the hospital gown and my fingers brushed my own bare butt cheeks. They took my clothes while I was knocked out! Stripped me! And changed me into this flippy little robe, on backwards, so my ass was hanging out. I could have died right there.

Keenan quickly turned away so I wouldn't catch him smirking. Too late.

"Where the hell are my jeans?" I screamed.

A thin, nervous-looking woman came running with a white plastic bag in her hands. I wouldn't let go of my gown to take it, so she set it on the bed. A stack of neatly folded clothes slid out. "We, uh, had them laundered for you," she stammered.

I tilted my head and stared her down. "Gee, thanks. That totally makes up for torturing me."

The woman backed up, ducked through the gap in the curtain, and escaped.

"Out! Everybody out," Dakota ordered. "Let her change clothes in peace."

People shuffled away. With a jingle of hanging metal rings, they closed the curtain around me. I sat on the bed, double fistfuls of crisp white hospital sheet pressed hard to my mouth. *What the hell have they done to me?*

Over my head, in a tiny glass vial, traces of silver flowed together into globs. In slow motion, I reached out and stroked the vial with my right index finger. The globs crawled to the side of their prison, inchworming along the glass, as close as they could get to me. Their front ends rose up, so for a couple of seconds they looked like baby slugs. Then they melted, fused together, and ran off like quicksilver.

The nanites wanted in. Most of them already were. I bit down on the sheet to keep from screaming.

***

Back in my own clothes, I burst through the round door of the big clinic building and reeled down the tunnel. Sunshine blazed through the clear plastic roof, stabbing my eyes. Filtered air blasted through vents, clean and cold, carrying the barest hint of burning varnish from squatters' campfires. Ash hovered nearby, one tentative hand at my elbow, not quite touching me. He might've been afraid he'd get his head bit off if he tried, or maybe it was about the 'bots in my veins. I didn't blame him. I wouldn't touch somebody who'd just mainlined a dose of that shit, either.

Dakota tugged on my other sleeve, trying to stop me. I resisted, and after a few seconds he gave up and let go. I couldn't even look at his face. He'd seen me humiliated in the worst possible way, tied down and deliberately infested. It didn't matter to me if Graham said these nanites were different. I felt unclean, right down to the bone. Nobody would ever want me again, not really. Not like before.

I slouched along with my head down, hands deep in the pockets of my old gray hoodie. When I cut across the giant waiting room of the hospital, the boys stuck with me, not speaking. Our new sneakers squeaked softly on the polished tiles. Without exactly meaning to, I wandered into the second tunnel, toward the biosphere. Two men in navy blue pants and white button-down Security shirts followed us at a distance. Three more guards hovered in the circular portal behind them.

"Dakota?" I muttered.

"They were waiting outside your hospital room," he hissed back. "You didn't notice?"

I shrugged. "Guess not."

I kept moving along the semi-transparent tunnel. Ash, Keenan, and Dakota followed me, and the train of Security dudes followed them. On a better day, it would have been funny. Just to mess with them, I slammed a palm into the wall. The hollow boom echoed in the confined space. Guards snapped to attention, all straight backs and wide eyes. Obviously they were there to make sure I didn't get loose and run off into the city. I turned my back on them. The back of my neck prickled under the weight of their stares. We reached the tiny, overhead sign that read *Biosphere*. Stuart might be there, and he had a lot of questions to answer. I broke into a run.

At the portal, I skidded to a stop, panting clouds of steam into the cold air. The plastic strips hung limp over a new barrier. Behind them, the dome was gone. I pressed my face against the hazy wall. An enormous circle of bare dirt proved it had been there, just like I remembered, so I wasn't crazy.

Dakota caught up with me first. "They moved the biosphere out to the launch pad. It's inside the ship now."

"No way," I breathed. "The rocket isn't wide enough to hold it."

"It's bigger than you think. The launch pad's like a mile from the main road," Dakota said. "The rest of our guys are over there right now, with that weird little doctor."

"Stuart?"

"Yeah, him. He's giving the boys the run o' the dome, an' it's pissin' off the Committee somethin' awful. You ready to go see your crew?" Dakota gave me a tentative grin.

I didn't smile back. A dull ache filled my chest. "It's your crew now, Dakota."

Ash and Keenan froze. They didn't even breathe.

"Guys...Dakota's your chief now," I told them. "Look, I can't take care of kids and fight the pox all at once. I'm afraid she'll...she'll..." I forced the words out. "Use 'em against me." The tears I dreaded didn't appear. I was all cried out, thanks to Graham and his sicko medical team.

Ash nodded. He let out a slow, defeated breath. "I get it. The kids come first."

That stung worse than any nasty thing he could have said. Because Ash would have made a good chief. Probably better than Dakota. But Dakota was two years older, and that made all the difference. If I handed the crew over to Ash, Dakota would leave. Some of the boys would go with him. Divided, they'd be easy prey.

Then I remembered how none of that mattered anymore. The pox was coming, in stolen bodies, rivers of them wide enough to fill highways. My crew ought to get as far away as they could from me. Run, and keep on running. I had to admit, if I was the Committee, I would've killed me already. Burned the body. Then scattered the ashes, just to make sure.

The Committee had to be furious at Graham and the other doctors. They still needed me for bait, but if I got compromised, Bianca would score big. A primary host, conveniently infested with Class Three nanites? Her people would gain the ability to heal. She'd be unstoppable then.

I couldn't let that happen.

Clearly, the Committee had come to the same conclusion. Their soldiers padded down the tunnel, coming closer, footsteps silent on the rigid plastic floor. Black holsters bulged on their belts. About twenty feet away they slowed, and then stopped. For the first time, I met their grim, sorrowful eyes with something like gratitude.

The younger one, a lanky guy with a pale, angular face, touched his burly partner on the arm. Both men stopped. They took a look at me and backed off a little. I heaved a shaking sigh and let my rigid back go loose. They weren't going to kill me. Not yet, anyway. Up close, I saw how young they both were, hardly out of their teens, with a few stubborn pimples still marking their cheeks. They gazed at me with hooded eyes, full of dread, like prisoners being marched to the gallows, and not executioners at all. Up in my own head like I was, I hadn't seen it before. Those guys weren't murderers. They hated their job.

A wave of sympathy mixed with my fear, and the combination made me sick to my stomach. I told myself they were doing me a favor, making sure the pox didn't take me. My eyes scanned the black nylon pouches on their thick belts. What weapons were hidden inside? Would they be enough? The 'bots would heal me, but I'd still feel the pain, wouldn't I? Rapid, anxious breaths shook my chest.

My lip trembled a little when I tried to smile, so I pressed two fingers to my mouth and blew the young soldiers a shaky kiss. "Stick around," I whispered, the sound of my voice almost lost in the hum of the fans. "I'm prob'ly gonna need you."

The pale one nodded. He raised his chin a little and took a deep breath, like I'd lifted a weight off his chest. Something inside me let go. My reapers were on the job. That was good, especially since I was probably too chicken to pull the trigger on myself. Like angels of death, my soldiers settled in and began their vigil.

I decided to head back the way we'd come, but the boys weren't moving. Keenan's golden eyes locked on Dakota's steely blues. The air between them crackled with hostility. No one spoke for a long moment. I flinched when Keenan turned his predatory gaze on me.

"So he's Chief, without earning it? No vote, no contest, nothing," Keenan snapped. He whirled to face Dakota again. "You didn't win this. You're not a real chief, no matter what she says."

"Oh, shut the fuck up, Keenan, you loser," Dakota spat.

He wouldn't back off, even though Keenan crowded him bad. I saw a fight coming, and both of them had knives. The thought made my stomach ache. My thighs started to shake, warning me I'd pushed too hard, too soon. I swore under my breath. The boys didn't seem to notice.

I put one trembling hand on Keenan's shoulder, half expecting to get slapped for trying. The muscle between his neck and shoulder went all ropy, and his body stiffened. Keenan wouldn't look at me. I couldn't turn him. Stepping sideways, I wedged my shoulder into the narrow space between the two boys. I felt small there, with them glaring at each other over my head. The sharp, acrid scent of their sweat touched the back of my throat. The smell of it set off alarm bells in the animal part of my brain. Keenan and Dakota were both on edge, adrenaline pounding, ready to have it out. I'd seen enough knife fights to know it would end with one or both of them dead.

Dakota wouldn't back off, not even enough to give me a little breathing room. I felt a little safer with my back to him, even if he was being a jerk. So I faced Keenan, my fingertips resting softly on his wiry biceps. If he reached for his knife, I'd be ready.

"Hey, Keenan," I whispered, keeping my voice low and soothing. "Remember that day, right after the riots, when you and me were scavenging in the Mini Mart, and that nutcase set his pit bulls on us?"

He barely nodded. I took a shallow breath, resisted a powerful urge to flee, and choked out a few more words. "And we hid in that back room with the smashed-up door?"

Keenan surprised me by answering. "Yeah. Their snouts came through the holes, and you beat 'em back with the trash can. We screamed for the man to call 'em off, but he wouldn't. If Joe hadn't showed up, they woulda killed us."

"Yeah. So, um…" I glanced over my shoulder at Dakota's furious face and forgot where I was going with the story. I had nothing left but the truth. I rose up on my toes to whisper it. My lips brushed Keenan's neck. Cool, filtered wind blew strands of his tawny, shoulder length hair against my cheek. "Keenan…please don't tell anybody, but…I'm scareder than that right now."

Keenan's muscles went loose under my hands. He let out a breath. Its warmth stirred my hair. "Oh, baby, I'm sorry."

Relief sent a wave of weakness through my body. I'd managed to talk him down after all. Nobody had to die.

Then Dakota jacked it all up. He yanked my arm, pulling me backward. "I think she's told you enough times. Don't call her that."

Figures. Just when I needed to not be a wuss, my knees went soft on me and I collapsed. Pain flashed through my jaw as my head hit the floor. I wish I didn't remember what an idiot I looked like, lying across their boots with the ridged floor pushing my lip back from my teeth.

"Oh, shit," one of them said.

"This is all your fault, ya little prick," the other one answered.

My head swam. Hands dug into my armpits. The boys lifted me. They settled me against someone's warm chest, half sitting up. In a moment I realized I was leaning on Ash. I felt dizzy every time I tried to open my eyes, so I squeezed them shut tight. I was lying over the train tracks, so a hard plastic ridge dug into my butt, but I didn't care.

An electronic chime sounded. I cracked an eye. Keenan had my cell phone, which I'd forgotten all about. He pushed a few buttons. A ring tone chirped, and someone answered.

"Hey, asshole," Keenan said into the phone. "Get over here. With a car."

The peeved voice on the other end had to be Adam's. That whine was unmistakable.

Keenan's tone could have stripped paint. "Not for *me,* numbnuts. Jackie needs you—she just collapsed. Get your ass over here. You know where we are." Keenan hit the red button and pocketed my phone like he owned it.

I sighed. *Whatever.*

I leaned against Ash, grateful for his body heat. He tucked a warm hand inside my double hoodie pocket, right over my stomach, and wrapped it around both of mine. The other boys stood over us, leaning on the wall. Adam took a long time to show up. I let myself slide into a dreamy state, not quite asleep.

With an electric hum, a tiny, teardrop-shaped capsule glided down the tracks toward us. Adam sat inside, under the round, clear roof. I yanked my legs off the track. Ash hauled me to my feet, startling a raven from his perch over our heads. When the big black bird spread his wings to fly, I gasped. Every feather stood out in perfect focus, so I saw exactly how they caught air. In three flaps the bird soared away, over the treetops. Even through the filters, I could have sworn I smelled the warm, dusty scent of his feathers.

I moaned under my breath. *Oh my God. The nanites. They're changing me.*

"What?" Dakota demanded. "What's wrong? Is it poxy? Was it spying on us?"

I shook my head. Tried to form a sentence. Gave up. Keenan led me to the capsule, practically poured me into it, and closed the passenger side door. Then he went around and spoke to Adam in low tones. I dreamed, eyes wide open, rapt with the glowing, multicolored lights on the dash. Adam said something to me. After a second I processed it and clicked my seat belt for him. We took off, soaring in near silence down the smooth tunnel.

I leaned back and tried to let the rushing air blow my pain away. My fingers touched my chin and came away smeared with blood. Another rub revealed smooth, healed skin. Too bad nanobots only worked on the outside. My heart still felt raw. As we rounded the corner I looked back at the boys I loved. All three of them stood in the tunnel, shoulders slumped. What had it cost Keenan to call in another guy for help? Did Dakota even care?

Our little car arrived at the decontamination chamber, but it took a different fork in the road, one I hadn't noticed before. This track swerved to the right, and then our car stopped with a jerk. A steel barrier rolled down in front of us, and another one behind, leaving us in pitch darkness. I gasped.

Adam's hand briefly covered mine. "It's okay. This is the first of three separate, automated airlocks. State of the art technology. Nothing from outside will get in."

I spoke into the darkness. My voice came out sounding more nervous than I wanted it to. "You know, if you just watch what you eat, you're pretty much okay outside. Long as you don't get bit."

Adam snorted. "Pretty much isn't good enough."

The door slid open and our capsule rolled forward into a lit section of tunnel, not much longer than the car. Somewhere, hidden machines hummed. Their vibrations came through the floor, so I felt them in my feet. We slid forward. Another long thirty seconds in darkness, and the cycle repeated. I sighed in relief when the last barrier rose, releasing us outside. The capsule accelerated to a breathtaking speed, soaring along tracks so smooth, it felt like we were flying. Lovely, large homes lined the road, but the yards stood deserted, their winter-brown gardens abandoned. Far away, a few other capsules zipped along the tracks between buildings. They were the only signs of life.

"Don't worry. The air you're breathing is filtered, just like it is inside the complex," Adam said, his hands steady on the controls.

"I'm not the one who's worried. You guys are ridiculously paranoid. Besides, nobody gets pox by breathing it," I said. "When's the last time you were outside, Adam? Really outside. This doesn't count."

"Four years ago. I was thirteen. I remember how it rained that day. I stood at the last window and smelled the air until the construction workers sealed it up," he said wistfully. That made me sorry I asked.

Our weird little pod began to decelerate. We had arrived at the launch pad. A tall wire fence separated the site from the rest of the Center. Space-suited guards stood at the gate. Adam stopped the car at their station and pressed his credentials to the window. Then it was my turn.

I squirmed. "Um, sorry. I don't have any ID."

The guard bent to look into my face. "Oh my God. You're Jacqueline Stuart!" Even through the filters, I caught the salty chemical smell of the balogna sandwich he'd just eaten.

I opened my mouth to argue. Stuart wasn't my name. Then I remembered that it was. I'd been adopted. "Um, yeah. That's me."

A second guard came over to stare. "That's really her? Take her in, get her inside, right away," he said to Adam. He hurried off to pull the big red lever that operated the gate.

As the mechanized gate slowly rolled open, the two men whispered from the doorway of the guard shack. It must have been some trick of the wind, but I heard every word.

"I guess we ought to issue her some credentials," one of them said.

"It don't matter," the older man grunted. "She ain't comin' back out. Committee orders."

"Hey, hey, no, no, don't!" I rattled the door, but it was locked. Guards surrounded us. "Back up, Adam. Quick, back up the car!"

Adam pulled forward, ignoring my pleas. He wouldn't even look at me. The gate slammed closed behind us. I was trapped.

Chapter 19

I slapped the dashboard. "The fucking Committee! They locked me in. I knew we couldn't trust them. Adam, turn the car around, take me back to the gate, right now."

Adam refused to answer. He kept on driving, his right hand gripping the lumpy joystick tight. A mile of newly laid blacktop stretched out ahead of us, with tracks down the middle. At the end of the line, the rocket stood sharp against the gray sky.

I released my seat belt. Fumbled with the door handle. An alarm began to buzz and red lights flashed on the dash. I wrenched the emergency release lever.

"What are you doing?" Adam shouted, grabbing for my arm. The capsule bumped against the rails, and sparks flew.

The car door suddenly flew open. I leaned out, Adam still gripping my arm. "Let me go!"

Adam abruptly released me. "Fine. Jump, then."

I lost my balance, screamed, and made a wild grab at the door frame. Pavement sped by, inches from my feet. Adam shoved the stick forward. The engine whined, and cold wind whipped my hair. Outside the open door, roadside weeds blended in a sickening blur.

Adam shot me a sidelong glance through narrowed eyes. "What's wrong? Scared?"

I wouldn't have admitted it to save my life. By then I was desperate to close the door, but it had swung out of reach. I made a halfhearted attempt to pull it in, chickened out, and leaned back, hanging on anywhere I could.

The engine whined as Adam eased back the stick, slowing the pod. "Seatbelt on," he snapped.

I hated myself for obeying. But I did it. Adam touched a button. The door slammed itself closed, barely missing my fingers.

I hunched in my seat, angry and embarrassed.

"I've got orders to bring you in. And I intend to obey them," Adam said.

"Good little minion," I said sarcastically.

"Shut up."

Seconds later, our crazy ride was over. A cavernous building squatted next to the rocket ship. Adam putted toward it, all careful and responsible again. He kept poking at a keyboard and scanning the rapidly changing screens. "Not contaminated, thank God. Never open a door to the outside again, Jackie. That was dangerous."

I rolled my eyes and refused to answer. One soapy decontamination wash—for the car, not for me—and another set of airlocks later, we were in. Adam parked the capsule. I got out on shaky legs and walked over to the tallest window I'd ever seen.

"Holy shit," I muttered, craning my neck to stare up at the gleaming white rocket outside.

The ship loomed over us, every bit as big as an urban skyscraper. A russet-painted scaffold rose on both sides of it, ragged jaws around a sharp, white tongue. High above the ground, tiny jumpsuit-clad workers rode lifts or inched along catwalks. On the ground below, a long, jointed cylinder, three times my height, stretched horizontally between the gaping jaws. It took me a minute to realize the scaffolds were set on giant hinges, so they'd gape open as the rocket thrust skyward.

Three elevators at the base of the scaffold opened in quick succession. A stream of workers trudged out. Their empty hands hung slack, and their faces were gray with exhaustion. Stoic replacements lined up, entered the lifts, and disappeared. The Committee was pushing hard to get this thing off the ground. I let out a bitter laugh. I would too, in their place. I'd be fuckin' killing my crew, just to save a few of their lives. What other choice did we have?

The reality of the whole situation hit me. The power these people had. The money. What was I thinking? I couldn't beat the Committee. Sure, we had a deal. But then the bastards locked me in.

Stuart's behind this. He convinced the Committee it's the only humane option. I'll be on that rocket when it launches. Without Dakota. Without the boys.

I crossed my arms over my stomach and hugged myself.

Another silver capsule idled on the tracks outside. The young soldier's clear, gray eyes stared at men through the window. There'd be no chance of sneaking off. Not that I ought to anyway, with a pox army converging on me. The thought gave me chills. What was coming this way? Hordes of infected animals? Huge, transformed wasps?

Oh, God, I hope it's not bugs. Anything but bugs.

That thought made the rocket seem like a pretty good alternative. I lost my balance every time I leaned back to gaze at its conical tip, but I couldn't quit doing it. Which part held Stuart's dome? I couldn't tell. I gawked, mouth open, and took a wobbly step backward. Then I bumped someone lightly on the shoulder and turned. A pretty blonde-haired girl in a pale blue jumpsuit glared at me. Her outfit matched Adam's exactly.

"Oh, sorry," I said automatically.

"You should be," the girl snapped. She looked me up and down. My holey sweatshirt looked ragged beside her crisp uniform, and I needed a wash. "Well. What do you know. The famous Jacqueline Stuart has come in off the streets. Somehow, I thought you'd be…tougher."

A hot flush crept across my face. I didn't answer. I felt this huge stupid wave of insecurity, and tried to let it go. *We have more important problems,* I told myself. It didn't work at all. My insecurity stuck around, persistent as bedbugs.

A group of teenagers sat behind us on a long, low wall. They all wore matching blue nerdsuits with spiffy astronaut patches on the shoulders. When they saw me talking to their teammate, they got up and came over. Every last one of them walked like a goddamn crew chief. Those kids were the chosen ones, the Center's top students. They glared at me with open hostility.

"What's your problem?" I snapped.

Adam touched me lightly on the shoulder. "There's some…sensitivity right now. This is my team. We've trained together for years. Only now, one of us has to stay behind."

"Why? Because Stuart wants me on the ship?"

Adam nodded. "The biosphere has limited resources."

"So kill another goat," I said.

"Jackie, we already killed all the goats."

"Oh." I fell silent.

The blonde girl looked me over, eyes narrowed. I had to admit, she had a pretty good reason to be pissed. Adam knew about the pox, so she probably did too, whether her parents told her or not. Normally, I would've been bitchy to her right back. But this close to the end, I didn't have the heart for it. I just felt sorry for her. For all of them.

I took a deep breath. Let it out slow. When I spoke, I took a soft tone, like the one I used to talk Keenan out of his tree. "I really am sorry," I said, holding her with my eyes. "Look, I don't want to go. My boyfriend's staying. So are all the other people I love."

None of the Center kids answered, but they listened, and that was worth something.

I took half a step closer. "I made a deal with your Committee, and…and …we even shook on it, but they…" I choked up and had to stop talking.

A handsome dark-skinned boy gave me a soft smile. He kind of reminded me of Ash, or what Ash might have looked like if I'd been able to feed him better. "You made a deal with the Committee," the boy repeated. “Isn’t that kind of like American Indians signing a treaty with the U.S. government?”

His friends laughed. I didn’t know what treaty he meant, and I didn’t want to advertise my ignorance, so I changed the subject. “They said they’d give me a shot at the pox-boss. Bianca. You know who I mean, right?”

People cast nervous glances from side to side. They knew who I was talking about, but they obviously weren’t supposed to.

“If I kill Bianca, I get to stay on Earth with my crew,” I said. “Until then, the Committee feeds us all we can eat. And we’re supposed to be able to come and go however we want.”

“Right. You believed them. And then they locked the gate behind you,” the blonde chick finished. She didn’t seem so angry any more. “So, is it true what they say about you?” The girl checked with Adam, who shrugged a reluctant go-ahead.

I knew what she meant, so I didn’t make her spell it out. “Yeah, it’s true. I’m a primary host. Distant relative of President Monroe. It wasn’t like I did Christmas at the White House, though. We never even met.”

I wasn’t prepared for their reaction. People subtly shifted their stances, so they weren’t quite so close to me in case I pounced. It made me want to jump on somebody, just to fuck with them.

The girl didn’t edge away, though. She stood right at my shoulder, like she had nothing left to lose. “What are you going to do, Jackie?”

“Good question.” I felt shaky, so I walked over to the wall and sat down, well back from the passing stream of workers. People gathered around me. It almost felt like having friends. “Whatever happens, I’m still gunnin’ for Bianca,” I told them. “I’m gonna burn that bitch alive.”

The Center teens flashed me nervous grins.

All except the black boy. He looked grim. “You think, if you win, they’ll set you free.”

I sat still, eyes wide. “Yeah?”

The boy spoke real slow. “I got to level with you, Jackie. I don’t know for sure, ’cause Committee meetings happen behind closed doors. But I’ve seen our politicians in action, and I think there’s…another possibility.”

I waited two breaths, then three. “Spit it out,” I snapped.

The boy glanced at the exhausted workers, still streaming out of the elevators and past us, down the wide, indoor avenue. None of them seemed to be eavesdropping. He lowered his voice anyway. “You’re the bait, Jackie. They’ll use you against the AI, but win or lose, you’re a liability. You could get infected and turn on us.”

“Oh my God. You’re right. Of course you’re right,” I hissed. “Their best bet is to make sure I don’t survive the fight. Why didn’t I see that?”

Adam squeezed my shoulder. "Don't be too sure. Doc Stuart wants you on the launch team, I know he does."

The Center teens watched me, waiting to see what I'd do.

"Which one of you has to stay behind?" I blurted.

No one answered.

"There were a bunch of cuts this week to get the crew to a sustainable size," Adam finally told me. "We thought we were done. But then, a couple of hours ago, the Committee announced one more. Alanna."

The team gazed sympathetically at the blonde girl, who stared at her feet, red-faced. She must have been the slowest kid on the genius squad. The worst of the best people. Doomed now, because of me.

"A couple of hours ago…" I mused. "Right around the time they could see I'd survive the Level Three nanites."

Everybody winced when I said that. They'd heard of the treatment. I didn't want to talk about it, though. My mind was stuck on the puzzle.

"It doesn't make sense, Alanna," I said. "If they don't plan on letting me live, I'm not taking your place. Why cut you now? Just to make everyone believe I'm on the team instead?"

Alanna shrugged. She rubbed her red-rimmed eyes with her knuckles and didn't answer.

It might have been wrong of me, but I was desperate. So I blew on the embers of her hope. "Look…you want to go, and I don't," I said. "Want to make a deal?"

Alanna's chin snapped up. Sky-blue eyes pierced mine. "Yes. Yes, I do. What do you have in mind?"

***

Less than twenty minutes later, a pair of green-uniformed technicians came to get me. I followed them away from Adam and his friends, feeling lost. The two men, a fat one and a skinny one, led me across the giant lobby, past the elevators, and over to an official looking counter, where they signed me in.

Then the chunky one held open a government-green door for me, standing way behind it so I didn't brush against him by accident. Maybe nanites would leap between us like invisible fleas and infest him. Shaking my head, I stepped past him into a hallway decorated with photos of grinning astronauts.

"Congratulations, and welcome to the space program. We are thrilled to have you aboard," the fat man recited in a dull, lifeless voice.

I couldn't blame him. Frankly, I wasn't that excited to be there either. Besides my crew, all I cared about was Stuart's array. I wanted to practice with that, not wait around in the hall while they dug through a stack of astronaut uniforms. Of course there wasn't one small enough for me.

"She's practically child sized," the skinny man griped from inside the narrow, dimly lit closet.

"Bianca doesn't give a shit what I wear," I pointed out.

They both ignored me. The fat man shoved his way into the cramped space and pointed over the other guy's shoulder. "Just take that one. It's cut slim enough for her. She can roll up the cuffs if she has to."

When they came out, I reached for the uniform, but the thin one snatched it out of reach. "Don't touch it until you've showered."

They pushed me into an industrial shower room, pressed a couple of bottles into my hands, and snapped the door shut in my face.

"Hey," I yelled through the door. "Can I get some regular shampoo? This is the louse-killer kind. I haven't needed that since me and my whole crew shaved our heads, like, three years ago." I tugged the door open.

The men yanked it closed again from outside. "Use what you are given."

"Aw, hell. This stuff stinks." I took the Betadine surgical scrub and the nasty pesticide shampoo into the shower stall and got started. As stinky iodine-yellow suds rolled off me, I reflexively plotted to steal their delousing shampoo. That stuff would make valuable trade goods back home. In the end, I left the bottle on the shelf. No point now.

I came out of the shower and found my clothes missing. Along with a clean towel, the one-piece coverall hung neatly on the bathroom rail, with brand new underwear, socks, and a pair of those high-tech flexy shoes Center teens wore.

They had no right to take my stuff! And that was my best hoodie, too. I took a breath to shout through the door, but let it out slow through my nose. As I dressed, the same old thought circled around to bite me in the butt. *I'll never need those clothes again.* Bianca was coming, with her pox army. They'd probably arrive in force tomorrow. After that, there'd be no more tomorrows, unless my plan worked.

And that was a long shot.

Still, I had more faith in Alanna than I had in the Committee. The astronaut team was her crew, just like my boys were mine. She would fight to stay with her people. I'd kill to stay with mine.

A rapid, insistent knock sounded on the door. The men were getting tired of waiting. I emerged, sanitized for their protection, wearing a sky blue astronaut uniform. Still rolling up my sleeves, I followed the dour pair to an elevator. "Oh, we're headed for the rocket, aren't we?" I exclaimed, trying my best to be friendly. "Cool, we finally get to see inside."

"No, *you* get to see inside," the thin one said bitterly. "*We're* not allowed in. *Our* education doesn't qualify us for those positions."

I wondered if that was his subtle, nasty way of making a point. Maybe word got out that I hadn't quite finished sixth grade before the epidemic closed the schools. Could be the teens weren't the only ones who resented me. I tried to shrug it off, but inside, I failed. The heavyset man pulled a key card from his pocket. He swiped it, the elevator door opened, and I had to walk through alone. The doors closed in my face.

No one said goodbye.

I stood real still, reading the panel and trying to figure out what floor I wanted. Only a few floors had lit buttons. Most of the rocket must be engine, with just a small living space for astronauts. Number 14 was labeled *Biosphere*. I brightened. *That's where my crew is! Eating free food, just like the Committee promised.*

And then another thought hit me. *Have the little ones heard I'm infested? Will they understand, or shrink away when I walk in?*

My finger hovered over gold-lit button14, wavered, and pecked a different one instead. Level 15, Observation Lounge. Hopefully no one would be there. I needed to be alone to get my head on straight. The elevator surged upward. I put a hand on the wall, knees bending over heavy feet. The lift ground to a sudden halt and its doors slid apart, releasing me into a long, curved hallway. I took a clockwise path around the half-moon corridor, my new, soft-soled shoes whispering on the polished floor. From waist height up, the wall gripped a strip of thick-paned window, bordered by a curved stainless steel railing. Outside, the clouds parted. Sunshine poured in the window, warming my wet hair.

I put a hand on the cool, slick rail. After the rocket launched, Adam and his children would stand in this spot and look out at the blue planet below. Earth might fill half their sky, but they'd never be able to land. Bianca waited there. She'd survive for centuries, riding her victims almost to death and then jumping to a new body before the last one expired. I shook off the creepy thought and moved along the rail. Something spidery crouched on the ground, far below.

That jolted me for a split second, but the thing didn't move. It was only a machine, not a huge transformed insect. I bellied up to the rail and peered down. My stomach did a slow flip, and I felt like I was tumbling forward, over and over. I clung to the rail and resisted the urge to back away. The spider-thing reminded me of a carnival ride, with eight long, multi-jointed tentacles, each ending in a deep, open topped bulb. From where I stood, I couldn't be sure, but it looked like the bulbs held seats. Some hidden operator switched on ultraviolet lights, and pale purple beams spiked off the arms.

Oh my God. That's the array.

I thought the array would be some kind of flashlight, not a moveable, jointed frame as big as an apartment house. From the size of the thing, Stuart expected Bianca to send something big, way bigger than the horrid yellow-white amoeba that had come out of Adam's mom and filled the hall.

More lights checkered the rim of each pod, a last ditch defense, if the construct trapped me high in the sky. A fall would be fatal. Except not to me, thanks to the nanites in my blood. If I fell, I'd suffer, and then heal. Bianca would get a functional primary host. I wondered all over again what weapons my reapers had. Would they do the job? How bad would it hurt? Was it even possible for me to die?

Out on the array, lamps on the pods lit in sequence, one after another, purple splotches chasing each other round and round in dizzy circles. Violet light glinted off ladders that ran three stories up the tentacles to the seats on top. Even from the fifteenth floor, the glare was blinding. Steel cables crisscrossed the frame of the array like spider webs. I swallowed hard, imagining working my way along them, hand over hand, to escape the construct. I clenched my fists, already battling the pox in my mind. I'd run and dodge and hide, hitting light switches, incinerating chunks of construct while giant, shape-shifting snakes snapped at me. Just thinking about it made me want to vomit all over their shiny new floor.

On either side of the array, chain link fencing extended in a wide V shape, with a gap in the pointy end near the base of the array. I stared at the mile-long funnel, mystified. Then I pictured a horde of infected animals, sensing my presence, homing in. The fence would route them right to me. And make sure I couldn't get away.

I heaved a deep breath. My chest shuddered like I'd been crying, even though I hadn't. I turned my back on the array and sank to the floor. No one was watching me, expecting me to be strong, to act like a chief. I covered my face with both hands. My chest hurt with an intense, piercing pain, but the sobs stayed inside, denying me relief.

This is it. It's over. Even if I kill the pox-boss, the reapers will kill me. I have to make sure my crew is safe before I die. But where should I send them? Is anywhere in the world safe? Maybe...space? My heart pounded at the daring idea. *Could my crew take the place of Adam's team? Are we tough enough, clever enough, to pull it off?*

I winced at the idea of betraying Adam. Then another worry hit me. What if we did steal the ship? Would we be able to fly it, without training? Probably not. Besides, my boys would go stir-crazy in there. They'd be fighting before the first week was out, killing each other within a month.

I wanted nothing more than to stay with my crew, except for them to survive—with or without me. Reluctantly, I went back to the plan I'd made with Adam's team. Everything hinged on the courage of a bunch of sheltered rich kids, people I barely knew. I pulled myself to my feet and leaned forward to look down. Something moved along the array.

A tiny, blue-clad figure worked its way up a ladder. With a human on it for scale, the array looked higher and more frightening than ever. Late afternoon sun found its way through a gap in the clouds and touched the climber's hair, turning it a brilliant gold. I recognized Alanna by her sky-blue coverall and yellow hair, and felt an irrational pang of jealousy. *What's she doing on my array? Isn't that my job?*

Then another thought hit me. *She's not wearing a protective suit, or a helmet. Why? She doesn't care if she gets infected?*

Alanna made it to a pod, but instead of climbing in, she let go of the ladder and reached up with both hands, grasping at an overhead cable. She arched her back, struggling with something above. I gripped the rail harder. Alanna slipped. Her body dropped off the scaffold and arced away through open air. I squealed.

I clapped a hand over my mouth, hot breath hissing between my fingers. My racing heart slowed. She hadn't fallen, the cable was a zipline! Alanna swung three hundred feet through the air to the other side of the array, where she grabbed a ladder, unclipped, and started climbing. I started having second thoughts. The girl looked like some kind of circus freak, swinging on her trapeze. I was no gymnast. I couldn't do half as well, and it wouldn't get any easier once Bianca showed up.

I swore, pushed off the railing, and strode back to the elevator. Inside, I hesitated, torn between seeing my crew and racing out to the array. My crew won out, so down I went to Level 14, Biosphere. The elevator doors hissed open, and the scent of orange blossoms filled my nose. I breathed in, feeling tense muscles go loose. Diffuse sunshine glowed from the semi-transparent walls. I could almost believe I was outside on a summer day.

Children's laughter came from somewhere in the branches of the big central tree. A shout went up when the kids spotted me. Little faces popped out of the shrubbery, and five boys raced down the staircase that spiraled around the thick trunk. "Jackie, you're back!"

Tito hung on my arm with sticky hands. When he got my attention, he held out a fistful of raspberries. Red juice stained his lips. "You gotta twy dese, Jack."

I didn't have the heart to correct his pronunciation. Tito had given me food. In our crew, that was a milestone. I remembered my mother telling me how I brought her my first flower, a dandelion from the lawn, when I was three. These days, a gift of food was better than any flowers. Just to be nice, I sat on the edge of a planter box and ate a couple of gross, half-crushed berries from the little boy's hands.

Tito beamed. "See, Paco? I bwought food, all by myself."

"Good job, Tito," Paco answered. "Feedin' your crew, like a big guy."

The berries tasted better than they looked. Delicious, tart sweetness filled my mouth. My empty stomach growled. "Wow. Those are good. I'm starving."

Boys reached into their pockets. Apples, walnuts, and red grapes tumbled into my lap.

"Thanks!" I grabbed an apple before it rolled off and sunk my teeth into it. Sweet juice ran down my chin. I'd never tasted anything so good.

My crew sat in a circle on the weird indoor lawn, eating together like family. I gazed at each face. Paco, still thin from his infection, but healthy and happy. The red streaks had disappeared from his arm. Tito was absorbed in picking walnut crumbs out of a broken shell. Caleb and Marc sat elbow to elbow, eating apples.

Old Joe was missing, along with Dakota, Ash, and Keenan. Caleb caught me looking for them. "Everybody's here."

"Joe made it? I didn't see him, going out."

"Yeah. He's upstairs with the big guys, talking to Doctor Stuart," Caleb said.

I leaned back to check the upper deck and found it empty. "Then this is a good time for us to talk. Because tonight, you guys need to move on. Get out of Colorado." Their protests almost drowned me out.

"But this place is great," Caleb yelled.

"This place is leaving. Going into space," I said.

Sarcasm edged Caleb's voice. "I think we all know that, Jack. It's a *rocket*. That's kind of hard to miss."

I let the half-eaten apple roll into my lap. "It's leaving for a reason. Listen up, you guys. I've got news. Bad news."

Everyone stopped eating and looked at me, eyes wide. Boys shifted nervously, eyeing my pale-blue astronaut uniform.

I bit my lip, refusing to cry. "The pox is coming, with a whole army of infected animals, or people, or . . . I don't know, something. And the thing is . . . she wants me. So you have to get as far from me as you can. Get your gear together. Crew's leaving in the next hour. And I'm staying here."

No one spoke. I breathed into the silence, feeling some small satisfaction that I'd gotten the message out without breaking down.

Caleb threw an overripe plum against the trunk of a tree, not that far from my head. The splat made me jump. "You are so full of shit, Jackie."

Kids giggled. I gaped like a moron. "What?"

"Whaaat?" Caleb mimicked my high, girlie voice. "Did you think we were gonna buy that? Sure, the pox wants *you*. Like you're *sooo* special. If you wanted to leave the crew, you coulda just said so."

"You dumped us and joined them, without sayin' a word," Paco said.

He shared a disgusted glance with Caleb. “See, she’s already wearing their uniform.”

Tito started to blubber. His snot soaked the shoulder of my crisp, one-piece suit. “I’m not abandoning the crew,” I cried, hugging the little one. “I’m trying to save your lives here.”

I struggled to my feet, the child heavy on my narrow hip. Tito’s arms squeezed so tight around my throat, I could barely talk. “I can’t let you die. That’s why you need to pack your gear. You’re leaving tonight.”

I pried Tito off my neck and pushed him on Paco. The stunted ten-year-old staggered under the child’s weight, but he did his best to hang on. Tito howled and thrashed, reaching for me. Turning away from him was the hardest thing I’d ever done.

“Pack your gear. That’s an order,” I snapped.

Nobody obeyed. Tito’s cries echoed off the high, curved walls of the dome. People looked away.

I followed their gazes and turned to face Dakota, coming out of the elevator behind me. Ash and Keenan flanked him, a few steps behind.

“You don’t give orders, Jackie.” Dakota said, staring me down. “Remember? You’re not Chief anymore.”

I took a stunned step backward, wrapping my arms across my hollow stomach. Dakota had the power now, and he wasn’t gonna give it up. He didn’t plan on listening to reason, either. That just figured. A bitter taste filled my mouth. *I never should have made him Chief.*

“Dakota, poxy animals are filling the highways. There’s so many, they show up by satellite. Ask Stuart if you don’t believe me. We can’t win this one. Please, please, get the boys out of here,” I cried, hating myself for begging.

Dakota’s expression settled into the rigid, unreadable mask it took on during fights. I’d never been on the receiving end of that before. It kind of shook me up.

Dakota folded his arms, looking me over. “This crew’s never left a member behind. Not unless that person was already dead. You’re not dead, so nobody’s leaving.”

“This is real, you gotta believe me,” I howled. One rogue tear escaped down my cheek. I flicked it away.

“I believe you, all right,” Dakota said. “I’ve been talking to Doctor Stuart about the nanobots. He showed us old news clips, and satellite images from just a couple of hours ago. All hell’s coming down on us, Jackie. I’m not leavin’ you to deal with it alone. We’ll talk later, okay? I’ve got work to do. Try and get some rest. Eat something.”

He brushed past, shoulders back and head high, walking like a boss. Kids scooted out of his way. Keenan and Ash followed their new chief into the cage elevator. The doors banged closed behind them.

I sat down on the edge of a planter box and stared blindly into space. *I'm not Chief anymore.*

Dakota was willing to sacrifice the whole crew for me. For nothing, really, because our little band had no chance against Bianca. And I had no power to stop him. I should have known Dakota wasn't the type to be a puppet. If I gave him power, he'd wield it.

Caleb made like he was going to walk away, but then stopped in front of me. He looked down and scuffed the grass with a toe. "I'm . . . uh . . . sorry. Guess you weren't lyin'."

"Wish I was," I muttered. "You don't understand what we're up against. If you stay, you're dead."

Caleb shrugged. "I'd be dead already if you hadn't taken me in. I owe you, Jack."

Over Caleb's shoulder, I scanned the pinched young faces of my crew. Paco sat on the grass, holding Tito on his lap. Marc, the new kid, hung back, half hidden behind a tree.

I felt despicable for going behind Dakota's back. But I had to try. "Listen, you guys. It's stupid for all of us to die when the pox is only after me. You could get away clean."

"Tell that to Dakota," Paco said.

I blinked back fresh tears. "I tried, he won't listen. And the pox is coming."

"Da pox is coming," Tito repeated solemnly.

My lower lip trembled. I didn't even try to hide it. "Yes, baby. Yes, she is," I whispered. "I am so sorry. I don't know what to do."

"Maybe twy to make fwiends," Tito said.

"She doesn't want—" I stopped myself. "Okay, sweetheart, I'll try. I'll do my best."

Tito went back to eating walnuts. Near the ceiling, giant fans began to turn, sending tiny dead leaves raining down. I crunched over them on my way to the door.

"Jack! Where you goin'?" a deep voice yelled.

I turned, saw who it was, and went running back. "Joe! Where have you been? When we rolled out, I thought you didn't make it."

"Almost didn't. We were up talkin' to the Doc. Tryin' to figure out a way t' beat this thing."

My words came out in a rush. "Joe, Dakota needs to take the crew and get out. Maybe head south, into New Mexico. Get the kids someplace safe."

Joe shook his head. "That ain't my call."

"It could be! It could be, if you wanted. They'd listen to you."

"That's what I thought, honey," Joe said, his voice husky. He reached out an arm to me, and I crept into the hug, feeling like a kid. He spoke low in my ear. "I tried. I'm sorry, Jack, but I did. I told him to leave you. I tried with Ash and Keenan too. And they wouldn't."

"So now the whole crew has to die?" I sobbed into Joe's checked flannel shirt. "You know how much worse that makes it for me?"

"Jack. Jack!" Joe grabbed me by the shoulders and looked me in the eye. "You got no choice. Make yer stand here. Here, with everybody who loves you."

I looked up at Joe's lined face, blurred with tears. "There's . . . there's a lot o' poxy animals comin' after me, Joe."

"But only one that matters. The boss. Bait her in. And kill her."

"I . . . I'll try."

"You gotta do better than that. Those boys are countin' on you. New Mexico ain't far enough. Hell, South America ain't even safe. This is our one chance, Jackie."

I wanted to dry my tears and charge off, all fired up for war. The best I managed was a shaky nod. "Okay. I'm gonna go on out and practice on the array."

Joe patted my shoulder. "Good girl."

Chapter 20

I don't remember making it to the elevator. Somehow I rode it downstairs. Two familiar men intercepted me the second the doors opened. They carried a lot of gear, with pistols and short-barreled shotguns showing, and weird, lumpy black bags strapped to their backs.

"Hello, reapers," I said.

The gray-eyed man and his burly partner both cringed a little.

"Sorry. But that's what you are. Might as well make your peace with it." I rubbed my damp eyes on the sleeve of my coverall.

The young soldiers watched me with identical haunted expressions.

"It's all right," I said. "Don't feel bad. We'll get through this. Or, uh, not." I barked a laugh, and was heartened when the big guy cracked a smile. I didn't ask their names, even though they knew mine. It seemed easier that way.

"Doc says you can go without your respirator if you want," the gray-eyed man said. "There's no way to carry enough compressed air, anyway, and the tanks are too heavy to climb with."

"I've lived without it this long," I said.

We stepped through the airlock into the cold outdoor air, and our breath instantly turned to fog. The men inhaled deeply and shared a smile. I wondered how long it had been since they'd been outside. Bianca had robbed them of that simple pleasure. I wanted to make her pay.

I shivered in my pale blue coverall, wishing I still had my hoodie. A warmly-dressed crowd milled around, peering in through the fence at the array. About half of them wore respirators. The rest had apparently decided it was too late to worry about it. People murmured and nudged each other when they saw me. My reapers cleared a path, and we slowly made our way toward the narrow gate in the funnel shaped fence that surrounded the array. The pale purple UV lamps cast an eerie glow in the fading light. The rocket loomed over our heads, standing stiffly beside its skeletal scaffold. Blue-uniformed guards stepped apart as we reached the gate. I would have passed between the men without a glance, but one of them spoke to me.

"Excuse me, Miss Stuart?"

I paused and looked up at the muscular Latino soldier. "Yes?"

"I just wanted to say thank you, miss. That's all."

The crowd took up his words, so they rippled backward, spreading out like rings from a stone thrown into a pond. "Thank you . . . thank you." Softly, from the back of the crowd, came a final, collective whisper in a breath of wind. *"Thank you."*

A hot stinging sensation in my eyes warned me of another flood of tears. I got a grip, though, and turned to face the throng. "You're welcome. I promise—" My voice broke. I choked out the words. "I'll do my best."

A derisive snort came from my left. A line of identically dressed men and women stood in front, against the fence, wearing long, black woolen coats and striking gold scarves. I gulped.

The Committee.

Committee members didn't add their voices to the echoes of thanks. And they didn't look one bit happy about my temporary celebrity. The hawk-nosed woman with the round glasses made an impatient gesture. The gray-eyed reaper immediately took hold of my arm. He walked me through the gate, and then I could breathe again. There was plenty of open space in the fenced-in funnel leading to the array. Nobody wanted to be inside that cage.

I craned my neck to look up at the array. Alanna climbed around up there, wearing dark goggles, even in twilight. I saw why when she began switching on and off giant, glaring UV lights. She finished at one pod, clipped on a zipline, and soared off to test another one. The crowd let out a breathy "oooh."

I rolled my eyes. *End of the world, and people still show up for the spectacle.*

Stuart came through the gate to join me. "What do you think of my array? Quite the accomplishment, if I do say so myself."

"It looks like a carnival ride," I said. "Only bigger."

He raised an eyebrow. "Where do you think I got the frame?"

I had to smile. "What's the world coming to, when the Center starts scrounging with the rest of us?"

Across the pavement, one of the white-coated technicians raised an arm to signal. Alanna acknowledged with a wave and began climbing down a ladder into the center of the tentacles, where the mouth would be if the array was the octopus it resembled. She reached the bottom, a technician shouted a warning, and I shut my eyes just in time. A painfully bright blast of pale purple light shot right through my closed eyelids, leaving splotchy after-images on my vision. Then every bulb on the array went dead.

"I call it the Bomb," Stuart said. "If you use it, the system overloads. It can take up to three minutes to recover."

I blinked in a useless attempt to clear my vision. "That's my last resort, then."

"Yes. Don't use it unless you absolutely have to."

Stuart walked me closer to the darkened array. It loomed over us like some nightmare insect. The ladders seemed to disappear into the gray sky. I clenched my fists at my sides. I had to win up there. Win, or watch my boys get taken.

Stuart's fingers dug into my arm. "I had hoped that Bianca would arrive to find you gone. Unfortunately, the ship isn't ready. We're cutting all the corners we dare, but there's no way we'll launch before the nanobot army arrives."

"You can't just get in and go?" I asked.

"It's not that easy. A rushed launch will end in disaster. An explosion, or a crash." Stuart leaned close to whisper. "I've done everything I can for you. Called in every favor. Twisted arms, even. But…not everyone has the same attitude that I do."

I understood. Stuart was the bleeding heart type, desperate to find a humane solution when there was none. Most of the Committee probably disagreed with him. I would too, in their place. Hell, if I was them, I would have had me executed a long time ago.

Stuart glanced over his shoulder. A paunchy technician was making his way toward us. We didn't have much time. The little doctor spoke rapidly, his lips close to my ear. "Jacqueline, if you prevail, your top priority is to make your way immediately to the ship. Certain members of the Committee see you as a liability. No matter what you do for us, for humanity . . ."

"I know. They want me dead," I whispered. "They're afraid of what'll happen if I'm compromised."

"True. And it is a very real concern. If I hadn't adopted you, the Committee would have had you executed already," Stuart wheezed. "But be aware, my protection will only last as long as I do."

The old man looked frail, and his breathing was more labored than ever. He probably didn't have much longer to live. On the other side of the chain-link fence, the Committee woman watched me, eyes cold behind her glasses. My shoulders slumped.

"Jacqueline, look at the ship," Stuart said, his lips barely moving. "About halfway up, there is a circular port, used for docking with the orbiting space station. See it?"

I craned my neck, searched, and finally spotted the outline of the closed door. "Yeah."

"It should be bolted before launch," Stuart muttered. "It will not be."

I shot him an alarmed look. I was no expert, but taking off with an unlocked door seemed like a bad idea.

"Adam and his teammates will open the port for you, and secure it after you make it safely inside."

I gaped up at the rocket. "You seriously mean for me to jump from one of those pods, into the open door? Do you have any idea how far that is?"

"If you come down to the ground, the Committee will almost certainly stop you from getting in the elevator."

"But Stuart, that's a big jump, I'm not sure . . ." I let it go. After all, getting onboard wasn't one of my priorities. "Just tell Adam to bolt the door on time, okay? Don't wait on me, because . . . I, uh, might not make it."

Stuart ducked his head, blinked rapidly, and rubbed his eyes with a gloved knuckle before he spoke. "If I don't see you again, good luck, my dear. It's been a privilege."

I should have thanked him. I could at least have said goodbye. But when I moved my parched lips, no sound came out.

The portly, middle-aged technician arrived at my side, still puffing from his brisk walk. He held out a pair of dark goggles by the elastic band. "Put these on. Alanna is waiting for you. She'll familiarize you with the array."

I put on the goggles and was plunged into night. A thin coating of ice glazed the metal ladder. I grabbed on. Cold bit into my bare hands. As I climbed, some of the ice melted under my grip, making the rungs even slicker. I sped up a little, trying to move before too much ice melted. About fifty feet up, both feet slipped and I banged my shin. Fear and pain made me cry out. Clinging madly with my hands, I scrambled back onto the ladder. My arms and legs shook. The pod at the top seemed impossibly far away. I made myself quit looking for it, and concentrated on climbing the s-shaped tentacle, one shiny rung after another. The horizontal section was the hardest, since I had to crawl along, staring straight down, with the ladder bruising my knees. After that, I was relieved to be going up again. Finally the black, bowl-shaped underside of the pod hung right over my head. I hauled myself in with the built-in handholds and flopped onto the plastic seat, clinging to the rim as the capsule rocked on its hinges.

Sweat had hardly cooled on my body when Alanna sailed in, unclipped her zipline, and dropped over the side of the pod, tipping it so far I thought I'd spill right out. I squealed.

"Get a grip, Jackie. If that scares you, we're already doomed," Alanna snapped. She settled into the seat beside me and loosened the scarf she'd wrapped over her face.

My witty comeback evaporated. Alanna's skin glistened with some kind of yellow-white slime that dripped from her chin and greased the roots of her blonde hair. She pulled off one black leather glove and pinched the opposite wrist. When she let go, the slime snapped back down like an elastic suit.

"Eeuw, what the hell is all over you?" I blurted.

Alanna grimaced self-consciously. "Don't look so revolted. It's made from your skin cells."

"My skin!" My jaw twisted in disgust. "But why?"

"Think about it."

"The doctors did this? To…oh my God." When I put it together, horror turned to sympathy, and my voice went soft. "To make the pox target you."

Alanna didn't answer. She pulled a little spray bottle out of a pocket and spritzed the slime with pink liquid, bravely pulling up her shirt to dampen her bare stomach. Cold wind wafted some of the pink mist over me. I edged away, suddenly worried that Alanna's second skin was made of false flesh, like pox construct. The odor wasn't the same dying-yeast smell, though. Instead, the scent triggered an older memory, a happier one, of the hospital microbiology lab where my mom used to work. Before she got sick, Mom sometimes took me there on weekends. When I closed my eyes, I could still smell the aroma that filled the room when she opened the incubator—the half-delicious, half-nauseating smell of warm agar.

The bittersweet memory took me back in time, to a summer day when I was small. I skipped down a shiny black staircase with my mom, my small hand in hers. On the way out of her lab, we always visited the black and yellow mynah bird in his cage outside the pharmacy. I loved that bird. He was the best thing about the hospital, as far as I was concerned. The memory faded, leaving me sitting in an open-topped capsule, winter wind blowing down my neck, with a girl who smelled like something that grew in a petri dish. Grief rose up, a dull ache in my chest.

A flap of my lab-grown skin sagged off Alanna's jawline, hanging in flaccid wrinkles that vibrated in the wind. I shuddered. "So, whose idea was this, uh, skin thing?"

"Doc Stuart's," Alanna said, closing her eyes to spray her face. She raised a hand to scratch, resisted the urge, and dropped it back into her lap. "He heads the liberal faction here. It's mostly made up of doctors, psychologists, those kind of people."

"They're the ones who want to let me live."

"They're not as benevolent as you think," Alanna spat. "Committee psychologists got me cut from the team. So I wouldn't hesitate to risk myself where necessary, they said. Without the space program, I have nothing to live for. And they know it."

I squirmed under her freakish glare. "They must think it'll give us an edge, if the pox doesn't know which girl is really me."

"Yep. So much for our secret plan," Alanna said bitterly. "If we switch places, and I try to board the ship, Bianca will trail me right to my friends. She'll kill them all."

"Not if I kill her first. Alanna, you can still get on the ship. I can still get back to my crew. But only if you're willing to show me the ropes up here."

Alanna huffed, looking away. In a minute, she wiped her nose and stood, balancing lightly on the balls of her feet while the pod rocked beneath her. Tears streaked her nightmarish face. "Fine. Grab a climbing harness from the compartment under the seat. Strap it on. Let's go."

My legs trembled as I stood and reached down to struggle with the half-frozen hinges of the underseat compartment. The pod jerked and swayed with my movements. Alanna watched me, shaking her head at my clumsiness. I pulled out the wadded harness, closed the lid, and managed to buckle into it by sitting down and sliding in one leg at a time. Even on the smallest holes, the nylon harness hung loose on my narrow hips. If I fell, would my body slip right out?

Alanna stepped out of the pod onto a horizontal steel beam that gleamed with ice. Concentric circles of those beams ringed the array, running between tentacles at various heights. From above, it looked like a giant, circular spider web crammed into a funnel.

"Follow me," Alanna said. "The catwalks lead to spotlight stations. I'll show you those first. Careful, it's slick as hell."

I had to man up big time to follow her out of the tippy pod onto the narrow catwalk. Heart racing, I crept along the eight-inch wide beam with tiny, shuffling steps, clinging like mad to anything I could get a hold of.

Alanna shook my hand off her goo-soaked jacket. "Balance yourself, dammit! You'll pull us both off." With the grace of a dancer, she set off across the abyss, not even bothering to clip herself to a safety line.

I was dumb enough to look down, and I froze. Alanna kept going. She didn't even glance back once to check on me. I stood there alone, stomach clenched, gripping a support strut with all my strength. Rapid, shallow breaths hissed in and out of my lungs. Ahead, the enormous white rocket blotted out a slice of darkening sky.

Alanna can't save me, I told myself. *Nobody can. I have to do this myself.* In my heart, I set my life aside. Gave it to Dakota, and my crew. I relaxed my grip, forced my fingers to let go. Head up and shoulders back, I stepped out onto the narrow beam. Wind flowed under me, and little gusts pushed at my body. Steel flexed slightly under my feet. Hands outstretched for balance, I walked the tightrope into midair.

About forty feet out, the beam connected to a small landing made from see-through metal mesh. I let out a relieved breath as I stepped onto it. A giant oblong spotlight had been mounted on the guard rail. Alanna grabbed the handles on either side of it. "The light pivots, see? But only so far. It doesn't go behind you, so watch your back."

She stepped away, motioning me to give it a try. I switched on the power, and a pale-purple ultraviolet beam stabbed the hazy air. Taking hold of the sturdy plastic handles, I pointed the light down for a stomach-lurching look at the crowd below. The Committee stood where I left them, in a neat row along the fence. Just for fun, I swept the spotlight up and down their line. A few people put their hands up to block the glare, but the hawk-nosed woman stared right back at me, violet light reflecting eerily off her glasses. Behind the Committee, the crowd thinned as people straggled away. Folks stopped to watch me annoy their dear leaders.

"Quit it, Jackie!" Alanna slapped the spotlight aside. "Don't make things worse than they already are."

"Okay, okay," I giggled. Reaching out with one chilly finger, I switched off the light. "Not that things could get much worse." I snuck a sideways peek at the teenage girl beside me, and my manic grin faded. Her second skin sagged in lines of despair, making her look like an old woman. It pierced my heart. "I'm sorry, Alanna. That they put this gross skin on you. And that you got cut from the astronaut program because of me."

"The program was my life," Alanna said softly. "All I ever cared about. But it's not your fault I got cut. The Center's gone to hell. This is the last ship. Parents are fighting to get their kids on board, or to defend them, if their son or daughter already made the team. My parents aren't here to fight for me. That's why I got cut."

"I know how you feel. I don't have parents to fight for me, either."

"Mine didn't die of pox," Alanna said impatiently. "They left two years ago to join the orbiting colony. Our separation was supposed to be temporary, but now . . . I'll never see them again."

"Orbiting colony?" I repeated. "I never knew there was a colony."

"What, you thought they were going to send a bunch of kids into space, all alone?" Alanna sneered.

"Why not? I've been on my own since I was eleven."

"Oh. Um, sorry." The monster-girl shifted her feet, looking down. Goo dripped from her shiny chin. After a long moment she muttered, "It would have been easier if you weren't so damn nice."

I laughed. I couldn't help it.

Alanna scowled. "I just want to hate you, you know?"

"Yeah, I get that. But the only way either of us has a chance is if we work together. We can split Bianca's forces, if part of her army chases you. I need to get the pox-boss alone and kill her." I pivoted the dark spotlight around, imagining the coming fight. My palms grew damp with anticipation.

Beside me, Alanna clutched the rail harder. "What's the pox boss?"

"Whatever body Bianca's in, that's the boss. She can jump from one body to another. I've seen her in a rat, and a pigeon. And once, in a woman. Sophia." The name brought back images of razor-sharp Chihuahua teeth, pain, and blood spreading through dark water.

"So, when Adam's mom was infected, was that the pox-boss?" Alanna asked.

I shook my head. "Nope. Regular old pox. It has a hive mind, though—a collective consciousness. So talking to Clara was kind of like talking to a piece of Bianca, if that makes any sense."

I didn't tell Alanna about the weird construct heads hanging from the infected woman's fingertips. Bianca knew what I looked like when I was ten. That had to be because the nanobots in Adam's mom were isolated, so their information was out of date. And my mother? The pox knew her too. Even six years ago, Bianca must have suspected that I'd turn out to be a primary host.

"How do you recognize the boss?" Alanna asked, interrupting my thoughts.

"When she looks at you, you'll know. You'll just know. She gives me a chill, right here." I put my fingertips lightly on the center of my chest.

Alanna pursed her slimy lips. "Oookay, if you say so. Assuming you manage to kill her, will her army give up?"

"Who knows? Somehow I doubt it. They'll have orders to catch you. Or me, I mean. That reminds me, I need to show you something. See that pod, the one closest to the ship?" I pointed at a tilted capsule on top of a faraway tentacle. "We need to go over there. Want to teach me how to work that zipline?"

Almost immediately, I was sorry I asked.

Alanna reached up to an overhead cable, pulled down a nylon strap, and clipped it with a carabineer to my harness. "Hook on, jump off. It's that easy. Watch the landing or you'll get bruises."

Somehow, I expected more. Like for her to actually train me or something.

Alanna tugged me toward the edge of the platform by my climbing harness. I dug in my heels, but the harness pinched in personal places. I gave up a step, then two. "Hey, hey, not so fast. Wait a minute, wait!"

She pushed me. I let out a shrill scream as I fell. The harness caught my weight with a painful snap. I clung desperately to the line so I wouldn't flip upside down and slip loose. The ride only lasted seconds before another catwalk loomed out of the dark. I was approaching way too fast. I pulled my knees up, skidded onto the landing, and went tumbling across ice-slicked metal mesh. Just before I slid under the railing on the far side, my flailing hand latched on to a pillar.

I scrambled upright just in time to see Alanna land on her feet and go into a perfectly balanced slide. I sidestepped, whipped a hand out and slapped her hard. Her feet flew out from under her, and she crashed down on her side. Hanging on to the post with one hand, I got a foot on her ribs, in that sensitive spot under the armpit.

She struggled, cursing and thrashing. I didn't let up, even when she went after my shin with a fist. Bloody pieces of her skin—or mine, really—tore off and stuck to the icy platform, making her look like some kind of alien. By then, I was too scared to let her up.

So I dropped a knee on the crazy girl's stomach, pinned her hands over her head, and waited. "You ready to listen?" I growled.

She wasn't, so I leaned a little harder, panting with the effort. "Hard to breathe?" I grunted. "I bet it is. I lived with boys for five years. Shows, huh?"

"What the hell is wrong with you, Jackie?" Alanna gasped.

"What's *wrong* is that you have no idea of how to be part of a crew. What were you thinking, pushing me off like that? We're partners here. All you have to do is cooperate for two days. One really, since today's mostly over."

"Okay. All right!"

I let her up. Alanna rolled to all fours and then struggled to her feet, murder in her eyes.

"Don't try it," I warned. "I'm still clipped in, and you're not." I held up the carabineer I'd taken off her harness, and felt a little surge of satisfaction at the surprise on her face. "If I think my chances are better without you, I'll make that choice." I twitched my chin abruptly toward the precipice.

Alanna recoiled from the edge, eyes wide. "No, no, don't, please don't," she babbled. "I'm sorry."

"Cool. It's over, then." I stuck out a hand. "Come on, then. I'll show you how you're gonna get on board the ship."

Alanna refused to shake my hand, but she did follow me over the short section of catwalk leading to another pod. I clipped in to an overhead cable for that little trip, just in case, since she was behind me. My fading adrenaline rush took me as far as the new capsule, where I collapsed on another plastic carnival-ride chair. Alanna hesitantly climbed in, blinking in surprise when I reached out to steady her.

"What is with you?" she muttered. "You threaten my life, then you're like, oh, that was nothin'."

I shrugged. "That's how it is when you're part of a crew. You gotta forgive people, 'cause you can't live without 'em. I said my piece. We can be friends again, if you want."

"Yeah. I'd like that." Alanna hunched in her seat. Part of her second skin hung in a flap down to her neck. I felt sorry for her.

"Your, uh, face is falling off." I reached out a tentative hand, but couldn't bring myself to touch the swinging skin. "Eeuw. Maybe you can stick it back on."

We both started to giggle. It got out of control. I laughed so hard tears rolled down my face, and hardly any sound came out. My stomach was killing me by the time it was over.

Alanna carefully lifted her Jackie-skin and tried to mush it back on. It folded and slid back down, dripping slime. "Damn. Doc Stuart's not going to like this."

"He can fix it later. I wanted to show you that." I pointed at the circular outline of the docking port. "It's your way in."

The view across to the hulking white rocket wiped the smiles off our faces. The docking port hung at a forty-five degree angle below the pod, thirty or forty feet away. Way too far to jump. I knew I'd never be able to get in there on my own, even with the door hanging wide open. Maybe Alanna could. But she'd have to fucking fly to do it.

"When the fight's over—win or lose—get over here as fast as you can," I said. "Then you've got to make that jump, somehow."

"Into the docking port?" Alanna breathed. She leaned forward, focused on the shiny white wall of the ship. "No way. I can't jump that far. Besides, how would I get in?"

"Adam's in on this. He'll be there to open the door. Stuart told me so," I admitted, leaving out how the doctor thought I'd be going instead of her.

I hadn't leveled with Stuart yet about my determination to stay on Earth. Come to think of it, I'd probably never get the chance. He'd have to be surprised, along with the Committee and most everybody else. Dakota crossed my mind then, and that gave me a pang. I hadn't had a chance to tell him about my plan. Had Stuart told him I was going into space? Was Dakota upset about it? I didn't know. One thing was for sure—if Dakota knew, he'd tell the crew. Keenan might already be going nuts.

With an effort, I focused on our problem. "Alanna, get a message to Adam. Tell him to sneak a rope on board. Whatever happens, don't go down to the ground and try to use the elevator. There'll be thousands of poxy animals here by tomorrow. Not all of them can fly or climb."

The blonde girl gulped. "Right. So we're better off up here. And, um, I'd get in huge trouble for telling you this, but . . . if you win, and I get on board, you'd better run. A lot of people would thank you. But more of them want you dead."

"I know. That's what my reapers are for. You know those soldiers who follow me around? They're not bodyguards. If I get taken, they're supposed to put me down."

"Orders of the Committee, no doubt." Alanna pulled up her feet and curled into a ball on the seat, knees to her forehead. Her muffled voice came out, a low moan. "Oh my God. I cannot believe this is happening."

I put a gentle hand on her shoulder. "It's all right. Well, it's not really all right, but I see why they have to do it."

Alanna peeked at me over one arm.

"See, I was born a primary host. Then Doctor Graham treated me with Class Three nanites, to heal my broken ankle in a hurry. Look what happened." I pulled my folding knife from a coverall pocket, opened it, and cut a thin line across the back of my hand.

Alanna squirmed, watching that. A long, tense hiss escaped her lips. The wound healed in seconds.

She sat a moment in horrified silence. When she finally spoke, her voice came out small and scared. "Class Three? We learned about those in school. They're illegal! Banned for being inhumane. Did it . . . did it hurt as much as they say?"

I nodded. "Worse. But that's not all. If Bianca gets me, she'll get the healing power too. Right now the pox is only limited because creatures she infects eventually sicken and die. If I'm compromised, my body won't get sick. It may never die, even if my mind is . . . gone. In me, she'll be unstoppable. So seriously, please. Don't stop the reapers. Don't let anyone stop them."

Alanna groaned softly.

I squeezed her shoulder. "Hey. We can do this. We'll get you on board the ship. Then I'll grab my crew and run. We'll get away clean, like we always do." I looked her in the eye, and tried to make both of us believe it.

***

For the next hour, we climbed all over the array, trying out UV lights and flying back and forth on ziplines. When the full moon rose, low and fat, over the horizon, Alanna called it quits. "That's enough. We can't have you coming out tired and sore tomorrow."

"I'm okay," I argued. "Besides, I still crash half the time when I try and land off the zipline. I want to practice a little while more."

Alanna wouldn't listen. "No. You're done." She headed for the ladder.

I reluctantly followed her off the array. Reapers shadowed us all the way to the airlock, where they checked us in with the door guards. I didn't have any ID, but it didn't matter. Everyone knew who I was.

Walking across the lobby toward the elevator, the blonde girl limped slightly. I felt a little bit guilty about it. I'd been banged up too, but on me, every last bruise had already healed. She wasn't so lucky.

We said goodbye outside the elevator. That reminded me that my partner had a house to go back to. I couldn't go home to the diner. The territory might not even be ours anymore. Feeling bereft, I gave Alanna a hug by the door. Slime got on my cheek. That grossed me out, but I hid it well. Or at least I hoped so.

"Um, try and sleep," Alanna said.

"I'll try. Eat some food, too, even if you aren't hungry. And I will too." I didn't know if I could keep that promise. Dread settled in my stomach, making me nauseous. I didn't want to eat. Probably wouldn't hold it down if I tried.

Alanna stood, legs a little apart, arms wrapped her across her slim body. "Okay. Guess this is it. My orders are to wait for the Committee to ping me. They'll get us up when Bianca's army is a few hours away."

"Come get me if I don't wake up," I joked. "I don't want to oversleep and miss it."

The elevator doors opened, and Ash popped out. "Oh good, I was just coming to look for you, Jackie. Dinner's on, and—" He spotted Alanna's slime-slicked face, with that blood-streaked flap of skin hanging off, and his jaw dropped. "What the . . ."

Alanna cringed, like she wanted to melt into the floor and die.

"Never mind, Ash, we'll talk about it later," I interrupted. Taking his arm, I dragged him into the elevator. "Good night, Alanna," I yelled, as the doors closed.

The elevator started up. "Try not to embarrass her, because—" I began.

"She's infected, isn't she?" Ash yelled. "Her face is melting. What the hell is that stuff? She got it all over you! Pox. It's got to be pox." Pulling up the hem of his oversized white t-shirt, Ash started scrubbing my face. I backed up, but he trapped me against the wall of the elevator, insisting on wiping off every last trace of slime.

"Ugh. I can't believe these people! They don't even have the decency to put that poor girl out of her misery." Ash yanked his shirt over his head, wiped my face one more time with it, and tossed it into a corner.

I stayed where I was, slumped against the wall, hoping his neurotic hygiene episode was over. It was. Ash sighed and put an arm around me. I leaned against the warmth of his bare skin, grateful for the comfort. One of his arms wrapped my waist. With his other hand, Ash stroked my hair, sending sweet shivers down my spine. That got my attention. A simple hug was one thing, but he'd never had the balls to touch me like that. Not with that kind of energy. Delicious as the sensation was, I reached up, gently tugged his fingers down, and held him at arm's length, so our clasped hands came between us. From his anguished expression, I knew. Stuart told him I was leaving.

I wanted to tell Ash I wasn't really going through with it, but a tiny red light winked from a high corner. That had to be another of the Center's security cameras. The whole dome was wired for video, elevators and all. If I admitted that Alanna and I planned on switching places, I might as well ping the Committee. I held my tongue, and it burned me up inside.

Ash had this look in his eye like he was holding in something painful or tender or profound. Time slowed down for me. I couldn't believe our life together was really ending. My heart felt like it could rip in half.

Ash parted his lips, real slow. Took a breath. "Jackie—"

I never found out what he meant to say.

Our elevator arrived at the biosphere, and the doors opened. Under the dome, day had turned to night. A dim green bulb cast a patch of sullen light along the curved metallic wall.

Dakota stepped from a shadow into the eerie glow. In a flash, he took in Ash's bare chest, my flushed face, our clasped hands. "Making the best of your last day on Earth, I see," he said, kind of deadpan, with no real feeling to it.

"Oh *please*," I said. I admit, my nerves were fried, so the words came out tinged with sarcasm.

That irritated him, I could tell. Dakota held me with his eyes, just like a chief. I wanted to yell at him, tell him it wasn't what he thought. But I didn't have the patience for the same old stupid conversation. Not that day. I was too tired, too scared, and I didn't want to fight. My shoulders slumped.

Ash spoke first, saving me. "Dude, it's her last day. Don't let it end like this."

Dakota's gaze snapped to Ash. They stared each other down, soft brown eyes against icy blues. A long minute later, Dakota nodded. I let my breath out.

"I'm gonna go take a shower," Ash muttered to me. "You should, too. Get that shit off you."

"It's not pox," I tried, but Ash wasn't listening.

"Dakota. Don't let anybody touch that t-shirt, there on the floor," Ash snapped. "It's contaminated as hell."

When Ash started up again about Alanna's poxy face, I gave up and went off to take advantage of the Center's free hot water. Ash and Dakota stood together, talking under the weird green light.

I took Stuart's little two-man cage lift up to the second floor deck, where the living quarters were. At least the lights were on up there. The green ones downstairs gave me the creeps. Just off the aquarium room was a hall leading to the fancy bedroom I'd used before. I padded across soft blue carpet, feeling like an intruder in somebody else's house, and pushed open the bedroom door. The pretty wood furniture was gone, replaced by a pair of lightweight, utilitarian sleeping bags attached to the wall with nylon straps. That mystified me until I realized that sleeping in space was different. People couldn't sleep in beds, they'd float right out.

Sadly, the big bathtub had been torn out. In its place was a weird vertical tube of clear plastic. I stripped, stepped in the tube, and touched the single button. Warm water jetted from spouts all around. After about ten seconds it switched to suds. I felt like a car in an automatic car wash. One quick rinse later, and I was done. A vacuum switched on by itself and sucked off every last drop, leaving me almost dry. Warm fans finished the job. The whole thing took two minutes, tops. I guess I was clean enough afterwards, but the process wasn't near as satisfying as sinking into a bath.

I shimmied into my only suit of clothes, the pale blue coveralls, which had taken a beating. Each bloodstain was a reminder of another crash, another failed lesson on the zipline. Smooth, new skin showed through gashes in the cloth, giving me a grudging appreciation for Class Three nanites. Still wasn't worth it, though. Not that I had a choice.

I left the bedroom and rode the lift down to the garden. A gravel path led to the giant tree, the one in the center with the spiral staircase around it. What I saw there took my breath away. Electric torches had been pounded into the indoor lawn, filling the space. My boys sat in a circle inside the ring of light. When they saw me coming they stood up, but stayed in formation under Dakota's watchful eye.

I wove between primal islands of jungle-thick vegetation. Up close, those turned out to be collections of herbs and vegetables, berry bushes and fruit trees. Low-hanging branches of the central tree brushed my head. A few walnuts snapped off and fell. I let them go. Everything made food here, food to eat and oxygen to breathe in space. The oxygen *they'd* breathe, I reminded myself. I was relieved not to be going. For a building, the biosphere was huge. Huge enough to live in for the rest of my life? Not.

My steps slowed as I entered the spell cast by the torches. Tiki torches— electric, real fire, whatever—those meant security to me. The third night after the epidemic landed us on the streets, me and Dakota got up our nerve and broke into an abandoned hardware store. Nobody stopped us, so we hauled off some bamboo camp torches and as many jugs of fuel oil as we could carry. Fire made all the difference as we huddled under the black sky, afraid to go home for fear of finding our families staggering around, minds gone, with the pox looking out of their eyes. Pretty quick, other surviving kids copied us. With no parents left to maintain control, we raged around the streets, waving lit torches. I know, a few people came to bad ends. But I had fun.

I walked between the golden lights, anxiety rising in my chest. Keenan was missing. I scanned the circle twice to be sure. Joe, Ash and Dakota stood together, apparently unconcerned. It bugged me that not everyone showed up, since . . . I pushed thoughts of tomorrow out of my head. Keenan had to be around, climbing Stuart's giant walnut tree, or wandering the dark paths around it.

Off to one side, a blanket lay on the grass, piled with food from the garden dome and some Earth-side luxuries too, like packaged cookies. Those had to be from Adam's team. Everyone had pulled together to make my last night on Earth a good one.

Near the middle of the circle I stopped. "Thank you all for being here. You know, everything's gonna be okay, because . . ."

Joe caught my eye, made a slashing gesture with one hand, and cast a meaningful glance at a tiny red light on the wall. I knew he was warning me of the cameras. I hadn't forgotten. But that meant Joe suspected the truth—I wasn't really going. It gave me hope. Maybe Dakota knew too.

All eyes were on me. I forgot what I'd been trying to say, fumbled for words, and came out with something I would have been embarrassed to say a week ago. "I love you all."

A long silence followed that. I didn't know how to fill it.

Dakota made a hand signal I didn't understand. The crew did. Our circle split into two groups on either side of me. For a second, I didn't get it.

Then Dakota bellowed, "Game on. Keep away!"

Paco launched a sealed package of Oreo cookies over my head. A giggle burst from my lips. That was my favorite game, and Dakota knew it.

I made a half-hearted grab at the prize, but I was too tired to be much of a threat. Laughing and shouting, the boys taunted me, tossing the package enticingly lower. Finally Ash snagged the bag out of midair, tore it open, and poured a pile of broken cookies into my cupped hands. I collapsed on the grass with my crew, eating chocolate crumbs. Buoyed by the fun, I made it through my share of the cookies and half a peanut butter and jelly sandwich before my stomach rebelled. Something waited in the green-tinged light by the elevator—a row of tattered daypacks and duffel bags. My crew's stuff, stashed by the door for a quick getaway.

My fingers loosened on their own, and the peanut butter sandwich slid onto the grass.

Dakota noticed, and put an arm around me. "I told them you'd want it this way."

I leaned my head against his shoulder. "Yeah. You're right. Good call. You're gonna be an excellent chief, Dakota."

He opened his mouth to speak, choked up, and said nothing. Until that moment, I hadn't realized that my opinion mattered to him at all.

Dakota had obviously told the crew to make my last night a happy one, but as the evening went on, their forced cheer wore thin. A few at a time, boys came to say goodbye. Paco was first.

I hugged him close. "You'll be fine," I whispered, my nose buried in his straight, black hair. "You're ten now, almost as old as I was when things changed. You've got a crew, which is more than I had then. Stay with Dakota and do what he tells you. You'll make it."

I wasn't so sure I was telling the truth.

Paco bit his lip, fighting for control. He moved over to make room for Caleb and Marc.

I hugged them both at once. "You guys aren't kids anymore," I told them. "You grew up good. I'm proud of you both. Help Dakota keep the boys in line."

The boys nodded, blinked away their tears, and shuffled off.

I made time to talk to each member of my crew that night. The same stuff came out, over and over. "You'll be fine. Don't worry, I'm gonna win this one." *Yeah, sure.* I felt like a liar, but people needed hope more than they needed the truth.

The only truly happy person was Tito. Nobody told him what was going on. That was probably for the best.

Ash and Dakota wandered out to the edge of the circle together, pretending to get more food. Thanks to my nanite upgrade, I overheard every word.

"After tomorrow, I don't know what I'm gonna do. How I'm gonna…" Dakota muttered. He looked down, fiddled with his food, and flipped the whole thing into the garden, plate and all.

Ash put a hand on his shoulder. He glanced back at me. "I know. I feel the same way," he said softly. "Damn. She is beautiful."

I glanced away, embarrassed, but I couldn't help hearing Dakota's answer. "I know you're in love with her."

Ash got quiet. He took a step back, dark eyes alert.

"It's okay," Dakota said. "I love her too. But we need to be crew here, because, y'know, pretty soon …"

"It'll just be us," Ash whispered.

"Yeah."

I gulped. They both expected me to die. If I had to be honest, so did I.

In a minute both guys came back, cheery grins pasted on. Ash held out a fresh paper plate. "Hey, look, Jackie, remember those canned Vienna sausages? Haven't seen those in years. We saved you some."

"Awesome, thanks," I said, in my happy voice. I took one of the gelatinous little meat sticks and forced it down.

My effort didn't fool anybody. Ash caught me gazing over his shoulder, toward the elevator. His smile faded.

"Ash, where's Keenan?" I asked softly.

"That's the thing. We, uh, don't know." Ash looked down. "I woulda gone after him, but . . . I couldn't miss this."

"You think he left? On his own? I can't believe it." All the strength left my body.

"He'd never do that," Dakota said. "Jackie, you know I'm not much of a Keenan fan. But he's loyal as hell—at least to you. He'd never leave, not while you're still . . ."

Alive. Yeah. I didn't say it out loud. None of us did. That would make things too real.

The party ended with Joe and Dakota herding the kids off to wherever they'd been sleeping. I shook the crumbs off the picnic blanket and stretched out on it.

Ash went around switching off electric torches. His voice came from the shadows. "Jack, wake me up when the call comes in. You don't have to go out there alone."

"Okay. I will."

Ash disappeared into the darkened garden. I laid there alone for a long time. Above, fans kicked on, spinning the sweet scent of some exotic, night blooming flower through the humid air.

The crunch of shoes on gravel told me Dakota was back. "Jackie? You awake?"

"Uh huh," I murmured. I didn't admit I was afraid to sleep. Afraid of the nightmares. Afraid to miss a minute with him. "Keenan still missing?"

"Yeah." Dakota pulled off his boots and stretched out beside me, warm against my back.

We cuddled in silence for a while, spooning, his arm around my waist. Dakota sighed. "So much I wanted to tell you. So many plans that'll probably never happen now."

I rolled over on my side to face him. My fingertips stroked his hair, the line of his jaw, the scar on his cheek. In that moment, I loved him so much it hurt. "It's not over," I whispered, pressing my forehead to his. "I can still win this."

"Don't lie to me, Jackie."

"Don't kill my hope, Dakota."

"Sorry, I'm sorry," he whispered, one hand cradling my head against his chest. "But Stuart showed us the video. Of you, fighting that thing that came out of Adam's mom. I'm not stupid. I can see the size of the array. I know what that means."

I huffed a heavy sigh, pulled away, and propped myself up on an elbow. "Dakota, listen. You're chief now. The crew is your first responsibility, not me. If you really expect me to lose, what are you still doing here? You ought to take the kids and get out."

"I can't."

I sat up, hugged my knees to my chest, and waited. Dakota said nothing.

"Why?" I had to work to keep from snapping.

Dakota slowly sat up too. When he spoke, his voice sounded low. Husky. Heartbroken. "A couple of reasons. Mainly because I love you. I can't leave you to face this thing alone. Our plan was to send Ash off with the kids, but . . . they aren't allowed out. We checked at the gate, and . . . we're locked in. All of us."

"That doesn't make any sense," I exclaimed. "They don't need you."

"But you do, Jackie! You do. Committee psychologists made the call. They think you'll fight harder with our crew trapped behind you. We're, like, hostages."

"I would have done my best either way!" My voice rose high and shrill. "You think a chain-link fence is gonna hold in Bianca? She's got the whole world already!" I spread my arms in a wild gesture, and one outstretched hand almost smacked Dakota in the face.

He trapped my fists, pulling them in to his chest. "Shhh, easy, take it easy," he soothed.

I wanted to fight somebody. Run outside and scream at the gate until they opened it. Shoot some guards, if I had to, just to get my kids out of there.

Dakota kissed my knuckles. Rubbed them lightly with one finger. "They're scarred, see?" he whispered. "Scarred from fighting. You're a fighter, Jackie. Maybe you can win this. Maybe you can win after all."

Somehow that derailed my anger. I guess I just wanted my Chief to acknowledge that I had a chance, however small. He did that for me. I leaned forward and kissed him on the lips. Dakota freed my hands.

The metal zipper pull on my jumpsuit felt cool against my fingers. I tugged it down a few inches. Then a few more. "You know, this could be our last night together," I said softly.

Dakota's eyes lit up. His breath quickened. He knew exactly what I meant. We kissed, lightly at first, then deeper, wilder. I let him unzip my sky-blue jumpsuit to the navel. His fingers slid inside, traced the lacy edges of my bra, and slipped underneath. He stroked my nipple, sending tingles through my body. I moaned, back arched, hungry for more. Our lips met. Tongues entangled, we tumbled to the grass, with him on top. I tugged the hem of his shirt up, desperate to feel his skin against mine.

"You sure?" Dakota breathed. "Here?"

Faint sounds of trickling water came from some pool, hidden in the shadows. Nothing moved but a few long-stemmed flowers stirring in the breeze. We were alone, and it was beautiful.

"It's perfect here. I love you." The words came to me easily, now that we were out of time. There's be no more days together, fighting and foraging in the city. No more nights cuddling on the red vinyl benches of Joe's diner. Tears leaked out of the corners of my eyes. I pulled Dakota closer, craving the comfort of his weight on my body.

"I love you too, Jackie. Always have. Always will." Still straddling me, Dakota leaned back and pulled his shirt off.

His rangy, broad-shouldered form blocked the faint light. I let my fingers explore his hard-muscled stomach, sliding an inch or two under the waistband of his button-fly jeans. I toyed with the top button but hesitated, suddenly shy. This was the moment I'd feared since rape gangs first hunted me when I was nine. I got away from them then, and every other time, too. But I wasn't unscathed, not really. Fear became a part of me, like a living thing, coiled in the back of my mind, always alert, always watching. But alone with Dakota, I could let go. I felt safe. Infinitely loved. And so hot for him I could hardly breathe.

He gave me a teasing smile. "Come on, do it. I dare you."

That familiar smile chased away the last of my fears. I popped open his top button. Then I looked deep into his eyes and reached down for the next one.

"Oh, fuck yeah," Dakota breathed. The seams of his jeans strained under the pressure of his erection, so the last few buttons gave way easily. Then he lay in my hand, the whole long length of him, rock hard and completely unleashed. We were in heaven, so in love that it felt like our hearts had melted together to become one ecstatic whole. I gently squeezed his cock, trembling at the thought of having that inside me for the very first time. Dakota groaned out loud. Whatever I was doing, he liked it. And I would have done anything to please him.

Arms braced on either side of my head, he bent to kiss me again. I tangled my fingers in his hair as he placed soft kisses down my neck, between my breasts, over the lacy softness of my white bikini underwear. The pressure sent tingles to my core. One strong hand behind my back lifted me so I could pull my arms from my sleeves. Dakota tossed my pretty new bra onto the grass, pushed me down on my back, and took my nipple in his mouth. His tongue made little circles over the flesh, and I moaned with pleasure. With a sudden motion, he gripped the fabric of my pants and pulled them off, panties and all.

He kicked off his jeans and we were naked together, reveling in the feel of skin on skin. Dakota slid his hand into that secret place between my legs and stroked me there, muffling my cries with kisses, until I was half out of my mind with desire.

He rolled on top of me at last, and I cradled his narrow hips between my legs. One of his hands dropped to my inner thigh, pressing it high and wide. His cock slid into me, just a few inches, and I gasped. He pulled back, slick against my wetness, and drove it in all the way. Sweet fire shocked a cry from me, but the pain quickly turned to ecstasy.

"Love you, love you, love you," Dakota whispered into my hair. "Forever, no matter what. You're my girl."

He pushed himself up on his arms, and our eyes met. At that moment, I gave myself to him, heart and soul. I'd never be the same. There was no doubt in my mind that I'd choose death over a life without him.

We rocked together, lips open, tongues entangled, our rhythm building to a frenzy. Pleasure like I'd never felt built inside me, driven higher by his powerful, insistent strokes. We peaked at the same instant, in tremendous, earth-shaking waves of sated desire, both of us gasping. Helpless in the grip of that unexpected ending, I gripped Dakota's back and tried to hang on. The tremors gradually stopped, leaving me feeling naked to the soul.

My love for Dakota overwhelmed me, and I saw the truth in his eyes. He wasn't just saying it. He loved me too. My Chief, my best friend, my partner since childhood. He loved me too. We lay together, with him still inside me, every little move we made sending delicious, tingling aftershocks through our bodies.

Dakota stroked a damp lock of hair off my forehead and kissed me there. "I want you to know something, Jackie. You come first for me. Before the crew. Before anything."

I shook my head, tears blurring my vision. "Don't ever say that. You're Chief now. You have to take care of all of us, not just me. Promise me." A sob caught in my throat. "Promise me, please."

Dakota's blue eyes took on a hint of ice. Up close, that was more than a little intimidating. "And if I have to choose between you and them? What then?"

"I can take care of myself," I said, not entirely believing it. "I need you to take care of the kids. When I'm up on the array, I have to know you're watching out for them, or I can't do my job." My fingers gripped his biceps so hard he winced. "Swear it."

Dakota dropped his forehead to the blanket, so his voice came out muffled. That didn't come close to hiding his pain. "All right! The kids come first. I swear."

Tears of relief flowed freely from my eyes as I hugged him. "Thank you. I love you so much for this."

"You're killin' me, Jackie," Dakota muttered into the blanket. "Killin' me."

I knew it was true, so I comforted him the only way I knew how, holding him close with my arms and legs wrapped around him. After I while, I felt his cock grow hard again inside me, and we started the whole glorious thing all over again.

But then a chime sounded from across the dome. The elevator's double doors hissed open. A frustrated growl rumbled from Dakota's chest. He rolled off me, irate as hell. In a second I saw why. Keenan stepped out of the elevator, into the spooky green light. I almost let him go on by. Traded him away for a few sweet hours with Dakota. After all, Keenan was the one who didn't bother to show up. Didn't care enough to say goodbye. But something was wrong with the way he moved.

I sat up, back rigid, fumbling for my clothes in the dark. Keenan took a couple of unsteady steps, one hand on the burnished silver wall of the dome. His gasps blended with the soothing hum of the fan. Fingers splayed, his hand slid down, leaving a dark smear behind.

In a flash I was up and dressed, running towards Keenan's crumpled form, taking in his bloody elbows and the torn-out knees of his jeans. I knelt by his side. "Oh my God! What happened?"

"Crashed," Keenan grunted. "Thought I had it that last time, but then . . ." He held up his left hand, showing me a deep gash on his palm. It bled black in the faint, green light. "Fucking zipline."

"You were out on the array, all this time? Alone? Why didn't you tell me? I would have helped you! Alanna would have helped you."

"Terms of the deal," he muttered, and started to cough. "That was the only way they'd let me up there. That Committee bitch said she didn't care if I broke my neck or not. I don't matter. She said I'm . . . disposable."

"You are not." I got a shoulder under Keenan's armpit, tried to lift him, and failed.

Dakota came over, bare chested, his skin still glazed with my sweat. We both smelled of sex, and at that range, Keenan couldn't have missed it. I flushed, acutely aware of my bra and underwear lying in plain sight on the grass.

"Come on, I'll get you upstairs, wake Joe and Ash," I said. "We can ping Doctor Stuart, get him over here to stitch up that hand."

Dakota stepped in to help. "Jackie, stop it, he's too heavy for you. We can't have you pulling a muscle. Not tonight."

I wanted to tell Dakota that if I did strain something, it would heal in under a minute. That I owed Keenan, after what he did for me, going up on the array, at night, all alone. Bianca had to be planning to unleash some gargantuan construct on me, and Keenan fully intended to get in her way.

I wasn't sure how well all that would go over. So I only said, "Okay, I'll help you get him into the cage lift."

"No," Dakota snapped. "Go get some rest. That's an order."

I'd pulled that same shit on Dakota before. Played the chief card to get my own way. Now it was coming back to bite me. I didn't have much choice. He was Chief now.

"Okay, Dakota." While he hauled Keenan to his feet and started for the lift, I trudged back to the darkened lawn and sank to my knees on the blanket.

Dakota's low voice carried from halfway across the dome. "I gotta hand it to ya, Keenan. That was badass, getting' up there by yourself."

"It's . . . way worse than it looks from the ground," Keenan muttered as they boarded the tiny cage lift for the second floor deck. "But I learned something out there. Something you need to know. It's up to you if you wanna tell Jackie."

"What?"

The whine of the lift's motor almost drowned out Keenan's answer. "They've got a last-ditch plan, for if . . . if we lose. If she gets taken. It's really hard core."

"Tell me."

Keenan spoke slowly, every word an effort. He sounded utterly exhausted. "When Stuart gets over here, ask him about . . . the autoclave."

"The autoclave?" Dakota repeated. Their lift halted at the second floor. The boys disappeared through a door, and I couldn't hear them anymore.

I flopped down on the blanket and stretched out. I didn't know what an autoclave was, and at that point, I was past caring. I already knew about the reapers. All I really wanted was Dakota, and he wasn't there. My eyelids forced themselves closed. I told myself Dakota would finish his business upstairs. I'd hear him walk in. We'd hardly lose a minute of our magical night. Lulled by the hum of the fans, I succumbed to exhaustion.

Rhythmic alarm bells woke me from a deep, dreamless sleep. The sirens blared from all around us, making my heart pound. I lurched to a sitting position, bumping Dakota, who'd been sharing my blanket. He must have come back, found me asleep, and decided not to disturb me, not even for our last night together. Now it was too late.

I've never regretted anything more.

We threw off the blanket and scrambled to our feet. Orange emergency lights blinked on, outlining doorways and corridors. They cast the biosphere in a ruddy glow, like the ship was on fire. It set my stomach churning. Dakota pulled on a shirt, his face rigid.

"This is it," Keenan bellowed from the second floor deck. "Lock and load!"

Upstairs, kids' high, tense voices called out their own names, checking in as if for sentry duty. In a minute, their rapid footfalls raced down the spiral staircase.

"Oh my God," I whispered. "It's starting."

Silently, Dakota reached out and squeezed my hand.

The main elevator chimed its arrival. A pack of Center soldiers marched out in riot helmets and intimidating matte-black body armor. Two of them peeled off the group and headed right for me. It took me a second to recognize my reapers in their freaky new gear. One of them pointed at a wall camera. Someone on the other side cut off the alarm in mid-squawk, but emergency lights continued to blink from beside the speakers.

The gray-eyed man opened a duffel and pulled out a black, rubbery one-piece jumpsuit with weird segmented pads on the knees. Tall, black boots thudded to the grass at my feet. "Get dressed quick," he said. "We have less time than we thought. Bianca's forces are picking up speed as they approach."

I clutched the suit to my chest. "How much time?"

"Fifteen minutes. Maybe less."

"I was told I'd have two hours," I snapped.

"The Committee decided your time would be better spent resting until you were needed."

I swore.

The gray-eyed man and his muscular partner folded their arms and pointedly turned their backs to me.

Taking the hint, I stripped and wormed my way inside the rubbery black suit. I rolled to my knees and Dakota zipped it up in back for me. The jumpsuit fit tight across my chest, compressing my small breasts, but it stretched plenty well enough to breathe. I flexed, checking out the squishy armor on my knees and elbows.

"Hurry up and get your boots on," the burly reaper said. "We need to get you in position before the main force arrives. Scout species are already filtering in."

"Scout species?" Dakota asked. "What kind?"

"Our biologists can't identify them," the man answered. "It's a new kind of insect—apparently engineered by the nanobot artificial intelligence. By Bianca."

Dakota swallowed hard. His eyes went wide. "What species?"

"They appear to be . . . butterflies."

Dakota shrugged. He looked a little relieved.

"Not wasps," I muttered, lacing up the flexible, calf-length boots. "Good. Butterflies. I can handle that."

I stood up, leaving the torn astronaut uniform crumpled on the grass. No surprise, the boots were exactly my size, just like the suit.

"Wear these." The gray-eyed reaper handed me a pair of leather gloves and a black knit cap. "Doc Stuart sends his apologies. You should have had a helmet, but they don't make them small enough to fit you."

I only nodded, tugging on the cap.

The young soldier put a comforting hand on my shoulder. "Ready?"

I wasn't. Didn't think I'd ever be. Sweat trickled down my back. I looked my reaper right in the eye. "Yeah," I lied.

I clutched Dakota's hand with my gloved one. We began to march toward the door. Men fell into step around us. I suddenly stopped. "Wait. Where's Keenan?"

"Here." Keenan prowled out of the shadows. Orange emergency lights turned his tawny hair red. His catlike eyes reflected absent flames.

He reached out to me. A slight intake of breath betrayed my surprise. No bandage wrapped Keenan's injured hand. I turned his palm up. Ran my gloved thumb over his pale, perfect skin. Not even a scar remained.

Keenan's lip pulled back in a pained wince. "Level One nanites," he said. "Still hurt like a sonofabitch. Stuart said it was nowhere near the Level Three kind you got. I can't even imagine."

I knew Keenan hated nanites more than anything else in the world. Pox killed his family, same as mine. *He voluntarily took them into his body. Endured that. For me.*

"Thank you," I whispered. Images of black marbles filled my mind. My lower lip trembled. Transfixed by the sorrow in Keenan's eyes, I hardly noticed when Dakota's fingers slipped from mine.

Keenan pulled me into a rough hug. "You can't go out there like this, Jack," he hissed. "Lookin' like a scared rabbit. You do that, you're nothin' but bait. So man the fuck up."

"Right." I nodded, clenched my jaw and tried to get a grip.

With a slap on my armored back, Keenan pushed me away. "It's cool. Ash has the kids, see? They're all right."

My crew clustered near the main elevator. Paco huddled under Ash's arm, close to tears. Caleb glared at the Center soldiers. Marc just looked numb.

Across the dome, the cage lift opened. Joe stumped out, carrying a sleepy Tito, still wrapped in his blanket. A black-clad soldier prodded the old man in the back, hurrying him along. Joe stumbled on his wooden leg and nearly fell. Tito woke up and began to wail.

"Joe," I cried. He looked up, frightened eyes in a lined face. "Don't you dare push him," I snapped at the soldier, who ignored me.

Joe came down the gravel path, a long step and a short one. A long step and a short one. Tito screamed the whole way. As Joe limped past, Tito reached out his arms to me, his tiny, tear-streaked face framed by the pale blue blanket. I didn't hug my littlest boy. Didn't even speak to him. If I did, I knew I'd fall apart.

"We'll be fine, Jack. Focus on your job," Joe said. He joined the crew.

"All right, everyone. Positions," a soldier barked. "Let's do this."

Armed men surrounded my crew, pushing them toward the door. "Don't kick them out, not now," I howled. "It's cold outside. Dangerous. Bianca's army is almost here."

"Everybody out but the chosen colonists. The rocket launches today," a soldier said. He pressed a button for the elevator.

"Guys, get your coats on," I cried to my crew. "Don't forget your packs. Did you remember to take extra food?"

"Yes, Jack," Paco said patiently. He pulled on his grubby red jacket and put an arm around Marc's shoulders. Together, they followed Ash into the elevator.

My crew trooped in behind them, all except Dakota and Keenan. Ash caught my eye from his spot in back, against the wall. *"I love you,"* he mouthed.

"Ash, wait," I cried, surging toward him. Reapers caught me and held me back. The doors closed, and my crew was gone. I felt like I'd been punched in the stomach.

"Jack!" Keenan grabbed the padded shoulder of my suit and shook me. "This is not the time to lose it, okay? Not the time."

I gulped. Nodded.

The gray-eyed reaper looked at his watch. "Five minutes."

We boarded the next elevator and rode down in silence. I stood between Dakota and Keenan, holding their hands tight. The car bumped its landing. I let go of them both, squared my shoulders, and stepped out.

Chapter 21

Flash bulbs went off in my face. Nervous officials crowded the huge lobby. They all seemed to be talking at once. The sour tang of fear filled the stagnant air. Red-faced men started shouting questions the second they saw me. "How do you feel, Jackie?"

"Can you win this?"

"What's the plan?"

"How do you think she feels, moron?" Keenan snapped, straight-arming a pushy photographer out of my face. "Fuck off." Nobody obeyed him, but Keenan's hostility earned him a few seconds of fame. He blinked against an onslaught of flashbulbs, one hand up to block the blinding lights.

As my reapers towed me through the press of bodies, onlookers crowded around. People clapped and cheered for me, yelling out last-minute advice and encouragement. Women sobbed. One hooded man muttered death threats. I wanted to stop, just for a second, to tell them I understood. I didn't blame them. I'd win, or die trying. After all, I couldn't save myself without saving the Center, too. I never got the chance. Reapers strode rhythmically forward. Dakota and Keenan stuck close to me on either side, doing their best to fend off a multitude of grasping hands. We reached the airlock and stepped outside into the misty night. Cold air on my cheeks was a relief, but it quickly chilled the sweat that trickled between my breasts. I gazed up at the dark, foggy sky and shivered. Spotlights swept the clouds, searching for Bianca's spies. Tiny crystals of snow fell through the beams, glittered like jewels, and winked out.

More soldiers fell in around us. They quick-marched me across the crowded pavement as people scattered from our path. On our right, against the outer wall of the building, a group of Committee members in matching black coats and gold scarves stood beside an oven-sized box. Fat power cables trailed away from it. I resisted the tug on my arm long enough to get a good look. The wheel mounted on the door of the box was obviously made to hold tight against pressure. I'd seen something similar a long time ago, in another life. My mom had an oven like that in her lab, for sterilizing used petri dishes. The thing filled with superheated steam, like a giant pressure cooker. *Oh my God. That's the autoclave?*

I had a hunch it was for me.

With nanites in my system, will I die in there, or just burn and heal forever, until I lose my mind from the pain?

My thighs quivered, and I barely felt the ground beneath my feet. Long-legged soldiers hurried me toward the fence that enclosed the array. Something there had changed overnight. A new pen stood just inside the gate—a cage, really, with a sturdy wire roof over the top. To get to the array, we had to cross that pen and go out another gate on the other side. The nasty Committee woman keyed in the code on a lock box. With a rattle of chain, soldiers pulled open the gate. I walked in, along with the reapers, Keenan, and Dakota, leaving the crowd behind. My crew huddled inside the cage, half-hidden in the long shadow of the ship. Trapped.

"You cannot keep them here," I yelled to the soldiers, to the Committee, to anyone who would listen. "This was not our deal!"

Ash hurried over, with Tito bundled in his arms. "Steady, Jack. We were gonna wait for you anyway. Might as well wait here."

I couldn't scream in front of Tito and scare him, so I threw my arms around them both. Ash's warm lips pressed against mine. Flashbulbs splashed red light against my closed eyelids.

"Enough of this ridiculous behavior," snapped the hawk-nosed Committee woman. "Get her to the array this instant."

Guards pushed my crew aside. A tall, black-armored man grabbed my wrist in a painful grip. I let out a startled yelp, but he didn't seem to care. Strangers hemmed me in so I couldn't see my familiar reapers. That new soldier dragged me across the pen, walking too fast, so I had to run a little to keep up with his long strides. I twisted as he dragged me away, looking over my shoulder, trying to hold onto Dakota with my eyes.

The soldier shoved me through the inner gate and locked it, leaving me inside a giant funnel, made to route Bianca's army directly to me. I felt sick. The murmur of the crowd faded as I walked across the icy blacktop, swiveling my head, searching for Alanna. She wasn't there. I'd been counting on her, so that loss hit me hard. Another Committee betrayal, I figured. *Bastards.*

The gate squeaked again, and my reapers entered the kill zone. Keeping their distance, they split up, moving in opposite directions, until they had me trapped between them. The gray-eyed one caught me looking at him and gave me a reassuring nod. I nodded back once, then looked away. Obsessing over them wouldn't help.

Stuart met me by the ladder, without his protective suit on. He towed a little wheeled oxygen bottle behind him. Plastic tubes snaked up his nose. My eyes went wide. His body looked frail, even through his winter coat, and above the bright gold Committee scarf his cheeks were pale and sunken. Labored breaths wheezed from his chest.

I started toward him. "Are you okay?"

He warded me off with a sharp gesture. "There's no time to talk about me, Jacqueline. They're here." Stuart pointed up.

I gazed up, straining to focus through the storm, but I didn't see anything but snowflakes.

"Listen," Stuart hissed. "Listen!"

Granular snow hissed against my rubbery black suit. I folded my arms for warmth and quieted my anxious breath. A fluttering sound floated down on the wind. It brought back memories of long-ago summer evenings. Hide and seek games in our dark backyard. Miller moths around the porch light.

Moths?

Their metallic gray wings blended with the mist. By the time I picked out the first one, nine or ten more were already circling high above us. Not butterflies, like the man said, but moths. Each one was a thing of beauty, mottled with gleaming silver and as big as a man's hand. The Center's siren suddenly went off, making me cringe. I could barely hear my own voice over the earsplitting wail.

"Shut it off, shut it off," I yelled at Stuart. That high-pitched noise shot my nerves to hell.

Stuart nodded and began puffing away, back toward the gate, his oxygen tank leaving tire tracks in the new snow.

Moths? Why moths? I thought frantically. *They aren't scary. It must be some kind of advance guard. Meant to weaken us before the army arrives. Weaken us . . . by infecting people? But how? Moths can't bite.*

"Dakota!" I dashed back the way I came. "Look out for the moths. Moths!"

I doubt the crew heard me over the siren, but they saw me all right. Boys lined up along the fence, their bare fingers hooked through gaps in the chain-link. The first of the moths dipped down, swooping gracefully over their heads. I pointed up as I ran, screaming nonsense. A moth passed between the wires, silver wings fluttering, and dropped within Ash's reach before he spotted it.

Ash ducked. Just then the siren cut off, so the whole crowd heard him swear. He ripped his coat off and whipped it at the pox-moth. Its fragile body hit the pavement with a sound like breaking glass. Tito squatted beside it, slowly reaching for one shattered wing.

"Don't touch," Ash bellowed. He smacked the downed moth sideways with his jacket, sending it through the fence and right into a cluster of Committee members on the other side. Distinguished men scattered, squealing in panic. A couple of my kids giggled.

The hawk-nosed woman let out an outraged noise and stalked toward the pen. "You nasty, foul-mouthed thug," she screamed at Ash through the fence. "I'll have you know, there will be consequences!"

She kept on raving, but I wasn't listening anymore. High above, a moth folded its wings and fell like a dart from the sky, arcing forward as it neared the ground. My shouted warning came too late. The moth slammed into the Committee woman's ear, half burying itself inside. Its sharp-edged wings twisted, slashing flesh. Blood soaked the woman's gold scarf. She shrieked and went to her knees, pulling out shards of pox-moth with her fingers. Committee members turned and ran, sending the crowd into a stampede.

"She's taken," I cried. Nobody heard me over the sounds of screams and running feet.

Less than a minute later, the only people left were my crew, two reapers, and a grim line of soldiers who refused to abandon their posts. Stuart had disappeared. I paced the fence, trying to keep an eye on the fallen Committee woman and the sky all at once. Dakota organized our crew into a tight knot, with bigger boys standing guard on the outside and smaller ones toward the center. Tito fretted from under a blanket in the middle.

Behind me, the infected woman struggled to her feet. I whirled. The pox watched from behind her eyes. "Jacqueline. Come here, darling," she purred, reaching out to me with bloody fingers.

I shook my head, stumbling backward, even though there was a fence between us.

"You are . . . the only . . . safe harbor," the pox breathed. She pressed the stolen body against the fence, running her tongue along cold wire, seeking a taste of me. Red-painted nails grated against chain link. "You are mine, Jacqueline, like your mother before you."

"I am not," I spat. The thing about my mom—that was a low blow.

"I am in control here," the pox said. "You are necessary. I will have you. So bow to the inevitable." Bianca's cold, authoritative tone reminded me of the original occupant of that body. The way I saw it, those two bitches belonged together.

Bianca moved along the fence, making for the gate. I figured she probably had the key code, since the Committee woman had known it. Her hand reached the lock box. She began to peck at the numbered keys.

"Shoot her," I screamed. "Somebody shoot her!"

The burly reaper drew his pistol and lined up his shot. Everyone flinched when he pulled the trigger. The infected woman dropped. I backed off a step or two, riveted by the bullet wound between her eyes. A shimmer of silver already rimmed the bleeding hole, gathering itself into a red-tinged stream.

"Jacqueline, stay back, stay away from the body," Stuart gasped.

My jaw dropped when I saw him coming through the blowing snow. The old man had traded his oxygen tank for a flame thrower, probably the very same one Adam had pointed at me. Stuart trudged forward, laboring under the weight of the big fireproof jacket and the fuel tank on his back. He raised the nozzle and aimed it at the silver stream of nanobots flowing over the woman's broken glasses.

I scrambled to get out of the way, slipped on the ice, and crashed to hands and knees. Stuart let loose a blaze of fire. I pressed my forehead against icy pavement as the blast stung the skin on the back of my neck. I could have sworn I felt the little hairs there curling and going up in smoke. A thick, oily cloud passed overhead, carrying nauseating smells of spent fuel, burnt hair and cooking flesh. We all stared at the woman's charred corpse in shocked silence.

With a sound like a thousand whispering voices, more moths arrived. They swirled peacefully above me, a sight of infinite beauty. I let out a strangled scream of horror, hands slapping pavement in a frantic search for anything to use as a weapon.

"Stay down," Stuart yelled. The little old man stood over me, nozzle to the sky.

I curled up in a ball, arms wrapped around my ears. The fluttering cloud coalesced into one giant, single-minded organism and dived. Stuart lit them up. Burning moths lit their brothers on fire, becoming plumes of flame that scattered, drifting in glowing, red-gold flakes to the snow covered ground. Fallen insects crawled after me, wings on fire. I rolled away, staying low in case the doctor accidentally torched me too. The last pox-moth thrashed and died. I lay still, panting for air. In that moment, I felt the vibrations through my fingers.

Hoofbeats.

Dakota must have felt it too. "She's coming! Get up there, Jackie, get up there," he yelled, waving a wild arm at the array.

With a strangled cry, I pushed off the ground and sprinted for the ladder. Wind swirled snow around the array, sending man-sized whirlwinds spiraling off into the night. Over the storm came the sound of Bianca's army, a low collective groan and the footfalls of thousands of galloping animals. Ravens jetted through the blizzard, passed within feet of my head, and disappeared.

Caught up in my terror, I couldn't worry about the icy ladder. Grippy gloves and padded knees made all the difference, so I climbed fast. I made it over the level section of the bent ladder and started upward again. The geese caught me there. The sound of their wings got lost in the storm, so the first I knew of them was when the leading edge of a wing hit me in the temple, nearly knocking me off the ladder. Pain lanced through my head. Flapping and spinning, the heavy body of an injured Canada goose careened toward the ground. Hot blood ran into my eye. I flattened myself against the ladder and clung while three more bird bodies slammed into mine.

Reaching up with a glove, I wiped blood off my newly healed skin. *Am I already infected?* I felt the same, still me, but trembling so hard I didn't think I could climb. The starlings changed my mind about that. Their angry, high-pitched cries gave them away as they swept in, circling the array, no doubt looking for me. I made it another twenty feet up before they hit. This time I was ready. I hooked one arm through the ladder, hid my face in the crook of my elbow, and protected the back of my neck with the other hand. Sharp beaks ripped at my tough suit, biting at my legs, my hat, my hair. Bianca threw the whole flock at me, spending their lives in a storm of feathers, soft little bodies falling all around. Some struck the catwalk above, broke wings, and dragged themselves after me in pathetic desperation. I felt a tremendous wave of sympathy for the flock, taken by Bianca and wasted in her tantrum.

Alone in the dark, surrounded by death, my compassion turned to fury. *Bianca called them her children. But they aren't precious to her. She doesn't love them. I do.*

I gripped the icy ladder and began to climb again. A faint odor blew on the wind, moist and rank, like a feedlot or a zoo. The hoofbeats grew louder. I clung to the array as Bianca's army pounded in. Their hot breath sent clouds of steam into the night air. Tossing heads appeared and disappeared through the fog—horned cattle, elk, deer, bear, horses, moose, dogs, and countless smaller creatures who somehow avoided being crushed by the churning hooves. Low, rumbling moans filled the air.

Maybe they smelled me. Maybe the birds told them I was there. Somehow, they knew. The herd thundered down the funnel, veered left, and circled the array, their runny noses and possessed eyes aimed up at me. More animals pressed in until they ran shoulder to shoulder, covering every square inch of pavement in a sickening vortex of diseased flesh. I scrambled up the ladder as fast as I could.

The pod came within reach, but it didn't feel like much of a refuge anymore. I swung onto the catwalk instead, buckled on a harness, and clipped to an overhead safety line. *I should keep moving, so the birds don't surround me.* Standing still with wind flowing under my boots, I strained my senses. No flutter of wings came my way, no sign of the enemy but the huffing breaths of the herd below. *No more birds? Didn't she bring some kind of creatures that can climb?*

Then the horrible truth dawned on me. *People can climb.* Bianca had hordes of infected humans. They had to be on their way, following behind the faster four-legged animals. When the poxy humans arrived, they'd swarm over the array. Cleverly block my escape routes. And take me.

My reapers felt so far away.

Keep moving. Taking confidence from my safety line, I bounded down a narrow catwalk, with no real destination in mind. A dark figure suddenly appeared out of the fog. I dodged. My boot slipped on the icy metal. Arms waving, I lost my balance and fell, screaming, into the air. The harness caught me with a spine-twisting jerk. I hung, dangling like a worm on a hook, with nothing in reach to grab.

"Swing," Alanna shouted. "Get yourself swinging."

My innards melted in relief at the sight of her ghastly face, sagging folds of Jackie-skin and all. *Alanna. It's only Alanna.* I kicked my legs, feebly at first, gaining strength as I got moving. She grabbed my line for a final assist, and I snagged a support strut.

I crawled onto the catwalk.

"Get up, get up!" Alanna tugged on my harness. "Come on. We are so fucked. Doc Stuart thought sure the nanobots would attack in construct form, but they're staying in their host bodies. We've got no weapons up here but UV lights, and those are useless." She hauled me to my feet. "Jackie, what are we going to do?"

I didn't want to admit that I had no clue. "Keep moving. Don't let 'em trap us."

Alanna led the way across the catwalk, not even pausing at the wide spot where the giant UV spotlight was mounted on the rail.

"We might as well leave the lights off," Alanna whispered over her shoulder. "The nanobots are safe inside their hosts. Lights will only pinpoint our position."

"Won't matter. I bet the birds know exactly where we are." I gazed nervously into the shadows. "Why do you think she stopped sending them?"

Alanna shrugged and kept going. The wind died down to a light breeze, and the air began to clear. I felt exposed without a screen of thickly falling snow to hide behind. From the dark sky around the array came the harsh cries of ravens. *They see us now.*

As if she heard my thought, Alanna pressed herself against a pillar and peeked out. The black birds around us were invisible in the dark. "I came out here earlier than I was supposed to," she murmured. "Stuart got me past the guards. I rigged some lines."

"For getting in the docking port, you mean?"

Alanna's earnest nod almost pissed me off. *She's plotting her escape.*

Leaving me to deal with this mess alone. But I couldn't blame her. If it was my crew on board, I'd do exactly that, in a heartbeat. *Must be nice. So long, suckers. We're out of here.*

"Adam pinged me this morning," Alanna whispered. "They're going to launch the second they're ready. Probably at dawn."

"Fine. Whatever."

"You don't get it, Jackie. When that rocket goes up, anyone on the array will be incinerated. Be on board by then, or be gone. You can't just sit up here."

"The Committee never told me that," I whispered. *Not even Stuart.*

"Why do you think they set up the array where they did?" Alanna asked acidly.

Figures.

The infected herd still milled below us, gradually slowing their crazed gallop to an agitated, high stepping trot. A giant black bull pointed his nose up, sniffed loudly, and snorted. He smelled me for sure.

We moved on, across the next narrow catwalk, and paused at a landing where another useless UV light hung from the rail. I leaned out and looked down, trying to see my crew. An impact suddenly rocked the array, almost jolting the railing from my grip. I let out a shriek.

Alanna snatched me away from the edge. "Something big just rammed us."

We crouched in the center of the landing and stared in sick fascination as the herd flowed backward, into the wide part of the funnel, like a tide going out to sea. Heads lowered, the animals paced backward, hooves stepping in perfect unison. A spotlight played over Bianca's army, and eerie red eyes reflected it back. Their collective intake of breath sounded like wind through trees. The herd charged. A colossal wave of flesh, horn, and bone galloped toward us.

Chapter 22

Bulls, grizzly bears, and huge wild bison slammed into the central pillar that supported the array. It sounded like a train wreck when they hit. Some of the bolts ripped free. The whole array lurched, and part of the conical frame sagged. Alanna and I both screamed. Animals in front went down under the weight of those behind, slender legs snapping with audible cracks. Bianca forced more animal bodies through the narrow end of the funnel and sent them against the fence. With a shriek of broken metal, chain link stretched, separated, and collapsed under their weight. Horned cattle flipped over the cage that held my crew and ground it sideways against the pavement. Boys shouted in the dark. After that, I didn't hear them anymore. I couldn't see what happened to them.

"Dakota?" I shouted. "Dakota! Keenan! Are you guys all right?" No one answered.

Automatic gunfire erupted from the perimeter.

"Soldiers are gunning down the herd," Alanna cried.

"Shit!" I yelled. Bullet holes would let out the pox construct, way faster than Bianca could release it on her own. Near-constant gunfire rocked the night, and deeper booms too, some kind of heavy artillery I'd never heard before. Those I felt in my bones. I covered my ears, but that didn't block out the explosions and the agonized bellows of dying livestock. In the aftermath, spotlights hovered over any animal that moved, no matter how small. Snipers picked them off.

"Lights, we need to get to the lights," I gasped, crawling across the icy platform. It wasn't level anymore. Gravity threatened to pull me into a slide. I worked my way downslope anyway, heading for the UV spotlight that now hung crazily from a bent railing.

"Wait," Alanna barked. She tugged on my safety line, testing it. The clip fell from above. Its long, nylon line pooled between us.

I picked up the carabineer, feeling kind of nauseous over that little fuckup, and clipped on to a different overhead cable, not knowing if it would hold or not. I jerked the line once. It seemed okay. Gloved fingers gripping cold metal mesh, I let myself slide toward the edge of the busted platform. It sagged under my weight, getting steeper. "Ah, ah, ah," I cried, picking up speed.

My left hand snagged the rail. With a surge of triumph, I hooked a leg around a post and grabbed the plastic handles of the UV light. That would hold me, unless the whole platform came down. I tried not to think about it. “Alanna! Can you take a zipline, get over to the next light?”

She peered into the dark. “I think so. The platform closest to the ship looks intact.”

“Perfect. Stay near the docking port if you can.” I lowered my voice. “Remember, Bianca might not know about the UV lights, so don’t switch ’em on ’til you can get her good. Go!”

Alanna clipped on and jumped off. She soared away into the night. Without her, everything was scarier. The last groans of the herd died out. Things got way too quiet. Even the reapers had disappeared. The silence was broken by occasional pops of gunfire, whenever Center snipers spotted a survivor. Cold wind swirled the smell of death around the array, and I shivered. I tried not to feel sorry for the animals. Failed. Switched to worrying about my crew instead. I leaned out as far as I dared, tracking the long beams of the spotlights as they skimmed the ground. Light brought heaps of slaughtered animals into gruesome color, but no human forms lay among them. No young voices called out from the crushed remains of the cage.

Maybe Dakota’s keeping ’em quiet. They could be sneaking off right now. They’ve got to be.

The sweeping beam of a searchlight caught the top of a round head peering over the back of a fallen elk. *A human!* I tensed, ready for the sound of gunfire, but apparently nobody saw him but me. The searchlight moved on, leaving the mysterious person in darkness. I sucked in a breath to shout out, but paranoia stopped me. *What if that’s Dakota? I could get him shot.*

The cloud cover thinned, and stars began to peek through. The searchlight moved back and forth across the ground, left and right and left again, in a hypnotic rhythm. *Too predictable. I’d yell at my sentries for doing stupid shit like that.* My eye was drawn, not to the stripes of light, but to the dark sections between. *Did someone move down there? Did he freeze just before the light touched him?*

With gargled cries, a group of poxy humans rose from hiding and ran for the ladder. The searchlight jumped to them. Their shambling strides told me they’d been infected a long time ago, ridden nearly to death. They wouldn’t live much longer in any case. Hidden gunmen mowed the infected men down. A few seconds later, a second group arose in another place. The grisly scene repeated itself until the base of the ladder gleamed with free nanobots.

Just like Bianca intended.

I pointed the UV light at them. My fingers itched to switch it on. I made myself wait. Burning up pox wouldn't help if Bianca was left alive. It was her I wanted. Only her.

I turned away from the searchlight and stared into the darkness behind me. Tiny metallic creaks and huffs of breath came from the pillars that held up the array. A chill crawled up my spine.

Alanna's panicked shout came from across the array. "Climbers! Climbers on the ladders!"

Center soldiers began to shoot them down. Loose nanobots flowed across the ground, shining silver wherever spotlights touched them. The unmistakable rotten yeast scent of pox construct tainted the winter air.

Across the littered battlefield, a valiant plume of flame lit the night. "Die, Biancaaaa!" A coughing fit cut short Stuart's war cry.

The little doctor surged forward, burning enemies from his path, but he stumbled over the legs of a dead cow and fell. The flame died out. I leaned forward, eyes riveted to the spot where he disappeared. After a nerve-wracking moment of darkness, his flame blazed to life again. Stuart marched on, small but mighty, lit by starlight and fire.

"Whoohoo!" I threw my head back and cheered. From across the array, Alanna's victorious shout joined mine.

Starting at the horizon, stars winked out as a band of blackness spread slowly up the night sky. A wet squishing sound, horribly familiar, rose with it. A spotlight caught the oozing yellow-white tissue and tracked it upward, thirty feet into the air, then fifty. An enormous false-flesh snake construct loomed over Stuart. The construct swayed forward and back, a cobra ready to strike.

Stuart's flame looked like a spark in comparison. He knelt and aimed it up. I pivoted the big UV spotlight into position, flicked it on, and let Bianca have it. Alanna's beam came to life, intersecting mine. Nasty yellow tissue sizzled and popped wherever the pale purple ultraviolet light touched it. Stuart burned at the base of the construct, charring it faster than it could heal. As Center soldiers cheered us on, Alanna and I drilled a blackened hole right through the head of the snake.

Which didn't slow it down at all.

Under the searchlights, the hole seemed to gaze down on us, a single, horrible eye. I moved my beam down, holding it over charred sections of the construct. I'd found a weak spot. The snake-thing shuddered in unmistakable pain.

"Got you now, bitch," I muttered.

The snake whipped and thrashed, making it hard to burn through any one spot. Following it with the light, I leaned crazily from side to side, forward and back, clutching the plastic handles. The construct reared up and shook as burned chunks of false-flesh rained down around it. It thinned and flattened, so our glowing purple beams easily tore through the fragile tissue.

"Yes," I shouted, punching the air.

Stuart began to run. Then I realized our mistake.

The giant sheet of suffocating flesh tipped forward, rippling and billowing. As it fell, it pushed a wave of humid, stinking air over me. The tissue landed with a heavy, wet flump. Stuart's tiny light went out. I held my breath. A minute passed, then two. Spotlights played back and forth over the liquefying mass. Nothing struggled beneath it. The little doctor was gone.

Alanna's scream tore through the air. She began to sob.

Faint squelching sounds came from behind me. I whipped the light around as far as it would go, which wasn't far enough. In the faint glow, tens of thousands of thin, whiplike tendrils appeared, coiling up the metal frame of the array. Their pointy tips waved in the air, sniffing for me. Every last one of them came up behind the spotlight, where they couldn't be burned. Bianca had been paying attention.

I sprang to my feet, cursing. *That snake was one hell of a distraction, and I fell for it.*

"Alanna, we have to risk it," I called. "Climb down and hit the button for the Bomb."

She didn't answer. I couldn't tell if she heard me or not. Maybe she was already slipping down a ladder, sneaking between rising tubes of yellow-white flesh. I almost hoped she wasn't. If Alanna tripped Stuart's emergency button, every UV light would blast at once, and then go out. We'd be trapped for three long minutes in utter darkness.

Tendrils spiraled toward me across slick metal mesh, making me forget everything else. I shuffled backward, eyes wide. Coils of false flesh pushed me right to the edge of the sloping platform. Off to my left, beyond the mangled guard rail, was nothing but open air. I clung to the railing and backed around the perimeter of the platform, closer to the catwalk and escape. *Almost there.* Then my safety line snagged on something overhead.

I jerked on the line a couple of times, but that didn't free it. Yellow-white roots grew closer, tempting me to stomp on them. I resisted the urge. That might be exactly what Bianca wanted me to do. Under the rubbery suit, sweat rolled down my back. The safety line stretched taut. I panicked and unclipped it. Arms out to the sides for balance, I walked onto the icy catwalk. Tendrils of construct whispered after me. It took all my self-control not to run.

I reached the zipline as the first thread wrapped around my boot. There was no way to test the line and make sure it wasn't broken, no time.

Fingers fumbling in my haste, I clipped on and leaped. For one heart-stopping moment, I was in freefall. Then my weight hit the harness with a jerk. I flew through black sky. Cold wind froze my face and leaked through gaps around my goggles, making my eyes water. Something tickled my ankle. A broken tendril writhed around my foot, feeling for a way through the tough suit.

I squealed, kicking like crazy, trying to shake it loose. Part of the nasty thing broke off and fell, but a wormy strip clung to the laces of my boot. In seconds, the platform appeared, dull gray under starlight.

I skidded to a landing, somersaulted once, and came up on my feet. An intact UV light hung on the rail. A quick blast incinerated the fragments of construct that still clung to my boot. I lifted each foot, bathing every surface in cleansing purple light. Blackened soot drifted away on the wind. No tendrils had made it to the top yet, not on this side of the array, but every tiny sound made me jump. *They'll be here soon, and then what? What happens when they cover the whole array?*

A thin strip of indigo glowed on the eastern horizon. Bianca was running out of time. Sunshine wouldn't do the naked nanobots any good. I'd have the same problem when the rocket launched. We could both fry together.

Behind the platform, glaring electric lights reflected off the enormous rocket. This close, the ship took up half the sky. A dark, round hole showed on the side. *The docking port is open.* I swiveled my head, searching for Alanna. I'd sent her down the ladder. If she didn't make it on board, it would be my fault. "Alanna, the docking port's open," I shouted. "Get up here."

A pod tipped above. Her feminine outline showed up against the white-painted rocket. Oddly, she wasn't moving. Wasn't trying to get to the port. Hadn't I watched her climb down? How had she gotten above me?

"Alanna? Alanna! It's time. You've got to go." She didn't answer. "What's wrong? Are you hurt?" I unclipped the zipline, grabbed the ice-slicked sides of the ladder and started climbing.

The cables she'd strung hung ready, a giant sling between two pylons, with a loop-swing below. *It ought to work, if she'd get her ass over there. How long 'til Adam gives up on her and closes the door?*

"Hey!" No answer, but her head turned, just a little. She saw me coming, I was certain of it.

Arms burning with the effort, I pulled myself onto the catwalk. Alanna didn't even bother to offer me a hand up.

"What the fuck—" I began.

Her head turned. I wasn't five feet away. And the woman in the pod wasn't Alanna.

"M-Mom?"

My mother looked different, older and smaller than I remembered, fragile and worn. Her dark, wavy hair had gone frizzy and gray. But she recognized me. Her laugh lines crinkled, and my heart leaped.

"Jackie, thank God you're all right," she said. "Oh, how you've grown. My little girl, all grown up."

"Mom? What are you doing up here?" I tipped my head, peering at her eyes. She sat in shadow, so I couldn't tell if she was infected or not. "I thought you were dead."

"Come here, sweetie, and I'll tell you everything. I know where Daddy is. We're going to live together again, as a family."

I scrubbed my smeared goggles with gloved knuckles. Slowly, I crouched down, trying to look into my mother's eyes without getting too close. Shadows hooded them.

"I hear you've adopted some little boys," my mother said. "I'm so proud of you for that. They can come home with us, and be your brothers. Daddy and I will help you take care of them."

That wasn't anything like Bianca's cold, reserved tone. *Could this really be Mom? Uninfected? Then how'd she get up on the array? Who brought her here?*

It didn't add up. I was suspicious as hell. Desperate to get a look at her eyes, I took a trembling step closer. Tendrils grew up from beneath the pod, coiling around pillars. They stretched closer to her, threatening her.

My mother gazed at me, love shining from her eyes. "Oh, my darling girl, I've looked for you for so long," she whispered.

Yellowish tentacles crawled closer, mere feet from her thin arms. My mother saw them and her small fingers reached out for mine. A powerful, protective impulse rose up inside me. I wanted to step forward, to offer a helping hand, but in that instant Alanna set off the Bomb. Every lamp on the array lit up at once, turning the whites of my mother's eyes a beautiful, alien shade of lilac. The blinding flash revealed a spider's web of construct engulfing the array.

Bianca's false flesh blackened and burned. Sizzling coils slipped limply from the scaffold to splat against pavement below. Sluggish, oily smoke rose through the air, carrying the nauseating odor of rotten yeast. All around us, UV lamps slowly brightened and began to overload. Their low electric hum built until I could feel it in my teeth. As pox died, my mother screamed, over and over, like a witch being burned at the stake. When she covered her face with both hands and wept, that simple, human gesture nearly broke my heart.

A scorched tentacle as thick as my thigh slid off the scaffold above my head and fell, smoking, to break in half on a horizontal beam below. The thing must have been seconds from wrapping around my neck, and I never saw it coming. That frightened me into moving. I hadn't taken two steps when every single light at the Center went out. Every streetlight, every window, every spotlight on the rocket died. Arms outstretched, I balanced on a six-inch beam over empty space, completely blind.

My mother whispered from the dark. "Jacqueline. Jacqueline. Help me."

Her voice made my skin crawl. Without my mom's familiar face distracting me, tearing at my heart, the undertone in her voice was unmistakable. *Bianca.*

Belated panic made my body shake. *I nearly let her grab me. Stupid, stupid!*

A rhythmic squeak told me the pod was tipping on its hinges. My mother must have climbed out. She was coming for me, moving fearlessly over the slippery steel beam. I held my breath and took a silent step backward. Faint footsteps followed me. Heart racing, I slid back another few inches. My shoulder blades touched a mess of sagging steel cable behind me. I seized it and leaped off the catwalk. My mother's grasping fingers slipped off my arm.

Tangled cables tore free. Heavy, silver coils fell from above, whipping my shoulders and the back of my head. Gritting my teeth against the pain, I clung on, the sticky pads on the palms on my gloves gripped tight around slippery steel. Twice the cables snagged above me, and twice they let go, dropping me a few feet with sudden jerks. I thought the whole snarled mess was going down, but something caught in the dark above me. I swung, exposed and helpless. Wind blew gritty ash across my cheeks.

As my eyes adjusted, the shadowy outline of the array appeared against the sky. The eastern horizon brightened. My exhausted arms began to give up, and steel cable slid through my hands. When I reached the broken end, I'd fall.

Someone above tugged on the line, starting me into a gentle sway, just like Alanna had. Was it her? On the third pass I glided close enough to a beam to grab it. Trembling, I pulled myself onto the bent, funnel-shaped frame of the array and crouched there. My mother knelt on the horizontal beam just above me. She had pulled me in, not Alanna.

My mother saved me. That means she's not infected. Bianca wouldn't help me, would she?

Shock made me feel weak. I made it up the nearest ladder to the catwalk above, where my mother waited near the empty pod. I wasn't twenty feet from her when Alanna appeared out of nowhere, grabbed me by the back of my collar, and yanked me back.

"Jackie, Jackie, no! That's not her."

I slapped Alanna's hand off. "Yes it is. She saved me."

"Because you're a primary host," Alanna muttered darkly.

"No, I talked to her, she doesn't sound at all like Bianca. Talk to her yourself. Mom, this is my friend Alanna."

My mom came toward us, but she didn't smile. Didn't recite the typical welcoming lines to my friend. I had a sinking feeling about that. Mother was always big on manners.

Alanna pulled off a glove, reached up, and ripped at her own face with her fingernails. A huge, bloody swath of Jackie-skin tore off. I winced as she threw the gob of skin onto the cold plastic rim of the pod, where it stuck.

My mother instantly lost interest in me. She hunched over the bloody skin, inhaling deeply. "Jackie, thank God you're all right," she cooed to the skin-gob, her sweet voice filled with all the love I remembered. A soft smile lit her face. "Oh, how you've grown. My little girl, all grown up."

I could have vomited. Alanna shot me a horrified look. She tugged on my jacket again. I moved backward, one deliberate step at a time, trying not to attract attention.

My mother didn't even glance up. "I know where Daddy is. We're going to live together again, as a family," she told the skin-gob.

Alanna and I backed down the catwalk. She took to the ladder first. I couldn't pry my eyes off what was left of my mom. I'd been so sure she was dead, but this was worse.

"Come on, Jackie," Alanna hissed from below.

I knelt and let my legs dangle off the catwalk, feeling for the rungs of the ladder with my feet.

"I hear you've adopted some . . . little . . . boys?" my mother said haltingly. Her voice trailed off into a confused-sounding question. The skin-gob had crisped and shriveled in the cold, dry air. She tilted her head and stared down at it with a perplexed look. Apparently Bianca's processing power was spread kind of thin, with the war and all. Her people weren't usually near that slow.

I tried to ignore her, ignore the pain in my heart, the awful, rekindled sense of loss, and focus on reaching back for the slippery ladder. With no safety line, that first step off the catwalk was a bitch. Sparrows fluttered in all around us, swirling around my pox-mother, landing all over her. She suddenly leaped into the pod, making it tip wildly. The flock of birds exploded in all directions.

"Adopted some boys, have you?" my mom snapped, in a new, aggressive tone. "Boys like this one?"

I looked up from the ladder and locked eyes with Bianca herself. A cold chill hit me in the middle of my chest. The pox-boss had jumped into my mother's body. Bianca bent, and from the space by her feet, she pulled out what looked like a big toy doll.

When my mind made sense of the picture, I let out an agonized scream. "Tito!"

Pale tendrils of pox construct supported Tito's back and head, holding his little body rigid. He saw me and began to cry, struggling to free himself from the ropy strands. Bianca stood in the tippy pod, riding the waves with perfect balance. It took me a second to see that tendrils had attached themselves to her back too. Under the pod, a million new tentacles rose up. Hissing and whispering, their disgusting off-white tips stroked her back, her face, her hair. She smiled and held out her hands to them, letting them lick her fingers.

In slow motion, I climbed back onto the catwalk. "Okay, Bianca. You win. Let him go. Get him safely to the ground, and I'll let you take me."

I didn't mean it for a second. Somehow, I'd grab Tito and make a break for it. I just wasn't sure how.

"You want him, come get him." False-flesh tendrils lifted the toddler and abruptly dumped him on the catwalk, two hundred feet above the ground.

Tito clutched the side of the swaying pod as the tentacles withdrew. He looked down, seemed to register how high up he was, and sobbed. "Jack, Jack!"

He didn't sound infected, but how could I be sure? "Stand still, Tito," I ordered, my voice tight with tension. "You're way up high. Hang on, don't fall."

Bianca made no move to leave the pod. She watched me with a satisfied smirk on her face. Tito was well inside her reach. If I tried to grab him, she'd get me for sure. The sky continued to brighten. Yellow warning lights began to flash on the rocket's russet-painted scaffold.

"In a few minutes, we're all going to burn," I told her.

"Of course. When the rocket launches," she said evenly. "Then I'll have you."

"There won't be anything left to have," I snapped.

"Enough for my purposes." Bianca laughed, a high, grating sound.

Poxy ravens fluttered in and landed on the array, all around my mother's stolen body. Bianca put out a hand, and one of the big, black birds hopped onto her wrist. *That's her ride out.* "All I need is a few cells. A little DNA, and I can regenerate you."

"No. You're lying." I mouthed the words. No sound came out.

"Jackie?" Alanna called. Her voice sounded far away.

"Go! Just go," I yelled.

From a faraway platform, a tiny gleam of light reflected off the scope of a rifle. *Oh my God. Reapers.* Yellow lights flashed on the scaffold. The reapers were about to fry too, right along with me. We were all out of time.

I pulled myself up onto the slippery catwalk and stood there, trembling with indecision. *They'll shoot me down, throw me in the autoclave. But Tito, what will happen to Tito?*

I leaned forward, bent my knees and sprang. I got Tito by the arm, jerked him off his feet, and swung his little body around behind me. Tito's feet slid on the icy beam. His weight hung heavily from my hand, unbalancing me. My pox-mother lurched from the pod and came after us, silver-tipped nails out. I screamed, backed up, and stumbled into my little boy.

A feral howl came from up high. Keenan dropped from above, falling free through the air, with no safety line. He grabbed a horizontal bar. Swung both feet hard at Bianca's chest. And knocked her off the catwalk.

Yellowish tentacles pressed close to one another, catching her, supporting her weight.

More tendrils hissed, reaching for Keenan's dangling legs. With a fluid motion, Bianca spun around on her sea anemone bed and grabbed at him. Tito and I both screamed. Keenan jerked his feet up and climbed higher.

"Tito, move," I hissed. I scooted backwards on the catwalk, pushing the scared three-year-old along. He refused to walk backward on the narrow beam, so I had to lift him. His wiggling unbalanced me. My free arm wind-milled, and I almost fell.

Keenan's arm arced over his head. His knife flew, flipped once, and buried itself in the base of my mother's throat. My mom fell backward against the bed of tentacles, blood spurting. I sobbed like a child as I lost her all over again. Ravens flapped madly around her face, so I couldn't see her anymore. I backed farther along the icy catwalk, still clutching the baby, my eyes blurred with tears. The rocket's yellow warning lights turned red. People shouted from somewhere below, but I didn't care.

A low, oiled double click of a pump-action shotgun sent a jolt of fear up my spine. I knew that sound well. I froze against a pillar, holding Tito tight against my body. The gray-eyed reaper had me in his sights. At twenty feet away, he couldn't miss. The first rays of morning sun lit his face, making him look so young. He pressed his lips together in a silent apology.

Poxy ravens walked on my mother's dead body. Bianca strutted among them, croaking her laughter through a pointed beak. Pale tentacles loosened, and Mom's corpse began to slip through. A siren wailed its final warning. The jaws of the scaffold rolled open. Takeoff would be any second now. We were all going to burn.

The reaper tightened his grip on the shotgun.

"Not yet, please," I whispered through dry lips, though I knew it was time. I shifted Tito to protect him with my body, thinking about what would happen to him . . . after.

The reaper abruptly swung the muzzle left and pulled the trigger on the ravens instead. Black feathers vaporized in a cloud of blood. "Go, Jackie, go," he bellowed, chambering another round. He pulled the trigger again.

Crazy Keenan dropped from his perch, wrapped his arms around me and Tito, and deliberately dragged us both off the catwalk. We all three fell, screaming.

Chapter 23

A net caught us in midair. I cried out. Harsh nylon cord tore at my face. Keenan's bony hip ground against mine as the edges of the yellow net rose, rolling us together. Tito struggled beneath me, trapped between my body and the tough mesh. Some hidden mechanism inside the open docking port whirred, pulling us in. We struck the side of the rocket with sickening force. Keenan yelped. My shoulder crunched, then healed in a blaze of pain. Tito grunted and fought, trying to tear free.

The net slid up the side of the rocket and pulled our tangled bodies over the rubbery edge of the vacuum seal. With a hydraulic hum, the winch tugged us another ten feet or so across smooth, cold floor. Rolled up in the net like that, I couldn't see much more.

Adam's amplified voice blasted through speakers. "Clear the docking port. Clear the port for liftoff."

Kicking and thrashing, we loosened the drawstring at the top of the net and crawled out. The round automatic door was already rolling closed, but our cable was in the way.

"It won't seal. All our air will leak out," I gasped. Hand over hand, I pulled on the cable, scrambling madly for the big metal clip on the end. The damn thing was made for a man's strong hands. I couldn't open it.

Keenan dumped Tito out of the net, shouldered past me, and threw the whole thing out, cable and all. As the giant, round door rolled closed, I got a glimpse of the gray-eyed reaper on top of the array. In a minute he'd die, and he must have known it. He could've tried to run, but he probably wouldn't have made it. So he stayed at his post, blasting poxy ravens with a shotgun. I carried his sacrifice like a heavy weight in my chest, and it humbled me.

Adam's amplified voice came through the speakers, loud enough to hurt my ears. "All systems clear. Prepare for liftoff."

"I can't believe that douchebag is fucking flying this thing," Keenan said. "That net was his doing, too. Hurt like a motherf—"

A roar filled the air, and the whole ship began to vibrate. "Prepare for liftoff? How?" I asked, nervously circling the dock. The round metallic doors to the interior of the ship were sealed. Keenan and I exchanged tense shrugs. No reclining astronaut chairs for us.

The ship surged up. “It’s moving,” I cried. Unbelievable force drove me to my knees.

“Jackie, get down,” Keenan exclaimed.

I didn’t have much choice. I ended up flat on my back on the floor, holding Tito on my lap, with Keenan lying beside me, squeezing me way too hard around the waist. Tito wailed and crunched his miniature stomach muscles, trying to sit up. In a minute the back of his small, dark head collapsed to my chest. He laid still, whimpering.

As my mammoth adrenaline rush subsided, I started to shake. Keenan slid a hand under my head and pulled me onto his shoulder. We roared into the sky, leaving Dakota, leaving everyone. At least we had Tito. That would have to be miracle enough. I hid my face in Keenan’s tangled hair and refused to cry.

After a while the g-force lessened. Our bodies lightened. “Whoa,” I squealed as I floated off the floor.

Keenan laughed—the first pure, delighted sound I’d heard him make in years. He looped an arm through a handhold, and we played airplane with Tito, holding him around the middle and flying him between us. We all giggled at how funny the others looked with floating hair. After a while Tito got tired, so Keenan rigged him a hammock out of the Velcro straps on the wall. The kid actually fell asleep like that, floating with his straight, black hair fluffed around his head.

Keenan and I played some, flying and spinning, but we were both worn out. After a while, we linked arms and floated together, resting our aching muscles.

“Jackie, we gotta count this one as a win,” Keenan said. “We got away. We saved Tito. The crew—”

“Don’t say it, please don’t.”

“No, I was gonna say, I think they got away too. After our cage got bashed, a bunch of soldiers were taken by the pox. They marched in and stole Tito from us. That’s when I climbed the array. Soon as I could, Jack. Soon as I could. I had to leave the crew to do it, but . . . it wasn’t even a choice.” He pulled me close and kissed me once on the forehead. Our eyes met. Instead of the angry, pinpoint pupils I was used to, his gaze was soft, with glowing rings of gold around huge, dark pupils. “From up there, I could see the crew. Dakota was gettin’ ’em out.”

“Dakota.” I breathed a lifetime of longing into that one word.

“He had to choose the crew over you, Jack. He had to, once you made him Chief.”

I knew it was true. Once he became Chief, Dakota changed. His attention was split, and responsibility weighed him down. He became more like me. And I tied it by making him swear that oath.

"Tell me they're back at the diner right now, Keenan," I whispered. "Make me believe it."

"They're safe. I can feel it, right here." Keenan guided my hand gently to his heart.

I spread my fingers. Keenan's heart beat under my hand, slow and strong. "We'll never see Dakota and Ash again," I said softly. "Or the other boys."

"Never say never. We're goin' into space. We'll get us some kickass ray guns and come on back."

I doubted the space colonists had much need for ray guns. Instead, they probably had shitloads of greenhouse supplies. I didn't say that out loud. Keenan needed his dream, like I needed mine. I leaned against his shoulder, closed my eyes, and floated, picturing my boys stretched out on the red vinyl benches of the diner, their bellies full of good canned food.

"I know you miss the crew. I do too. But it's just you and me now, Jack," Keenan whispered. He wrapped a hand around my waist and pulled me a little closer.

I saw the way he looked at me. Couldn't blame him. He'd earned that right. But my heart still ached for Dakota, and it didn't feel like it would ever stop. I tried to remember that Keenan had lost crew too. He must have been hurting. He just hid his feelings better than I did. *Either that, or he just got what he always wanted.*

I didn't know, and it didn't matter. I looked over the feral, wounded boy across from me. Somehow, despite everything, he was still capable of love. *Without Keenan, Bianca would be wearing my face right now.* Gratitude filled my heart, and it pushed out some of the pain.

I put my hands on Keenan's shoulders, and the movement started us into a slow spin, so the room seemed to rotate around us. "I gotta tell ya," I said. "That jump you made at Bianca was epic. Two hundred feet up. No tether or nothin'."

Keenan tilted his head and smiled. "Thanks, babe. Sorry 'bout your mom."

My lower lip trembled a little. "I know. But she wasn't my mother. Not really."

"Yeah. Hang onto that, okay? Hang onto that." Keenan hugged me, and something inside me let go. It took me a second to figure out what had changed.

For the first time in five years, I felt safe.

"Y'know, Keenan," I murmured tiredly. "You're the bravest guy I know. It's hard to believe you're only fourteen."

"Fifteen. I had a birthday this winter."

"Oh. Right." I had a twinge of guilt over missing it, even though our crew never celebrated birthdays. They brought back too many memories.

We floated, and I must have dozed off, because a deep mechanical hum startled me awake. I about lost my shit when I woke up in midair. My spastic kick got Keenan in the leg.

"Ouch," he yelped, right in my ear. "Hey look, the door's opening."

A round portal to the interior of the ship rolled back, revealing a brightly lit tunnel big enough to drive a truck through.

"Come on, let's check it out." Keenan tried to tug me by the hand, but in zero gravity, the motion sent us both into a nauseating wobble.

Puking up there would be a mess, with nasty floating globules . . . I swallowed hard, pushing away the image. Waving an arm, I managed to snag a handhold on the nearest wall and tow Keenan in. We hung on the wall like monkeys, craning our necks to peer through the open door.

"What're ya waitin' for, Jack? Let's go."

Curiosity warred with my ridiculously overdeveloped maternal instinct. "Tito's still asleep. He'll be scared if he if he wakes up alone."

Keenan shrugged. "He's safe enough where he's at. If we hear him cry we'll come right back."

"I don't feel right leaving him." So I stole extra Velcro from the loading dock and strapped Tito to my back. He was super easy to carry, since he weighed nothing. The toddler fussed a little, then settled down and went back to sleep.

We floated toward the tunnel by pulling ourselves along handholds mounted on the wall. "Go to the light, Jackie," Keenan intoned in a deep, mystical voice.

I giggled. "Shut up, asshole. I'm not dead yet."

I reached the transparent tube first and ducked inside, careful not to bump Tito's head on the rim. We all floated down the passageway. Looking straight down through the clear floor made my stomach do flips. The pipe shot through the middle of a narrow, high-ceilinged chamber, about fifty feet up. A stack of seat-belt equipped bunks reached dizzying heights above and below us.

The cylindrical room seemed deserted. Then a portal opened near the top. Keenan and I braced our hands on the ridged walls of the tube and peered up. People floated in, their faded jeans out of place in the slick plastic-and-chrome world of the space ship.

Keenan grabbed my arm. "That's them, that's them, it's our crew!"

When I recognized the boys, I let out a joyful shout. Spinning and somersaulting, our crew flew through the air, occasionally colliding with each other or the wall-mounted beds. Their hair floated weirdly around their faces, and they were all laughing their asses off. Me and Keenan went nuts, whooping, hugging, and hollering.

"Dakota, Dakota!" I called, holding on with one hand and waving the other one like crazy.

He saw me and floated over to our tube, gripping the outside of it to pull himself lower. First his boots hung at eye level, then his long legs dropped down, in those familiar holey jeans. I could practically feel the soft cotton under my fingers. When his blue eyes met mine, my heart surged. "Oh my God," I whispered. "I thought I'd never see you again."

Dakota's lips moved. I couldn't hear what he was saying. He placed his palm flat on the glass, his eyes lit with joy. I put mine against it from the other side. Dirt and scrapes marred his handsome face, but his gaze was clear and steady. *"We made it,"* he mouthed.

"How?" I asked, full of wonder.

"Adam," Dakota mouthed. He pointed at the end of the passageway, where a crowd of blue-clad teens waved at us from behind a window.

"Look," Keenan said. "It's Captain Douchebag and his junior astronaut crew."

Adam's laugh came through a speaker. "That's Captain Weatherford to you, Keenan. We can hear you. The rest of your people can't. We had to launch in a hurry, so some of the speakers aren't working yet."

Belly down, I pushed off the ridged walls with both feet and glided to the end of the tunnel in one long soar. Keenan and Dakota scrambled to keep up. I was feeling pretty proud of myself until I slammed into the thick pane of glass on the far side.

It made a lot of noise, and all the astronaut kids flinched. Tito woke up and cried. I reached back and patted his shoulder, murmuring soothingly. My nose and elbows burned for a minute, then the pain faded. The bloody smear I left on the glass didn't. In the other room, one of the girls gave me a grin and a sarcastic thumbs-up. It took me a second to recognize Alanna. I'd gotten used to her nightmare face. She looked like a stranger with my transplanted skin scrubbed off and her long, blonde braid floating.

Alanna's lips moved, but her excited voice came out of the speaker to my right. I couldn't hear her at all through the window. "Jackieeee! Welcome aboard."

"You saved my crew." I pressed my fingers to my lips, overcome with emotion.

Alanna beamed. "Well, Adam did, really. His decision."

"In violation of about ten different regulations," Adam added. "I'll catch hell for it once we reach the space station. Probably lose my rank."

I had to ask. "Then why?"

Adam moved closer to the window. People floated aside to make way for him. "Jackie, we saw what you went through for us, up on the array. It was the least we could do. But the truth is, I didn't plan this. When Bianca's army took down the fence, the boys ran inside, into the lobby. The front of that building is mostly glass. It wouldn't have held for long. So I gave the old man a flamethrower. He held the door while the kids escaped up the elevator."

"The old man?" I repeated, my voice rising. "You mean the one-legged man? Joe?" My head whipped around, and I did a fast scan.

Joe was missing.

Adam saw my stricken look. "Last I saw, he was alive. Uninfected."

"Joe's all alone down there?" I breathed, blinking back tears. "We left an old man with ten thousand pox-infected animals. What's he gonna do? He's a cripple."

Keenan squeezed my shoulder. "Take a deep breath, Jack. Joe's a tough one. He'll be okay."

"I'm sorry, Jackie. I did what I could," Adam said.

Everyone got quiet. I watched my crew, playing and spinning around my clear tube. They knew about Joe. They'd had a little time to deal with the loss. We'd lost crew members before, to pox, turf wars, or plain old starvation. Just not anybody I really leaned on. I know, Joe never manned up like he could have. He would've made a better chief than me. Maybe he refused 'cause he thought it would make us stronger. Either way, he was our father. We were all weaker without him.

"Adam, did we get Bianca?" I finally asked. "I know she was in a raven when it got shot, but what does that mean? Did she die with the bird, or blow away on the wind and find another host?"

"We don't know yet," Adam said. "We're having trouble getting through to mission control."

"Trouble getting through to mission control?" I echoed. That gave me a chill. Tito felt it and shifted fretfully. "Adam, you know what that means—"

He cut me off. "It's bad, I know. But there's nothing we can do about it right now. Time for you to go inside. We have to sanitize the docking bay. There's a print-out of a personal decontamination protocol in your quarters. Follow it exactly . . . um, if you can . . ."

"Yes Adam, we can read well enough for that," I said numbly, looking for the door into the tower room, where Dakota waited for me. There wasn't one. "How do you want us to get in there?"

"I don't want you in there. Mainly because the only way is through here," Adam said shortly.

"We can't even pass you in the hall?" I sighed.

"Right." Adam nodded. "So you get separate quarantines. It's three days to the space station. Once we arrive, they'll test you and make sure you're clean. We don't have a lab on the ship."

I didn't argue. We couldn't bring pox into humanity's last refuge. Tito shifted on my back, and I reached back to pat him. The motion set me into a clumsy midair spin, arms waving. Tito whined about it from his Velcro backpack.

Alanna grinned. "You'll learn to handle yourself better after a bit."

A panel beside their window slid open. Beyond was a tiny one-room apartment, with a wide, seat belt equipped sleeping bag tethered to the wall.

"That's supposed to be officer quarters, but we're making an exception for you," Adam said. "There's a food dispenser in there and a computer you can use."

I turned in time to see Keenan taunting Dakota behind my back, silently mouthing words through the glass. I caught the last few. *"Oooh, baby. Three . . . whole . . . nights."*

From Dakota's glare, he read lips well enough to get the message.

"Keenan, stop it," I said. "It's not happening, so don't get your hopes up." I caught Dakota's eye and slashed my hand through the air in an emphatic *not happening* gesture. Caleb cheerfully mimicked me.

Adam cleared his throat to interrupt. "Into your quarters now."

My crew gathered at the window. Dakota grinned and blew me a kiss. Paco threw his arms over his head in a giant victory sign. Keenan pulled me backward, through the door of our quarters. My feet never touched the floor.

"Clear," Adam said. The door hummed closed.

We were alone, floating in a tiny, super clean apartment. It felt surreal, like a crazy, never-ending dream. The whole place smelled of soap and plastic. We found our disposable UV goggles and got to work cleaning ourselves with the handheld UV light. I spent extra time on Tito, even though I doubted Bianca had infected him. An infected hostage was of no value.

When we were finished, I gave him an awkward smile. I'd never felt so uncomfortable around Keenan before. "Well, we did it. Mostly."

"Yeah. Except for Joe. That still pisses me off."

"And they lost contact with Mission Control. You know what that means," I said. "This isn't over. We have to get ready and go back down there."

Keenan kicked himself into a slow flip and answered upside down, without looking at me. "Yeah. I ain't giving up the whole fuckin' planet. Not without a fight."

"Good. Me neither." I let myself drift over the sleeping bag, the food dispenser console, and the computer station with its Velcro seatbelt. The tiny bathroom seemed to be equipped with some alien vacuum system. That would be a disaster with Tito. But for the moment, he slept.

“We gotta get ourselves ready,” I mused. “But how?”

Keenan arced down from the ceiling in a graceful dive, grabbed the one chair and pulled himself in. He attached the seatbelt and looked up at me. “For now, we learn all we can. We need to build weapons—better ones than those UV lights. I barely finished fourth grade, you know. I have a lot of catchin’ up to do.” He switched on the computer and laughed. “Look what’s here.”

I leaned over to see cartoon characters dancing across the screen, holding the letter B. “Oh my God. Adam left this for us to find.”

“Good. At this rate, I can finish high school before we make it to the station.”

I rolled my eyes. Keenan thought he was great at everything. Not that I’d tell him so, but it was mostly true. Still, academics might not be his strong point. We’d see.

I didn’t have the energy for kindergarten, so I maneuvered myself and Tito into the vented sleeping bag and attached the straps. It felt weird, because we didn’t rest on anything at all. As exhausted as I was, I couldn’t sleep. Every motion we made started us rolling, and the straps brought us up short. I closed my eyes, wishing Dakota was there. Happiness filled me at the thought of him, and the rest of the crew too. We’d be together. A few days wouldn’t matter much.

About fifteen minutes later, Keenan unzipped the bag on the other side of Tito, deliberately not crowding me. My eyes flew open anyway.

“Don’t panic, Jack,” he drawled. “It ain’t happenin’ ’til you beg for it.”

I couldn’t help laughing at him for that. “Keenan, you’re an amazing guy. You really are. But there isn’t gonna be any begging. I’m in love with Dakota.”

An ironic smile touched his lips. “Sure you are, for now. But you’ll change your mind, ’cause I’m the better man.”

I swallowed all my snappy comebacks. Didn’t even roll my eyes. Keenan didn’t deserve that. Not after what he did for me. I tried to look away.

Keenan stroked my hair, and his gaze pulled me back in. His voice was a deep, soothing purr in my ear. “That’s right, babe. I’m the better man. I proved that to you today, and I’ll keep on proving it. I know, I’m younger, and you don’t take me seriously because of it. But that won’t matter when I’m nineteen and you’re twenty.”

My treacherous hormones kicked on then, like he was a good choice. Which he wasn’t. I knew better. I’d just been scared a lot lately, and he was the most dangerous guy I knew. From Keenan's smirk, he could tell I was tempted. I turned away from him, away from the lure of those golden cat eyes. It was gonna be a long three days.

The End . . . until book 2

About the Author

Courtney Farrell lives on an orbiting space station, where she pens novels while evading pox-infected animals. She tweets messages from behind enemy lines as @CAFarrell.

Where to connect with the author

Blog
http://www.courtneyfarrell.com

Facebook
https://www.facebook.com/pages/Courtney-Farrell/405475149467821

Twitter
https://twitter.com/CAFarrell

Goodreads
http://www.goodreads.com/user/show/7894049-courtney-farrell

Amazon
http://www.amazon.com/-/e/B001JPBU6S

Other books by the author

The Enhanced Series

Enhanced
Sacrificed

The Mexican Drug War
Gulf of Mexico Oil Spill
Terror at the Munich Olympics
The Abortion Debate
Methane Energy
World Population
Mental Disorders
Green Jobs
Mongol Dawn
Children's Rights
Human Trafficking
Save the Planet: Using Alternative Energies
Plants Out of Place
Build it Green
Save the Planet: Keeping Water Clean

www.ingramcontent.com/pod-product-compliance
Lightning Source LLC
Chambersburg PA
CBHW030545200626
46808CB00024BA/332
9780990444909